Sign up to my newsletter, and you will be notified when I release my next book!

Join my Patreon (patreon.com/jackbryce) to get early access to my work!

lordjackbryce@gmail.com

Cover design by: Jack Bryce

ISBN-13: 9798862664454

JACK BRYCE

To Dimples of Venus.

Chapter 1

The subway was crowded. Sweating commuters pushed together, most of them dreary-eyed and pale. Like me, they were not looking forward to another day at the office.

And many of them had worse jobs than I did. Ever since the Upheaval, when our dimension collided with the world of Tannoris, mankind had found itself in a new world. Cities and towns were still largely what they had been before the Upheaval, but *the Wilds*…

Well, the Wilds were exciting… An unexplored and new frontier. But they could also be dangerous.

The elves had helped humanity through the worst of it. They were natives of Tannoris and better suited to deal with its threats and the System that the collision had introduced. Together with the elves, mankind had reinforced our cities, making some look almost like medieval fortifications. We now shared those places with the elves.

It might sound exciting, but life had become much more boring. For our own safety, normal humans weren't allowed to leave the settlements. The Coalition made sure that everyone was safe, even when 'safe' offered little excitement.

For me, that didn't parse. I used to go out there, camp in the wilderness. I'd gone hunting a few times, fishing, and I loved hiking and discovering new trails. I didn't mind a little adventure. I dreamed of the Wilds. I wanted to go back out there — be in nature and fend for myself. I wanted to make my own place away from the city.

Sure, cities were fun, especially if you were looking to

party and meet a lot of people. But I had come to a mindset where I wanted to be *out there*. I wanted to carve out a little spot for myself. Maybe have a family — people to love and care for and spend my days with. In peace.

But for most humans, the options to go out there and chase the outdoorsman's dream were limited. If the System hadn't assigned you a Class, then you were vulnerable.

And I didn't have a Class.

Unless you'd call 'call center agent' a Class. I worked as a helpdesk technician at a company downtown, and the job was painfully monotonous. Every day was the same — answering call after call about mundane computer issues and staring at my screen waiting for the clock to hit 5 pm. I longed for something more. In the past, my hiking and camping trips had brought excitement, but without a Class, I could no longer go out there.

An electric chime roused me from thought. The train arrived at my station, and I joined in the usual press of bodies to get off.

Unlike some of the ganglier office drones, my build made it relatively easy to push my way through the masses. Even as I did so, my eyes drifted to a man overseeing it all. Dressed in a medieval-looking breastplate, he wore a cape with the clenched fist logo of the Coalition. Something about him crackled with power, not in the least his purple-glowing eyes.

A Blade Warlock or a Tempest Mage, perhaps. Not impressive Classes, but certainly good enough to oversee daily routine in the city.

I had to admit to a little envy. Before the Upheaval, I could have gone toe-to-toe with most people. But now that the System had – seemingly at random – doled out Classes and I wasn't among the lucky ones, the world had gotten smaller. And even though the Coalition was generally benevolent and not at all as autocratic or dystopian as some people would have thought they would be, I still had a feeling there was a whole world out there that I couldn't experience because I had no Class.

I moved up the stairway, foregoing the crowded escalator, and emerged into the sunlight. So close to the edge of New Springfield, I could see the watchtowers rise over the office buildings here and there. I kept my chin up and joined the droves of people heading to their workplaces for the day.

When I got to the office, I immediately noticed something was different. Everyone was crowded into the meeting room, crammed together and murmuring with hushed voices. I squeezed in and saw the CEO standing at the front, solemnly looking over the crowd.

"I'm afraid I have some very bad news," he announced gravely. "Due to financial difficulties, the company is declaring bankruptcy and ceasing operations effective immediately."

Shocked silence reigned for a moment before everyone began yelling out questions and panicking all at once. I just stood there as the chaos erupted around me. Sure, I had the same questions as most of them did, but I didn't feel the panic. I had always managed to pull through hard situations; I knew how to handle myself.

But I had to wonder — did my knowledge still apply in today's world? After all, I was suddenly out of a job without any warning or safety net to fall back on. Living expenses in the well-protected town of New Springfield were high, and I wouldn't be allowed to leave the town to simply get by on my own or move to a cheaper place.

"You can all report to the Coalition's Labor Division," the CEO said, making calming gestures. "We have reported the bankruptcy to the Coalition, and they will do their utmost to make sure that everyone is allocated to another job. You will not be left to fend for yourself."

Screw that, part of me thought. It felt too much like being herded to a new place.

I turned away and left the room, even though the CEO was still going on. I wasn't interested in any of this. I gathered my meager belongings from my desk into a cardboard box. This meant I'd have to start over completely – searching for a new job, figuring out my benefits situation, updating my resume. The tasks felt daunting, especially since I hadn't been job hunting for years, but I would do it on my own.

I wasn't going to get 'allocated' like I was just an asset that could be offloaded anywhere. In fact, with every passing second, I realized I was pretty much done with all this sheltered and shielded stuff. Maybe this was an opportunity to start afresh.

I shuffled out of the building that had been my workplace for three years. My emotions cycled between dread and excitement – the weirdest emotional cocktail I'd had in a long time. Normally fairly perceptive, I was almost too far gone to notice that a man in a suit and a long coat had been following me ever since I'd left the office.

Maybe even longer… He had his hood thrown back, and his face was familiar – like someone I'd seen before. As I walked on, I dug in my mind, soon enough realizing that the guy had been on my subway almost every day during the past week. He had stood out because something about the way he looked was impeccable — a little inappropriate for the subway.

Great. Now I was imagining people following me.

I decided to get a coffee and try to calm my nerves before figuring out what to do next.

At the cafe, I sat staring vacantly out the window. It was hard to focus my mind on a single thing.

One moment, I saw myself rolling out of New Springfield's gates in a rugged 4X4, a rifle wedged between me and the passenger seat, ready to carve out my own place in the world — Class or not — and screw the System. The next, I dwelled on the safer option to find another job. Maybe there would even be something a little more adventurous. I knew the Coalition sometimes used regular mortals for deliveries to outposts or needed us for engineering and construction work as they carved out a new place in the Wilds.

My future was now a big uncertain void, and I had no idea how to proceed. After about thirty minutes of spiraling, I was jolted out of my thoughts when an unfamiliar voice spoke.

"Rough day?"

From across the table, a familiar face looked up at me – the older man in the impeccable suit from the subway. I hadn't even noticed him slip into the seat.

I cleared my throat, feeling my guard rise. "Hm," I just hummed. I wanted to tell him to go; after all, it was pretty impolite to just take a seat at someone's table, even in crowded New Springfield.

He chuckled wryly. "I can tell you had a rough day because you let your coffee get cold," he said.

Then, he passed his gloved hand over it, and it immediately began wafting steam again, spreading the aroma of hot coffee.

A spellcaster.

I sat up, narrowing my eyes at him. "What do you want?" I asked, feeling the hairs on my forearms rise: a familiar sensation when magic was at work nearby.

The man noticed it since I had the sleeves of my shirt rolled up. The sight of my physical response to his spell seemed to please him, for a smile formed slowly before he fixed his steel-gray eyes on me again. But the light in them was not unkind. It was a little disarming.

"I don't *want* anything," he said. "I come to present

you a business proposal."

I eyed him warily. After the day I'd had, a sketchy job offer was the last thing I needed. But I was also in no position to be picky, and something about the man conveyed sincerity. "What kind of business?" I asked hesitantly.

"It's quite simple really," he said smoothly. "But I must ask that you promise secrecy before I explain further."

I hesitated. This whole thing seemed weird, and I still half thought it was some kind of scam. But I found myself genuinely curious, and it wasn't like I had better options. Plus, a promise of secrecy wasn't that much.

"Alright, I promise I'll keep whatever you tell me secret," I conceded.

"Excellent!" He smiled and leaned forward. "Now, my name is Mr. Caldwell. I represent a group of investors looking to back promising individuals such as yourself..."

I raised an eyebrow. "Promising individuals?"

He nodded and jerked his head in the direction of my forearm. "Yes," he said. "You're sensitive to magic. You have potential. You could have a Class."

At that, my heart jumped. I managed to conceal it, and I almost felt a little silly for having such an emotional response of child-like glee to the concept of acquiring a Class. In that moment, though, I realized that it was exactly what I had wanted for a long time.

I wanted agency, to be an actor. I wanted to forge my own path in my own way.

Could this man bestow it on me?

"Well Mr. Caldwell, you have my attention," I said. "But I'll still need to hear details about the actual work before I agree to anything further."

He nodded. "Of course, of course!" He looked around to see if anyone was listening. The place was fairly crowded, and it was impossible to say how far our conversation carried. If he had secrets to dispense, *this* certainly wasn't the right place.

"Mr. Wilson," he began, giving me no chance to interrupt and ask how he knew my name. "Have you ever seen the view from the city walls of New Springfield?"

Chapter 2

Caldwell led me up a narrow staircase that wound its way up one of the watchtowers. It was quite the climb, and I couldn't help but feel that Caldwell was testing me when he turned to ask if I was getting tired. I was fit and made it up easily, so I shook my head.

At the top, we stepped out onto a small observation platform. Caldwell gestured grandly at the landscape beyond the city walls. "Feast your eyes, my friend. The view up here is like nothing else."

I moved to the railing and looked out. My breath caught in my throat.

Past the walls, the land stretched on for miles in every direction, undulating with hills and valleys, dotted with farms that exploited the fertile soil. But this was not the world I remembered from before the Upheaval.

Strange, vividly colored vegetation covered the landscape, so dense in places it looked almost jungle-like. In the distance, I could see a shimmering azure lake nestled between the hills. Wisps of rainbow-hued mist drifted here and there across the terrain. It was beautiful, yet profoundly alien.

"Magnificent, isn't it?" said Caldwell, joining me at the railing. "This is what we fight daily to reclaim and civilize. The Frontier Division's great purpose."

I nodded, still drinking it all in. "It's incredible. And a little intimidating too, to be honest." I chuckled ruefully. "Not sure I'd last ten minutes out there on my own."

Caldwell smiled and put a hand on my shoulder. "With the proper training and tools, you'd be surprised what you can handle."

I nodded, my eyes scouring the magical Wilds ahead.

"First," Caldwell said, "let me explain a bit more about the Frontier Division. We're an elite force of pioneers, scouts, and outriders. The Coalition tasks us with exploring and securing the Wilds beyond civilization."

He gestured out at the landscape. "Lately, we've started an initiative to recruit regular folks, people like you, to join us as homesteaders. You'd live on your own plot of land near one of our outposts. Now and then, we'd ask the homesteaders to assist the Frontier Division — maybe scouting some magical anomalies or helping with other tasks," he continued. "So you'd be kind of a freelancing member, contributing your skills while still being self-sufficient."

Caldwell looked back at me. "Make sense so far?"

"Yeah, I think I've got the gist," I replied with a nod. "You want to get more boots on the ground taming the Wilds, and homesteaders can be a big help with that."

"Exactly. We provide basic combat and survival training, then set you up with your own plot of land near one of our outposts," Caldwell said. "You'd be part of a community of like-minded pioneers working together to start a new life amidst the Wilds."

It sounded daunting, yet exhilarating at the same time. Still, I furrowed my brow skeptically. My instinct was to accept his offer here and now, but I needed to temper my enthusiasm, to learn a little more before I'd take the offer.

"And the Coalition asks for nothing in return? All I have to do is uproot my life and risk it all in the wilderness?" I made it sound like a give, but I was honestly getting pretty excited.

Caldwell held up a hand. "Please, hear me out. Of course, it benefits the Coalition as well to have independent, self-sufficient settlements flourishing. But for you, it's a chance at a new beginning. To have purpose." He lowered his voice. "And yes, to gain a Class."

My eyes widened at that. Caldwell grinned and continued. "We have an Awakening ritual. It's intense, sometimes dangerous, but success means unlocking your inner power. If you have the spark, as I almost certainly know you do."

My pulse quickened. This man was offering everything I'd secretly yearned for since the Upheaval. A chance to prove myself, to find my own goal and meaning. And to gain a Class, achieving the power and control that came with it.

I didn't have to think about it very long – this was clearly the chance of a lifetime. "Alright, Mr. Caldwell, you've convinced me," I said, meeting his eyes firmly. "I accept your offer."

Caldwell beamed and vigorously shook my hand. "Excellent! We'll begin preparations for the Awakening ritual at once. In the meantime, I have a homeland deed for you to review." He handed me a scrollbound document. "Your new property lies just east of Gladdenfield Outpost, near a lovely spot by the Silverthread River."

I scratched my chin thoughtfully. "I have a lot of questions about all this. What exactly will the training involve? How dangerous is this Awakening ritual? And what kinds of skills and equipment will I need to survive out there?"

Caldwell nodded. "Those are all excellent questions, Mr. Wilson. Let me address them one by one."

He went on to answer my questions in great detail. The Awakening ritual did carry risks, he admitted, but their magicians took every precaution. As for skills, sharpshooting and scouting abilities would be particularly valuable on the frontier, but there were also more rustic skills like farming and hunting. However, since time was of the essence, they would assign me a partner who had experience and could give me pointers when necessary. We'd get started pretty fast that way. It helped that I already knew a lot from my own experience and interests.

I listened carefully, chiming in with a few more specific queries. Caldwell answered each one patiently, continuing to refer to me formally as "Mr. Wilson."

After the third or fourth time, I chuckled and held up a hand. "Please, call me David."

Caldwell looked a bit abashed, but then smiled back. "My apologies, David it is." He went over some more details about the homesteader initiative, emphasizing the shared purpose I'd find with my fellow pioneers. We'd have to rely on each other a lot, and we'd be trading and working together often.

Eventually, we moved to discussing the Awakening. Caldwell explained it was an intense ritual using rare reagents and elven magic to unlock a person's latent abilities. There were always risks involved, but his team had taken every precaution to minimize them.

When all my questions had been answered, at least for now, Caldwell led me back downstairs. We agreed to meet in two days, after I'd had a chance to tie up my affairs in the city and prepare for the new chapter ahead.

I emerged from the building feeling dizzy with possibilities. The Wilds called out to me now more than ever. Thanks to Caldwell and the Frontier Division, I finally had the chance to answer that call. My new life was just beginning.

Chapter 3

Taking a deep breath, I stepped into the stone chamber where the Awakening ritual would take place. Torches flickered from sconces along the walls, and arcane symbols were etched into the floor. At the far end stood an altar, with several robed figures gathered around it.

As I approached, the magicians turned to face me. Caldwell was among them, along with a couple of other human mages and three elven spellcasters. The one leading the ritual was a rather plain-looking elven woman, her mousy brown hair hanging lank over her shoulders. She regarded me with a bored, seen-it-all expression.

"Welcome, David," she said tonelessly. "Please, stand in the circle and we will begin." Her attitude reminded me of a surgeon before surgery — to the person undergoing the procedure, it was often a life-changing event; to the surgeon, it was just another day at the office.

I moved into the outlined circle at the center of the room. The magicians began chanting in a strange, lilting language I didn't recognize. Caldwell lit incense at the four corners surrounding me, wafting trails of fragrant smoke into the air.

I glanced around warily. This was some serious magic they were invoking here. What if something went wrong? Still, I shook off my doubts. I had to stay calm and trust the process. Sheltered life in the city might be good for many, but it was driving me crazy. I needed freedom and purpose, even with the dangers. This ritual was the key.

The chanting grew louder as the magicians raised their arms. The circle beneath me began glowing faintly.

At first, I felt nothing, but then a tingling sensation started spreading through my body. It grew steadily, soon becoming almost unbearably intense. I gritted my teeth, determined not to cry out.

Vivid images flashed through my mind — places and people I'd never seen before. Strange whispers echoed in my ears. The tingling gave way to searing pain, radiating to my very core. This was it, the Awakening was upon me! I fell to my knees, jaw clenched against the powers that roiled within.

And then, as suddenly as it began, the pain receded. Gasping, I lifted my head and blinked, trying to gauge if I felt different from before. I didn't…

The magicians peered at me silently. Caldwell hurried over and helped me to my feet.

"Well done!" he said. "The ritual has awakened your inner gift. In the coming days, your Class will become clear."

I nodded, exhilarated yet puzzled. I didn't feel too different yet. "How will I know what Class I am?"

"Come, let's discuss it over coffee," Caldwell said, leading me from the ritual chamber.

In a lounge area, Caldwell poured us mugs of dark coffee from a thermos he requisitioned from a bar. Many others were taking a break here, all of them elves or humans in service of the Frontier Division. It felt strange to realize I was part of them now. As we drank, he explained more about Classes and their roles.

"Some common Classes are Riflemen — they need no further explanation, I think. Then there are Warriors who wade into melee battle and expert Archers who pick off foes from afar," he said. "For spellcasters, Pyromancers control fire while Toxicologists concoct strange elixirs and lob them like grenades. We also see many Tempest Mages, who focus on lightning magic, and the hundreds of subtypes of Warlock, who are less useful as they often require aid from outside — such as from a demon or devil — to learn new spells."

He took a sip of coffee before continuing. "The Frontier Division heavily favors Classes that focus on scouting, trading, crafting, and building. We are not combat-focused, although we can pull our weight when needed. What drew me to you was your affinity for magic combined with your personal experiences as an outdoorsman. The System…" He considered his words for a moment. "The System allots a Class based on the recipient's preferences and a random chance factor. The combination of outdoorsmanship, survival skills, and the randomly allotted magical affinity that you have mean you might be a spellcaster with natural affinity."

He leaned forward, focusing his intense gaze on me. "That is rare and extremely valuable."

"What kind of Classes are like that?" I asked.

"First and foremost, Druids," he said. "Then there are Stormlords, Green Mages, and several more. Of course, there are also some exceedingly rare and valuable subclasses, like the Pioneer Elementalist, the Frontier Summoner, and the Outrider Magus. It is my personal hope that you are one of those."

I nodded, fascinated. The possibilities seemed endless. Then, I looked back at him. "And you?"

"Magebreaker," he said with a grin. "Basically a combat Class; I am strong against other mages. But I can also detect them." He smiled. "That is how I found you. My Class allows me to be a talent scout of sorts." He chuckled and shrugged. "I greatly prefer that over any military role. I like finding the right people and helping them along their path."

Caldwell looked at me intently. "Keep an eye out for your interface appearing. It's different for everyone, so pay close attention to your thoughts and instincts over the next few days."

I made a mental note to stay alert for any changes or new sensations in my mind. According to Caldwell, that would signify my interface awakening.

As we finished our coffee, Caldwell stood and gripped my shoulder. "Go now, settle your affairs in the city," he said. "Then return here in five days to begin your new life in earnest. I expect your Class will have revealed itself by then as well, and we can discuss its merits in more detail."

I nodded, my excitement growing. In less than a week, I would embark on this new path. I had a lot to do to get ready. But soon I would be leaving sheltered city life behind for the wild frontier. And I couldn't wait to get started.

"I'll be back in five days," I promised Caldwell. My great adventure was so close I could taste it. All that remained was letting go of the old me and uncovering and embracing the power within.

Over the next few days, I busied myself tying up loose ends in the city before my departure. I gave notice at my apartment, donated or sold most of my belongings, and said goodbye to the few friends I had here. There weren't many, and they weren't very good friends to begin with. I had been a solitary figure mostly.

It would hurt the most to say goodbye to my grandparents, who had raised me from an early age, but I wouldn't be able to see them in person, as they were still in Louisville's well-protected ward. Travel – especially on such short notice – was difficult and expensive.

A phone call would have to do for now. And I made that call on the final day of my preparations. My grandparents – tech-savvy for their age – put me on speakerphone, and I announced to them that I was heading into the Wilds, that I would get a Class and become a homesteader, working alongside the Frontier Division. A silence followed, and it was grandpa who spoke first.

"Wish I could come with you, son," he said. "You always were the adventuring type, just like your mom and dad."

"Yes, you are," Grandma agreed. I could hear the emotion in her voice, but she was happy for me. "You go and do it, son. You deserve it. Your grandfather and I have always known living in the protected wards wasn't for you."

Grandpa chuckled. "That's right. You go out there and see the elves and the kin and live like your parents did."

"Just don't get lost like them," Grandma put in, some grief edging her voice as painful memories returned.

I smiled, savoring how much they wanted me to be happy, even though I knew they would personally have wanted me to just stay in New Springfield where I was safe. That was love too; to let go when you know your loved one needs to strike out on their own.

"Thanks, Grandma and Grandpa," I said. "I shouldn't have to say it, because you already know it, but I love you guys."

And I did. They could've tried to discourage me from the adventuring life and to sway me into staying in New Springfield. After all, they had lost their son and daughter-in-law to the dangers of the Wilds.

But they didn't. They wanted me to find my own place, make my own way.

"Just… just try to be in touch when you can be, alright son?" Grandpa asked, his voice close to breaking.

"I will," I said. "I promise."

After that, we spoke a little more about the adventuring life, with my grandparents reminiscing about how dad had been when he was young. How, when the Upheaval had come, he had quickly chosen the adventuring life and how mom had joined him.

"They were fighters and explorers, son," Grandpa said and chuckled. "Why, I couldn't have stopped them if I'd wanted to."

Grandma laughed and agreed. "It was their path."

"And it's yours too," Grandpa said. "I felt it in my bones when I saw you growing up."

I laughed, feeling warmth in my heart for them. "I'll try to make them — and you — proud."

"Oh son, we're already proud of you," Grandma said.

"Hm-hm," Grandpa agreed. "We're proud of you no matter what you do. And so are your parents — wherever they are now. We don't care about how much you explore, how much money you make, or how many monsters you defeat. We just want you to pursue your own happiness and make your life into what you want it to be."

I smiled. "I will," I said. "I feel this is the right path."

"Then it is," Grandma said with that tone of voice she had that ended any discussion.

We talked for a while longer. But at long last, everything we could say had been said. I hoped that there would be ways to stay in touch in the Wilds, but I expected that the frontier would limit my options quite a bit. In the Wilds, where Tannoris and Earth had collided, the old Earth technology became unreliable and finicky, especially when it came to electronics. But I would try to keep my loved ones updated as best I could.

By the final night, all my affairs were settled. My backpack and duffel bag contained everything I planned to bring with me into my new frontier life. It wasn't much, but I hoped it would be enough.

Caldwell and I hadn't discussed in great detail what the Frontier Division would provide for me, but I had to assume that it included most of the supplies I'd need to survive until I had my place — whatever and wherever that would be — set up. After all, the stores in New Springfield didn't sell survival equipment anymore: there was simply no demand as everyone stayed in the city.

Sitting on my bed in the empty apartment, I felt a swirl of emotions. Excitement, nervousness, sadness about leaving this place I'd known for so long. But mostly eagerness for the unknown adventure ahead. Part of it felt impulsive. I had accepted the call to adventure on little more than a gut feeling, but I sensed that embracing it would do me well.

And somehow, it felt fitting. My parents had been explorers as well, with Classes of their own. Their fate was unknown — likely the Wilds had claimed them — but if so, they had fallen doing what they loved most, braving the wilderness.

I lay back, thoughts drifting. Would I really be able to survive out there? What if this Class powers thing didn't work out? Doubt crept in, but I pushed it away. I had to have faith in myself. Caldwell had seen the magic in me; he would not be wrong.

And I had sensed it all my life. A feeling of destiny. Something greater was waiting for me.

Eventually I drifted off to sleep. My dreams were fragmented and confusing. I saw shimmering rivers cutting through vivid jungles, mist-shrouded mountains looming in the distance. Strange creatures moved through the landscapes — things both beautiful and terrifying.

I saw fields laden with harvests, smiling in the sun while the gentle lapping of rivers sounded in the background. Towns and outposts stood on crossroads along rutted frontier roads, where folks lived simple and honest. And there was adventure, for those who sought it. There were mysteries to uncover and secrets to learn.

I awoke with my heart pounding. Gray predawn light filtered through the window. The dreams had seemed so real. I knew they were a glimpse into the life that awaited me out there. A life of magic, adventure, and of making my own place in the world.

I smiled, ready to embrace it all. Rising, I quickly washed up and got dressed. I did a final check of my bags and then slung them over my shoulders. It was time.

I took one last look around the apartment that had been my home for years. It seemed small and confining now. With a nod of resolve, I turned and walked out the door for the final time.

At the Frontier Division's facility, Caldwell greeted me warmly, waiting at the reception as if he knew the exact moment of my arrival. "David! Good to see you. How was your final week in the city?"

"Uneventful," I replied. "I'm ready to get started on something much more exciting."

Caldwell nodded knowingly. "I thought you'd say as much. And your Class?"

I shrugged, unable to hide my disappointment at not yet having had my Class revealed to me. "Nothing yet," I said. "And my interface hasn't activated either."

He considered that for a moment, his steel eyes fixed on me. "Nothing whatsoever?" he asked.

"Well," I said. "I *did* have a dream."

Caldwell nodded, a small smile surfacing. "Ah," he hummed. "Well, sometimes it takes longer for the Class to reveal itself. That is, in itself, not a bad thing at all. But dreams are often portents. They may offer insights on your emerging Class. Can you tell me some of the details?"

"Sure," I said, and I described the vivid dreamscapes again — the fields, the rivers, the towns, and the hint of adventure.

Caldwell listened intently, brow furrowed in concentration. "The environments certainly match reports from our scouts about the central frontier regions," he mused when I was finished. "And they match my own experiences as well. As for adventure, well, many roles are needed out there. But I do not believe that the dreams reveal anything I can unravel just yet."

I nodded, feeling both excited and apprehensive about the mystery. "Do you think the dreams were a vision of what's to come?"

"It's possible," Caldwell replied. "The Awakening can attune one's mind to the energies of the Wilds.

What you saw may have been glimpses of your destined path."

That thought sent a thrill through me. I couldn't wait to discover the role I had to play out there.

Caldwell went on to assure me there was no real cause for worry. My Class would reveal itself when the time was right. Patience and attentiveness were key.

"But first things first," he said. "Today, you and I will venture out into the Wilds together. I will accompany you to Gladdenfield Outpost near the Silverthread River, where we will introduce you to the townsfolk you will deal with on a daily basis."

I nodded enthusiastically. I was looking forward to it all, and the prospect that Caldwell himself would accompany me was a good one. I was beginning to like the old man in his impeccable suit with his polite mannerisms.

He grinned. "First, we will see about our transport. And I have a feeling you will like it..."

Chapter 4

Caldwell led me outside to a fenced-in area filled with rugged off-road vehicles. My eyes went wide at the sight. After years stuck in the city, part of me had started to think that cars like this no longer existed.

"Go ahead and take a look," Caldwell said, gesturing to a Jeep Wrangler Rubicon emblazoned with the Coalition's emblem on the doors. "This will be your ride out to the frontier, on loan from the Frontier Division as long as you're working with us."

I let out a low whistle as I walked around the muscular off-roader. "Now this takes me back," I said with a grin. "My dad had one kinda like this when I was a kid. We used to go camping and fishing with it."

Caldwell nodded. "A fine, reliable vehicle. The Rubicon trim is top of the line — reinforced suspension, upgraded axles, front and rear locking differentials."

I nodded, impressed. "And I see you fitted it with woodland camouflage too. Smart thinking."

Caldwell smiled. "Of course. Blending into the surroundings can be crucial out there."

He tossed me the keys. "Why don't you take a seat up front and get a feel for it?"

I hopped inside eagerly, taking in the leather seats and shiny dashboard instruments. Turning the key, the engine rumbled to life with a throaty purr.

"Feels good, doesn't she?" Caldwell said. "Why don't you take us on a little test drive?"

"Don't mind if I do!" I put the camo Wrangler in gear and tooled around the obstacle course behind the motor pool. She was responsive and handled well, but I was so excited for the adventure that I would have beamed a smile even if I'd had to get out and push...

After parking, I hopped out, grinning from ear to ear. "This thing is amazing! I can't wait to really open it up out in the wilderness."

Caldwell nodded approvingly. "She's all yours then. The Division wants our homesteaders to have dependable transportation for their work assisting our missions."

I furrowed my brow skeptically. "Seems like an awful lot to entrust to someone you just met. Aren't you worried I might just take off with this sweet ride and never look back?"

"Perhaps some might," Caldwell conceded. "But I believe you'll utilize our equipment responsibly."

I nodded thoughtfully. "I appreciate the vote of confidence. And don't worry, I know contributing to the community is key to thriving out here. I intend to do my part."

"Excellent. Now let's go over the rest of your Coalition-issued equipment," Caldwell said.

He led me to a storage room lined with shelves holding tools, survival gear, and more. "You'll find axes, saws, shovels, and other implements here to establish your homestead."

Next, he indicated bins loaded with packaged food. "These preserves and MREs will sustain you until you can harvest your own crops. If I may make a suggestion, I would try to procure fresh supplies from Gladdenfield Outpost before using the MREs. They are fine emergency rations, and the Wilds are very unpredictable. You never know when a natural or magical event will cut you off from civilization for a while."

Finally, we came to a locked cage holding racks of firearms and ammunition. Caldwell passed me an unloaded semi-automatic rifle chambered in 5.56 NATO and a forty-five as a sidearm. "These are for protection," he said. "Use them only when absolutely necessary."

I nodded, carefully stowing everything in the Jeep's cargo area. My pulse quickened, realizing how well supplied I was for the challenges ahead.

"Now, why don't we load up your belongings and get underway?" Caldwell said.

After securing my meager personal bags, I gripped the wheel with eager anticipation as Caldwell settled into the passenger seat.

"Gladdenfield Outpost is located along the Silverthread River, about two hours in a general western direction from here," he informed me, consulting a map. "I'll navigate us there. It's a safe drive, but the roads out there are in a poor state."

"Sounds good to me," I replied. I shifted into four-wheel drive, and we rumbled toward the fortified gates of New Springfield.

As we approached the checkpoint, elf guards eyed us warily, rifles glinting in the sun. Beyond the massive walls, the world was untamed, full of both wonder and danger. But I was ready to leave the choking confines of the city behind. Out there, I could find purpose on my own terms.

With a nod to the guards, we passed through the gates onto the open dirt track. The wild frontier lay before us, strange and alluring. I took a deep breath, optimism rising in my chest.

The unknown called, and I would answer.

As New Springfield's walls shrank behind us, the wild landscape opened up on all sides. Strange vegetation and soaring rock formations I'd only glimpsed from the city now surrounded us. I breathed deep the fresh air, savoring my freedom.

With my rugged new ride rumbling beneath me, the open frontier awaiting, I was feeling good and in control of my fate.

Chapter 5

As we drove over the rugged terrain, I gazed at the towering light brown trees, so much like the pictures of the great redwoods I had seen in some of the textbooks on old Earth flora and fauna. Strange flowers in vivid hues bloomed here and there amid the emerald grass.

"Magnificent, isn't it?" Caldwell said. "When Tannoris merged with Earth, it created something entirely new. Not quite one world or the other anymore."

I nodded, making sure to focus more on the rutted road than on the enchanting forest around us. It wasn't easy.

"I've never seen anything like it," I said. "Well, not outside of picture books anyway." The state of the Wilds was documented, and there were occasional documentaries and sensational movies about it. Most people in the safe towns took an interest. I suppose it was the same as people appreciating Westerns, space operas, or other entertainment that told of a time of a lawless frontier.

Still focused on the road, I asked a question that had been bothering me for years and that no one so far had produced a satisfactory answer to. "Does anyone know why the worlds merged in the first place?"

Caldwell shook his head. "No one knows for certain. The elves may possess more information, but they remain secretive as always."

The answer was not as insightful as I had hoped. The Upheaval was a subject of great speculation, and many people expected the mysterious elves knew more about it. But if they did, they were keeping it to themselves.

He went on, "The kin believe it was the arrogance of

the elves that brought about the Upheaval – the calamity that joined our realms."

This sparked my curiosity to learn more. But Caldwell changed the subject to discuss the inhabitants of this land, almost as if he didn't want to talk about it too much.

"You'll find all manner of beasts out here. And of the sentient kin – well, there are catkin, foxkin, deerkin, and several more. The elves stand apart from the kin, and we do not categorize them as kin. It is the same with dwarves and kobolds, orcs and goblins. And, of course, there are many new species that arose after the Upheaval. Adaptations and hybrids we still struggle to catalog."

I shook my head in wonder. "This is a lot to take in. What of the native sentient beings? The 'kin' you mentioned?" I had heard of them and knew they existed, but they were never seen in the secure cities and towns.

Caldwell nodded gravely. "Ah yes, many kin have made their own places in the merged worlds. They have changed and adapted. As denizens of the Wilds, they are often savage or uncivilized, but they are more adaptable. They are often insular but can be friendly. The Frontier Division cooperates with the more civilized kin a lot. Many of them are contractors and freelancers."

I listened intently as he elaborated on the different groups. The diversity was astounding. Caldwell stressed the importance of being open-minded with the kin. Stereotyping would only breed resentment.

"Remember, to them, we humans are just as much outsiders and newcomers to this land," he advised. "This is not just *our* Earth anymore. It is also *their* Tannoris; Cordial relations must be built over time. They have their own customs. For instance, foxkin and catkin do not shake hands like we do. To them, touching hands is very intimate — something reserved for spouses and lovers."

That fascinated me, and I wanted to ask more, but we crested a hill, and an ominous vista opened up below, smothering my questions before I could ask them as I gawked at the display. A pyramidal structure with Gothic arches and buttresses rose from the valley floor. It sat on an island in the middle of a stream, with arched stone bridges, crumbling and battered, reaching to the structure from either shore.

"That is one of the Dungeons," Caldwell commented. "Places of power, now home to all manner of fell creatures. Within are the secrets of the old elves of

Tannoris — secrets even their own descendants have forgotten. But they are dangerous places."

I stared at the foreboding building, imagination ignited. So much to uncover in this land. My heart was thumping at the thought of venturing into a place like that.

"In time, once you gain experience out here as a frontiersman, you may venture to some of these sites," Caldwell offered. "Gladdenfield Outpost is relatively secure, so you can explore these threats at your own pace, or not at all if you wish."

I nodded thoughtfully. The dangers here were real, yet exhilarating. With care and courage, I would find my path. Who knew what I would uncover? I shook my head in wonder, struggling to keep my eyes on the rutted road. This was all just amazing.

Smaller stone ruins dotted the rolling landscape as we pressed onward. Caldwell explained these were remnants of ancient Tannorian outposts.

"Few now remember their original purpose. But perhaps in time, their secrets will be revealed," he mused.

I imagined myself one day exploring those age-worn structures, uncovering knowledge lost for eons. The scope of mysteries in this world kindled excitement and purpose within me.

And so we continued onward, the Jeep rumbling sturdily over the untamed earth. I kept scanning the unfamiliar terrain, wary yet eager to discover its many secrets. What role might I play in this tale between worlds? I was determined to find my place here — a place uniquely my own.

But first things first: I had to get my homestead.

After two hours of driving, we crested a hill and Gladdenfield Outpost came into view below. It was a small medieval-looking settlement, with timber buildings and dirt roads enclosed by a tall palisade wall of sharpened logs. There couldn't be more than fifty buildings within, offering a home to perhaps as many families.

As we approached, I could see elven guards with rifles patrolling the top of the wall. The main gates stood open, and a few traders were leading pack animals laden with goods in and out. Some of the creatures were strange and ostrich-like — beasts of burden the likes of which I had never seen before.

"Here we are, the central trading hub for the region," Caldwell said. "You'll be coming here often to resupply and socialize, though your homestead lies just outside."

I nodded, taking in the rustic look of the place. It reminded me of historical dramas before the Upheaval or artists' impressions of medieval villages in the Old World. It had a powerful charm with its muddy roads and cozy wooden buildings – something sincere and pure that New Springfield had been unable to offer.

We rumbled through the gates, which immediately swung shut behind us as the elven guards watched us with tight eyes. The buildings were rough-hewn but solid. Townsfolk eyed us curiously as we passed – mostly humans and elves, with no kin in sight right now, although Caldwell had assured me there were plenty of them in Gladdenfield.

At Caldwell's instructions, I brought the Jeep to a halt in front of a large tavern bearing a sign reading 'The Wild Outrider.'

"Let's go inside – I believe your partner is waiting to meet you. Don't worry about the vehicle and the supplies – people don't steal around here."

I followed him in, confused yet excited. Caldwell hadn't mentioned meeting my guide here in town. "My partner?" I hummed, a half-question, but he heard me all the same.

He smiled and nodded. "I told you we would set you up with an experienced frontiersman. What better place to find one than the frontier?"

There was no arguing with that logic. I shrugged and followed him inside.

The tavern was dim but cozy, with timber walls and a crackling fireplace. Spicy aromas filled the air. Caldwell procured a table while I glanced around eagerly, having no idea who my mentor might be. There were a lot of people inside, and most faces and other features were concealed by the shadows. There were no electric lights — perhaps due to the disturbance in electronics that was the result of Tannoris' magical energies?

Soon enough, Caldwell beckoned me to follow and sit with him. A barmaid brought us two mugs of frothy ale. I took a sip of the bitter yet refreshing drink.

"So tell me more about this settlement," I said to Caldwell. "How long has it been established?"

"Ah, Gladdenfield is one of the Frontier Division's oldest outposts," he replied. "It was founded about 5 years after the Upheaval first merged our worlds. Back then it was just a tiny fort manned by a few intrepid Coalition members. But it's grown into a thriving trade town. Others have grown much, much faster, but

Gladdenfield is solid and reliable."

I nodded along, intrigued by the history. "And who lives here now besides the elven guards?"

"Well, there are the human traders and craftsmen of course – blacksmiths, carpenters, leatherworkers and the like," Caldwell explained. "Plus elf merchants who bring goods to and from the cities and safe Coalition settlements to trade. The occasional dwarven prospector passes through too, seeking new mineral deposits in the hills."

"It seems like a real melting pot," I observed.

"That it is," agreed Caldwell. "You'll find all types gathering here from the surrounding region. It makes for a lively community."

I smiled. "That sounds up my alley. I can't wait to meet more of the locals and really get to know the place."

Caldwell returned my smile. "I'm glad to hear your enthusiasm. Now, in terms of the landscape, the area provides opportunities but also hazards."

I leaned forward, wanting to understand the terrain.

"To the north lie the Shimmering Peaks," Caldwell went on, "named for their iridescent mineral deposits. The mountains are rich in ores but also home to unruly bands of kobolds and goblins."

I furrowed my brow. "Good to know. I'll be sure to avoid wandering that direction."

"Indeed," said Caldwell. "To the west, the Wyvern Wood is thick with valuable timber but teeming with, well, wyverns." He grinned. "The name quite gives it away. Oh, and not to mention giant spiders."

"Spiders," I muttered. "I take it the Frontier Division is still working to make that area safer?"

"We do our best to curb the more dangerous beasts, but threats remain," Caldwell conceded. "Southwards you'll find verdant farmland and grazing pastures along the Silverthread River where your homestead lies. That region is more secure, if still untamed."

I felt relief hearing my lands were in the safer zone. "And the east?" I inquired. "The forest we just passed through?"

"Springfield Forest," explained Caldwell. "While relatively safe, it is home to at least three Dungeons and several ancient elven ruins. Those places are best avoided at low levels – especially since your Class hasn't awakened yet."

My mind swirled with thoughts of discovering those forgotten ruins. But I knew such exploration would need to wait until I had much more experience in these parts.

"I'll be sure to thoroughly explore the safer areas before venturing anywhere too hazardous," I assured Caldwell.

He nodded approvingly and took another long draught of his ale. I followed suit, feeling the strong drink warm my belly.

Then, Caldwell stood abruptly. "Now... Let's go meet your partner, shall we?"

Chapter 6

My pulse quickened as I followed Caldwell to a table in the back corner. A lone figure sat with their back to us. Before we reached the figure, the enticing aroma of lavender met me. It was subtle but powerful enough to trump the scents of ale and sweat of those drinking in the tavern.

It was fresh and full, something I would want around

me. A scent I could truly get used to, and I felt myself almost distracted from this important meeting, wondering where the scent came from.

But as the mysterious figure stood and turned, I was brought back into the here and now. My eyes went wide, and I did my best not to stare.

She was a foxkin — slender but curvy in the right places, with pointed vulpine ears and a gorgeous foxtail swishing behind her. Flowing black hair framed her delicate features, turning to fur with white highlights around and on her fox ears. Striking sapphire eyes locked intensely onto mine. There was an edge of the wild there — something untamed and free and unlike anything I had ever seen in my days.

She was mesmerizing.

"David, meet Diane Whikksie, your partner," Caldwell said.

Diane smiled, flashing dainty fangs. Her melodic voice sent a tingle through me. It had a slight hoarse quality that resonated in my soul. "Hello, David," she said in an accent that seemed almost French. "I've been looking forward to meeting you."

'Daveed,' she made of my name… And it sounded like music to my ears.

I gave her a smile and a nod. It wasn't easy keeping

my cool and not staring at her perfect figure wrapped in a beautiful loose shirt, tied at the waist, and offering me a fair sight of her ample bosom, but I managed somehow. The fox ears though, made me do a double take, and she noticed, signaling so with a slight smile.

The truth was, I liked those ears. I liked them a lot.

"The pleasure is mine, Miss Whikksie," I said, satisfied with how cool my voice sounded.

"Please," she said. "Come sit."

She extended a hand toward a seat, and a momentary misunderstanding was all it took.

On a whim, I stepped forward and extended my hand to shake hers, taking her gesture to sit down as an invitation to shake hands — a pretty common way for strangers to introduce themselves.

Of course, I had forgotten all about what Caldwell had said before we arrived in Gladdenfield Outpost, although the words now reverberated in my mind as if he was shouting them at me through a bullhorn.

"For instance," he had said, "foxkin and catkin do not shake hands like we do. To them, touching hands is very intimate — something reserved for spouses and lovers."

Oops.

It was too late. I gripped her hand. Her touch was

electric; her blazing blue eyes widened, almond-shaped in all their natural beauty, as her plump lips pouted a little.

The tavern around us seemed to grow quiet. Several faces looked up — other foxkin and catkin among them, and by the sparks in their eyes, I could tell this was going to be a very juicy piece of Gladdenfield gossip.

Great. I was already making a name for myself.

The moment lingered. My eyes on hers. She didn't seem... well, *unhappy*. She seemed stricken, but I knew women well enough to discern that she did not resent my touch. Still, I knew nothing about foxkin culture. It could go anywhere from here; she might even challenge me to a duel or something! I had no idea.

Instead, she smiled. Next to me and one step behind me, Caldwell cleared his throat.

"You don't waste time, do you, David?" she hummed in that delicious accent, her voice going straight down my spine and to my nether regions.

"I, uh..."

"Ahem," Caldwell interjected, and his voice severed the connection — for the moment. Our hands untangled, and mine fell to my side.

"David is from the city, of course," Caldwell explained. "I should have reminded him... He, uh... He does not know the customs."

"Indeed," Diane purred, her eyes still on me before giving a light chuckle. "Well, come sit. And please, call me Diane."

I kept my composure and sat down next to Caldwell and opposite of Diane, whose eyes never left me, twinkling with some spark of entertainment. This was going great; day one at the frontier, and I had already proposed or something to a foxkin…

I cleared my throat, trying to shake off my little cultural faux pas. "So, what's the plan from here? I'm eager to get started on this homesteading adventure."

Diane smiled, seemingly willing to overlook my unintentional proposal. "Of course. Let me give you a brief overview of how this will work." She unfurled a map across the tabletop, using empty tankards to weigh down the corners.

Leaning forward, I could make out the winding blue line of the Silverthread River, with small homestead plots marked out along its banks. Diane pointed to one near a bend in the river.

"This parcel will be your land. A sturdy log cabin is already constructed, with plots for farming and pasture."

I nodded, picturing myself living in that hand-hewn cabin. It would be rustic for sure but felt right for this untamed land.

Diane went on. "As your partner, I'll be staying with you at the cabin until you get your bearings and feel settled."

I felt a simmering excitement at the thought of Diane staying with me. There was clearly chemistry between us, though we'd only just met. Having her beautiful face be the first thing I saw each morning would make this strange new world a lot less intimidating.

Caldwell added, "And I'll be checking in from time to time to monitor your progress. However, business elsewhere may make my visits few and far between."

I smiled. "That's very reassuring. I appreciate you both looking out for me as the new guy around here."

Caldwell nodded. "Of course. It is our duty to aid those bold enough to venture forth and tame the Wilds."

"That makes sense," I agreed. "I imagine dangerous creatures are plentiful."

Diane nodded. "More than I can count, and new ones

appearing constantly. So don't go charging into battle just yet."

"Noted," I said. "I'll focus on getting my bearings first."

"A wise approach," said Caldwell. "In time, the Frontier Division may request your assistance with certain tasks to help keep the land around Gladdenfield Outpost safe. Scouting missions and such. Although we will make no such requests until we believe you are ready."

I nodded thoughtfully, excited by the prospects. "I'm happy to help in whatever way I can."

We discussed logistics a while longer, with Diane and Caldwell both offering helpful advice about the area. I was starting to feel well prepared for the challenges ahead thanks to their guidance.

When it seemed I had a solid understanding of my role, Caldwell stood up from the table. "Well, I'll leave you two to get better acquainted. Please, eat and drink your fill — it's on the Frontier Division tonight."

I stood as well to shake Caldwell's hand. "Thank you again for everything. I'm sure I'll be seeing you around Gladdenfield soon."

"Indeed you shall," Caldwell said warmly. He gave Diane a paternal smile. "Take good care of our promising new frontiersman."

"I will, don't you worry," Diane assured him.

With that, Caldwell took his leave, exiting the tavern and leaving Diane and I alone at the table together. I sat back down slowly.

Diane met my eyes with a playful smile. "Well now, shall we order some food? You must be hungry after the long journey here."

"Starving," I admitted, settling in across from her. The tavern was cozy and full of life around us, but in that moment all I could focus on was her captivating face in the flickering firelight.

Diane waved the barmaid over and began listing off dishes and drinks for us to sample. I didn't have much frame of reference, but everything sounded delicious.

As we waited for our food, Diane and I fell into easy conversation. With her, this strange new world already felt a little less daunting. I had a sense this was the beginning of something exciting.

Chapter 7

The food arrived shortly, and the aromas made my mouth water. There were meat pies with flaky golden crusts, bowls of hearty vegetable stew, and baskets of freshly baked bread. Two frothy mugs of ale accompanied our feast.

"Dig in!" Diane urged with an enthusiastic sweep of her hand.

I needed no further convincing. The journey had left me ravenous, and everything looked incredible. I tried a bit of everything, savoring the rich and hearty flavors.

"This is amazing," I mumbled through a mouthful of stew-soaked bread.

Diane smiled, looking pleased. "So glad you're enjoying it! The cook here, Darny's wife, is excellent. We'll have to come back often so I can show you all my favorite dishes."

I washed the food down with a swig of ale and grinned. "I like the sound of that," I said. "So, what do you eat around here most of the time?"

She laughed, and I loved the way it made her fox ears stand upright. I could get used to that laugh. "Well," she began, "we mostly eat whatever we can get!"

I joined her laughter as I took another bite from the meat pie, savoring the taste. "I doubt that," I said, "this pie tastes like heaven. If Gladdenfield Outpost has ingredients like this at its disposal, I doubt anyone out here is subsisting on grubs and leaves."

She grinned, looking down at her plate a little bashfully. "You're right," she said. "Our people have it good here, but we remember the older days." At that, her expression turned a little more sorrowful. There was a story there, so much was certain.

However, by the way she closed up a little, I expected it was not an easy topic to discuss for her. No doubt, there would be more such sensitivities for me to navigate if I wanted to get to know her better. I decided to let it rest for now, even though I wanted to know more about her. We had only just met, after all, and I did not want her to be uncomfortable.

We ate companionably for a few minutes. Conversation revolved mainly around the meal and the ingredients, and it was casual and relaxed. I was struck by how comfortable and natural it felt, even though we'd only just met.

Diane had a warmth that made me feel instantly at ease.

As I sampled more dishes, I noticed Diane seemed to favor the meat pies. She delicately picked the flaky crust apart with her fork to get at the contents.

There was something overwhelmingly cute about the way she delighted in the taste. When she caught me looking, she flashed a smile, her cute canines on full display.

"I take it foxkin are big on meat?" I guessed with a smile.

Diane's eyes glinted. "Very, very much so! Yes, meat is a staple of our diet. The forests provide plentiful game, so we've never lacked for it."

I leaned forward, curious to learn more about her kind. "What else can you tell me about foxkin? I'll admit I don't know much yet."

Diane tipped her head thoughtfully. "Well, others say we are known for our curiosity and cleverness. Foxkin enjoy learning, exploring, solving puzzles. We hunt a lot, but we are better trappers than we are at shooting game." Her eyes twinkled. "And we like to play a trick every now and then."

I chuckled. "Duly noted."

She went on, "We also have very strong senses of smell and hearing. Our night vision is excellent as well. All in all, we are better suited to the woods and the Wilds than, say, humans or even elves."

With that, she gave me a look that seemed to contain something of a challenge, and I understood from it that she was eager to see how I would do. I expected that, to her kind, skills of outdoor survival were important. They probably gauged an individual's worth by their ability to survive.

Maybe they even assessed potential mates on that metric…

That stray thought sent a little jolt down my body, and I knew I was already on that course. I wanted to get to know her better, though, and I would prove to her that my outdoorsmanship was fine — better than that of most. I was probably not at foxkin levels yet, but I certainly wasn't a pushover.

As my mind refocused, Diane elaborated on foxkin history and culture as we ate. I hung on her every word, captivated by her musical voice and lively storytelling. "The foxkin originally lived only in Tannoris before the Upheaval merged our worlds," she explained between bites of stew. "We made our homes in the forests there."

"Fascinating," I remarked. "So your people came here to Earth along with the elves and the other kin?"

Diane nodded, taking a sip of ale. "Yes, some of us ventured through the portals and rifts that opened up. We were curious about this new land. And Tannoris was dying, so we couldn't stay."

"That makes sense. And it seems like your kind has adapted well to life here?"

"Oh yes, quite well," said Diane. "Your forests are actually very similar to those in Tannoris. Plenty of good hunting and foraging."

I leaned forward, eager to learn more about her culture. "And what of your dwellings? Did you build new settlements here or continue as nomads?"

Diane chuckled. "We foxkin are wanderers at heart.

We don't care much for staying in one place."

"So you don't build permanent houses and villages?" I asked.

"No, not usually," she replied. "In our culture, living in a fixed house is seen as something only the wealthy and eccentric do. For most foxkin, we follow the seasonal migration of prey and make temporary shelters along the way."

I shook my head in amazement. "Incredible. I can't imagine living such a nomadic life, but it clearly suits your kind perfectly."

Diane smiled, tail swishing proudly. "It is in our blood. We are born to roam and explore. Though..." She gave me a coy glance. "Having a family might make settling down tempting."

I smiled and nodded, knowing what she meant. Before the Upheaval, I had been a little of a roamer myself. And I, too, longed for a place of my own and a family of my own now.

As the food was cleared away by the serving girl, we moved closer together, leaning in over the table. There was a natural draw to each other as I leaned in, fascinated, and she did the same, enthusiastic to teach me more about her ways.

"I think a great occasion to learn more about our kind

are the Hunters' Festivals we hold. They are aligned with... well, they used to be aligned with the seasons, but those were different on Tannoris. The festivals we've held here are usually when the moon gives more light for the night."

"Full moon?" I asked.

She nodded enthusiastically, one of her pretty locks slipping astray and framing her beautiful face. "Yes," she said. "The full moon."

"It all sounds wonderful," I said sincerely. "I'd love to take part someday, if I could be so honored."

Diane smiled softly. "Any friend of the foxkin is welcome at our gatherings."

I returned her smile, feeling a newfound kinship with this mesmerizing woman. As we lingered over the last dregs of ale, our eyes locked. An unspoken connection hummed between us.

At last, Diane smiled broadly at me. "Well, we should make our way to your homestead before dark. The woods around Gladdenfield are generally safe. Trouble won't find you unless you go looking for it. But it's much harder to navigate at night, and we shouldn't take the risk just yet."

I nodded, disappointed for a moment that this fun... well, *date*... was coming to an end. But then again, I was very excited to see my new place. "Yeah," I said. "Let's go have a look!"

She grinned. "Caldwell will settle the tab. Let's go!"

Chapter 8

Diane and I stepped outside the tavern into the mellow evening light. The sun was just about to touch the western horizon, which I could discern by the warm golden glow it cast over the landscape.

"What a lovely evening," Diane remarked, tail swishing contentedly as she turned her face to the fading sunlight.

"It really is beautiful," I agreed, admiring the way the light softened Diane's features. The softer light brought an exquisite glow to her enchantingly black hair. The way her cute fox ears perked upright had me mesmerized.

She turned to me and smiled, her sapphire eyes ablaze in the evening light. A silent moment passed, and it was far from uncomfortable. "Where is your vehicle?" she finally asked, fidgeting with the rebellious lock of black hair that had slipped free during dinner.

"This way," I said, gesturing in the direction where Caldwell and I had parked.

As we turned, I wondered for a moment how he would return to New Springfield if he'd left the vehicle with me. Then again, he probably had a few ways to move around, seeing as the Frontier Division was so closely tied to Gladdenfield Outpost.

We strolled unhurriedly, neither eager for the evening to end. The village was winding down from the day's bustle, a few merchants packing up their stalls for the night. Some curious eyes fixed on us as we walked along, and several of the merchants and townsfolk greeted Diane with a hint of reverence in their voices. By the looks and sounds of it, she was a well-known and respected figure in town.

"Thanks for sharing so much about the foxkin at dinner," I said as we walked together in the waning sunlight. "I was fascinated hearing all the stories and traditions."

Diane smiled. "I'm glad you found it interesting. We don't often get a chance to share our culture. I don't speak with many people, to be honest, and those I do speak with are usually accustomed to living in the Wilds. They already know much about us."

I nodded. "Well, if there's anything else you want to tell me, please do. I can't seem to get enough."

"Hmm, let me think…" Diane trailed off, tail swishing pensively. The fading sunlight brought out glints of white highlights around her fuzzy black ears, and she pouted a little as she thought.

At last she continued. "One thing that's central in foxkin society is our dens. They're our sanctuaries, our comfort."

"But I thought you were nomadic?" I said.

She grinned and nodded. "I see you've been paying attention! Very good. Yes, we are nomadic, but when the…" she blushed for a moment and turned her eyes to the packed dirt road. "When breeding time comes around, we make a den for the little ones and for those in the family who are pregnant."

"Are the women in the family usually pregnant at the same time?" I asked, trying to work things out in my mind.

She smiled sideways at me, dodging a heap of some pack animal's droppings. "Oh no, you misunderstand. Our families are big. Only a few foxkin are born male, and they usually take multiple wives. Our families are called packs."

I nodded. "Like the elves?"

"Indeed."

It had been one of the many cultural gaps between humankind and the elves that the Coalition had tried to smooth over. With elves, there was a similar ratio of girls to boys born as with humans. However, most males had very little… well, *interest* in the activities that resulted in children. They mated once every twenty to fifty years. As such, it was common for multiple women to flock to the rare males with an increased drive and who mated more often. The remainder of the males largely abstained.

One of the first things the Coalition had pushed for was official recognition of what was now called 'the Elven Marriage,' which was concluded between a man and multiple women. Once legalized, it had only taken a few months for the first human males to take multiple wives, although it was still much less common among humans.

"However, unlike the elves," Diane continued, "with us foxkin, the necessity comes from lack of males. Not from... *inactive* males."

I chuckled at that. I had not yet seen an elven woman who was ugly, but the vast majority of them were very plain. It was strange since humanity had an idealized picture of elves as beautiful and ethereal creatures, often inspired by fantasy fiction. In truth, while they were never ugly, there was almost nothing remarkable about them, and they seemed... well, dull.

But there were exceptions. And when an elf was beautiful, she was *beautiful*. And I mean hauntingly, absorbingly beautiful. Unfortunately, the beautiful ones were usually very aloof and icy.

"Anyway," Diane said, "we make dens when the mating time comes around. They are temporary, of course — meant to be a safe haven for mothers and children until the pack can move on again."

I tried to picture it. "So you decorate those dens in certain ways?"

"Oh yes," said Diane. "With soft bedding, natural objects like stones and feathers. Things that remind us of the forest."

Her description made me smile. "That sounds really cozy."

Diane chuckled, her sapphire eyes acquiring a faraway look as she thought back on the dens she had seen in her life. "The dens are private places, for family and mates. They are one of the few places where we are truly very safe."

I nodded thoughtfully. "I appreciate you explaining your customs. Learning more about them is interesting, but also useful to me."

Diane smiled warmly. "I know. That's why I don't mind your questions." She gave me a coy look. "Even the personal ones."

I laughed, feeling suddenly bashful. We walked in comfortable silence as the sun sank lower in the painted sky.

Diane broke the quiet. "I'm glad Caldwell assigned me as your partner. I think we'll work well together."

"Me too," I agreed. "You're already an amazing guide to frontier life."

Diane playfully bumped my shoulder with hers. "Just imagine the adventures we'll have!"

I grinned at the thought. Diane's spirit was infectious. As we neared the vehicle, I felt truly optimistic. Out here with Diane, the world seemed full of possibilities.

We reached the rugged Jeep, and I held the passenger door open for Diane. She smiled as she hopped in, tail swishing against the seat.

I walked around and slid into the driver's seat, turning the key in the ignition. The engine rumbled to life, and I pulled out onto the dirt track leading south out of Gladdenfield Outpost. Soon enough, the surrounding forest had swallowed up the sight of the charming little frontier outpost.

"Your homestead's about twenty minutes southwest," Diane informed me. "Just follow the Silverthread River till you see the old lightning-struck cottonwood on the right bank. There, we take a narrow ribbon of a road, and the going will be a little slower. Your cabin's a quarter mile beyond that."

"Got it, thanks," I said, scanning the landscape ahead. The last warm light of sunset painted the wild hills and forests in amber hues. Birds wheeled overhead, their calls echoing among the trees. This was truly out there — nature, the wild. Excitement brimmed in my very soul, and I took a deep, happy breath as I handled the

Jeep.

I stole glances at Diane as I drove. The fading light illuminated her elegant profile. Sensing my look, she turned and flashed a fanged smile.

"Excited to see your new home?" she asked.

"Very much so," I replied. "Still haven't wrapped my head around the fact that I own property out here now. Feels surreal after a lifetime in the city."

Diane nodded knowingly. "It's a big change for sure. But I think frontier living will suit you."

I certainly hoped so. This new path still felt impulsive, but my gut said it was right. And having Diane's guidance and company soothed any doubts.

The terrain grew rougher, the track meandering down ridges and gullies. I shifted into four-wheel-drive and picked my way carefully around rocks and ruts.

"You're a natural at this," Diane remarked as I maneuvered a tricky descent.

"Just don't look in the back," I joked. "Pretty sure everything's bouncing around back there."

Diane laughed, her ears perking up amusedly. The sound sent a pleasant tingle through me. Making her laugh felt like a goal in its own right.

"So," I said, eager to learn more about the foxkin. "Your people — do they drive?"

She nodded. "Some of us do. There were no cars or even combustion engines on Tannoris. I think the physics just... worked differently?" She shrugged. "I don't know how else to explain it."

I nodded. "It makes sense," I said. "After all, we see electronics failing in the Wilds as well. It might not be physics as much as it is some kind of magical interference. After all, we didn't have magic — insofar as I'm aware — on Earth before the Upheaval."

"That could be it," she agreed. "And maybe the Upheaval kind of watered down the magic so that some of your technology now works?"

"Maybe," I said, smiling at how eagerly she engaged in the conjecture. She was curious like she said, and I felt that was a good trait.

Before long, the shriveled lightning-struck cottonwood Diane mentioned came into view, lit up by the headlights.

"There's your marker," Diane said. "Head right at the next trail junction."

I followed her direction, spotting a small path cutting off the main track. It led through a wooded valley by the glinting river. It was a rough road, and I was grateful for the Jeep's excellent handling.

"Almost there," Diane told me with an encouraging

smile. She seemed nearly as excited as I was.

The trail ended at a clearing on the riverbank. Nestled against the flowing water was a cozy hand-hewn log cabin. Two small plots, one for farming and one for pasture, flanked the rustic dwelling. They needed some work to be properly cleared, but I could see someone had been here recently to make the place a little more ready for me.

I parked and stepped out, gazing at my new home in awe. It was perfect — exactly the kind of idyllic retreat I'd dreamed of finding out here.

Diane joined me, looking pleased by my reaction. "What do you think? Does it meet your expectations?"

"It exceeds them," I said sincerely. "This is incredible. It's secluded, but not too remote. And the scenery is beyond words." I turned to Diane, a jolt of excitement passing through me as she slipped her hand into mine, giving it a warm squeeze. "Thank you for bringing me here."

"Of course!" Diane replied, smiling back brightly. "I'm so glad you like it. Now come on, let me give you the tour!"

Still hand-in-hand, she pulled me eagerly toward the front door. Her enthusiasm was contagious, and it took me a moment to realize that the holding of hands —

which in this situation would have been a gesture of intimacy by human standards as well — was very intimate to the fox girl.

She seemed to realize it at the same time and drew her hand back, her cheeks turning a deep crimson. I smiled at that but decided to say nothing for the moment.

We entered the cabin together, and I used the electric torch provided by Caldwell until Diane had found an oil lamp and lit it. In the expanding glow, I found that the interior was rustic but cozy and well-equipped with furniture.

Diane showed me where everything was located, from the empty pantry to the woodpile for the stove and fireplace.

I felt right at home. With Diane as my partner, this unfamiliar world no longer seemed so daunting. I knew this was where I was meant to be.

Chapter 9

Before we did anything else, Diane and I thoroughly explored the cozy cabin. It was small and rustic, but what space it had was used efficiently. Upon entering the cabin, there was a small mudroom with a few built-in cabinets.

Next came the living room with the fireplace and the adjoining little kitchen. The only furniture in the living room was a simple but sturdy dining table with a few chairs. The kitchen featured wooden counters and a cast iron stove that connected to the stone chimney. A hatch in the floor led to a simple cellar where food could be stored, although there was also a roomy larder. There was no electricity.

The cabin had a pitched roof, and a pitched ladder ran up to a loft under the roof with just enough room for us to stand. Like the rest of the cabin, it was snug and welcoming, and there were four beds with thick feather mattresses and hand-stitched wool blankets. They were unmade as of yet. It was a little cramped, maybe, but nice and cozy.

After exploring, Diane and I headed back outside into the deepening darkness, lighting the flashlight again. The cool evening air carried the scent of pine and wildflowers. We walked around to the rear of the Jeep to start unloading my belongings and the generous provisions Caldwell had equipped me with.

I unlatched the rear door, and it swung open heavily. Diane stepped up beside me and let out an impressed whistle. "That's quite the haul! Mr. Caldwell wasn't kidding about setting you up proper."

I chuckled. "No kidding. I figured maybe a bag of dried beans and some matches. But this..." I gestured at the array of tools, weapons, food, and survival gear. "This is another level. I almost feel guilty accepting it all for free."

Diane smiled and nudged me playfully with her hip. "Oh hush, you'll need it. The Coalition wants you to succeed. It needs successful homesteaders out here to retake the Wilds. Now come on, let's take stock and get this inside before it's pitch black out."

We started removing items one by one and laying them out carefully on the floor of the cabin. There were shiny tools, including an axe, saw, and a shovel, coils of rope, an assortment of traps, a pile of packaged MREs, and a crate of preserves.

I also unloaded the rifle and handgun Caldwell had gifted me along with several boxes of ammunition. I hoped I wouldn't need to use them but felt reassured having them just in case.

In addition to the Coalition-provided gear were my own meager belongings — some clothes, books, camping supplies I'd managed to hold onto over the years. It wasn't much to start a new life with, but combined with what Caldwell had arranged, I felt well equipped.

It took several trips apiece to bring it all inside, but eventually we formed neat rows of gear across the hardwood living room floor.

Hands on my hips, I surveyed our haul. "Wow, this is a lot of stuff laid out like this."

Diane gave me an encouraging rub on my arm. "We'll tackle it together. I'm an expert organizer."

I could see a glint of mischief in her eyes, but something told me that a nomadic foxkin who had lived on the frontier all her life would indeed know a thing or two about efficient inventory management. "All right," I said, smiling at her. "Let's hear it!"

She glanced around the cozy space, contemplating. "Hmm, I figure we should put the tools and weapons in easy reach but out of the way in the mudroom entry. There's a little cabinet in the mudroom we can use for them. It will have to do until we make you a workshop."

"Good thinking," I replied, gathering up the tools and firearms. The small entry room to the cabin turned out to be perfect for stashing muddy boots and bulky equipment that we wouldn't need regular access to.

Next, we turned our attention to the food stocks, moving the crates and bags over to the pantry nook adjacent to the old cast iron stove. Diane showed me the hand pump at the sink for fresh water as well.

"It's an artesian well," she explained. "You won't run

out as long as you don't waste." She beamed a happy smile as she studied the pump, and I realized that — to her kind — having clean, running water at her beck and call was probably a great luxury.

Come to think of it, I had to agree with her. I made a mental note about water conservation and was once again happy that she was here with me. Her appreciation, enthusiasm, and knowledge would make this venture a lot more lively and a lot less lonely, even though I didn't mind a little solitude from time to time.

As we put things away in organized cabinets and drawers, I started feeling more settled. Diane's guidance was proving invaluable already. Within an hour, order was restored, and all the new belongings were distributed logically throughout the cozy space.

I stood back next to Diane to appreciate our efforts. "It's really coming together," she remarked, giving my arm an affectionate squeeze. "Looks like you still need some more female touches around here." She pursed her lips as she looked around. "We'll have to get you some decorations."

I grinned and gave her a teasing nudge. "I thought foxkin only decorated their dens?"

She blushed a little and mumbled a reply I couldn't make out before she perked up with foxlike enthusiasm.

"Oh! How about we get the fire going? The nights here can get cold!"

I laughed. "That's a great idea!" We lingered another moment, her hand still resting comfortably on my arm. An unspoken connection hummed between us.

Diane gave herself a little shake, as though coming out of a trance. "Well! You can get the fire, and I'll have a look in the bedroom and make sure the beds are made. Caldwell's guys had better left us some linens..."

I chuckled as Diane headed up the creaky wooden steps to the cozy sleeping loft under the pitched roof. I heard her rummaging around in the dressers, looking for some bed linen, and my pulse quickened thinking about sharing this intimate space with her. But those thoughts could wait for later. For now, there were still tasks at hand.

I gathered an armload of split firewood from the stack outside and carried it into the cozy cabin. There was a small but convenient supply of firewood, but I'd have to get more soon. The living area featured a beautiful stone fireplace, the only source of heat for the rustic dwelling.

I piled logs and kindling in the hearth, then struck a match to light the tinder. Soon, flickering flames licked over the dry wood. I added a couple of larger logs, watching as the fire grew, its light dancing across the room.

The warmth was welcome after the chilly evening air outside. I sat back on my haunches, prodding the logs with an iron poker to let air circulate. Orange embers swirling up the chimney promised many such cozy nights ahead.

This simple routine of building a fire stirred nostalgia in me. How often had I done this on camping trips over the years? Yet now it was for my own permanent home, not a temporary campsite. And sure, turning up the heating in an apartment was easier, but there was satisfaction to be found in doing things like this – taking your time.

I glanced around the bare walls, thinking the space could use some decoration. I'd have to ask Diane if she had suggestions – a nice tapestry or rug would liven up the place, and there had been one rolled up in one of the cabinets, so I'd put it down there. This was my view now too, no longer confined to the city, and I aimed to make the cabin feel more lived-in.

Picturing where I might place my few possessions, I moved the braided rug into the living room from its storage. As I placed it, I made sure it was far enough away from the fireplace to prevent it from catching fire. Satisfied, I looked around and decided some comfy chairs around the hearth to keep with the rustic vibe would be nice. I'd have to build bookshelves for my modest collection.

The popping fire drew my gaze again. Already this unfamiliar place was starting to feel like home. Adding personal touches would only reinforce that further, but for now, the simple fire was comfort enough.

I fed the fire two more logs to ensure it would keep burning steady, finding comfort and satisfaction in doing so. It had been a while since I'd made a fire for myself, and it was good to be out of the city.

The creaking ladder announced Diane's return from the loft where she had been getting the beds ready. She paused once her dainty feet touched the hardwood floor, tail swaying gently as she watched me tending the fire. The flickering light played across her fine features.

"There we go, that should hold us for a while," I said, dusting off my hands as I stood up. "Did you have any luck finding bedding?"

Diane smiled. "I did indeed – the dressers were stocked with blankets and linens. Nothing fancy, but it'll keep us warm. And there's a spare set for when we have to wash the linens."

"That's good news," I replied, looking around. "You know, this cabin already feels more welcoming than any place I had back in the city."

Diane moved to stand nearer the fire, holding her palms out to the warmth. "There's something special about a homestead, rough as it may be. The city keeps you safe, but it comes at a cost."

I nodded thoughtfully. "You're so right. I'd gladly accept some hardships for the freedom."

We stood in comfortable silence for a few moments, the fire popping and hissing gently. It was surprising how natural it felt already, the two of us sharing this space.

"So Diane," I began, "tell me more about Classes. Are they always something matching your skills and personality?"

Diane nodded. "Yes, your Class taps into your innate strengths and inclinations. It amplifies what is already within you."

"And do you get any say in the matter?" I asked. "Or is it just whatever the awakening ritual reveals?"

"The ritual simply unlocks what was slumbering within," said Diane. "But you can choose how to utilize and develop your Class."

I stroked my chin thoughtfully. Her words gave me hope I could cultivate my eventual Class in a direction of my choosing.

"You know, it's still so strange that I don't have a Class yet," I mused. "Have you gotten any hints about what mine might be?"

Diane tipped her head thoughtfully. "Not yet, but these things take time. Don't lose hope." She smiled. "My Class is Scout. We're natural pathfinders and survivors."

"That makes perfect sense," I said. "You really know your way around out here."

"I've lived in the wilds my whole life," Diane replied. "It's second nature. With time, it will become natural for you too."

I nodded, hoping she was right. Gaining useful frontier skills seemed key to surviving and thriving out here. Having an experienced Scout guiding me was incredibly valuable.

"Well, when my Class does manifest, I hope it's one that complements yours," I said. "We'd make a great team."

Diane met my eyes, smiling softly. The fire's glow framed her face exquisitely. "I have a feeling we'll make a good team regardless," she said. We gazed at one another as the world narrowed down to just this room, this hearth, this shared comfort.

A log split in the fireplace, sending up a burst of sparks that broke the spell. We both jumped, then laughed together at being startled.

Diane brushed a strand of hair from her cheek, looking bashful but still smiling. "It's getting late. We should rest up for tomorrow."

Chapter 10

After enjoying the fire and letting the cabin heat up a little, Diane and I decided to turn in for the night. It had been an eventful first day, and we were both eager for some rest.

"Well, I'm going to go get ready for bed," Diane said a bit shyly. A touch of pink colored her cheeks. "Let me know if you need anything."

"Sounds good, thanks," I replied, "I'll be up in a few minutes myself." I was tired and wanted to go to bed too, but I needed to keep an eye on the fire for a bit.

Also, I didn't want to impose. She needed some privacy to change for the night. Although I had to admit to more than a little curiosity as to what she looked like under her clothes.

Diane gathered her small bag of belongings and made her way up the creaky wooden ladder to the sleeping loft. I busied myself tidying up downstairs, stowing the fire poker and making sure the logs were safely banked for the night.

Despite my weariness from the long day, my pulse quickened thinking about sharing the intimate sleeping space with Diane. Our natural chemistry was obvious, though I didn't want to rush anything, especially since there was a cultural gap I didn't quite grasp just yet.

I had already accidentally given her the cultural equivalent of a proposal, and although she hadn't seemed to object, I didn't want to risk our budding friendship that I hoped to turn into something more.

After changing into a simple linen shirt and cotton pants using the small sink in the kitchen for washing up, I slowly climbed the ladder. I paused at the top, suddenly realizing I was entering a space where Diane might still be scarcely dressed.

"Uh, decent up here?" I asked politely.

"Oh! Um, yes, come on up," Diane replied. I detected a tremor of shyness in her voice.

I climbed the last few rungs and saw Diane perched tensely on the edge of the further bed, wearing a modest white linen nightgown with a deep cut that made my fantasies run wild.

Her bosom was firm and round with a slight glisten of sweat caused by the day's activities that spun my mind. She had let her long dark hair down, and it fell in waves over her shoulders.

My breath caught at how utterly lovely she looked.

The beds were close to one another, with less than an arm's length between them, and I swallowed at the realization of having her so close to me.

When Diane noticed me, her cheeks flushed crimson, and she hurriedly slipped under the blankets, turning her body away. I smiled at her shyness, and I almost told her she looked beautiful. But I did not want to cause her any distress or embarrassment.

"Well… goodnight then," she managed to say, her voice strained.

I smiled as I slipped into my own bed on the opposite side of hers. "Sleep well, Diane. I'm really happy that we met. You've been a great help, and you've made the beginning of this adventure a lot more colorful than it would have been had I been on my own."

I could hear her give a contented sigh, and I knew she was pleased with my sincere words. "I'm happy I met you too, David," Diane murmured back almost inaudibly. "And you're adapting… remarkably."

I grinned as I leaned over to blow out the oil lamp on the nightstand, cloaking the small room in shadowy darkness. "That's because this life is a lot more interesting than the one I had."

She yawned, and I could hear the slow in her speech as she replied. "Hmm," she hummed as she rolled up in her cozy blankets. "You'll… You'll have to tell me more about that someday."

"I will," I replied, folding my hands behind my head as I stared at the rafters in the darkness. It was nice to be here, with the scent of the woodfire still lingering.

I lay there on my back, listening to the occasional pops from the cooling fire below. Sleep felt unlikely with my heart hammering. I was acutely aware of Diane's presence just a few feet away in the intimate space, and my mind went spinning with scenarios of how she would sneak out of her bed and climb into mine – how my hands would go roaming, claiming her bountiful body, and...

To distract my racing mind, I tried thinking over the momentous events of the last few days. So much had changed so quickly in my life. Just a week ago, I'd been stuck in my dreary city routine. Now here I was in a secluded valley on the frontier, beginning an unknown future.

My restless thoughts latched onto the mystery of why I hadn't received a Class yet. Most Class powers awakened during the ritual itself. What did it mean that mine was delayed? Was there something wrong with me?

I must have sighed aloud because Diane's soft voice spoke through the darkness, husky and sleepy with her adorable accent. "Trouble sleeping?"

"Yeah," I admitted, rolling onto my side to face her. I could just make out her silhouette in the bit of moonlight from the window. "My mind doesn't want to settle, I guess."

Diane rustled around under her blankets to face me. Her eyes glinted as they reflected the faint moonlight bleeding in through the windows. "Anything I can do to help?" she asked gently.

There were definitely some things she could do, but I kept those thoughts to myself. "I don't want to keep you awake," I said apologetically.

"It's alright," Diane replied. "I don't mind." She propped herself up on one elbow so we could talk more easily. "What's on your mind?"

Her caring, attentive tone made me want to open up. "Mostly just thinking about my Class," I confessed. "I know I should be patient, but I'm hoping my powers manifest soon."

Diane made a sympathetic hum. "I understand, the waiting must be so frustrating. But these things unfold in their own time."

I knew she spoke the truth, yet patience had never been my strong suit. "You're right," I acknowledged with a heavy sigh. "I just... I want to feel like I have a purpose out here, you know? Like I belong."

"You already do have a purpose," Diane said gently. She reached out and gave my hand a brief, reassuring squeeze. Before I could ask what she meant, she lay back down facing away. "Try to sleep if you can. Tomorrow's a new day."

Her simple words and gesture, though subtle, struck a chord in me. She was right — I didn't need magical powers or a Class to have worth and purpose — although they would be nice, of course. Just being here, living freely and carving out a homestead, was meaningful. With that calming thought settling my restless mind, I finally drifted off to sleep.

Chapter 11

I fell into a deep sleep, exhausted from the long day of travel and the excitement of arriving at my new homestead. As I slumbered, vivid visions began overtaking me.

I found myself wandering through an otherworldly landscape of soaring mountains wreathed in rainbow-hued mists and forests carpeted in emerald moss.

Ancient elven ruins were scattered across the terrain, rich with fantastical carvings and icons.

Strange creatures flitted amongst the cliffs and trees. Tiny, slender sprites no bigger than my hand flickered through the underbrush, their bodies alight with shifting colorful flames. Wispy wraiths glided soundlessly past, their transparent forms billowing like smoke.

In the distance, stony beasts with heavy tread shook the earth as they rumbled by. Their craggy hides were etched with glowing runes. Everything felt intensely real, yet somehow, I knew I wandered in a dream realm.

I walked unafraid amongst the fantastic beings, sensing they would not harm me. I was at peace in their magical domain because part of me belonged here.

Then the earth fell away before me into a deep, shadowy ravine. Craggy boulders littered the steep path leading down into its depths. As I peered cautiously over the edge, I saw wispy forms moving about below.

The wispy creatures were mostly sprites, wraiths, and small elementals. Only one figure was humanoid in appearance — a woman with pointy ears, antlers, and a fuzzy little tail. She looked up and met my gaze, waving in a friendly gesture.

The woman was mesmerizing, her deer-like features adding to her exotic beauty. She was curvy and voluptuous – more so than the more toned and fit figure of Diane – and something about her spoke of femininity and fertility in a way that made the mind wander. It didn't help that she wore a simple outfit of rough fabrics and leather that scarcely concealed her ample curves.

As I watched, transfixed, the deer-woman beckoned me to come down and join them. I hesitated, wondering if I should turn back. But something compelled me forward. It was not just her beauty, but the sense of belonging I experienced here.

Carefully picking my way down the winding treacherous path, I descended into the shadowy gorge. The figures came forward eagerly to greet me as I reached the bottom.

"Welcome, Summoner," said the deer-like woman in a melodic, lilting voice. "We have waited long to meet you." The others swirled around us in a loose circle.

I blinked, utterly confused. "Waited for me? But who are you?" I asked. "And what do you mean by Summoner?"

The woman smiled patiently and full of admiration,

her emerald green eyes blazing as she took me in inch by inch. "We are your disciples, sworn to serve you, the Summoner. And you are the foretold one, destined to call us forth when the time comes."

My heart quickened as understanding dawned — this was a sign of my Class! Had the dream unlocked hidden knowledge within me?

The disciples watched me expectantly. I hesitated, unsure what to do next. "But how do I summon you?" I asked the woman. "I don't know how…"

She smiled reassuringly. "Trust your instincts, Summoner. The power lies within, needing only your call to awaken." The others swirled around me, awaiting my attempt. "Seek," she hummed, extending a slender arm with her palm up. "Seek within, Summoner. It is in you. It has always been in you."

There was something comforting in her words, reinforcing that sense of belonging.

I took a deep breath, seeking that power. At first, there was nothing as I searched my soul. But soon enough, I found… a pocket in my mind. A place where knowledge was concealed and kept — something to be awakened, something that was awakening. My hands rose of their own accord, directed skyward.

The disciples began to glow brighter, thrumming

with energy. With words that came naturally, I called upon those bound to me in this life and beyond. I intoned, my voice echoing powerfully, "Come forth, loyal ones! Heed the summons and appear!"

Crackling energy surged through me. A blinding magical burst lit the gorge. The disciples vanished. I waited, heart pounding. Had I banished them? Seconds stretched on with no sign of their return. Doubt crept in as the silence deepened.

But then the woman and wisps reappeared, more solid than before, as if I could reach out and touch them. She laughed, a tinkling of joy that made my own heart liven up. Her beauty became even greater as she gave into her joy and happiness, unrestrained and innocent and free as a creature of nature. It was as if my words had liberated her.

I couldn't stop myself from smiling at it. Part of me wanted to hold her, not even — or not just — out of the desire to touch her, but to share in her happiness and joy.

When she was done, she fixed those sparkling emerald eyes on me once more. "We are here and await your every summons," she said with a bow. "You will learn the spells, and we will come!"

I understood there was still much to learn, but now

knew my purpose — to call them forth. There were spells — magical words I would need to learn, but it would come, and I would grow.

At this realization, my dream form began drifting up out of the ravine, soaring over forests and seas. The disciples waved farewell, shining brightly.

"We will come to you when called, oh Summoner!" she pledged again.

And then, they faded.

With a gasp, I awoke in the darkened cabin loft. Early light peeked through the window. The vivid dream still burned in my mind.

"David?" came Diane's soft voice as she rolled over and studied me, her face still half-buried under her sheets, but her eyes big. "Are you okay? I heard you stirring…"

"Yeah, yeah… I'm fine," I replied. "I just had the most intense dream…" I wanted to tell her every detail, but the morning felt too fragile for now.

"Do you want to talk about it?" she asked, concern lighting up her pretty eyes.

"Let me make us some coffee, then we can talk," I suggested. Diane yawned and rose from bed, smiling. As she stood in her clinging nightgown, I was reminded that this was no dream. I was really here. With her. In this place.

Joy mounted in my heart as I almost sprung from the bed, eager to start this day in a way I had not been for a long, long time.

Chapter 12

I hurried down the ladder to start some coffee, my mind still spinning from the vivid dream. Diane followed shortly after, wrapping a shawl around her shoulders against the morning chill.

At the simple kitchen area, I busied myself grinding some coffee beans by hand and then adding them to the waiting pot of water on the cast iron stove. I carefully lit the stove and let it heat until the water began to bubble gently. The percolating coffee soon filled the small cabin with its rich, invigorating aroma.

While waiting for it to brew, I added a few split logs to the fireplace to rekindle the flames. We would need the extra warmth to combat the crisp morning air that crept in through the walls.

Once the fire was merrily licking over the dry wood, I joined Diane at the table near the hearth. She had tucked her legs up under herself on the chair and had her shawl wrapped tightly around her. Her eyes watched me expectantly over the top of it.

"So, tell me about this intense dream," she prompted, her ears perked and tail swishing with curiosity. "I could tell it really made an impact on you."

I took a deep breath, gathering my thoughts on where to begin and how much detail to provide. "Well, it all felt incredibly lifelike and real, like I was actually there," I started. "I found myself wandering through this vivid mystical landscape with mountains, forests, and ancient ruins scattered around."

I did my best to describe the sweeping vistas and fantastical scenery, emphasizing how real it had felt. I told her about the various creatures I had encountered, from the tiny flickering sprites to the massive lumbering beasts etched with glowing runes. Diane listened raptly, eyes wide, nodding for me to continue.

When I got to the part about discovering the ravine and descending into it, she leaned forward slightly in her chair. I made sure to set the scene carefully — the jagged boulders, the slippery path downward, the shapes swirling about the shadowy depths.

Diane's brow furrowed in concentration as I described the deer-woman in detail — her graceful antlers, fuzzy tail, and piercing yet kind emerald eyes. How she had welcomed me and referred to me as 'Summoner.' I recounted our conversation verbatim, watching Diane's brows rise at the mention of spirit disciples sworn to my service.

"It certainly sounds as if your Class is beginning to manifest," Diane said thoughtfully once I had relayed the entire dream. "Summoners are rare… Rare and powerful. If you are indeed a Summoner, I understand now why your aura called out to Caldwell and made him choose you…" Her eyes dwelled over me for a second. "Apart from your fitness."

I smiled at that. Out of another mouth, it may have been a mere statement of fact, but the slight blush — visible just behind the shawl — told me it was more in this case.

"Oh," Diane continued hurriedly. "The landscape you described sounds a lot like parts of Tannoris that I remember as a child. Perhaps you have some special bond to it? Either way, the power to summon other creatures is a great one!"

I nodded, staring into my coffee mug as I rolled her statement around in my mind. "It still seems bizarre to think I could develop such an incredible ability," I replied after a moment. "In the dream, it felt completely natural, like second nature. But awake here in the real world, it's harder to believe."

Diane smiled kindly and gave my hand a reassuring squeeze from across the table. "Believe it," she said. "Magic is real… although it is sometimes hard to accept to those who have lived on Earth before the Upheaval."

I gave her a thankful nod and once again felt happiness that she was with me. I knew I would have managed on my own, but it was so much better to make this journey in her company.

By now, the coffee was finished brewing. I eagerly poured us each a steaming mug full, savoring the rich aroma. Diane closed her eyes as she inhaled the fragrant steam.

"Mmm, it smells delightful!" she remarked. "Reminds me of the rare coffee those traveling elf merchants occasionally bring through Gladdenfield to trade and sell. Much better than my usual bare-bones campfire brew out in the wilderness."

We both chuckled at that. I made a mental note to thank Caldwell again for providing these luxuries along with the basic survival supplies. I was struck by how quickly this place was starting to feel like home. Diane added a small splash of coffee creamer to her coffee, and I was amused at the sight, smiling.

She smiled back, one eyebrow perked. "What's so funny?" she asked.

"Just… You're like this magical being to me. And yet you drink coffee… with creamer."

She laughed. "I'm hardly magical!" she exclaimed. "And while there was no coffee on Tannoris, I'm pretty sure that any Tannorian who's lived around humans has taken to the drink. It's one of humanity's greatest achievements!"

We both laughed at that, then slowly sipped the hot revitalizing drinks. As we drank, Diane's expression became pensive once more. "I wonder if that deer-woman you described plays some greater significance," she mused. "Since she seemed to take such a central role in the dream events, perhaps she is a guide meant to help you learn to use your abilities."

I blinked, impressed by her insight. "I actually wondered the same thing," I admitted. "If she's meant to be my… spirit mentor or something along those lines." It was puzzling yet deeply intriguing. I found myself eager to hopefully see the deer-woman again and learn more.

"She must be a deerkin," Diane mused. "They lived with us on Tannoris, but they kept to themselves as many hunted them."

We tossed theories and conjectures back and forth while continuing to sip our coffees. But soon enough, our conversation was interrupted by a loud extended groan from my stomach.

Diane raised an eyebrow, a corner of her mouth quirking upward as she covered her mouth to chuckle. "Clearly, all that intense dreaming worked up quite an appetite," she teased.

I chuckled. "Guess I better eat something."

"I'd be happy to whip up some breakfast for us both," Diane offered, standing gracefully from her chair. She glided over to our food stores and perused the options critically, her bushy tail swishing behind her.

"Let's see what we have to work with here… some potatoes, a few speckled eggs, strips of that dried cured mystery meat." Her nose twitched adorably as she investigated further. "And I think some wild herbs and spices in my personal pack..." She glanced at me over her shoulder with a wink. "My private little treasure!"

Before long, a mouthwatering aroma of frying potatoes and eggs filled the cozy cabin. Diane cooked the mixture deftly in a cast-iron pan over the stove, adding crumbled bits of the savory dried meat at intervals. She sprinkled dashes of various dried herbs, integrating them seamlessly. She was quite the cook, and I looked at her with admiration as she finished the meal.

"There we go — a real hearty wilderness scramble," Diane announced proudly as she scooped the cheese-laden concoction onto two wooden plates. She also pulled some bread out of her pack and toasted it over the fireplace flames.

"This looks positively delicious," I proclaimed as we finally sat across from each other at the table to eat. The first flavorful bite confirmed it — the potatoes were crispy, the cured meat added just the right savory kick, and the herbs provided depth.

Between hungry mouthfuls, I turned our speculative conversation back to my mysterious powers. "You know, if I manage to gain control of these summoning abilities like in the dream, I bet my spirit allies could be a great help around the homestead here," I pondered.

Diane's eyes lit up at the possibilities. "Now that would be tremendously useful if you could manifest them physically for tasks!" she responded enthusiastically. "It was wise of the Coalition to recruit those like you who might awaken such rare talents. Your gifts could aid the whole community."

I nodded, growing increasingly excited to discover the true extent of the abilities my vivid dream had hinted at. There was so much I hoped to learn and explore.

We finished our delicious meal while chatting more lightly about the day's plans and tasks ahead. As we cleaned up the dishes, Diane flashed me a playful wink, her stunning blue eyes glinting knowingly.

"But no more dreaming for now," she teased. "We've got a busy day ahead out in the wilderness! I want to show you the layout of the riverbank area. Awareness of your surroundings is vital. And we should also have a look at your plots!"

After breakfast, Diane and I headed outside into the crisp morning air. A thin mist hung over the Silverthread River, promising a hot day ahead.

"Let's start down by the water," Diane suggested, tail swishing excitedly. "I'll show you some prime fishing spots for when we need to stock up on food. I know how to smoke them, so they'll keep for a while."

We picked our way carefully down the rocky, shale-strewn bank. The stones were slippery with moss and algae, requiring sure footing. Diane moved with graceful ease, clearly at home in this environment. I didn't do too poorly myself, having hiked a lot through difficult terrain, but I was eager to pick up a few things from her — she was a natural.

When we got to the riverbank, Diane pointed out little eddies and riffles in the flowing water, explaining why fish tended to gather there. "See how the current bubbles over those submerged rocks? They trap insects for the fish to feed on, so they like to hang around close to them."

The churning patterns she identified would have been invisible to my untrained eye. But it made sense — the foxkin were masterful hunters and foragers by nature.

"Impressive," I said.

She smiled and shot me a wink. "Nature provides for us, so long as there's not too many of us, and we all have our space." She tapped the side of her head. "It's good for our minds, too, having our own place and... well, just subsisting from time to time."

At last, we reached the water's gravelly edge. Upstream, the river split around a wooded islet before winding lazily into the distance. The silver waters glittered in the climbing sun, forcing me to squint.

On the far bank, vivid magenta and azure wildflowers dotted the swaying grass. The diversity and saturation of colors reminded me this was no ordinary meadow. We were firmly amid the otherworldly Wilds now.

"It's so beautiful here," I breathed, taking it all in. "I can't believe this is all mine."

Diane smiled, her pointy ears twitching happily. "Just wait till you see it at sunset when all the colors deepen. It's unbelievable. This spot has some special energy."

We continued downstream at an unhurried pace, pausing occasionally so Diane could point out tracks in the mud or interesting plants. Apparently, my homestead was close to a favored drinking spot of local animals. I tried to commit as much as I could to memory.

"And these purple flowers are important," she said. "They help keep down a fever. Medical supplies can be difficult to get at times, so it's good to keep medicinal plants around."

I made a mental note as she showed me examples of both edible, medicinal, and poisonous plants. Her wilderness wisdom would prove invaluable in keeping me and others alive out here. And like she said, it was amazing what nature provided for us.

After about half a mile, we finally looped back inland toward the cabin. The two fenced rectangular plots lay adjacent to the rustic dwelling — one meant for farming crops, the other for livestock.

"Let's have a look at the state of these," Diane said. "We should assess how much work it is before we can get them ready."

"Sounds like a plan," I said, following after her.

The garden was overgrown with stubborn weeds and woody brush, but someone had already put some work into clearing it: there were no trees or larger boulders. Still, it would require much more work before we could sow.

Diane kicked at the tough, stringy roots stubbornly binding the soil.

"We'll need to put some hard work into clearing this

out before we can even think about planting," she assessed. "Luckily that's what all those shiny new tools are for."

I nodded, surveying the work ahead. This would require days of backbreaking labor, hacking and tearing up roots in the hot sun. The prospect was daunting, yet deeply satisfying too. This was the purpose I had sought.

We moved to inspect the livestock pasture next. It was in slightly better shape than the garden, with mainly scraggly grass and a smattering of bright wildflowers sprouting about.

Diane walked the perimeter, scrutinizing the sturdy wooden fence posts. She made sure to take note of any weak sections so we could reinforce them later. Luckily, there were only a few.

"This will serve as a sturdy barrier to keep animals safely contained," she finally proclaimed with an approving nod.

"Yeah, these fences seem really solid and well-made," I agreed, running my hand along the beams. "Hopefully they'll continue holding up to whatever creatures I'm going to put in here."

Diane shot me a sly sideways look, hands on her hips. "You mean whatever critters *we* put in here after careful consideration! Lesson one for out here — don't bite off more than you can chew."

I laughed, holding up both hands in mock surrender. "Yes ma'am, you've made that loud and clear!" Her guidance would prove invaluable, I knew. She would keep me from getting ahead of myself.

We spent some time walking the plots, envisioning together how we might arrange the spaces and what work would be involved to whip them into shape. Even for basic subsistence farming, the scope was daunting. Yet deeply satisfying too, this planning and visioning of a meaningful life's purpose.

When the sun had climbed high overhead, beginning to bake our necks, Diane suggested heading back. "We should get started on clearing that garden plot today, if possible," she said pragmatically. "But first, how about a quick dip? We're both already hot and sweaty from all this walking and surveying."

I blinked, unsure if I had heard her right. "A…dip?"

Chapter 13

Diane flashed a mischievous grin, her eyes sparkling with impish delight. Without warning, she suddenly took off sprinting for the riverbank, kicking up puffs of dust in her wake.

Halfway there, she called back teasingly over her shoulder, "Last one in's a rotten egg!" Then, in one smooth motion, she crossed her arms and peeled her shirt up and over her head, exposing inch after inch of her slender back.

I stood frozen stupidly for a moment, pulse thudding, as I watched her gracefully shimmy out of her pants next, hips swaying.

Although I only got to see her naked behind — and it left me hungry to see the front — she was beautiful. Full and toned, with just a slight tad of visible muscle definition. The world I used to live in was full of women who would murder for a fit body like that.

And from behind, as she shot me a sideways look, covering her nipples with slender hand and forearm, I could see the enticing bounce of her full bosom. Unlike many toned women, she was not lacking in that department either.

My body responded to the sight of her like this. And at the same time, my mind reeled. She had been so shy!? Why the sudden easy disrobing? Perhaps this had something to do with foxkin culture? Something I didn't yet comprehend about her and her people.

"Are you coming or not?" she called out as she headed toward the riverbank.

That jolted me out of my thoughts. Well, that *and* the enticing ripple through her voluptuous backside as she walked and threw me another look that was almost coy.

I gathered my wits enough and headed after her, hurriedly shedding my own clothing along the way. There was, however, one particularly upright problem, and I tried to conceal it to her sight as best I could.

Luckily, Diane didn't look at me to notice. Instead, she let out a gleeful yip as she splashed into the river's embrace. I followed shortly after, gasping as the bracingly crisp water hit my bare skin but happy my noticeable rod was now hidden underwater.

"It's cold!" I called out.

She laughed. "Uh-huh! Something to wake you up after a long day!"

"It sure does," I agreed, laughing.

We laughed and shouted playfully, swimming about as we washed off the sweat and dust accumulated from our long trek along the riverbank. Diane's soaked black hair clung alluringly to the slender curve of her neck and shoulders, and I could only look at her whenever the sunlight fell on us and dug into the blue water, revealing an enticing glimpse of her.

Catching me staring, she flicked water at me with her tail, eyes glinting impishly. "Eyes front, mister. Don't make me dunk you!" But her voice held a teasing lilt rather than a true warning.

"Alright, alright," I said, laughing.

I surfaced from a deep breath and turned away to dunk my head underwater again, as much to cool my flushed cheeks as to clear the exotic vision of Diane frolicking mermaid-like from my mind. Life out here in the Wilds with her would certainly never be boring!

Diane swam closer, an impish smile on her face. Before I knew it, she playfully dunked me underwater!

And in that delightful moment, as I turned with surprise toward my assailant, I caught sight of her beautiful body underwater.

She was perfect — a fit hourglass figure with curves where they needed to be, and the exotic appeal of her fox tail only added to it. For a brief moment, my mind was running with images of all the naughty things I wanted to do with her.

Then, I came up spluttering as she laughed merrily, the sound like tinkling crystal. "Oh, so that's how it is?" I grinned, wiping the water from my eyes.

I lunged for her legs under the surface to try and upend her in retaliation, but she adeptly twisted away, her lithe body as slippery as an eel.

"You'll have to be quicker than that!" Diane taunted, smirking. We proceeded to chase each other through the shimmering azure water, our laughter echoing between the trees.

I finally managed to catch her slender waist from behind, wrapping my arms around her as I pulled her in, laughing and pulling her down. She gave a yelp, and we sank below the surface together, bubbles streaming around us in chaotic patterns.

Diane's long dark hair swirled hypnotically as we spun slowly in the emerald underwater world, tendrils of black locks enveloping me. My arousal rose as she allowed herself to be enveloped by arms, and our bodies touched underwater – how could they not? Her skin was soft and wet against mine, and for a timeless moment we hung suspended, neither wanting to surface.

It was a lovers' embrace – something of a promise.

At last, we broke the surface together, gasping for breath. I released her, although I had to apply some willpower to not hold her and let my hands roam instead. Part of me told me that would have been too soon.

Diane's cheeks were endearingly flushed as she smoothed back her sodden hair. "Not bad," she allowed with an impish grin, cocking her head.

I chuckled. "I got you in the end," I said. "But you're a slippery one."

"Hmm," she hummed. "Let's swim for a while

longer, David. I don't want to get out just yet."

"Yeah," I agreed.

We lazily circled and swam around each other, our hands and feet occasionally brushing under the water. I floated peacefully, gazing up at the vivid azure sky framed by the towering trees along the banks as my mind replayed the tender moment between us.

Diane's frolicking shape occasionally crossed before me, blocking the sun in the most pleasant way. Here in this glittering oasis, there was only joy, laughter, and the beauty of nature and each other.

After a blissful time, we reluctantly headed back toward the rocky shore. I couldn't remember the last time I'd felt such uncomplicated, wholesome joy.

"Now," Diane said as we came close to the bank. "Look away! And don't peek! I'll get us some towels."

I chuckled and complied while Diane emerged from the water. Of course, I had already seen a bit, but I was not going to play foul. Part of me had a feeling these were little foxkin mating games, and I liked the build-up of the tension between us. I would revel in it, take things slow, and get to know more about her and her culture before…

Well, before I would make a move.

"You can look now."

I opened my eyes to the sight of Diane wrapped in one of the towels the Frontier Division had provided. It was a small towel, and it left very little to the imagination. Her ample bosom almost spilled out, and most of her wet, glistening thighs were exposed. She laughed and threw me a towel before turning around herself.

I had no such qualms as she had, but I wasn't going to say that and make it awkward. Instead, I quickly toweled down, then wrapped the towel around my waist before signaling it was okay to look.

We strolled companionably back to the cabin, clothes clinging damply to our cooled bodies. I knew many trials and hardships awaited on the frontier, but perfect moments like this would make it all worthwhile.

Diane gave me an affectionate nudge as we walked. "You know, you're not such terrible company, for a human," she teased. Then, more softly she added, "I have a feeling we'll make a great team out here."

I smiled back warmly at her, my heart swelling. "I think you're absolutely right, Diane."

As the cabin came back into view, we slowed, neither quite ready for the magic of the moment to end.

Diane skipped a few steps ahead, then turned and walked backward, facing me with a grin. "I suppose we should get to clearing that garden now. But later, I'll teach you how to fish the river. And I'll make us a nice lunch!"

I laughed at her enthusiasm. "That sounds perfect."

With the promise of good work and good company ahead, I went to find my work gloves, my mind swimming happily at the thought of the moment she and I had just shared.

Chapter 14

After our refreshing swim, Diane and I got dressed and had a quick lunch before we headed to the supply shed to gather tools for clearing the garden plot.

Inside the small wooden shed, an array of farming implements hung neatly from pegs on the walls. Diane perused them with a critical eye, idly swishing her fluffy tail and keeping her fox ears perked upright as she did so.

"Let's see… we'll need scythes for cutting back the tall weeds and brush," she mused. She selected two curved long-handled blades and handed me one. I tested its weight — heavier than expected but it felt balanced in my grip.

"And pickaxes and shovels for digging up the roots once the stalks are cleared," Diane continued, passing me the other tools.

I hefted the pickaxe experimentally, judging its heft and balance. Though bulky, I could tell with some practice I'd get the hang of swinging it accurately.

"I haven't used farm tools much before but I'm a quick learner," I said confidently. The frontier work would be rough but deeply satisfying.

Diane smiled approvingly. "You'll get the hang of it soon enough. I'm sure of it. The most important thing is pacing yourself — don't overexert on the first day."

I nodded, appreciating her vote of confidence. She was right; with the scorching afternoon sun, it would be easy to push myself too hard too quickly.

Carrying an assortment of scythes, axes, picks, and shovels, we made our way out to the overgrown garden plot. I did some warm-up stretches of my arms and back, loosening up for the labor ahead.

Gripping the curved hardwood scythe handle, I swung it in a wide sweeping arc, feeling it slice cleanly through the tangled overgrowth with a satisfying swish.

Beside me, Diane whirled her own scythe gracefully, severing stalks and scrub brush left and right with practiced ease. "This is the easy part," she called over the rhythmic ringing of the blades on vegetation. "Just wait till we start tilling up those stubborn roots!"

We steadily cleared a wide swath along the edge of the plot, the sun beating down on us. Soon, my linen shirt was soaked through with sweat despite the shade provided by the encroaching trees. The sustained physical exertion felt good, using muscles that had atrophied from years cooped up in the city. Out here, I was making tangible progress — transforming the very land with my labor.

After an hour of hard work, we finally paused to drink some water. I marveled at how much ground we'd managed to cover already. Diane leaned on her scythe handle, wiping her sweat-slicked brow beneath the disheveled locks of hair but grinning with satisfaction.

"Not bad for your first morning of frontier work," she remarked appraisingly. Then her tone turned wry.

"But now comes the real labor — tackling those stubborn taproots!"

I gulped the last of my water, bracing myself. Gripping the heavy pickaxe, I swung it down with focused force, driving the chipped stone tip deep into the densely packed earth. Beside me, Diane dug in with her pointed shovel, scooping up loose dirt to gradually expose more and more of the thick woody roots.

The networks of roots clung tenaciously to the soil, resisting each jerked tug and chop. Before long, my arms were burning with exertion. After just thirty minutes of determined hacking, my swings had slowed considerably.

Diane paused, leaning on her shovel handle as she eyed me critically.

I straightened, rolling my aching shoulders to loosen them. "I'll admit, dislodging these roots is tougher work than I anticipated," I conceded. "But I'm determined to keep chopping away as long as I can."

Diane nodded approvingly. "That's the right spirit. Still, no need to wear yourself out on the first day. Tell you what — let's trade off tools frequently to stay fresh."

We swapped back and forth between the heavy pickaxes and the shovels at intervals. Having Diane's assistance made the work go noticeably faster. Bit by bit, we hacked, sawed, and tore up gnarled root after stubborn, gnarled root.

Around mid-afternoon, I finally lodged the sharp shovel deep under an enormous central taproot and heaved upward with a roar of effort. It tore loose in a shower of dirt.

"By the gods, look at the size of that beast!" Diane exclaimed, impressed. "I'd say making that kind of progress deserves a good long break and a nice snack!"

I wearily agreed, grateful for the respite. My hands were blistered, my back and arms ached from the hours of ceaseless labor. But I also felt deeply fulfilled looking over the exposed, overturned soil we had managed to prepare.

While I carefully cleaned the tools, Diane prepared a simple but energizing afternoon snack back at the cabin, with strips of dried smoked meat and handfuls of sweet berries. We ate gratefully in the shade of the dwelling after washing up.

"I have to say, David, you're a natural at this," Diane said through mouthfuls. "I know every muscle must be sore and aching, but you barely broke stride, just kept powering through without complaint. That kind of perseverance will serve you well out here on the frontier."

I chuckled tiredly, taking a long drink of water. "Let's just say I have no doubts I'll sleep very soundly tonight." I rolled my stiff shoulders, trying to massage some life back into them. "But I also feel deeply proud of the progress we made today. Hard work is fulfilling when you can step back and see tangible results."

Diane nodded, eyes shining. "My sentiments exactly. At this rate, if we keep up this pace, we'll have the plot totally cleared and ready for planting in three days tops."

I couldn't suppress a slight groan at the thought of several more days of nonstop digging, chopping, and shoveling under the baking summer sun. But Diane's visible enthusiasm and encouragement helped keep me motivated. I could endure the agony for the sake of transformation.

She must've seen my expression, though, because she laughed. "Don't worry! We won't be doing *only* this. I suggest tomorrow we drive down to Gladdenfield and visit my friend Leigh. She's a regular frontier girl, and she is the best supplier of seeds and farming supplies, including... magical ones. You should get to know her as you'll be buying most things from her. She can also take a lot of stuff you grow off your hands and will offer a fair price."

"Sounds good," I said, thankful for an activity that would keep things interesting during the coming days.

After our snack, we returned for a final few hours of picking away at the remaining roots and scrub brush while the daylight persisted. My muscles screamed in protest, but I pressed on, my second wind keeping me going.

When the sun had finally dipped low, beginning to cast long shadows from the encircling trees, we set down our tools nearly in unison by unspoken mutual consent.

"First day down," Diane declared, looking immensely satisfied as she surveyed the swath of exposed, freshly overturned soil.

I joined her, gazing out over our combined handiwork. I felt a wave of weary pride and accomplishment wash over me. It was just the very beginning, but a hugely gratifying start.

Diane bumped her hip against mine and gave me a coy look. "So! How's it feel to be a real frontier farmer and homesteader now?"

I laughed. "Ask me again when my aching muscles recover." But then I grinned broadly. "Honestly though – it feels pretty damn good."

That evening, Diane and I worked together to prepare a simple but hearty supper in the cabin's small kitchen. I was exhausted from the long day of labor in the fields, but I enjoyed having Diane's cheerful company as we chopped vegetables and stirred fragrant pots and pans on the old cast iron stove.

As I roughly diced some preserved vegetables for a stew, Diane rummaged in her worn leather pack. "How about some music while the stew gets ready?" she suggested brightly, producing a well-worn fiddle and bow. "My mother taught me to play this old thing as a girl."

"I'd love to hear you play," I said sincerely as I set the rough-hewn wooden table with plates and mugs. Soft music would be a soothing balm after the day's toils.

Diane carefully rosined up the bow then tucked the fiddle under her chin. She closed her eyes in concentration and began playing a lively frontier reel, her slender fingers making the bow dance nimbly over the strings.

The quick, merry notes of the fiddle soon filled the

cozy cabin space, complementing the lively popping and crackling of the fire in the hearth. Diane's foot tapped along as she played song after song from memory, lost in her own music.

When she had established a rhythm, Diane began singing along to the fiddle tunes in her sweet, melodic voice. Though the words were in a language I didn't understand, the emotion and warmth in her singing stirred my heart. Her voice was like a tonic, washing away the weariness of the long day.

The tunes were familiar, although the words were not, and I was brought back to happy days by them, finding myself humming along. Diane's spirited fiddle playing and singing was a welcome tonic for my weariness after the long day's work taming the land.

As we finally sat down to eat the savory stew by firelight, Diane setting aside her fiddle, I commented on her impressive musical talents. "Your singing was so beautiful, Diane. You have an amazing gift."

Diane smiled, her cheeks flushing slightly. "Thank you, David. That's so sweet of you to say."

"How long have you been playing the fiddle?" I asked before scooping up another spoonful of the hearty stew.

"Oh, since I was just a little kit," said Diane fondly.

"My mother started teaching me simple songs on a child-sized fiddle when I was five or so. Singing helps time pass swiftly, and it lifts the spirits. My mother sang through all our chores and while preparing meals too. Music connects us to the generations before."

"That's a nice thing to share with your mother," I remarked. "And this particular song that you played? The melody was familiar."

Diane chuckled. "Well, we stole it!" She winked at me.

I laughed. "Stole it?"

"Hm-hm," she hummed, watching me with those big eyes of hers. "After the Upheaval, we learned the melody from the humans with Classes who we met in the Wilds, just as they learned some of *our* music. I thought I'd play it for you." She blushed a little. "I hoped you would like it."

I smiled, appreciating the sweet gesture. "I did."

"But I'm not a Bard," she added with a grin. "So it's no magical music."

"I don't know about that," I joked. "It was kind of magical to me."

She laughed and gave my arm a playful pat. "Oh, you! I should've been a Bard, I guess."

I laughed along, but her remark soon enough turned

my mind to the topic of Classes. The dream had been the last development in that area, and there had been disappointingly little magic springing forth from my fingertips during the day.

"You know," I began after swallowing a bite of the freshly made stew of jerky and vegetables. "But I have to admit, part of me had hoped my special powers would be revealed by now."

Diane nodded in understanding, her expression sympathetic as she passed me a slice of crusty bread. "I know, I know. It's always hard waiting for something you want so badly." She smiled. "But these supernatural awakenings happen in their own time, not ours."

I sighed, knowing her words were wisdom, yet still feeling impatient and purposeless without my powers. "You're right, of course. I just can't help feeling like I'm stumbling around in the dark without my Class to guide me."

"Not at all!" Diane protested. "Just look at all the progress we made together on your homestead today. You're literally building your future with your own two hands – planting seeds for sustenance, shaping the very land. That's real purpose already, Class or no Class."

I gave her a grateful smile, touched by her encouragement. "Thank you, Diane. I'm lucky to have you here keeping me grounded." It was true – her friendship and guidance were a gift.

We ate in a tired but contented silence for several minutes, simple sounds of night seeping in through the cracks in the walls – owls hooting, wind rustling the trees. Eventually, I looked back to Diane and spoke my curiosity aloud.

"Can you tell me more about your own Scout powers and how they work? I'm so curious to better understand how these Class abilities function once awakened."

Diane brightened at my interest, setting down her fork. She sat up straighter. "Well, let's see… As a Scout, I have preternaturally heightened senses which help me track prey or enemies. I can move through any terrain easily, almost like I'm one with the land itself. And I can remain unseen and hidden, even in open spaces."

She demonstrated her last point by suddenly vanishing before my eyes in the chair, only to peek around the corner of the kitchen a moment later with an impish grin.

I stared open-mouthed. "That's incredible!" I breathed. "Are all Classes so… supernatural in what they enable?" I shook my head, mind spinning at the implications.

"To varying degrees, yes," said Diane with a sage nod, retaking her seat. "Each Class enhances the bearer's intrinsic talents and gifts, pushing them into almost superhuman realms. Like extraordinary strength and toughness for Warriors, healing and life-giving for Healers, and so on."

"And summoning otherworldly beings and spirits for Summoners," I mused aloud. The idea still seemed fantastical to me, yet thrilling at the same time. To command such unfathomable power…

She smiled. "Exactly, but it is important to remember that the enhanced abilities are no substitute for skill won the old-fashioned way. Yes, I can disappear and move silently, but if I hadn't spent a lot of time hunting in the wild and honing my skills, there were many aspects of subterfuge that I would not grasp. For instance, the play of light, practicing patience when necessary, and knowing what terrain helps concealment the best."

I nodded. "That makes sense."

"Which is exactly why we're doing well, even though you don't know your Class just yet. These skills at farming and landscaping are vital for a homesteader, and the System could never replace them."

Before long, we were settled comfortably beside each other on the braided rug before the softly popping and hissing fireplace, weary muscles glad for respite.

As we sat relaxing, I turned to Diane. "Can I ask you something? It's been on my mind since we first met back at the tavern."

Diane looked at me curiously. "Of course, ask away."

I took a deep breath. "That first handshake... I know it has special meaning in foxkin culture. I didn't intend to, you know, *propose* or anything. Did you mind?"

Diane laughed lightly. "Don't worry, I realized it was an innocent misunderstanding. You didn't know our customs. I didn't mind at all."

I nodded, relieved. "Still, I feel badly. I never wanted to be disrespectful."

Diane smiled and touched my arm. "You weren't. Really, it was rather sweet." She blushed slightly. "No one's ever proposed to me before, even accidentally."

I grinned teasingly. "Well, maybe someday I'll do it on purpose."

Diane's eyes widened in surprise, but she smiled back shyly. The fire crackled merrily as we gazed at each other. The words I had spoken — half-jokingly — lingered, and I believe that we both understood in that moment that there was truth to my joke.

Diane was the first to break the silence. "We should go to bed," she said, her cheeks crimson. "Tomorrow's a long day!"

I grinned and nodded. "You go on ahead. I'll clean up here and make sure the fire is out."

She made to hop to her feet with her vulpine grace. But she hesitated, leaned in, and gave me a peck on my cheek. Warmth radiated from where her lips had touched me.

I smiled at her, unable to keep the sparkle out of my eyes, and she giggled before hopping up, this time for real, and making her way to the ladder.

Chapter 15

The morning sun slanted through the cabin windows as I sipped my coffee. Diane and I had risen early to put in a few hours of work clearing more of the garden plot's tangled overgrowth.

I slowly rolled my shoulders, feeling the pleasant ache in my muscles from the hard labor out in the field. My back and arms were stiff, but it was a good kind of soreness — the result of honest work transforming the land with my own two hands.

Diane stood humming yesterday's song over the cast iron stove, deftly using a fork to turn slices of potato frying in one pan while scrambling a heap of speckled eggs in another. The sizzling aroma made my mouth water.

"Eat up while it's hot," Diane said cheerily, sliding a generously heaped plate stacked with the eggs, potatoes, and toasted bread in front of me. "You'll need fuel for the exciting trip we've got planned today! And while we're in town, we might as well get some more food. The longer we can put off starting on the MREs, the better!"

I nodded eagerly, already shoveling a big bite of the fluffy scrambled eggs. Diane's frontier cooking was simple yet incredibly delicious, filling, and energizing.

"And I can't wait for you to meet my good friend Leigh," Diane added as she sat down across from me with her own plate. "She's got all sorts of interesting wares for sale, some infused with a touch of magic. And I think you two will get along famously right from the start."

She shot me a meaningful look that I couldn't quite place.

"That sounds good," I said.

She smiled and nodded, giving me no further hints of what that look had meant.

We hurried through the hearty breakfast, both eager to get on the road. The morning air still had a crisp chill when we stepped outside, but the cloudless azure sky promised another scorching afternoon ahead. Our breath fogged faintly in the shaded parts of the yard as we loaded up the Jeep with empty sacks and burlap bags to hold our purchases.

Just to be sure, I also tucked the rifle into the Jeep with us, carrying the handgun on my body after plenty of assurances from Diane that it was allowed to carry openly in town.

I slid behind the wheel of the rugged off-roader as Diane settled into the passenger seat beside me. She shot me a happy look, and I smiled back before I turned over the engine. Soon we were bouncing down the winding dirt track away from the secluded homestead, tracing our route back to the main road.

"Feels good to take a little break from the hard work for a fun excursion, doesn't it?" Diane remarked over the roar of the wind whipping her long dark locks around her face. When I glanced her way, her eyes were bright with excitement, ears perked upright.

"It really does," I agreed, nodding and returning my focus to navigating the bumpy trail. My muscles were still pleasantly sore and stiff from the previous days of labor, but my spirits were high. "I'm looking forward to seeing more of the frontier and meeting some of the locals."

The vibrant wilderness sped by in a blur around us – soaring trees with copper-hued leaves, vivid flowering bushes dotted among the vibrant grasses. Strange new birds with long iridescent tail feathers swooped through the sky overhead while lumbering herd beasts with shaggy coats grazed placidly in the grassy clearings. The sheer diversity of flora and fauna never ceased to amaze me.

As the rutted dirt road carried us nearer to Gladdenfield's fortified log palisade walls and guard towers, traffic gradually increased. We began passing laden wagons guided by elven and human traders, their heads wrapped in bright scarves to block the dust kicked up by their plodding beasts of burden. Diane waved cheerily out the window to acquaintances, shouting jovial greetings that were lost to the wind.

There were several foxkin among them as well, and I realized not all looks that met me were friendly. A foxkin male, short and wiry, shot me the nastiest look as we drove past his caravan.

"Who's that?" I asked Diane once we'd passed him, nodding back in his direction.

"Oh, that's just Anwick," she said, giving a dismissive wave. "I told you foxkin males were rare, right?"

I nodded, catching the male's stink-eye again in the rear-view mirror. "Yeah, you did."

"Well, despite their rarity, Anwick still hasn't found a single mate, let alone begun his harem." She laughed and shook her head. "He's a spiteful and jealous thing. Just ignore whatever he does and says."

I shook my head and chuckled. "Gladly."

At the gates, the elven guards recognized us from our previous visit and waved us through with a smile. I carefully navigated the winding, deeply rutted streets, following Diane's directions toward the rambling general store she had enthusiastically told me about.

"Here it is!" she chirped, very excited. "Time to introduce you to Leigh!"

After I parked, Diane hopped out and headed straight

for the entrance. I followed her a moment later, taking a bag with me to carry the wares we would need to purchase.

Inside, the aisles and shelves were stuffed to overflowing with tools, dry goods, bolts of cloth, seeds, and countless other items.

But that was not what caught the eye. Oh no…

The woman behind the counter did. She was a first grade wilderness gal, wearing a cowboy hat, cowboy boots, and scuffed jeans that hugged her ample curves in a way that sent my head spinning. Long blonde locks and a buttoned plaid shirt — the buttons of which struggled to contain her bouncy chest — completed the picture. She had that look of maturity about her — a little older than Diane and a little more experienced, but she was still in her prime.

And those blazing blue eyes said she knew exactly what kind of effect she had.

"Well, howdy!" she called out, giving Diane a wave. "Diane! So good to see ya!" She had a delicious southern accent that suited her just fine — wild and free; the way I liked them.

"Leigh!" Diane called, greeting her friend.

Diane rushed over to embrace her friend warmly. They laughed together, rocking back and forth as they hugged, and I won't lie — seeing the two of them hugging was *very* nice.

Diane finally detached from the hug and turned to introduce us. "Leigh, meet my friend David who just recently moved to a new homestead out near the Silverthread. David, this bubbly ray of sunshine here is my dear friend Leigh."

"Welcome to Gladdenfield, David!" Leigh exclaimed, eagerly shaking my hand in both of hers. As she did so, her blue eyes took me in boots to crown, and I could tell she liked what she was seeing. "Diane told me someone new would be comin' to our little neck of the woods, but she didn't tell me it'd be a good-lookin' man."

I grinned at that. "Well, surprise. Here I am."

She nodded, wetting her lips for a moment. "Here you are, indeed."

Diane giggled as well, and that was a weird one to me. Obviously, her friend was flirting with me. And either I was crazy, or Diane and I had a thing going on. And yet here she stood happy as a ladybug.

Then I recalled her earlier words about harems and foxkin sharing men. Another cultural thing I still needed to understand better.

"Well, it's great to meet you too, Leigh," I replied sincerely. "You've got quite the operation going on here," I added, gesturing around at the diverse wares filling every nook and cranny of the rustic space.

"Oh gosh, ya think?" she hummed, looking around with those big blue eyes. "Most days it's barely controlled chaos in here." She followed up with an infectious, almost musical laugh. "But I really do enjoy running the business. Why don't the two of y'all come on round the back? I wanna show you two some of the new specialty shipments that just arrived earlier this week!"

Threading through the crowded aisles, Leigh led us to a far corner that was stocked to the exposed rafters with farming equipment, seeds, fertilizers, and other agricultural supplies. My eyes widened as they roamed over the incredible variety available, including many plants and tools I'd never encountered before on Earth.

Leigh enthusiastically showed me magical seeds she called moonlight taters. "Like the name says, these babies will grow in moonlight and in just about any temperature so long as it ain't freezin'. They need plenty of water, but around the Silverthread that ain't much of a problem."

"Amazing," I said, studying the seeds. They looked so mundane, I thought for a moment she might be bullshitting me. But Diane was looking on with those big sapphire eyes and nodding enthusiastically.

"Here," Leigh said, handing me a packet of moonlight potato seeds. "On the house. As a welcome-to-the-neighborhood sorta thing, y'know?"

"Leigh," I said, sincerely moved. "You don't have to…"

"Oh, go on now!" she said, then pushed the packet into the pocket of my jeans. Her slender fingers on my hips kindled a fire, and she shot me an enticing wink from under the brim of her hat. "I like to help out."

"Well, thanks!" I said.

"See?" Diane hummed. "I told you Leigh was great."

She shot Diane a warm smile before continuing the tour of her store. She had many of these kind of seeds, and there was just a little too much information from the bubbly blonde for me to commit it all to memory, but most of the magical crops were varieties of mundane crops, except they grew faster or in different conditions. While amazing, I had not yet seen anything otherworldly.

"And I buy whatever ya grow," she said when she completed the tour. "Now, I'm no hack, so I'll tell ya right now what Diane could tell ya: you'll make loads more if you sell it to the elven traders directly. But they ain't always in town, and when they are, they're gonna haggle. So if you wanna do it the convenient way, sell your produce to me, and I'll sell it to elves. You won't have to stick around till there's an elf who wants to trade, and you won't have to deal with their shrewd hagglin'. How's that?"

Diane nodded. "I do the same with what I hunt," she said. "Some of the elves are… well… they're…"

"Miserly vultures," Leigh finished her sentence for her.

The two girls broke out laughing, and it was impossible not to join in. There was something about Leigh that said fun followed in her wake — she seemed the type to always have a joke ready, a great idea to pass the time. Never a dull moment. Diane was sweeter and softer, more shy and intimate, and yet the two seemed to complement each other perfectly.

"Well," I said. "I'll do a few deals with the elves myself when the time comes. Out of curiosity, if not anything else, but I'll happily have you as a middle woman."

She licked her lips as she gave me a naughty look. "I prefer the term go-to-girl… for all your needs."

I laughed and nodded. "Go-to-girl it is."

She clapped her hands and smiled. "As Diane knows, you two will always be welcome here. Now, I'm thinkin' David brought that big old burlap sack for a reason and y'all are looking to buy some supplies."

Diane nodded, her smile fading a little. "Yeah, about that..."

Leigh waved it away. "Don't worry. We gotta help each other out, and not many starting out have a lot to spend. Why don't you two bring what ya need over to the register, and I'll keep a tab until the money comes rolling in, huh?"

"That's nice of you, Leigh," I said. "I appreciate that!"

She smiled warmly. "Around here, we stick up for each other. Now go ahead and let me know what you need."

The three of us spent the next hour or so chatting and shopping. With Leigh hanging around and catching up as we did our shopping, it didn't go very fast, but it didn't have to. I could already feel that out here, things happened at a different pace. It was a pace that suited me a lot better.

Besides, it was entertaining. Seeing Diane's easy, affectionate friendship with the energetic Leigh was incredibly heartwarming. The frontier folk truly cared for one another.

When we had everything, Diane shot me a meaningful look. "We should be on our way again,

David."

Leigh, leaning on the counter in a way that give me a fine look at her ample, freckled bosom, looked up and nodded. "Ya don't wanna be out there when it's dark," she said. "Still, y'all should have a couple of hours before nightfall to make the trip."

Diane nodded, blushing a little as she looked at me. "Yeah, we do... but, uh, I wanted to grab a drink together with David at the Wild Outrider. Maybe? If... If you want to? My treat?"

The way she asked it was too cute. I couldn't have refused if I'd wanted to.

"Hmm," Leigh hummed, narrowing her eyes at me. "Can't say I blame you for wantin' a drink with this man, Diane."

I chuckled. Leigh's constant flirting was making me more than a little fiery, but I wanted to keep my cool. Still, I had little doubt that something might happen here if I saw Leigh more often.

I smiled at Diane and nodded. "Yeah, great idea! Let's go grab a drink."

Chapter 16

The frothy ale and lively shared laughter in the cozy tavern were the perfect capper to our delightful outing. It wasn't as crowded as it had been the last time we were here; apparently, it was a slow day in Gladdenfield. But that suited us just fine.

Diane sauntered up to the bar and ordered us each a drink, returning to our small corner table with two overflowing mugs. I couldn't help but feel proud and happy to be sharing the company of such an exotic, sweet woman. The way her eyes kept finding mine told me she greatly enjoyed my companionship as well.

Her bright blue eyes fairly shone with optimistic excitement as she sat down across from me and raised her drink. "To new friends and new beginnings!" she exclaimed merrily, holding it out towards me in the gesture of a toast.

"To new friends and new beginnings," I echoed with a smile, happily clinking my frothy mug against hers. I felt incredibly lucky to be sharing in this quest for meaning and purpose out here with Diane by my side.

We both tilted our drinks back, the crisp taste helping wash down the dust from the road. Diane set her mug down with a satisfied sigh.

"Hit the spot, didn't it?" she remarked. "Emrys brews the best ale for leagues around. He gets the hops from local farmers."

I took another swig of the amber ale and nodded. "You're right, it's delicious. Nice and cold too on a hot day."

We chatted amiably about our favorite parts of the day's excursion as we slowly drained our drinks. Around us, the tavern hummed with life — traders laughing together, a Bard plucking out tunes in the corner. But Diane's lovely face across from me held all my focus.

As we lingered over the last sips, I turned the conversation to our new acquaintance. "Leigh seems like a real gem. How did you two meet?"

Diane's eyes crinkled fondly at the memory. "Oh, it was maybe a year or so after I first wandered into these parts. I was in a bad way, no money or shelter." Her expression clouded briefly.

"Leigh took me in, gave me a job helping in the store. Fed me, kept me safe." Diane smiled. "Her compassion changed everything. I'll always be grateful."

I listened intently, always eager to learn more of her past. "She seems an incredibly warm-hearted person. I'm thankful you had her kindness."

Diane chuckled. "Don't tell Leigh this, but she's also a shrewd businesswoman! She taught me a lot about bartering and appraising goods fairly."

We shared a laugh at the amusing contradiction of Leigh's savvy dealings contrasted with her bubbly persona. I was quickly coming to appreciate how the locals here looked out for each other.

Too soon, the lowering daylight outside the smudged windows told us it was time to begin the trek home. But we lingered a few moments more, neither of us eager for the magical day to end.

At last Diane pushed back her chair and stood, eyes dancing. "Suppose we should get moving before it's full dark out there."

I nodded and followed her out into the street, rolling my shoulders in the pleasant sunlight and fresh open air after the cozy tavern. I was really growing to like this place and its people.

The streets were still full of life with townsfolk and visitors going about their day. Everything seemed amiable – people nodded in passing or, if they recognized Diane, greeted us or made short inquiries before going on their way. In that manner, I met several people before we could even climb into the Jeep.

I cranked the engine and steered the Jeep back out onto the rutted dirt road leading home. Diane nestled comfortably into her seat, gazing dreamily out at the vibrant passing scenery.

"I'm so glad you got to meet Leigh today," Diane remarked after a short while of companionable silence. "She's been a good friend to me since I arrived here. She's really important to me."

"I could tell right away that she has a big heart," I replied, briefly meeting Diane's eyes. "And I appreciate the chance to start meeting the locals and building connections."

Diane nodded. "It takes time, but you'll come to feel at home here. The frontier folk look after their own." She gave my arm an affectionate pat. "And I, for one, feel like you're part of us already."

I smiled, buoyed by her reassurance. "It means a lot that you say that, Diane. Thanks."

She hummed affectionately, her fox ears perking upright, and her soft hand stayed on my arm.

The winding track climbed steadily into the hills. Below, the vivid valley gradually came into view once more. There, nestled against the shimmering Silverthread, stood our cozy log cabin. Home.

Diane's keen eyes made it out through the trees before I did. "There it is!" she exclaimed gladly.

The Jeep rumbled faithfully along as the sun dipped lower above the forest. Soon we were pulling up beside the house, eager to unpack and share dinner together.

Diane hopped out and came around to meet me, eyes dancing. "I'd call that a pretty great day, wouldn't you?"

"One of the best," I agreed sincerely. "Come on, let's unpack before we get something to eat."

As we arrived at the cabin, the last rays of the sun streaked the sky orange and pink. The evening was serene, the only sounds being the soft rustling of leaves and the distant murmur of the river. It felt good to be home after the bustling day in Gladdenfield.

Home. It felt like that already — more so than any other place I had ever lived.

I parked the Jeep near the entrance of our property, and Diane and I started to unload the supplies we had bought. So far, we'd only gotten some fresh food to liven up the preserves, as well as the packet of moonlight tater seeds, which was a prized possession to me — my first magical crop.

Of course, the result would be potatoes. That wasn't very magical, but the growth process would be. I could grow them year-round, barring winter, and that would keep us fed — both by the potatoes themselves and by the profits that selling them would bring in.

Or so I hoped. Honestly, I didn't know much about the profits on produce out here in the Wilds, but I expected Leigh would cut me some honest deals, so I stood a fair chance of making it out here. One thing was sure: I didn't want to fall back on the Frontier Division and ask them for help unless it was absolutely necessary. As much as I appreciated and liked Caldwell, independence was important to me.

"Let's take these inside," Diane suggested, her melodic voice and enticing accent breaking me out of my reverie as she grabbed a bag of fresh produce. I gave her a nod and started carrying the remaining supplies into the cabin. The interior of our home was cozy, the lingering scent of the woodfire still in the air.

As we unpacked, I could not help but marvel at the delightful simplicity of my time here so far. Out here, there were no administrative requirements, no bookkeeping, no complex dealings with landlords and employers. The simple act of preparing for our livelihood, of making a home in this wild frontier, was deeply satisfying.

Diane seemed to sense my thoughts. "It's a different life, isn't it?" she said, her voice soft. I glanced at her, and our eyes met. Hers were filled with understanding and a hint of amusement.

I nodded in agreement. "It sure is. But I wouldn't have it any other way." I meant every word. I perked up an eyebrow at her. "But how would you know?"

She laughed, pointing at me with an eggplant as she narrowed her eyes. "Think you're the first one from the city to come traipsing by here?"

I chuckled and rubbed the back of my neck. "I hadn't thought of that."

She winked. "Most people who come here, especially those who have unlocked a Class, feel like they're finally free."

"Well, I can relate," I said.

We finished unpacking the supplies, and Diane started to prepare supper. Using the preserved food we had, as well as some of the fresh produce we had purchased, she made another of her signature frontier stews. I watched her for a moment with an approving smile as she chopped the vegetables and stirred the pot.

Then, I went about setting the table. Leigh had tucked a bottle of wine into our bag — free of charge — and I uncorked it. For lack of glasses, we had to drink it from mugs — 'like savages,' some of my former colleagues would have said — but that did not diminish the fruity bouquet in the slightest.

We laughed, talked, and drank as the cabin filled with the delicious aroma of the cooking food, making our stomachs rumble in anticipation. The sun had set by the time supper was ready. We sat across from each other at the small table, the only light coming from the flickering flames of the fireplace. It cast a warm, cozy glow throughout the cabin.

Diane served the stew into our bowls, and we dug in. The food was simple but hearty, perfect for our tired bodies after a long day. We ate in comfortable silence, the only sounds being the crackling of the fire and the occasional clinking of our spoons against the bowls.

As we ate, I found myself stealing glances at Diane. The firelight highlighted her features, making her look even more beautiful. I felt a familiar warmth spreading through my chest as I watched her. I was lucky to have her by my side in this new life.

Diane caught me looking at her and smiled, her eyes twinkling in the firelight. "What are you looking at?" she asked, a playful tone in her voice.

I chuckled, feeling a bit embarrassed. "Nothing. Just thinking how lucky I am," I said.

Diane laughed, a sound that was warm and comforting. "Well, I'm lucky too," she said, meeting my gaze. "To have a partner who's so willing to learn and adapt."

I felt a surge of happiness at her words. It was nice to know that she appreciated my efforts and was happy to be here with me. "Thank you, Diane," I said, my voice sincere. "I appreciate that."

She smiled. "You know, I didn't know what to think of it when Caldwell came to me and asked me to help out one of the new homesteaders. I… Well, I've always been a bit of a loner. But something about the offer felt right… And I'm happy I agreed."

"So am I," I said. "Very much so."

We finished our meal in companionable silence, both of us lost in our thoughts. After clearing the table, Diane suggested we take a walk outside to enjoy the cool evening air, taking a flashlight with us.

We stepped outside, and I was immediately struck by the beauty of the night. The stars were out in full force, their twinkling lights illuminating the landscape. The moon was a silver crescent in the sky, casting a soft glow over the cabin.

We walked slowly, enjoying the quiet beauty of the night, our path divined by the cone of the flashlight. Diane pointed out various constellations, her knowledge of the night sky impressive. I listened to her, the melodic sound of her voice soothing in the stillness.

After a while, we decided to head back to the cabin. We were both tired, and the day had been long.

We prepared for bed, Diane heading to the loft while I occupied myself with the fire. I followed her up the ladder a few minutes later, the loft bathed in a soft glow from a candle on the nightstand. We said our goodnights and retreated to our respective beds. As I lay in the darkness, listening to the soft sounds of Diane's breathing, I came to an utter relaxation – a fulfilled tiredness of a simpler life and a busy day.

The events of the day replayed in my mind as I slowly drifted off to sleep. The bustling market, the unfamiliar faces, the unspoiled beauty of the land… it was all new and exciting. And there was much left for us to explore and discover.

Chapter 17

I drifted into slumber, lulled by the gentle chorus of crickets and the distant murmur of the river. As I slept deeply, vivid visions overtook me once more.

Once again, I wandered in that mysterious and mystical landscape from my previous vivid dreamscape – a place I had come to call Tannoris in my mind. I practically gawked at the fantastic scenery, marveling at the mountains that reached for the multi-colored clouds where birds with colorful and delicate feathers played and squawked. Then, letting my gaze drift down again, I stared at elven ruins of white stone, overrun with emerald crawling vines, serene and beautiful even in their decline.

And then there were the creatures… Among the mighty trees were lumbering beasts and weird critters. Small thing like elemental squirrels flitted and capered through the undergrowth, leaving flickering trails of multi-hued fire in their wake. Tiny sprites no bigger than my hand, their bodies alight with hypnotic flames, endlessly shifted hue as they seemed to contemplate my presence curiously. Larger luminescent elementals strode through the gloom, their wispy forms billowing like smoke.

And yet, I walked on unafraid amongst the fantastical menagerie of creatures inhabiting this mystical realm. My strides carried purpose, for my dream-self seemed to know exactly where he was going even if my waking mind did not understand. I sought the hidden ravine where I had first encountered the alluring deer-woman who served as my spirit guide.

At last, the ravine loomed before me, the cracked boulders and sheer rocky walls rising starkly from the verdant forest. I carefully picked my way down the steep, winding path leading into the shadowy depths below. Loose scree shifted treacherously underfoot, threatening to send me sliding into the gloomy depths.

But I persisted, bracing myself against the rough canyon walls until I successfully reached the ravine floor. Emerging from the claustrophobic passage into the ravine proper, I saw the deer-woman waiting just ahead amidst the swirling motes of light that were lesser spirit creatures.

Her appearance was as mesmerizing as I recalled – tall and slender, with fluffy ears that gave a little twitch at the sight of me. She nodded as I came, her intricate antlers bobbing with the motion of her pretty head. She stood serene and perfectly poised amidst the dancing spirits swirling around her in reverence.

"Welcome again, Summoner," she said in her rich, melodic voice that echoed magically around the gorge. Her large emerald eyes were intent upon me, yet filled with warmth and approval. The soft fur of her ears and tail shimmered iridescent in the rays of magical half-light streaming down from above.

I inclined my head respectfully to her in greeting, although I could not stop my eyes from taking in the beauty of her exotic form.

"I have returned," I said. "And I still have so many questions." My own voice echoed strangely, as if I were speaking underwater.

The deer-woman smiled, an expression of infinite patience and compassion. "In time, your powers will blossom, and true understanding will follow," she assured me in a gentle tone. "But come. I have something important to show you now. Something that will benefit you at once."

She turned with natural grace and glided deeper into the rocky gorge without looking back, clearly expecting me to follow without hesitation. The swirling motes of lesser spirits danced around me as I hurried after her, filling the air with whispered snatches of some strange unintelligible spirit tongue.

After several minutes of walking, we entered a large cave-like chamber with intricate glowing glyphs etched into the curving walls. More diverse spirits danced and swooped through the musty air, tracing chaotic patterns across the ceiling beams in time with their own inscrutable rhyme. They cavorted in the angled beams of sunlight streaming down through cracks in the high stony ceiling.

In the center of the rough stone floor was a raised circular dais carved all over with arcane runes. The deer-woman stepped lightly up onto it and then turned to face me once more, her hooves clicking delicately on the weathered rock.

"Behold — the summoning circle, a conduit for my kind to touch your world," she intoned. As she spoke, the elaborate etched runes began to glow. "Here a rare power will awaken within you — a Frontier Summoner."

I slowly approached, feeling energy radiate from the glowing circle. "A Summoner… A Frontier Summoner?" I asked hesitantly.

"Yes," the woman nodded. "One whose magic intertwines with the wild. Your bonds with nature spirits will be strong. It is a unique Class. Be blessed."

My heart quickened. This Class was ideal for life out here. Eagerly, I stepped onto the dais, raising my arms as energy flowed into me.

The cavern shook. The woman cried, "Now, reach out once more, man of the frontier!"

Even as my active mind wondered what she meant, part of me understood well enough — a primal part that spent little time navel-gazing or overthinking matters. I could call it instinct, perhaps, and that was what drove me to reach out and touch the mystical forces around me.

And with that, they flowed into me. Or, well… I *absorbed* them. They were understanding, skill, and prowess, while I felt something alter within me. As I did so, the spirits swirled around me as if in celebration.

The woman laughed delightedly. "Well done, Frontier Summoner! With training, your gifts will continue to grow. But today, you have begun them."

I turned slowly, marveling at the arcane power that thrummed in my veins. It was no mere illusion, not just a dream — I could feel something new blazing within me. Raw power that I would shape in the days to come.

The deer-woman regarded me warmly. "Go in peace, Summoner. The denizens of the planes await your call when you have awakened fully in the mortal realm."

As she spoke, the cavern chamber dissolved away into inky darkness.

With a gasp, I opened my eyes to see predawn light filtering through the cabin window.

My heart pounded as I sat up in bed, the realization still settling in. And the power was still there, raging in my channels with untapped potency.

I was a rare Frontier Summoner! One whose magic and skill would intertwine the arcane with the survival skills of an outdoorsman. My developing abilities would be the perfect complement to life out here.

I could hardly wait for morning to tell Diane every detail of the dream and its revelations. Her wisdom might help me unravel the full meaning of my destined path as this unusual Class. She was still asleep, and it was still early, so I would leave her for just a bit.

I rose and dressed quickly by the gray dawn light. There would be no more sleeping after the intense vision.

Chapter 18

I quietly made my way downstairs, carefully stepping over the creaky parts of the ladder to avoid waking Diane. Once downstairs, I got dressed. My mind was abuzz with all that had transpired in the vivid dream.

As I entered the main room, I became aware of a hovering translucent box at the edge of my vision. I had thought it to be a speck of dirt or something, but now that the initial excitement faded, I noticed it wasn't going anywhere.

Startled, I blinked hard several times, but it remained stubbornly in place. Focusing on it, the speck enlarged, and I realized it was a status display, showing a basic overview of my attributes:

Name: David Wilson

Class: Frontier Summoner

Level: 1

Health: 20/20

Mana: 10/10

My eyes widened in understanding. This must be my interface that Caldwell had mentioned, manifesting after the Awakening ritual!

The dream had unlocked it, displaying my health and mana points. I had actual mana points now! I could only hope that meant I could cast spells.

I quickly discovered that by focusing, I could open additional interface windows with more details on my abilities. One showed a set of skills available to me:

Skills:

Summon Minor Spirit — Level 1 (4 mana)

Identify Plants — Level 1 (1 mana)

Foraging — Level 1 (1 mana)

Trapping — Level 1 (1 mana)

There was a spell there… Summon Minor Spirit. Apparently, in the system that those with a Class had access to, spells were skills. That likely meant they could improve over time and with use. I nodded to myself as I reviewed it all. The skills fit the nature powers described as belonging to a Frontier Summoner in the dream.

Eager to properly test these newfound powers for the first time, I focused my mind and peered inwardly until I could sense the swirling currents of arcane energy from my vivid dream. I felt them pulsing within my core, raw and untamed.

Channeling my will, I extended my hand outward and spoke the words that came instinctively to summon forth this power. "I call upon the realms beyond. Heed now my voice! I summon you, spirit of beyond!" As I did so, my new interface offered me several options, which unfolded as I focused my eyes on them.

Spirit Type:

Earth / Air / Water / Fire / Storm / Woodland

On instinct, I chose fire. At first nothing happened, but then a flickering orb sprang into being before me, rapidly expanding until it took on a vaguely humanoid shape, composed entirely of shifting, swirling flames with two glowing embers for eyes. It was similar to the shapes that had flitted about me in the dream — no larger than my hand and full of vibrant energy.

I laughed aloud in pure delight. I had summoned forth my very first spirit from the realms beyond!

The creature hovered patiently, awaiting instruction. Knowing it would not last long in this plane, I quickly directed it to light the stove fire. It swooped over and, with a gesture, kindled a cheery blaze crackling merrily in the stove. Amazing! The creature obeyed my mental commands.

But the effort of calling forth this minor spirit had left me quite drained. Glancing at my interface, I saw my mana reserves had dropped from 10 down to only 6. I would clearly need to judiciously manage these mystical energies until I grew stronger.

But what an incredible first step!

My heart swelled with accomplishment and wonder. The raw potential was there within me, untapped wells of arcane might. With time and training, I could grow truly powerful. But for now, lighting a simple fire was momentous progress. I smiled broadly, scarcely able to contain my elation.

I played around with the spirit a while longer. It obeyed my mental commands without discussion or pushback, and it lasted much longer than I would have thought. It took several minutes before the playful little shape flickered out of existence, returning to the spirit realm from which I had called it forth.

Wanting to further test these newly awakened frontier abilities, I moved outside into the crisp morning air. Kneeling by some bushes around the cabin's edge, I activated my Identify Plants skill at a cost of 1 mana and instinctively knew them to be currant bushes.

The Foraging skill then helped me locate some ripe, juicy berries quickly at a cost of 1 mana. Using the magic of the spell, I easily skipped over the ones that weren't ripe yet, and I also avoided a batch because my magically infused instincts told me they were spoiled in some way, even though they appeared fine. Moreover, the bounty somehow seemed to be more than I would have thought, as if my Foraging skill magically increased the yield!

Popping one of the tart berries into my mouth, I smiled in deep satisfaction. The pieces were coming together. My powers as a Frontier Summoner provided a blend of mystical energy and frontier survival skills ideally suited to living and mastering this untamed land.

For my next test, I gathered some spare logs and branches. Acting on instinct, I used my Trapping skill at a cost of 1 mana to fashion a simple deadfall trap capable of catching small game. There was a kind of primal intuition to the process. This had been something I hadn't even been capable of doing before all this, and the knowledge came magically into my mind.

Constructing traps would let me supplement the food situation once our rations from the Coalition ran out, and it would also add some meat to the diet of potatoes. The frontier was shaping me into a survivor.

As I sat there in the sun, having just placed my first trap, I found myself brimming with excitement. I just wanted to share it with someone, and I decided to head back into the cabin to check if Diane was up yet.

Heading back inside, I noticed the sunlight slanting into the cabin. Diane would probably be rousing soon upstairs, but she was still asleep for now. I decided to surprise her with coffee, broth, and fresh berries as a celebration of my powers awakening.

Soon the rich aroma of brewing coffee filled the cozy space. As I was preparing a platter of foraged berries, I heard the creak of the loft ladder that signaled Diane was up.

"Something smells good!" she said brightly as she descended. Her eyes widened as she saw the spread of food and drink. "David, you didn't have to do all this!"

"But I wanted to," I replied with a grin. "Especially on such a momentous morning. Diane, my Class just activated! Just like you said it would."

Her eyes lit up and her ears perked in excitement. She then gave the cutest squeal, hopping up and down and clapping her hands. "I knew it! I knew it! I knew it would awaken in time," she enthused. "Tell me everything!"

As we ate the simple but energizing meal, I described the interface details and explained my basic frontier skills. I couldn't show her the spirit I could summon as I only had 3 mana left, but I described it in great detail.

"Incredible!" said Diane when I had finished. "A true Frontier Summoner! Those are extremely rare! I've only ever heard of them and never met one in progress." She shook her head, filled with wonder. "Oh, David, it's the perfect Class! The progress we'll make on the homestead with your powers." Her pride and enthusiasm spurred me on.

I smiled and sat back, utterly satisfied. "So… how does this mana come back?"

"A night's rest," she said. "Or with potions." She thought for a moment. "Maybe your Class will even offer you access to alchemy so we can brew our own mana potions! That would be great."

I nodded, already seeing visions of an alchemical laboratory to make such things for personal use… and maybe a few for profit? I shook my head in disbelief, smiling at the options before me.

Diane hopped excitedly again, sharing my delight.

"First things first, though," I told her. "We finish breakfast. And then, we need to finish clearing the land."

Chapter 19

After our celebratory breakfast, Diane and I headed out to the garden plot to pick up where we had left off clearing the stubborn overgrowth. My frontier skills had awakened, filling me with eager energy. As such, I was looking forward to starting the day!

I hefted my scythe and set to work slicing through the stalks and scrub brush along the plot's edge. Beside me,

Diane swung her own blade gracefully, severing vegetation with practiced ease. The morning air was still crisp, promising another scorching afternoon ahead.

We worked steadily under the climbing sun, the ringing of our scythe blades mixing with birdsong. By late morning, my linen shirt was once again soaked through with sweat. Diane showed no sign of tiring, effortlessly scything away the encroaching growth.

When the sun reached its zenith, we finally sat beneath a tree to eat a light meal and rest our weary muscles. Diane smiled at our progress, tail swishing proudly. "At this rate, we'll have the whole plot cleared by tomorrow evening," she proclaimed.

I nodded, gulping water gratefully. My hands were already blistered, but I forced myself to keep going through the afternoon. Diane and I traded off tools, attacking the stubborn roots in shifts.

As the daylight began fading, we set our implements down nearly in unison, backs aching but deeply satisfied. A wide swath of overturned soil now stretched before us. We had conquered a huge area in just two days.

That evening, I could barely lift my spoon to eat supper, my arms leaden with exhaustion. But I took pride in transforming the land through honest work. Diane's tireless energy inspired me to push my limits.

Before we went to bed, I checked the trap but had caught nothing. My new instincts told me that it would better to place snares and traps farther away from the cabin.

At dawn the next day, we quickly ate breakfast and headed out to the plot again. A renewed sense of purpose drove me forward, scythe swinging with fresh vigor. The physical labor energized me in a way my old city job never had.

By early afternoon, we hacked and tore the last of the scrub from the earth. I drove my shovel under another tremendous central taproot – the last that blocked the plot – and heaved with a roar. It tore free in a shower of dirt, exposing rich soil.

Diane let out a whoop, throwing her arms skyward in triumph. "We did it!" she cried, pulling me into an exuberant, sweaty hug. I laughed, hugging her back tightly. Her wild spirit was contagious, and hugging her was a delight. She felt just right in my arms, like she fitted there.

As she pulled back, our eyes met for a moment, and her cheeks tinged a slight rose color as her ears gave an endearingly nervous little twitch. I knew then –

although perhaps I had known all along – that I was falling for her.

And she for me.

She cleared her throat and pulled back from the embrace, smiling shyly, and I let her go reluctantly. I was not sure how much longer I would be able to keep at bay my growing feelings for her, and I decided I needed to bridge that gap between us – to understand what it meant in foxkin culture to be close in the way I wanted to be close to her.

And I had just the idea… But it would have to wait for a little while.

We did a final pass picking rocks and roots from the plot. Then I stood back with Diane, gazing out proudly over the wide swath of cleared, tilled earth awaiting seeds. It was deeply fulfilling to see such tangible results of our combined labor.

"Shaping a piece of the frontier with your own hands – that's the real magic," remarked Diane, voicing my thoughts. I nodded in heartfelt agreement.

After cleaning the tools and grabbing a snack, we headed to the livestock pasture next. This plot was already partly cleared, with mainly scraggly grass sprouting about.

Diane scrutinized the sturdy wooden fence,

inspecting for damage while I hacked away at clusters of thorny bushes with a hatchet. Before long, the pasture was clear and ready for occupants.

"There," Diane proclaimed with satisfaction, hands on her hips as she surveyed our work. "All prepped and just awaiting some critters to fill it."

I smiled, picturing the animals we might acquire – chickens, goats, maybe even a milk cow. "It's really coming together now. I feel like a true homesteader, getting everything ready to be self-sufficient out here."

Diane beamed. "You've come such a long way already, David. When you first arrived, you knew little of homesteading. Now look at you – you're a natural!" Her praise made my heart swell with pride.

We decided to do one final task while there was still light. I wanted to start a smokehouse to preserve meat and fish, so I constructed a simple lean-to roof while Diane cut and stacked firewood inside. Soon we had a perfect smoking hut that we could use once we started trapping and fishing in earnest.

As the sun dipped low, we washed up in the river and then headed inside for supper, pleasantly exhausted after another productive day. The cabin already smelled of home – woodsmoke, wild herbs and hearty stew.

After eating, we relaxed by the fire, muscles aching but spirits high. Diane brought out her fiddle again, playing lively songs that echoed happily off the log walls.

When she finally set the instrument down, I said, "Diane, your music is so beautiful. It reminds me of when my mom used to sing folk tunes around our old campfire."

A wistful smile crossed my face at the memory. "She didn't have a voice like yours, but she sang often and free. I don't think she even realized it herself. I have many happy memories of our home… before the Upheaval changed everything."

Diane's expression softened with empathy. "Tell me about it. What was life like for you and your family before?"

I gazed into the flickering fire, gathering my thoughts. "Well, we lived in a nice house out in the country. My dad worked construction, while my mom took care of the home. They both loved the outdoors, so we were always camping, hiking, and fishing on weekends."

Diane listened intently, her ears perked with interest as I shared memories of carefree childhood trips and my close-knit family. Her eyes clouded with sorrow when I described the chaos of the merging worlds.

"Everything fell apart so fast," I explained. "I was in Louisville with my grandparents when it happened. That turned out to be a lifesaver, as our own town was just swallowed up by the Upheaval. Nobody knows what happened to it. I ended up in my grandparents' care in the city, and I'm thankful for them. But I never saw our town or any of the people from it again. All I got were reports from the Coalition made public that showed the place where our town used to be had turned into the Wilds. Not a trace of it."

Diane reached out and squeezed my hand supportively. "I'm so sorry, David. That must have been incredibly hard to go through. And your parents?"

"The System assigned them Classes," I said. "Like so many, they were swept up in the adventures. My grandparents became my primary caregivers, but I have warm memories from whenever my parents came back. One day, they went on a mission and..." I shrugged. "Well, they never returned."

"Oh, David, that sounds terrible."

I nodded. "It really turned my whole world upside down. What about you, Diane? What was it like when the Upheaval hit?"

Diane's expression grew distant. "I remember it being

utterly terrifying at first. Rifts tore open the sky, and this world — it was strange to us then; we feared the cities and the metal and the concrete — appeared behind the rifts. Many foxkin fled for safety, but families were separated in the chaos."

She explained how she got separated from her parents and siblings when monstrous creatures, driven wild by the Upheaval and the magical energies it released, stampeded over their camp. "We all scattered. By the time the fighting ended, I couldn't find any of my kin."

I listened sympathetically as Diane described those harrowing times. "You must have felt so lost and alone," I said softly.

Diane nodded, ears drooping slightly. "For a while I wandered the wilderness surviving on my own. But eventually I made my way here to Gladdenfield and Leigh took me in. She became the family I thought I'd lost."

We sat in silence for a moment, hands clasped, sharing the emotional weight of memories long buried. It felt good to open up and share these things.

"Well, we've both come through a lot to be here now," I finally said. Diane gave a small smile and squeezed my hand gratefully.

We talked late into the night, sharing treasured memories and bonding over the roles our loved ones played in shaping us. I felt I truly knew Diane better now. Out here, the present was all that mattered, but the past remained woven into who we were.

Chapter 20

The next morning, I was up early, feeling energized and eager to put my plan into action. Diane was still asleep, so I headed downstairs and got busy making a hearty breakfast.

Soon, the aroma of frying eggs, potatoes, and fresh bread woke Diane. She descended the ladder, smoothing back her adorably disheveled hair. "My, something smells delicious!"

"Morning, Diane," I greeted her cheerily. "Have a seat, breakfast is just about ready."

As we ate, I set my plan into motion. "So, I was thinking of heading into Gladdenfield today for some supplies. We don't need much – some food, some seeds, and some stuff to help set up the traps – but I think we could both use a break from working the land."

Diane's ears perked up with interest. "That sounds lovely! Let me grab my things."

"Actually," I said slowly, "I was hoping to make this just a quick solo trip if that's alright? I have one or two personal errands to run. But I'll be back by evening so we can have dinner together. That way, you can take the day off and just rest! You've been a great help, but I would love for you to relax a little as well."

The truth was, I would have loved for her to come along. But for my little plan to work, I needed to head into town alone.

Diane looked surprised, her fox ears twitching for a second, but nodded agreeably. "Of course, no problem! It actually sounds nice to relax for a day. But... I can't sit still too long. I'll use some of the time to do some fishing around here. I'll make sure we have some fresh fish for dinner!"

I smiled, hoping she wouldn't feel I was avoiding her. But keeping my plans secret was necessary. "Thanks for understanding. I appreciate it!"

After breakfast, I secured supplies for the journey in the Jeep while Diane tidied up inside. Soon I was bumping down the winding path away from the homestead.

It felt refreshing to be behind the wheel alone with my thoughts, watching the vibrant wilderness flow past. The morning sun shone behind the vivid leaves, promising another hot day ahead.

Birds burst from the undergrowth in explosions of color as I navigated ruts and rocks. The solitude allowed me to gather my courage for the next phase in getting closer to Diane.

I knew she cared for me too, but the cultural gap remained. I hoped today's undertaking might bridge it. My palms grew sweaty on the wheel just thinking about it.

To calm my nerves, I focused on the present – sunlight on the stone-strewn trail, strange cries echoing from the forest. Out here, it was just me and the untamed land. Well, and all the strange creatures that called Earth home since the Upheaval.

After a while, the main road came into view through the trees, right next to the cottonwood. I shifted gears and steered the rugged vehicle onto the wider dirt thoroughfare.

Soon more travelers came into sight — traders with laden wagons and strange beasts of burden. Some of them were elven traders, traveling between the villages of the frontier to sell and buy. I exchanged friendly waves and greetings with them as our paths converged.

The bustle increased as I neared Gladdenfield's palisade. Homesteaders heading out to their own plots of land mingled with hunters and adventurers returning from forays. It was interesting to realize that — unlike in New Springfield — everybody here had a Class. These were all people of supernatural ability, very different from those in the city.

At the gates, the guards recognized me and waved me through with smiles. I navigated the crowded streets, following the road to my destination. In the town, I drove carefully and slowly, and my excellent vehicle — although it was in need of a wash right now — drew a lot of attention from the inhabitants.

After parking, I double-checked if I stood in a good spot and took a deep breath. This was it — time to put my plan into action.

I took a deep breath and pushed open the door to Leigh's shop. The bells jangled merrily to announce my arrival. Leigh looked up from behind the counter and broke into a broad grin.

"Well, howdy, David! This is a pleasant surprise," she said warmly, straightening up and smoothing her hands down the front of her jeans.

Leigh was her usual charming self — blonde hair escaping from under her cowboy hat, cheeks rosy from the heat. Her blue eyes lit up at the sight of me. My eyes were drawn to her voluptuous figure, and I found, to my delight, that she wore daisy dukes. She shifted her hips enticingly when she saw me.

I smiled as I approached the counter, glancing around the cozy, cluttered space. Shelves overflowed with all manner of goods and curiosities from the frontier lands. "Hey Leigh. I was hoping I could pick your brain about something."

She immediately perked up, leaning forward eagerly. "Well now, I do love being picked," she purred, shooting me a flirty wink. As she did, I couldn't help but notice two undone buttons at the top of her shirt, affording an enticing glimpse of freckled cleavage.

I chuckled, feeling my blood heat. Leigh seemed completely unabashed about her constant stream of shameless flirting.

"Actually, it's about Diane," I explained, trying valiantly to keep my eyes on her face. "And I know you and Diane are close friends. I figured you could give me some, uh… *insights*. I don't know much about foxkin and, well, their customs."

Leigh's eyebrows shot up, nearly disappearing under the brim of her hat. "Ohhh, I think I'm pickin' up what you're layin' down now." She grinned knowingly, drumming her fingers on the counter. "This about gettin' it on with a certain fluffy-tailed vixen that happens to be a mutual acquaintance of you and I?"

I cleared my throat. It wasn't often that I had to search for words, but Leigh managed to put me in that position. Her delicious body, her challenging blue eyes, and the way she leaned on that counter made my head spin. She was coming on hard – harder than I was used to. Here was a woman who knew what she wanted.

She laughed when she saw my response, placing a light hand on my arm. "I'm just jokin' around with you,

David," she said. "I saw what was going on between you and Diane the moment y'all came in here." Her smile warmed a little. "I'm happy she found someone she's interested in."

I rubbed the back of my neck. "Thanks… Yeah… Diane and I, we've been getting closer. And I really like her. But I don't want to risk offending her or messing this up by misunderstanding her culture."

She grinned and licked her plump lips for a moment. "Well, I heard you already proposed to her."

I chuckled. "I, uh, may have done that."

"And she didn't get mad. That says a lot, David." She nodded thoughtfully, glancing toward the window as if she could see Diane out there somewhere. "Mm, but it's real wise of you, coming to ask," she mused. "Okay then, let's have a sit-down and chat about this."

She came around from behind the counter and hooked her arm through mine, guiding me over to a small table tucked in the back corner. The sway of her full hips in those daisy dukes and the thick thighs underneath were mesmerizing to watch.

Part of it was a little confusing to me. I was pretty sure that I was developing profound feelings for Diane, but I liked Leigh a lot. Being near her was easy and fun, and I loved her bubbly, easy-going personality.

Obviously, I loved her body, too — and she was proud of it and confident. These were all attractive traits to me, even though she was very different from Diane.

I wanted them both.

I caught a whiff of Leigh's perfume as we sat down across from each other — something woodsy and wild, with a hint of honeysuckle. It suited her.

"Now, mating and courtship with foxkin is tricky for an outsider to fully grasp," Leigh began matter-of-factly, folding her hands on the tabletop. "They have very different views on romance and intimacy from how we humans see things. The first thing you gotta understand is, most vixens will only take one mate in their whole life once they decide to settle down proper."

I nodded. "Alright, so… it's a commitment for life."

"Hm-hm," she hummed. "Fox girls ain't for blowin' off steam or some fun-and-forget." Suddenly, her eyes turned a little harder. "Especially Diane," she added with an edge. "I care about her like a sister. So my first advice for ya is to think things through. I ain't gonna have nobody breaking her heart. At least not without me breakin' their bones."

I couldn't help but smile at that. The bubbly blonde had an edge, and she had it just where I liked it — when it came to friends, she considered family. It spoke for her character that she wasn't all playfulness and giggles.

"I'm dead serious," she said, misunderstanding my smile.

"I know," I said. "I can tell. Don't worry. My rash days are long behind me. I'm out here to stay. Don't forget: I'm already practically living together with her."

"I reckon that's true," she hummed in her delicious country accent, her blue eyes warming up a bit again. "I'm sorry… if I'm a bit protective. She had a rough time during the Upheaval. I just want her to be happy, y'know?"

I nodded and placed my hand over hers. "I understand."

Now she shot me a wry, knowing look. "All right," she hummed. "On to Diane… So here's the thing. You probably noticed that there are certain times when she ain't bashful or shy at all, right? I mean, a fox girl will get butt-naked and hop into a pool with you."

I laughed, nodding. "Yeah, that's definitely a side of Diane I've seen."

Leigh smiled, leaning back comfortably in her chair. "Well that's 'cause they're at ease in nature. They're not really ashamed of their bodies, but most of 'em – especially those like Diane who've been living with humans — will grow a little more self-conscious. The result is a kinda confusing mix of signals, right? Bashful one moment; bold the next."

I laughed. "Yeah… yeah, that's Diane."

She grinned. "So here's the thing. That behavior don't necessarily mean she's fixin' to get hitched just yet. Even if she seems sweet on you, Diane likely won't settle down permanent-like with one mate until she feels certain about him."

I nodded, eager to hear more of what she had to say. This was turning out to be a pretty interesting lesson…

I took mental notes as Leigh explained more about foxkin mating habits, feeling relieved to have help decoding Diane's behavior. With our different cultural backgrounds, I had found some of her shyness and reticence mixed with boldness and easy touching confusing, but this provided useful context.

Leigh went on, "So don't be too surprised if she seems hesitant about getting physical at first, even if she's flirting up a storm with you out by the well." She shot me a pointed look. "Building real trust and devotion is a big deal for foxkin when it comes to mating. It's not just casual fun times."

I nodded slowly, thinking back on a few moments with Diane that seemed to confirm this. "That makes a lot of sense, thanks Leigh," I replied sincerely. "I definitely want to make sure I understand where she's coming from and don't make her uncomfortable."

"Of course, hun!" Leigh patted my arm reassuringly. "Now, once a vixen decides she's found her match, there are some courtship rituals and customs you'll want to know about too before you make things official..."

As Leigh spoke, I noticed her hand was still resting lightly on my arm, her fingertips idly tracing little circles in a way that was proving highly distracting. I shifted in my seat, eyes once again drawn to the bosom those buttons were straining to contain. Damned if the feeling of her nails grazing my skin wasn't having a powerful effect.

I coughed discreetly into my fist, determined not to let my imagination run away with itself. "So, uh...what kind of courtship rituals do foxkin have, then?" I asked, steering the discussion back on track.

She smiled up at me. "First things first, stud. That proposal you made earlier?"

I nodded.

"You need to do it again or let her know you meant it the first time 'round. That'll be the start of it. After that, the two of y'all can go on a date."

A little confused at the required formal gesture — a shaking of hands — I perked an eyebrow. "So... I need to shake her hand again?"

Leigh laughed, giving a playful little squeeze on my arm. "Oh shoot, darlin', nothing that uptight! It's more like a holdin' of hands. You just gotta stick yours out and say somethin' like asking her out, y'know? Say you wanna court her."

I grinned and nodded. "I mean, we've held hands over the last couple of days a few times..."

She leaned in, pouting her plump lips in the dirtiest way as she fixed her bedroom eyes on me. I think I actually shivered at that.

"Holdin' hands, hmm," she hummed, her husky southern accent making my blood pump. "Very lewd..."

Despite my own arousal at her half-act, I still laughed and shook my head. "Leigh, you are wild..."

"You don't know the half of it, sugar," she purred, her fingernails making another teasing trail up my forearm.

That moment hung in the air, and I felt myself very close to acting on it. All the flirting with Diane over the past few days had already riled me up, and Leigh wasn't doing anything to improve the situation. At all.

"And that's another thing," she said, keeping her eyes fixed on mine. "They don't mind sharing their men."

The implication hung heavily in the air. My entire body was tense. "Yeah," I said, finding my voice a little hoarse. "She told me that."

Then, she pulled back, breaking the tension just like that as she gave a lighthearted smile, and leaving me in that chair as one heaving bulk of sexual tension.

"Well," she purred, hopping to her feet like nothing had happened. "That should help give you a good groundin' on how foxkin operate in matters of the heart."

I breathed out and sat back in the chair, trying to get my muscles to relax as I looked up at her from under my eyebrows, a crooked smirk on my face.

Tease. And the way her eyes sparked told me she knew it pretty damn well.

But I liked it.

"Thanks, Leigh," I said.

"Anytime, sugar," she replied. "Now, I got a couple

of elves comin' by in a few minutes for a trade, so I need to get my business hat on, baby. And I can't focus with a good-lookin' guy like you hangin' around. Nuh-uh."

I laughed and rose to my feet, struggling a little to hide the bulge that had formed. Her eyes dipped for a moment, and she didn't seem to mind at all.

"Tell ya what," she said. "You have that talk with Diane, and maybe you can come by, and we'll talk a little more about how ya should proceed, huh? We'll make a day of it, 'cause I could use a day off."

I smiled. "Are you asking me out on a date, Leigh?" I asked. It was my turn to put her on the spot a little.

But the country blonde wasn't easily put on the spot. She just cocked a delicious hip, tipped her hat up a little, and gave a playful shrug of one freckled shoulder. "I ain't no foxkin," she hummed. "When I like someone, I go for the throat."

With that, she narrowed her eyes, purred a 'rawr', and snapped her perfect white teeth at me.

I broke out laughing. What other answer was there? I liked her, and I couldn't help but wonder how crazy a day with Leigh could get. Probably pretty damn crazy. And likely a little dirty, too.

"Now, go on," she said. "Git! I need to do business. You're gettin' me all riled up!"

Still laughing, I let Leigh walk me over to the door. She leaned on the frame as I stepped outside. The dusty frontier town bustled around us under the baking sun.

Leigh stopped me before I left, her gaze a little less teasing and more serious. "Between just you and me, I think you and Diane will make a perfect couple," she added sincerely, giving my arm an affectionate squeeze.

I sure hoped she was right. Diane and I seemed to connect more deeply with each passing day. "Thanks again, Leigh," I said. "For everything."

"Of course." She smiled. "Now you go on and put some of that foxkin courting advice into action." She gave me a playful swat on the rear as I turned to go.

I laughed, waving goodbye over my shoulder as I walked down the creaky steps to the dusty street. Behind me, I heard Leigh call out teasingly from the doorway: "Y'all come back and see me real soon now, y'hear? We'll hang out and make a day of it. Can't have a handsome fella like you be a stranger around these parts!"

I chuckled and waved again in promise that I would return. As I climbed into the Jeep and pulled away down the bumpy road, I saw Leigh leaning in the doorway watching me go, arms crossed under her ample bosom, smile on her plump lips.

She was something…

Chapter 21

After leaving Leigh's shop, I had a lot on my mind as I drove back to the homestead. Her advice about foxkin courtship customs had given me plenty to think about. But I also couldn't stop replaying her shameless flirting in my head.

That curvy country gal seemed determined to get a rise out of me, figuratively and literally. And damned if she hadn't succeeded on both counts. I shifted in my seat, jeans still feeling a bit too tight. Leigh seemed to enjoy yanking my chain and pushing boundaries.

Not that I really minded her particular brand of mischief and teasing. But it left me wondering if something might happen between us, especially with her talk about sharing mates.

The potential for… *complications* was definitely there. But I knew that Diane wouldn't mind sharing me, although I still needed to understand more about these harem… rules. How would I go about all of it? Maybe that was another thing to discuss with Leigh.

I shook my head, trying to clear it and focus on the trail as the Jeep jostled along. I cared deeply for Diane and wanted to court her properly. No need to get ahead of myself.

The sun-dappled wilderness flowed past, its strangeness slowly becoming more familiar to me. I kept replaying my conversation with Leigh in my mind. Her advice about foxkin views on intimacy and commitment had been insightful. But some parts were still confusing me.

Like her insistence I essentially "re-propose" by asking Diane on a date. That seemed unnecessarily formal considering we already lived together. Then again, this was their culture, not mine. The more I considered it, the more I realized all I needed to do was openly convey my interest in courting Diane as my mate. No need to turn it into some overly ceremonious occasion.

I just had to be sincere about my intentions and desires. If Diane reciprocated, we could build our relationship gradually, respecting her more conservative pace regarding intimacy.

Rounding a bend, the glittering ribbon of the Silverthread River came into view ahead. Our cozy cabin awaited, tucked against the flowing water. I smiled, easing up on the gas pedal as the charming little dwelling grew nearer through the trees. Diane was likely down by the riverbank, her fishing pole cast into the rushing currents.

Soon I was pulling up beside the cabin, gravel crunching under the tires. As expected, I spotted Diane's shapely form down on the rocky shore. She turned at the sound of my approach, betrayed by the purr of my Jeep.

Her expression lit up, and she offered a cute smile. With unbridled enthusiasm, she waved eagerly for me to come join her. The sight warmed my heart — she had clearly missed me these past hours apart as much as I'd missed her.

I quickly gathered my nerves, parked the car, and headed down the winding path to the water's edge. It was time to have a heartfelt talk with this amazing woman who occupied my mind.

"Welcome back!" Diane greeted me brightly as I approached. She looked radiant today — her dark hair spilling loosely over one shoulder, cheeks endearingly flushed from the sun. She wore a light and simple dress that clung to her fit form. On most women, the garment would have been drab, but she made it look wonderful, her delicious bronze skin contrasting with the white fabric.

She grinned as I watched her, her fox ears perking up and her tail giving a little swish.

"Catch anything good?" I asked, nodding toward her fishing pole.

"A few nice trout," said Diane, nodding at the bucket beside her that held the bounty. "How was your trip into town?"

I rubbed my neck, feeling just a little anxious. "It was fine." I almost said I had picked up some supplies, but the truth was that I'd forgotten all about them. No matter: it had been an excuse more than anything else. We still had plenty of supplies, and I would make a trip to town again soon enough.

Her ears twitched and she studied me closely. I took a deep steadying breath. It was now or never.

"Actually, Diane, there was something I've been wanting to ask you." I lowered myself to sit next to her on the stones. And as I did so, I extended my hand, keeping my eyes focused on hers.

Diane's eyes went wide, one hand flying to her mouth in surprise. "David, what are you…?"

I offered her my open hand. "Diane, since the moment we met, I knew you were special. Our friendship has come to mean the world to me. And I want it to be *more* than a friendship."

Her eyes shimmered as she listened silently. This was it — time to take the plunge. "Diane Whikksie, would you do me the honor of allowing me to court you?" I asked.

For a breathless moment, Diane just gazed at me, unspeaking. Then a dazzling smile lit up her face.

"Oh, David!" she cried joyfully, pulling me into a tight embrace. I held her petite frame against me, my heart swelling with emotion.

After a long moment, Diane drew back to look deeply into my eyes. Her own shimmered with happy tears. "Nothing would make me happier than to have you court me," she said softly.

I broke into a wide grin, relief and elation washing over me. "You have no idea how happy that makes me to hear," I said.

Diane laughed, a musical, joyous sound. Impulsively she threw her arms around my neck again for another hug. I lifted her up and spun her around exuberantly as we embraced.

I reveled in that moment as long as I could — we both did. By the bank of the Silverthread and under the bright sun, I held my beautiful frontier girl, mind spinning with what was to come. There wasn't a happier guy in the world right now.

Setting her back down, I caressed her cheek tenderly. "I promise I'll do this properly and respectfully, in keeping with your traditions."

Diane smiled radiantly. "I know you will. That's part of why I care for you so." Her eyes were filled with affection.

"But please help me with it," I said. "When I do something that doesn't work for you, let me know. In my culture, relationships flourish only if there is good communication."

She grinned. "It's the same with us," she said. Then, she leaned in to give me a kiss on my cheek, and the touch of her soft lips was enough to roil up the fire in my heart. "I promise that I will."

I smiled warmly. "Shall we have dinner together tonight, to celebrate the first day of our courtship?" I suggested.

Diane's eyes sparkled. "I would love nothing more," she said, taking my hands in hers again. "But let's stay here for while longer. Sit with me by the bank of the river! I want this moment to last."

I couldn't agree more. I sat down beside her, finally holding her hand without wondering what it meant. We lingered there together on the rocks for a while, neither wanting this magical moment between us to end, and both savoring the future — the things that were to come between us.

Chapter 22

I wanted our first official dinner together as a courting couple to be special, so I spent the late afternoon decorating the cabin while Diane cleaned the trout and foraged some herbs to spice up our meal. I gathered wildflowers from around the homestead, arranging them in a simple vase on the dining table. Then, I lit candles and scattered some rose petals across the tabletop and floor.

When Diane came inside and saw my efforts, her eyes lit up. "Oh David, it's wonderful!" she exclaimed, clasping her hands together. Her fluffy tail swished happily behind her.

I smiled, pleased that she appreciated the touches. "Only the best to celebrate our new beginning," I replied warmly.

We worked together to prepare the fresh trout, seasoning it with wild herbs. The savory aroma of the fish frying filled the cozy cabin. I also toasted some bread and poured us some more of the wine Leigh had gifted us.

Soon, we were seated across from each other, the flickering candlelight playing softly across Diane's lovely features. Her blue eyes shone as we tapped our mugs together in a heartfelt toast.

"To new beginnings," Diane said softly.

"To new beginnings," I echoed. We both smiled and drank.

The trout was cooked to perfection, the flesh tender and flaky. Diane made the most adorable little hums of satisfaction as she ate. I loved seeing her enjoyment of the simple meal I had prepared.

Over dinner, we chatted about lighter, happier topics

— favorite childhood memories, the beauty of the changing wilderness seasons, hopes for the future. Diane's sweet laughter echoed merrily around the cozy cabin interior whenever we joked, and I was pleased to hear the sound.

As we lingered over the last sips of wine, I reached across the table and took Diane's hand, softly stroking the back with my thumb. Her fingers curled around mine, and she smiled gently.

"I'm happy right now, being here with you like this," I said sincerely, meeting her shimmering sapphire eyes.

"So am I," Diane replied, her voice hushed. "Happier than I've been in a very long time." Her thumb idly traced little circles on my palm, sending pleasant tingles up my arm.

When the food was finished, Diane shyly mentioned she had been working on a new song and asked if I'd like to hear it. There was something about the shyness in her voice that told me there was a story behind this song she had written herself, and I hoped she would tell me — if not tonight, then later.

"I'd love to," I replied eagerly.

Diane fetched her violin and rosined up the bow. Tucking the instrument under her chin, she began to play a melancholy melody. Then she started to sing in her beautiful, lilting voice with its exotic accent:

"Two souls adrift, drawn together,
A love unrealized,
My heart knows yours though words unspoken,
Through feelings undefined."

Her voice swelled with emotion as she sang the second part:

"Oh, let this be our love's dawning,
No longer shall I pine,
For I see in your eyes the missing piece,
To make my spirit whole."

I listened, enraptured by the heartfelt lyrics and the melancholic strains of the violin. When the final notes faded, I applauded enthusiastically. Her cheeks flushed, and she bowed her head in appreciation of the applause.

"That was breathtaking," I said. "What is the story behind it?"

Diane's eyes took on a faraway look. "It's an old folk tune my mother used to play for me as a child. It speaks of the bittersweet longing when two are not yet united in love. The joy of finding one's other half, but not yet knowing if it will come to pass. It…" She swallowed, obviously gathering her courage. "It describes how I have felt about you since we first met."

"It's beautiful," I said. "I feel the same, Diane. I just… I didn't want to rush things. You're from a very different place, and I needed to understand some things before I could… Well, before I could ask you."

Diane smiled softly. "I understand, David. Somehow, I had a feeling things would be all right."

I felt honored she had chosen to share something so meaningful. As she sat down beside me on the braided rug in front of the fireplace, her long legs folded under her, she held my hand. We talked more about songs that were important to us, and I hoped to one day teach her a few songs from my childhood.

"I would love to learn them," she hummed, her sapphire eyes fixed on mine. "Through music, we can learn more of each other. It often says more than words."

And as we sat there, me losing myself in her eyes, I could no longer stop it. Cultural differences and mating customs be damned. When the heart burns, caution is thrown to the wind.

I leaned in…

Diane's eyes widened for a moment as she understood what was about to happen. But she did not back away or stop me.

Instead, a sigh — almost like a whimper of release — escaped her plump lips. Her hands trembled slightly in mine as I closed my eyes, pining for the moment our lips would meet.

And when they did, I was swept away. Soft and full and tender. Warm. I lost myself in our first kiss, and so did she, surrendering herself to me in full.

For the first time, I felt her push her body against mine, her heartbeat near and blazing and full of life and longing. My mind reeled with how soft her skin was, with how delicious the curves of her hips were when I ran my hand over them, with the soft fur of her tail as I…

She drew back, her eyes big and vulnerable in the firelight. Her tongue flicked out for a moment, still tasting me on her lips, and then she smiled shyly, turning her eyes to the ground.

I smiled, taking a deep breath. I wanted nothing more than to carry her off to the bedroom, but Leigh's words came to mind: "Don't be too surprised if she seems hesitant about getting physical at first."

It felt as if a kiss alone was a big jump for her.

I held her hand and smiled. "So," I said, my voice hoarse. "Like I said, communication is important. I want to take you to bed, Diane. I know what it means to you, and I'm here to stay. But I need to hear if that is what you want, too."

She pressed her lips together as she looked up at me. Her cheeks were burning, and her eyes were hazy. "I want it too, David," she said. "But I can't yet. It's..." She bit her lip in the cutest way as she considered her words. "To us... it's different. It means everything to join a man's family."

I smiled and nodded, giving her a kiss on her cheek. "I understand," I said.

"It's not that I don't want to," she hummed, touching her cheek where I had just kissed her. "I could..." She bit her lip for a moment as she watched, her eyes turned hazy again. "I want to... every inch of you... But..." She shook her head.

I touched her arm lightly. "Hey," I chuckled, at least a little flattered by the obvious hunger in her eyes. "It's okay. It *will* happen. I feel that this is right. So we don't need to rush anything."

With that, she gave a happy nod and fell into my arms again. "Thank you, David," she hummed. "I'm so happy. And I think so too. I can't wait... It just needs to be the right moment. I'll… I'll know when it's there."

I couldn't deny the fire in my chest. I was a man after all, and my feelings for her meant I also lusted to have her share herself with me. But part of me realized that it would be all the sweeter for the wait.

Still… there had been a lot of flirting and teasing going on, and I hadn't had anyone in my life for a while in New Springfield. But I would wait.

We enjoyed the embrace a while longer as our minds cooled. Finally, we rested in front of the fire again, Diane shimmying her body against mine and holding me close as we watched the fire pop and crackle together.

This was the life. What we shared here and what we were building here were beautiful things — things that would last. Contentment filled me as Diane and I sat in comfortable silence, simply enjoying each other's closeness as the fire gradually died down.

Eventually, we retreated to our beds, both of us craving more but knowing we must be patient. However, it was her idea to push the beds together. Even though the gap between them meant we could not lie together too comfortably, we were close at least.

Diane curled up contentedly next to me, head nestled on her pillow. She kissed me goodnight, and the kiss almost pulled us into the play I so longed to share with her. But we restrained ourselves, and I rested my hand on her slender waist as she drifted into sleep.

Soon after her, I fell into a deep, peaceful sleep, Diane's heady scent still surrounding me. Her gentle breathing from just an arm's length away gave me peace and comfort.

Chapter 23

I awoke to soft sunlight filtering into the cabin bedroom. For a moment, I was disoriented, unsure where I was. Then I became aware of a warm, slender body pressed up against me, one arm draped lightly over my chest. Memories of the passionate kiss with Diane the night before came flooding back. Somehow, the fox girl had managed to squeeze herself onto my one-person mattress. Her own bed was empty.

It was a tight fit, but I didn't care. I turned my head to see her still sleeping peacefully, lips parted slightly as she breathed. Her silky black hair was endearingly mussed against the pillow. She looked so relaxed and content nestled against me.

Not wanting to wake her just yet, I remained still, idly tracing her slender waist with my hand as I listened to the sounds of the frontier awakening. Birdsong and the gentle burble of the nearby river heralded the day's fresh beginnings, and everything was quiet and perfect.

After a few minutes, Diane began to stir, nuzzling her face against my shoulder. Her sapphire eyes fluttered open and she smiled drowsily up at me. "Good morning," she murmured.

"Good morning, beautiful," I replied, kissing the top of her head.

Diane hummed contentedly, tightening her arm across me in a lazy half-hug. I reveled in holding her slender form against me, her body conforming so gracefully to mine. Our bodies responded to one another, and she gave a delicious sigh of contentedness and with a trace of desire as she arched her back and hugged me tighter. Her fuzzy tail brushed my leg – a feeling I could get used to.

We lay together a while longer, neither wanting to leave the cozy nest of blankets just yet. But eventually Diane sat up with a yawn, her fox ears giving an adorable twitch. "Shall I make us some coffee?"

"That sounds perfect," I agreed. We shared a soft kiss before Diane slipped from the bed and headed downstairs, her foxtail swishing behind her.

I rose shortly after and washed up at the basin in the kitchen. When I finished washing up, I gave Diane a kiss on her soft neck, winning a purr from my fox girl. I headed back up to get dressed for the day. By the time I descended the ladder again, the rich scent of fresh coffee permeated the cabin.

Diane stood at the stove frying up eggs for breakfast, swaying gently to a tune only she could hear. I came up behind her and slipped my arms around her waist, kissing her cheek.

"Smells delicious," I murmured against her skin. "And I don't mean the eggs."

She laughed and gave me a playful bump with her toned behind before leaning back against me with a contented sigh. "I hope you're hungry, I'm making a big frontier-style breakfast."

"Starving," I assured her, giving her petite frame a

final squeeze before releasing her to finish cooking. I began setting the table for two.

Soon we were sitting across from each other, steaming mugs of coffee at our elbows. The simple meal of eggs, jerky, and toasted bread tasted incredible.

As we ate, Diane reminded me of our plan for the day — to plant the magical moonlight potato seeds Leigh had gifted us. "With those little guys growing day and night, we should have quite the crop in no time," she said enthusiastically.

I smiled and nodded. "Hopefully they live up to their name and flourish even in moonlight. Extra harvests year-round would really help with provisions. Not to mention get us a little money to pay Leigh for all the stuff we got from her."

Our first crop… It was an exciting prospect. After all, this was what it was all about — why Caldwell had given me the opportunity to make my own way in the Wilds. We would become a self-sufficient part of the frontier.

"And I love potatoes," Diane hummed dreamily. Her eyes shone as she began to describe different potato dishes depending on the season — roasted potatoes in autumn, potato soup in winter, cheesy scalloped potatoes in spring.

I chuckled at her delight over humble tubers. She loved food, and she loved cooking — that much was apparent from our days together.

We discussed where to plant the moonlight spuds — rotating spots season by season to replenish the soil. Diane suggested fertile spots in our plot closer to the Silverthread River, knowing they would fare well there, especially at first.

As we finished eating, sunlight streamed in the cabin windows, beckoning us outside to the day's work. After breakfast, we worked together to tidy up the kitchen, hands often brushing as we moved about the cozy space. When the dishes were cleared, I pulled Diane into my arms for a moment.

She settled against my chest with a contented sigh, arms slipping around my waist. We held each other close, her warmth and sweet scent surrounding me.

I lifted Diane's fingers to my lips, kissing them softly. "Ready for the day?" I asked her with a wink.

She smiled, cheeks flushing. "Excited, in fact!" Her fingers gave mine an affectionate squeeze.

"Then let's get out there!"

The morning air was still cool and fresh as Diane and I headed out to the garden plot, tools in hand. I carried the precious packet of enchanted moonlight potato seeds Leigh had gifted us. Diane brought the shovel and hoe for tilling the fertile soil.

At the cleared plot, we worked together smoothing the overturned earth, breaking up clods. Diane hummed a cheerful tune as she hoed, ears perked and tail swishing in time with the music.

When the soil was prepared, I carefully opened the seed packet. The small seeds inside looked perfectly ordinary. I still marveled that magical properties lay hidden within.

Diane showed me how deep and far apart to plant them. We dug shallow trenches and dropped the seeds in one by one. The work was simple but satisfying – actively cultivating sustenance from the land using our own hands.

By mid-morning, warmth permeated the valley. I wiped sweat from my brow as I patted soil over the last planted seed. Our first crop was nestled in the earth.

The fences would keep out most of the critters, but we'd have to see if it was fully effective. If not, we might try to make a denser fence out of interlacing twigs.

"Just look at them all," Diane said proudly, tail curling as she surveyed our handiwork. "Before long, we'll have more moonlight potatoes than we know what to do with!"

I chuckled, sharing her optimism. "Let's just see how the first crop goes before we get all excited. I'm still not sure about this whole magical thing."

"Oh, you'll see," she said, shooting me a wink.

We washed our hands in the river, then sat beneath a shady tree to share some bread and dried fruit as midday came around. The sun-dappled meadow was serene, birdsong mixing with the gentle babbling of water over stones.

As we ate, Diane turned to me, ears perking curiously. "David, can I ask you something?"

"Of course," I replied.

She looked at me searchingly. "When you asked to court me yesterday, you knew exactly how to do it properly in the foxkin way. How did you learn our customs so well?"

I chuckled, rubbing my neck. No hiding it now. "Well, I had a very informative chat with Leigh when I went into town yesterday," I admitted.

Diane's blue eyes widened. "You asked Leigh about courting rituals?" She seemed torn between surprise and amusement.

"I wanted to be sure I understood your culture and didn't mess things up," I explained. "Leigh was incredibly helpful. She explained the importance of being direct and sincere about my intentions to court you. And not rushing intimacy before you were ready. She also told me to repeat the whole… proposition thing if I was serious about wanting to be with you."

Diane blushed but looked touched. "That's very thoughtful, David. I appreciate you taking such care." She smiled softly as a little twinkle lit up in her eyes. "Though I can only imagine what else Leigh had to say on the subject! I bet a lot!"

We both laughed at that. The light in her eyes told me there was something going on here — she and Leigh might have even talked about it before I did.

"Well, she sure had some things to say," I said carefully, not wanting to presume.

Diane nodded, tail swishing pensively. "Leigh has always been very open about such things. She knows us foxkin don't see intimacy the same way humans do sometimes." She looked at me earnestly. "You were right to talk to her about it. It's very sweet of you."

I smiled. "I'm happy she took the time."

She nuzzled against my shoulder gratefully. We sat in cozy silence as finches twittered in the branches above.

After a time, I spoke again. "Leigh did explain some things that helped me understand foxkin courtship better. Like how hand-holding signifies a serious intention to court when done ceremonially. And how foxkin females usually take just one mate."

Diane perked up, clearly intrigued I had gleaned these cultural insights. "Very true," she said with a sage nod. "Our mating habits are quite different from human norms."

"I'm thankful Leigh was so willing to teach me," I replied. "I should have talked to her before we first met. I could have avoided an accidental marriage proposal!"

We both laughed, reminiscing about that amusing misunderstanding back at the tavern when we first met. It seemed so long ago now.

"Well, I liked that you did it. It was..." She touched her plump lip with a finger for a moment. "It was disarming. And the way you dealt with it showed me you were willing to learn." She eyed me for a moment, her eyes lidded. "It also helps that I think you're... well... hot."

I laughed, and she gave me a playful swat. "I mean it! I never liked how foxkin men look!"

Remembered the scrawny one we saw on the way to Gladdenfield — I had already forgotten his name — I had to agree.

Diane's expression became thoughtful. "Leigh has always embraced the spectrum of sexuality and intimacy. She sees the beauty in all kinds of relationships. She's really open-minded. And so confident about these things!"

I nodded slowly. Diane and Leigh's openness regarding matters of the heart was refreshing compared to the social norms I'd grown up with. Out here on the frontier, forging bonds of trust and affection took precedence over rigid propriety.

"I noticed," I said. "She seems very open about those things."

Diane bit her lip, looking at me for a moment. "About that… You probably noticed Leigh flirting with you rather shamelessly."

I chuckled. "It was hard to miss."

Diane smiled. "Well, I want you to know I don't mind if you and Leigh want to… get to know each other. Among us foxkin, it's not uncommon for sisters to share a mate, and I consider her a sister. As long as there is openness and consent between all involved."

My eyes widened in surprise. This was very different from the human norms I knew. "That's not something that's really accepted for humans," I replied carefully. "I mean… We don't usually do that."

Diane nodded in understanding, taking my hand. "I know, your customs are different, so I don't expect you to embrace ours fully. If you don't want to court other women, I'll accept that. I only mention it so you know I would not be upset if you wished to be intimate with Leigh too." She smiled shyly. "Actually, it might be nice… if we were harem sisters."

I blinked, repeating the words in my head… *If you don't want to court other women, I'll accept that.*

"Hold on a sec," I said, holding up a hand. "You'll 'accept' if I don't want to court other women?"

"Well," she hummed, misunderstanding me. "I… Of course, I would like it better if you did. But I like you enough, David, to accept if you don't want to."

I was speechless for a moment. This was one of those cultural things. I decided to address it right away. I smiled at her and took her hand. "I'm not saying I don't want to," I said. "I was just amazed that, in your culture, it's actually appreciated and encouraged."

She nodded, a little confused. "Of course it is! It's…

well, there aren't a lot of men… But even if there were…" She considered it for a moment. "Yeah, I mean, it's good to have friends and a big family. Harem sisters are like close friends that you can share anything with. And we can help each other out. And when there's… y'know… little ones…" She blushed for a moment. "Well, it helps if there's more of us. If you need a night's rest, you can leave the kids in the care of one of your harem sisters."

I grinned and nodded. "You don't need to convince me. It sounds amazing to me. But you don't get jealous?"

She shook her head. "No? Why would I? I like you. I want you to be happy. I mean, it would be different if I wouldn't like one of my harem sisters." She thought for a moment. "But maybe Leigh would get jealous? I've not heard of a lot of harems with humans in them."

I chuckled and shook my head. "I have no idea. I don't even know if she actually wants to be in that kind of relationship or if she's just fooling around."

"Well, find out," Diane said, prodding me playfully, that twinkle returning to her eyes.

I narrowed my eyes suspiciously. "I'm getting this feeling *you* already know."

"Maybeee," she hummed, letting the word trail off

before she rested her cheek against my chest, her fox ear tickling my chin. "But that's between you two."

"Alright," I chuckled. "I see how it is."

She giggled, snuggling closer to me. By the looks of things, I was going to have to pay Leigh another visit soon.

Chapter 24

After our lunch, Diane and I decided to spend the rest of the sunny afternoon fishing together. We gathered up our poles, tackle boxes, some bait, and a bucket for the catch, then made our way down the rocky bank to the river's edge.

I took my time selecting the perfect fishing spot, eventually settling on a promising little eddy where the water bubbled energetically over submerged stones. Diane stood beside me, keen eyes scanning the river's surface. She pointed out a few prime locations, impressing me again with her innate ability to identify the best areas to drop a line.

"Right there looks perfect!" she said, indicating a swirl of current flowing around a partly exposed boulder. I nodded and moved into position, carefully casting my line out. Diane had already flicked her line expertly into a foamy back current nearby.

We stood shoulder to shoulder, eyes fixed on the glittering water. Within minutes, Diane's rod bent sharply as she hooked a decent-sized trout. It fought valiantly but was no match for her reflexes honed by a lifetime of wilderness living. She reeled it flapping onto the rocky shore.

"Nice catch!" I said appreciatively as she unhooked the fish and tossed it into her waiting bucket.

"Thanks! Now let's get you one too," Diane replied with an encouraging smile. Her fluffy tail swished excitedly behind her, indicating her levels of energy at this activity.

I turned my focus back to my own line, staring intently at the red and white bobber floating near the churning eddy. It bobbed a couple of times as curious fish investigated the bait, but none committed to a full strike. Meanwhile, I heard two more splashes from Diane's bucket as she landed additional trout.

I didn't mind her pulling ahead in the catch count – it was just nice being out by the river with her on this sunny day. A pair of exotic long-tailed birds with brilliant emerald and violet plumage swooped down over the shimmering water. I smiled at the sight – even common animals here in the frontier lands were impossibly colorful and strange.

After twenty minutes without a bite, I decided to try my luck at a new spot. I carefully reeled in my line and looked to Diane. "Mind if I move just downstream a bit? Maybe I'll have better luck around that fallen tree sticking out into the current."

"Go for it!" Diane said. "If the fish aren't biting where you are, it never hurts to experiment."

I crunched over the loose stones to the new locale. The half-submerged fallen tree created an eddy that looked promising. As I cast out again into the churning water, I saw Diane unhook another wriggling trout from the corner of my eye. She tossed it into the steadily filling bucket.

"That's number five for me now," she said with an impish grin when she noticed me watching. "Don't you worry though, fishing takes a lot of practice. You just have to keep trying different spots and baits until you get a feel for it!"

I laughed. "Clearly you foxkin are natural masters when it comes to hunting and foraging of all kinds."

Diane looked pleased, her fox ears twitching happily at the compliment. "Well, when you spend your whole life roaming and surviving out in the wilderness, you pick up a few tricks," she replied modestly.

I nodded, peering at my bobber bobbing among the ripples by the fallen tree. I appreciated Diane's encouragement, but my competitive instincts still wished I could catch up to her ever-rising count.

As I pondered the situation, an idea suddenly came to me. I still had a fair bit of mana left. Perhaps I could use one of my newfound skills or frontier magic to help even the odds?

Activating my interface with a thought, I quickly reviewed my options. The Identify Plants skill likely wouldn't be very useful here. But maybe my Summon Minor Spirit spell could somehow lend aid?

Yes, that was it! With a spirit's help attracting fish, perhaps I could close the gap with Diane. Eager to test this, I focused my will and cast the summoning.

I extended my palm, willing the mystical energies to

coalesce. The interface popped up again, offering me a choice of affinities for the spirit. I chose an aquatic affinity, hoping this would make it adept at aiding with fishing.

With a flickering burst, a small swirling orb of elemental water magic took shape before me. It expanded rapidly, colors shifting hypnotically across its translucent form. I had to squint against the dazzling magics at play.

Within seconds, the orb materialized into a diminutive humanoid shape. Its features were simple — two luminous blue dots for eyes and a small slitlike mouth on an otherwise smooth watery head. Rivulets constantly dripped down its surface as it hovered patiently before me.

The summoning spell now complete, I focused my thoughts toward the liquidy creature. "Help me catch some big fish!" I directed it mentally.

The sprite bobbed its dripping head in acknowledgment and immediately dove into the rushing river without hesitation.

I watched closely for any signs of its influence. At first, nothing seemed different, my line still slack in the current. But gradually, trout started practically leaping onto my hook as the elemental herded them toward me from below!

Initially, I thought it had some kind of control over the fish, but it simply seemed to herd them — almost like a shepherd dog — in a way that did not intimidate or frighten the fish, and they converged on my bait.

In no time at all, I was hauling fish after fish onto the shore, barely having time to rebait between casts. My bucket rapidly filled to match Diane's. With the minor water spirit's help, I had completely turned the tide!

I let the spell dissipate once it waned, not wanting to exhaust myself completely. The creature winked out of existence with a faint pop, spraying droplets.

Diane looked quite impressed as I set down my rod to rest sore arms. "Wow, using your magic to summon that fishing helper was clever thinking!" she said. "It seems like your abilities as a Summoner will really change how we're able to work out here."

I smiled, pleased she appreciated me putting these skills to practical use. "I figured why not try to give us a little boost where possible," I replied with a shrug. "No sense letting these powers go to waste if we can have spirits lend a hand!"

She pouted a little. "Hey, you even caught more than *I* did!"

I laughed. "Well, it's not a fair competition. I used my

magic."

At that, her eyes took on a mischievous light. "I… might have used one of my Class abilities as well."

I perked an eyebrow. "You what?" I said, feigning indignance as I got to my feet and placed my hands on my sides. "You cheater!"

She laughed and hopped to her dainty feet swiftly, leaving her bucket and rod where they were. She stuck her tongue out at me and began running.

Grin on my lips, I began my pursuit of the sprightly fox girl down the riverbank…

Laughing, I ran after Diane down the winding riverbank as she laughed merrily, deftly leaping from stone to stone. Her lithe acrobatics made it challenging to catch her, but I was determined to try.

Diane's melodic laughter rang out as she nimbly darted and wove through the rocky terrain, her bare feet finding sure purchase on the smooth round stones. She shot me an impish grin over her shoulder, eyes alight with mischief and delight at our spontaneous game of chase.

"You can't catch me that easily!" she called out, laughing as her fox tail swished enticingly behind her. She had cut a hole into her light summer dress for it, and the sight of it was just too cute. Diane's natural grace and agility gave her an advantage, but I pushed my muscles to pump faster, breathing hard as I scrambled after her slender form.

The exhilarating burn of exertion quickly spread through my limbs, but I pressed on determinedly. Diane's musical laughter and the swishing flash of her tail around trees and boulders spurred me to pick up speed. I relished the challenge of trying to catch this swift and sprightly vixen – the thrill of the pursuit was half the fun.

We rounded a rocky outcropping dotted with vibrant wildflowers in a rainbow of hues – deep magentas, sunshine yellows, and vivid azure blooms that only seemed to grow in the magical wilderness. Their cloying fragrances mingled in the warm air.

At last, the stony riverbank opened up into a sunny grassy meadow, blades swaying gently in the breeze. Spying an opportunity in the open space, I dug deep and managed one final burst of speed, laughing breathlessly as I closed the distance and wrapped my arms around Diane's slender waist.

She let out a delighted yelp as we tumbled together into the soft, lush grass. The momentum sent us rolling until I had her pinned beneath me, both of us panting and flushed from the exhilarating chase. Diane's silken hair was endearingly mussed, inky locks spilling across the grass. Her cheeks were flushed a rosy pink, eyes sparkling.

"Gotcha!" I exclaimed triumphantly between heaving breaths. Diane squirmed playfully beneath me, but I held her fast, our bodies pressed close. I could feel her chest rising and falling rapidly against mine, our hearts still racing.

Diane looped her arms lazily around my neck, deftly threading her fingers into my hair. "Okay, okay, you caught me fair and square," she conceded with a grin, batting her thick lashes coquettishly.

I gazed down at her, utterly enchanted. "So tell me, what's my prize for managing to catch such a swift fox?" I asked teasingly.

Diane pretended to consider deeply, absently twirling a lock of my hair around her finger. "Hmm… how about… this?" she purred. Before I could react, she pulled my head down to hers for a sudden, passionate kiss.

My eyes fluttered shut as our lips met, the kiss

rapidly deepening. Diane melted against me, hands trailing down my neck and shoulders to pull me tighter to her. We clung together amidst the gently waving meadow grasses.

I was acutely aware of every inch of Diane's lithe body conforming to mine, her curves cushioned against me. Our kisses grew hungry, more fervent. When we finally broke apart for air, our faces remained just inches apart, noses touching.

Diane's cheeks were adorably flushed, lips kiss-swollen and parted enticingly as she struggled to catch her breath. Her crystal blue eyes were darkened, pupils wide with desire. Seeing her obvious enjoyment sent a thrill coursing through me.

This vixen was pure fire. The softness of her skin under the summer dress, and the way the loose garment offered a sight of her enticing bosom made me heady and needing more.

"Mmm… I'd say that was a more than satisfactory prize," Diane purred throatily, nuzzling her nose affectionately against mine.

I grinned down at her. "I'd have to agree," I murmured. Unable to resist, I leaned in again, capturing her lips in a series of soft, lingering kisses.

Diane responded eagerly, as though she could never

get enough. We took our time indulging in long, lazy kisses, our hands beginning to wander and explore each other's bodies through our clothing.

My pulse raced wildly at each new discovery – the enticingly soft fur of her fox tail, the alluring curve of her hips, the way she arched into my touch ever so slightly. Our mutual longing was quickly growing harder to deny.

With great reluctance, I slowly withdrew from the kiss, gently caressing Diane's flushed cheek as our labored breathing slowed. The depth of intimacy we'd shared out here in the wilderness had my mind spinning deliriously. But I didn't want to rush her, knowing how seriously foxkin viewed physical bonding.

But even as I pulled back, she gave an impatient mewl, drawing me into her embrace again. My eyes widened as she kissed me with a passion. Then, with a move as swift as fire, she rolled me onto my back and straddled me.

Her body pressing down on me, my mind whirled... Where was this going?

Chapter 25

The afternoon sun forced my eyes into a narrow squint, but even that couldn't dim the breathtaking sight before me.

Diane, her body poised above me, was a vision to behold. The summer dress she wore seemed painted onto her voluptuous figure, clinging to every curve and dip. The sight of her nipples' contour, pushing against the thin fabric, sent a surge of blood coursing through my veins.

An audible sigh of longing slipped past her lips, the sound wrapping around me like a seductive whisper.

The vibrant hue of sapphire in her eyes glittered against the sunlight's backdrop as they locked onto mine. A playful sparkle whirled within them, flickering like a beacon of mischief.

"David," she murmured, her voice low and sultry. The twitching of her foxlike ears, almost reacting to the intimate note in her voice, tugged at my heartstrings.

I pulled her in.

Our lips collided in a fervent embrace, our tongues dancing as she began grinding on me while she still straddled me. Her hands weaved their way into my hair, latching on with a gentle force, while my fingers dug into the soft flesh of her hips, anchoring her against me. I wanted to slip my hands under the hem of her dress — to feel.

I could feel the rhythmic grinding of her hips against mine, her escalating heat seeping through the tantalizing barrier of her scant panties and my jeans. I was hard, eager, and my mind swam with need.

"You're driving me crazy," I managed to breathe out against her lips, my breath hitching as she undulated against me.

My words drew a smile from her, her fingers tracing the lines of my chest through the worn fabric of my plaid shirt.

"I want you, Diane… so much."

Her mouth curved further into a teasing smile as she ground on me, her hips gyrating and driving me crazy. Her bushy fox tail swished animatedly behind her, a playful accompaniment to her tantalizing game. I could see the blazing fire in her eyes, a reflection of the same desire that was undoubtedly burning in mine.

I frowned, confusion wrinkling my forehead, my hands restless on her hips, eager to explore more of her enchanting body, but…

"We'd best stop," I muttered. "Or I'm gonna go completely crazy."

"I don't want to stop," she smoothly continued, her voice dropping to a sultry whisper that ruffled my senses. "There are… things we *can* do, David."

A wave of anticipation crashed against my chest, my heart thudding against my ribcage in response. "Things?"

She licked her lips.

As she pushed herself up, a tantalizing distance was created between us. Her hand drifted downwards, finally settling on the bulge straining against my jeans.

"Can I touch you?" she asked, her voice barely above a whisper.

It surprised me — I had considered her shy and would never have thought she'd ask something so straightforward. It went to show that there were things about her — about her kind — that were different.

But hell yes.

A nod was the only response I could muster, my hands instinctively moving to my fly. The button yielded easily, the zipper following suit in eager complicity.

Her hand slipped inside my jeans with an assured ease, her slender fingers pulling my throbbing cock free.

A gasp of surprise, tinged heavily with delight, escaped her lips as she wrapped her delicate fingers around my pulsating shaft. "It's so beautiful," she murmured, her eyes wide with wonder and a hint of awe.

A guttural groan rumbled in my throat, the feel of her gentle touch sending a wave of pleasure coursing through me.

"Diane," my voice strained with desire, my plea hanging in the warm summer air.

Her fingers moved, slow and deliberate, stroking my

length in a teasing rhythm that left me gasping. I watched her cheeks flush a rosy pink, her eyes clouding over with unadulterated desire.

As her hand explored me, my own were not idle. They roamed her body, tracing the enticing contours of her body through her dress. Unable to resist and meeting no objections, I gently pulled down the collar, revealing her breasts.

Taut and firm, her nipples strained against my palm as I roamed over them with hungry hands.

A breathy moan escaped her lips as I kneaded her breasts, drawing a shudder from her. I pulled her down, taking one of her nipples into my mouth. She gasped, her grip on my cock tightening reflexively.

Her taste was intoxicating, a divine blend of sweet and salty that danced on my tongue. I sucked eagerly on her nipple, my tongue flicking against it in a rhythm that matched her hand on my cock. Her back arched, pushing her chest further into my mouth, a silent plea for more.

"Do it..." she purred. "Touch me... Touch me everywhere..."

I grunted with delight as my free hand roamed downwards, sliding under the hem of her dress. The fabric of her soft panties greeted my fingers, clinging desperately to her heat.

I teased her over her panties, my fingers tracing her folds. She bucked against my hand, her breath coming in ragged gasps.

"Oh yes… Hmmm, David." Her voice was a needy whimper, her plea echoing around us. My name on her lips sent a surge of desire coursing through me, my body throbbing with need.

Her hand left my cock, moving downwards to her panties. In a swift move, she pulled them to the side, revealing her pussy.

I had been yearning to see her naked, and the sight of her cute little pussy was breathtaking. A glistening treasure, slick and ready for me, with a small strip of black hair above it. Irresistible. A groan of longing rumbled out of me, my body aching for her.

These games were driving me to the edge, my desire for her threatening to consume me.

Entranced by the sight of Diane's alluring pussy, peeking out from beneath the hem of her summer dress, I reveled in her soft hands trailing my rock-hard cock.

Her pink panties, playfully pulled aside, offered an invitation that was beyond any man's capability to resist. The mere sight of her feminine allure caused my body to respond, my cock throbbing with a primal and possessive urge as ancient as time itself.

And she was so close... She had only shimmied down a few inches, and my rod grew harder, so close to her delicious flower. I longed to enter her, to feel her around me and thrust into her — to give her all of me.

"David," she whispered, her voice a gentle ripple that shattered the tranquil silence of our forest sanctuary. Her plea was as raw as it was needy — an echo that hung in the air, entwining with the rustle of the leaves overhead, the soft murmur of the Silverthread River, and the faint whispers of the wind.

She inched forward, and I groaned with lust as her wet pussy touched my rock-hard cock. The warm, slick heat against my tip was almost unbearable.

She was now mounted on top of me, her slender legs draped across my waist in an intimate embrace, her sweet pussy rhythmically grinding against the evidence of my pulsating desire. Her tail, mirroring the deep black and silver streaks of her wild, untamed hair, twitched and quivered in anticipation of the pleasure yet to come.

As she slid her slit along my length, I growled with desire, and a little bead of precum connected us. She let out a pleased moan and began grinding faster, her perky tits bouncing cutely as she sought a rhythm.

"That's… ahhn… That's it," I whispered as she found her rhythm, grinding and sliding on my cock, making sure my throbbing tip connected with her clit each time she slid over me.

Her captivating sapphire eyes, hauntingly beautiful and deep pools of desire, held me captive. A fiery spark of lust and longing burned fiercely within them, threatening to consume us both.

"I need… I want… ahnn… I want to cum on your cock, David," she murmured, now arching her back as she gyrated, pleasing herself on my cock without letting it slip fully into her wet heat.

Once again, her bold words caught me off guard, but I was too immersed to dwell on it. Her breasts bounced with every movement, and my hands instinctively found their way to those enticing orbs.

"Do it, Diane," I groaned.

As she increased the tempo, my hands found their way to her round ass, my fingers sinking into the softness of her flesh, guiding her sinuous motions as she rode me.

I could feel the damp heat of her arousal against my pulsing length, marking me with her heated essence. With each passing moment, Diane moved with a frenzied and erotic urgency, her grinding hips pressing her exquisitely tight, wet core against my cock. More than once, she aligned her tight little flower with my tip as she slithered up and down, and the proximity — the sense of almost slipping into her tight little pussy — nearly drove me insane.

"Ahn, Diane," I groaned, the raw pleasure from her movements causing pure ecstasy to roll back my eyes.

My hands roamed her body, exploring her curves, pulling her nearer, my lips yearning for the peak of her breasts teasingly peeping out from her dress. Her skin tasted sinfully sweet, the sensation of her hardened nipples against my tongue pushing me deeper into the abyss of desire.

Diane whimpered in response, her fingers digging into the broad expanse of my shoulders as she continued her erotic dance against me.

"I'm so close, David," she breathed out, her voice barely audible, a desperate plea echoing in my ear, her body tense with anticipation.

Her movements grew increasingly frantic and uncontrolled as the peak of her pleasure approached.

My hands explored her trembling body, my fingers teasing her hardened nipples.

Diane's soft cry of pleasure and desperation filled the air as she threw her head back, her hair cascading like a dark waterfall. Her motions became more frenzied, her body grinding on mine in a desperate plea for release. Faster and faster, she rubbed her little nub along my cock, wet with her juices, and she tensed up.

"Cum for me, Diane," I urged, my voice strained with arousal and anticipation. Her response was a faint whimper, her body writhing uncontrollably above me.

"Hnn… Yes… David… I'm cumming!"

I watched in awe as her orgasm washed over her, her body quaking in the throes of a pleasure so profound it seemed otherworldly. My cock, slick with her juices, throbbed against her, my own climax dangerously near.

Diane's body went limp with satisfaction, her breaths coming out in ragged gasps as she descended from her peak. I remained hard against her, my cock pulsating with unsatisfied need, yearning for my own release.

Gently, I traced light patterns on her back, my lips pressing soft, comforting kisses against her flushed, heated skin. With barely a shift from Diane, her body slowly relaxed and her breathing leveled.

I held her close, my hands still cradling her ass, my

cock pulsing with restrained desire. Diane looked up at me; her sapphire eyes were dark and filled with unspoken promises. Her lips, swollen and flushed with desire, parted softly.

"David," she breathed out, her voice barely audible. A sigh of pure contentment filled the air as the tremors ceased wracking her beautiful body.

When she gazed up at me once again, her sapphire eyes flickered with renewed longing, her full lips warm and inviting.

"David," she hummed again, her voice brimming with adoration. "That… Hmmm…" She ran her tempting tongue over her lips as she shot me the naughtiest look. "Now it's your turn."

Still flushed from her climax, Diane looked exquisite in her ruffled summer dress, her ample breasts spilling out, pink nipples an invitation to lick and to kiss. Her silky pink underwear was still askew, revealing her tight little pussy, nub swollen after her orgasm.

I was consumed with an almost primal urge to devour her.

She teased me with a sensual movement of her hips, causing my swollen length to rub against her folds. Her fluffy tail flicked with anticipation as she seductively rubbed herself against me. Her sapphire eyes were alight with playful mischief and unspoken desire.

"Oh, David," she sighed, pouring raw lust into every syllable. "Your cock… it feels so good on my pussy. I can feel you are about to explode!"

Her words, filled with pure desire, caused me to groan. Her body was the epitome of sensual perfection, her movements driving my desires wild. The sight of her fox tail, twitching with excitement, threatened to push me over the edge of self-restraint.

With a tantalizing smile that promised untold pleasure, Diane slithered down my body. Her fingers moved deftly, unbuckling the buttons of my plaid shirt with practiced ease. The sensation of her hands dancing over the hard planes of my chest was electrifying. They continued their journey lower, her fingertips trailing down to my cock, which bucked at her touch.

"Do you mind if I… taste you?" The husky whisper stirred my blood, filling my already heated body with an overwhelming anticipation. "C-can I please?"

I only managed a nod, my mind drowning in vivid fantasies of her soft lips encasing my eager length.

Her wicked grin grew as she grabbed a firm hold of my pulsing cock. Her eyes widened in anticipation, her tongue darting out instinctively to wet her lips. The sight of the fox girl on her knees, breasts bared and frilly pink panties pushed to the side was so lewd, it took all my self-control not to cum on her lips right then and there.

Lowering herself, her raven hair formed a veil around her face. My heart pounded wildly in my chest as I felt her pliant lips envelope my rigid length, the warm wetness of her mouth sending jolts of pleasure up my spine.

The sensation was beyond exquisite; her mouth was a cozy haven of warmth, her tongue a teasing delight. She took me deeper with every bob of her head, her enthusiasm igniting my base desires. The sight of her, kneeling to the side of me in the grass, her generous breasts spilling out of her dress, was indescribably alluring.

The pace of her movements picked up, her hand providing a rhythmic accompaniment to her mouth on my erection. Her muffled moans vibrated against me, the intense pleasure coursing through my veins in waves. The familiar tension was building, a tautly coiled spring of pleasure in my lower belly.

"Cum in my mouth, David," she hummed as she took me out for a moment, her whisper a delight against my length, and it was all I could do to grunt in response. My thoughts were a whirlpool of pleasure, completely centered around the bliss she was bestowing upon me.

Without hesitation, she resumed her assault, sucking and stroking with renewed vigor. The heat within me was building to a crescendo, the mounting pleasure threatening to consume me.

I watched, mesmerized, as her body moved in the summer light, her tail flicking with excitement, her breasts exposed and bouncing with her movements. The sight of her, combined with the sensations she was teasing out of me, was too much.

With a primal groan, I climaxed, my seed spilling into her eager mouth.

Diane didn't miss a beat, she swallowed every drop, her eyes locked on mine, an intimate connection in the heat of the moment. The sight of her, lips wrapped around my length, swallowing my essence was unforgettably powerful.

"Ahh," I groaned, twitching as I gave her another rope of cum, my hands digging into her raven locks streaked with silver.

And she took it all, kept her plump lips firm around

me until I had given her all I wanted to.

When my climax had passed, I was left panting, my body pulsating with the aftershocks of my intense orgasm.

Diane sat back on her heels, a satisfied smirk playing on her lips as she swallowed the last bits. Her eyes sparkled with mischief, her disheveled appearance only adding to her allure in the sunlight.

She wiped her mouth with the back of her hand, her tongue darting out to lick her lips. "That was… a lot of fun," she said, her voice husky and breathless with a hint of self-satisfaction.

I laughed, my heart still hammering in my chest. "That sure is one way to put it," I replied, my voice raspy from the overwhelming satisfaction.

Diane crawled back up my body, her dress still disheveled, her tail swishing contentedly. Her head rested on my chest, her silky hair sending ticklish sensations down my skin.

"I can't believe we just did that," she murmured, her breath still coming in short gasps. "That was so very exciting!"

I chuckled, pulling her even closer to me. "Believe it, Diane," I said, my voice brimming with contentment.

We lay there, in the grass, basking in the afterglow of

our shared pleasure. Diane's tail curled around us, its soft fur a comforting blanket that added to the warm and content atmosphere.

The sun was lowering in the sky, its rays kissing our skin with warmth. The Silverthread River whispered its soothing lullabies nearby, the soft gurgling a peaceful soundtrack to our post-coital bliss.

I looked down at Diane, her sapphire eyes twinkling with post-orgasmic happiness. Her black hair was in disarray, her summer dress wrinkled, and her panties still pushed to the side. She was beautiful as she lay there, the embodiment of raw, satisfied lust.

We lay there on the grassy bank, our bodies entwined, and I watched the white clouds drift by with the sweet symphonies of nature for company.

Something beautiful had happened here today…

Chapter 26

Still catching my breath, I lay staring up at the vibrant blue sky through the gently swaying meadow grasses. Beside me, Diane nestled close, idly tracing circles on my chest with her fingertips as the warm breeze caressed our skin.

I turned my head to see her smiling contentedly, cheeks still endearingly flushed. Our passionate encounter in the secluded meadow had been utterly magical.

After all the teasing and flirting these past days, finally taking our affection to the next stage out here amidst the wilderness had exceeded every expectation. Sure, we hadn't gone 'all the way' yet, but now I knew that we would.

And considering how fiery she was, I also knew it would be amazing once our relationship came to that point.

I leaned in for a soft, lingering kiss which Diane returned eagerly, confirming she too had found the experience profoundly intimate and joyous. When we parted, her eyes were tender.

"That was amazing," she murmured, nuzzling against me.

"You took the words right out of my mouth," I replied, stroking her silken hair. I reveled in our closeness as we held each other in the swaying grasses.

After a blissful time simply savoring the afterglow, we helped each other clean up and fix our disheveled clothes, exchanging occasional tender kisses and caresses. The walk back was unhurried, our arms looped.

"Want to do some more fishing?" Diane asked, her

cute fox ears perked. "I feel like sitting by the water a little longer!"

"Hmm," I hummed. "There is nothing I'd like to do more than relax with you by the riverbank and laze in the summer sun. We might as well catch a couple more fish while we're at it."

She laughed and nodded, giving my arm looped through hers a squeeze. "You make it sound so delightful!"

I grinned. "Well, it *is* delightful!"

Though it was still only mid-afternoon, the fishing gear and full buckets of trout awaited right where we had left them. No birds — or worse, predators — had taken the opportunity to grab a fish or two, and that was just plain lucky. We'd have to be a little more careful next time.

And there would be a next time.

I lifted the heavy bucket effortlessly, renewed vigor and energy flowing through me. Diane retrieved the abandoned poles with a playful smile. "Shall we try our luck a while longer?" she suggested brightly.

"I'd love nothing more," I agreed, spirits soaring. We took up our former spots along the glittering river's edge, lines recast into the foamy currents. Peaceful silence descended, but it was charged now — an intimacy in our shared glances not present before.

Within minutes, Diane was reeling in another wriggling trout, her reflexes as sharp as ever. She tossed her catch into the waiting bucket with a satisfied flick of her tail. No doubt, the foxkin vixen had activated her Class ability again. She was a little competitive, this one, but I liked that about her.

I smiled watching her skill, buoyed by our new closeness. When I turned back to my own line, I was delighted to see my bobber jiggle and vanish below the surface. Gripping the pole, I swept it up sharply to set the hook.

The trout fought mightily, but I expertly worked the reel, drawing it steadily closer until its silvery form emerged from the rushing water. I whooped triumphantly as I deposited my catch into Diane's bucket since mine was already full.

Diane beamed at me. "Nicely done!" Her bright smile warmed me. Together we turned back to the glinting river.

We continued fishing companionably as the afternoon waned, conversation minimal. But the silence was charged with intimate energy, our hearts having found unity on a whole new level. My rod regularly bent and bobbed as trout after trout struck the bait.

By the time the sun hung low above the shimmering waters, staining them crimson, both buckets were heaping full. Diane tucked back an errant lock of hair, grinning at our combined impressive haul.

I smiled, remembering my delight at how useful my elemental summon had been. But any triumph in fishing now paled next to the pure joy of my deepening bond with this amazing woman.

Diane suggested we smoke some of the trout to preserve them for selling and storing. I agreed it was a great idea.

We slowly climbed the winding path from the rocky shore up to the cozy cabin that was the beginning of my homestead, the tranquil evening enclosing us. Diane swished her tail happily, carrying her overflowing bucket. I followed a few paces behind, eyes roaming unabashedly down her shapely silhouette.

We began by taking our catch into the kitchen. There we cleaned, bled, and gutted the fish. I had not done that before, but Diane was quick to explain it. She also told me the cabin had a drain that led back to the river, and we should be careful what we pour in there. Cleaning the fish wasn't that hard to do, especially not with the sharp knives that Caldwell had so kindly provided me with. Life on the frontier fared best when one had the right tools.

As we worked, Diane gave me the occasional playful bump with her hips or shot me a warm smile. It was clear that what had happened today had deepened our bond and made us get to know each other even better.

And we both liked what we had seen and experienced. I smiled to myself, happy with life here. I could go on like this forever, finding simple satisfaction in providing for myself and my loved ones, living in tranquility by the banks of the Silverthread River.

Soon enough, we finished up and headed outside with the prepared fish. When we reached the little log smokehouse we had built, we laid the cleaned, scaled trout side by side on the racks within. Our hands brushed often, eliciting smiles as we found joy in this task together. Soon fragrant alder smoke from the small fire we lit beneath the fish began wafting into the darkening sky.

With the fish in the smokehouse, we washed our hands in the kitchen, then headed back outside. I held her close as we watched the sun arch and dip toward the horizon above our cozy homestead. After that, I chopped some firewood while Diane relaxed a little.

After a while, when I took a break to wipe my brow clean of sweat, she came over and wrapped her arms around me. "Come on," she said. "Let's have a bite to eat while the fish smokes. We've done enough for today."

Within the snug cabin, I stoked up a hearty fire while Diane prepared a simple but delicious meal. We moved in easy unison, exchanging occasional tender caresses. At times I still caught her gazing at me with almost disbelieving joy, as though she too could hardly believe our passion had flowered so beautifully.

Seated across from each other at the wooden table, we raised our mugs in a toast, eyes locking as we finished the last of the wine that Leigh had gifted us. After today, we were truly partners in every sense of the word. Companions not just in labor and friendship, but now also in love.

We ate slowly, focused only on each other's presence. Occasionally beneath the table, our feet would play. The fire crackled a joyful rhythm, complementing our high spirits as we talked.

"I think I'll go into town tomorrow," I said. "I can try to sell the fish to Leigh."

"That's a great idea," Diane said. "I'm sure she has a few buyers for fish from the Silverthread River." Her eye twinkled a little as she watched me. "And I bet Leigh would love to see you again."

I laughed and nodded. "Well, she's good company. That's for sure."

"The three of us should do something together someday," she hummed, thinking for a second before she focused her sapphire eyes on me. "But all in due time. I'll stay here tomorrow and make sure we have some traps set out. I also saw a few berry bushes on the far bank, nice and ripe. I'll swim across and do a little foraging."

"That sounds perfect," I agreed.

When the meal was finished, Diane came into my arms. We stood swaying slowly to music only we could hear, her head nestled contentedly upon my shoulder. All was right in our tiny corner of this strange, joined world. We cleaned up and went outside to check on the fish.

When the trout were adequately smoked, we transferred the bounty into storage barrels, preserving them for future meals. Our productive fishing session would help keep us fed, and it might make us a little money as well.

As twilight deepened, we stood hand in hand to enjoy the cooling air. Finally, we headed inside and to our beds — still joined together — and there, we once again hungered for each other and did a step-by-step repeat of our earlier afternoon activities.

Chapter 27

The next morning, I awoke to soft sunlight filtering into the cozy cabin bedroom. Diane was still curled up beside me, her head nestled on my shoulder and one arm draped lightly over my chest. I gently stroked her silken hair, not wanting to wake her just yet.

After a few blissful minutes, I carefully extricated myself from the bed so as not to disturb Diane's slumber. I dressed and tidied up before heading downstairs to start some coffee. The rich aroma soon filled the cabin.

I put together a simple breakfast from our stores, then brought a tray upstairs for Diane. She awoke with a smile as I set the food beside her. "What a lovely surprise," she said, sitting up and giving me a soft kiss.

We ate together, chatting happily about the day's plans — Diane would continue improving the homestead while I drove to Gladdenfield to sell the smoked fish. I was looking forward to sharing my new closeness with Diane with her dear friend Leigh.

After breakfast, I gave Diane another lingering kiss goodbye before departing. The drive to town was pleasant, sunlight shining down through the vivid leaves overhead. Birds swooped out of the way as I came, disappearing between or above the soaring trees that lined the winding road that led to Gladdenfield Outpost.

In Gladdenfield, folks nodded in friendly recognition as I drove past. It amazed me that I was already becoming a familiar face after a relatively short time out here. At Leigh's store, I parked and unloaded some of the smoked trout to sell.

The door chime jangled merrily as I entered. Leigh

looked up from behind the counter and broke into a broad grin. "Well hey there, darlin'!" she said. "Been wonderin' when you'd stop by again." She looked me up and down as she spoke, shifting her hips, and I just knew she was gonna give me a hard time again.

Literally.

I laughed. "Good to see you too, Leigh." Her bubbly energy was infectious. I hefted the bucket of smoked fish. "Fresh catch from the Silverthread to sell, if you're interested."

"You bet I am!" said Leigh. As she came around the counter, I couldn't help noticing her low-cut top and how it showcased her freckled cleavage. But I kept my eyes politely above neck-level.

Leigh evaluated the fish, looking impressed. "These sure do look tasty. Y'all are mighty fine anglers!" She named a fair price that I happily accepted. It was enough to cover the outstanding bill and leave a little for us to spend as well. Good news because I wanted to peruse her collection of seeds; we needed more crops.

Together, Leigh and I carried the trout to her storage room before returning to the front counter.

"So, I'm guessin' things are goin' real well between you and Diane?" Leigh asked, leaning on the counter as her eyes roamed over me. "I can just tell; you've got that happy glow about you."

I chuckled. "Your intuition is spot on as always, Leigh. Diane and I decided to officially court. Things have been amazing between us since. And it was your advice that helped us out!"

Leigh's face lit up. "Aww, well that just warms my heart!" she exclaimed. "I could tell right off that you two have a real special connection." Her expression turned playful. "And I bet you've been gettin' real close now that it's official, hmm? Don't lie, baby, I can see that glow."

I chuckled, feeling a bit flustered. "We have grown… closer, yes," I said. "I care about Diane tremendously and want to build something lasting together."

Leigh smiled knowingly. "Oh I believe that, hun. And I know Diane feels the same way 'bout you." Her eyes twinkled impishly. "But I gotta say, David, for her to have… taken a few steps with you." She clicked her tongue and gave me a wink, indicating we both knew full well what she was talking about. "Well, that's still surprisingly fast. She must really like you."

I had to laugh. "Well, I hope so," I said.

Leigh giggled delightedly in response. "Hey now, no need to be embarrassed," she said, giving my arm an affectionate squeeze. "I think it's sweet how smitten you two are. Diane deserves to find happiness again after everythin' she's been through."

I nodded. "You've been a good friend to her. I appreciate you helping me out."

"Of course!" Leigh waved off my thanks. "You fit right in around here. And between you and me, having a handsome man on the frontier is always a welcome sight." She shot me a flirty wink.

I laughed, by now used to Leigh's shameless brand of humor. "Well, I'm officially off the market now," I joked. "But the compliment is still appreciated."

Leigh laughed. "Oh, I'm pretty sure Diane doesn't mind a little friendly company now and then," she said with a wink as she leaned forward a little, affording me a more generous view.

I grinned. She was crazy. I loved it.

"She may have said something along those lines."

"See?" she hummed, her eyes turning a little smoky. "There's all kinds of benefits to living on the frontier. We do things differently around here. And we have a lot of fun." She trailed a slender finger down my arm, her blazing blue eyes almost making me grunt with need.

Then, Leigh gave me a warm, sincere smile. "But truly, I'm real happy for you both. Diane deserves a devoted partner after all she's overcome."

"I'll do my very best to be that for her," I promised.

"I know you will," said Leigh confidently. She drummed her fingers on the counter thoughtfully. "So, how about we get to business, huh? After that, you and I can talk some more, okay?"

After we concluded our dealings with the fish and settled my outstanding tab, Leigh beckoned for me to follow her toward the back of the store.

"C'mon round the back, I got a real special shipment of seeds that just arrived," she said eagerly. "With that lovely plot of yours, I bet you and Diane could grow some incredible crops out there! And these are some actual magical crops."

That was more like it! I was curious to see what kind of magical crops a farmer could grow out here. Intrigued, I trailed after Leigh through the crowded aisles until we reached a corner overflowing with sacks of seeds, gardening tools, and farming equipment.

Leigh gestured proudly to the abundant selection. "Now I know these may look pretty ordinary to you, but lots of 'em got magical properties the likes of which you ain't never seen on Earth. It's Tannoris and the Upheaval that brought us these!"

My eyes widened as I scanned the incredible variety, reminded again of how much strangeness this merged world contained. Leigh went on to explain the origins of some of the most interesting seeds.

She hefted up a large burlap sack labeled 'Aethershine Wheat' in ornate calligraphy. "This here grain actually glows when it's grown! Real pretty to look at when it's swayin' in the moonlight, I tell ya. And the elves love it for a very light ale they brew. Fetches a mighty fine price from them." She winked. "If it's money you're after, you could start with a harvest or two of that. It'll set you up nice!"

Next, she showed me a woven parcel holding dried leaves of 'Masander,' a medicinal herb from Tannoris. "This stuff in tea form can cure just about any headache or bellyache, provided it ain't too serious. Tannorians swear by it, and we've found it works like a charm here too! Works wonders for hangovers!"

Another sack held 'Silk Beans,' a climbing vine producing beans wrapped in a fine, satiny fiber. "The elves go crazy for the silk these make," explained Leigh. "Real soft and delicate, perfect for their fancy underthings." She gave me a wink and pulled out a strap of her lacy thong over her shorts. "I even wear 'em myself," she added teasingly.

A pulse went through me at the sight. The idea of that lacy thong hugging Leigh's luscious curves was enough to make any man go crazy. And she knew it, too.

"See anything you'd like?" she purred as she tipped her hat, her blue eyes smoky as they roamed over me again.

I grinned and licked my lips, keeping my eyes fixed on her. "I sure do."

She gave me a gentle push. "Oh, go on now," she cooed. "I meant the seeds, baby."

Chuckling, I turned to them. As I examined the odd assortment, one group of seed packets caught my eye – they were labeled 'Alchemy Seeds.'

Noticing my interest, Leigh picked one up and explained, "Now, these seeds grow plants to produce reagents that alchemists use for brewing all kinds of potions and elixirs. I'll admit I don't know too much about 'em. I sell the potions: I don't make 'em. But anyone with a green thumb and an interest in alchemy surely should have a look at 'em."

My pulse quickened. This could be perfect for

creating mana potions to restore my magic energy!

Leigh went on describing the various Alchemy Seeds. There were gnarled 'Thauma Roots' that were used to create a kind of paste that served as a vital reagent of most potions. There was 'Wispsilk,' the leaves of which were important in some way Leigh didn't understand, and there were 'Magebread' flowers that were vital ingredients of mana potions.

"With these babies planted on your land, you'll have easy access to alchemical ingredients," Leigh said. "And if you can't make the potions just yet, you can always sell the ingredients to me. I know a few alchemy traders who pass by Gladdenfield on occasion, and I'm sure I could get a good price. Anyway, this is my whole supply of stuff that might be useful in alchemy. My shop ain't the biggest in that respect. Other towns on the frontier specialize more in that kinda stuff."

I nodded, my mind racing with ideas. Homegrown potion-making supplies would be invaluable. I would not need to purchase expensive concoctions from others, and I could make a handsome profit selling them. Of course, it would be another skill to learn.

But why not? Alchemy sounded fun and useful. Who knew what I could come up with? Plus, I wanted to summon many, many more creatures, and mana was a bottleneck. Potions would help.

"Leigh," I said. "I think some of these Alchemy Seeds could really benefit my magic and skills. Is there any way I could get a few packets of the Thauma Roots, Wispsilk, and Magebread to start an alchemy garden?"

"Well, of course!" Leigh replied. "I'd be happy to set you up with some. Let's ring you up a nice starter bundle."

We returned to the front counter where Leigh carefully wrapped packs of the three essential seed types I had requested in brown paper and string.

"There ya are! With these seeds, you'll have a thriving alchemy garden in no time," Leigh proclaimed.

I smiled, envisioning the future harvests. "This is perfect, Leigh. Thank you! Once my alchemy skills improve, having homegrown potion ingredients will be invaluable."

"Of course!" Leigh replied. "You let me know if you ever need more seeds too. I'm always gettin' new shipments from exotic places."

I laughed. "Will do. I'm pretty keen to explore this whole alchemy business."

"Hmm, it can be profitable for sure, sugar. Now let's ring you up!"

After settling my bill for the Alchemy Seeds, I tucked

the precious parcels carefully into my pack. My mind swirled with ideas for the most fertile spots to plant near the cabin and how to incorporate the spell reagents into brewing. I'd have to consult with Diane as well; she knew much about such things.

Noticing me pondering all the new possibilities, Leigh tipped back her hat and chuckled. "I can see you're starting to see the charm of life out here on the frontier, huh?"

"You've got that right," I agreed fervently. "Every day seems to bring some new wonder."

Leigh smiled warmly. "Well, speakin' of wonders, how's about you and I head over to the tavern and have a drink together? My treat this time, as a thanks for bringin' me that delicious smoked fish."

I grinned broadly. "You bet."

Chapter 28

After ordering our ales, Leigh and I settled at a small table tucked away in the rustic tavern's corner. Sunlight streaming through the windows illuminated swirling dust motes. Leigh scooted her chair close, leaning forward eagerly.

"So David, tell me about yourself," she prompted before taking a sip of ale. "I've been curious about you!

What's your story? How'd a strapping man like you end up out here on the wild frontier?"

I chuckled at her curiosity. "Well, it's kind of a long story," I began. I gave her the broad strokes – my monotonous city job, getting laid off, and feeling aimless. Then meeting Caldwell and getting the chance to relocate and start fresh as a homesteader in the Wilds.

"It sounded like a pretty good opportunity," I said. "And as it turns out, I made the right choice. Already, this place is starting to feel like home. The work is rewarding, and the company is great." I shot her a wink.

Leigh chuckled warmly; chin propped on one hand as she studied me with those big blue lookers of hers. "Mmhmm, that Caldwell sure knows how to pick 'em," she remarked with a wink. "But you chose your path – can't imagine every unemployed city boy jumps at the chance to rough it out here."

"No, you're right," I agreed. "I've just always loved the outdoors and adventure. The frontier life called to me." I smiled wistfully. "My parents were explorers themselves before…" I trailed off, old pain surfacing.

Leigh reached over and gave my hand a comforting squeeze. "You're followin' in their footsteps, baby. I'm sure that would make them proud."

I nodded gratefully. "It feels good to embrace that adventurous spirit again. What about you, Leigh? How'd you end up way out here?"

Leigh laughed. "Oh gosh, that's quite a tale!"

"Well, tell me!" I said, sitting back with a smile.

"Hmm… Well, where to begin. I grew up on a ranch in Oklahoma. It sat close to a little town, but no cities worth mentioning anywhere. We were happy, but my family was one of the old-school kinds, if you catch my drift?" Seeing I didn't, she smiled and leaned forward. "The ranch had been in the family for years, but we never expanded. We never made it more… economical. Time passed, and others just overtook us. Our way of doin' things was too expensive, and the market just too competitive. We were small time, a family business, y'know?"

I nodded. It was a story I'd heard before; small businesses getting pushed to the side by the bigger ones.

"The ranch was foreclosed on," she said. "We had nowhere to go but a trailer where my drunk-ass uncle lived."

For the first time since I'd met her, something like pain passed over Leigh's beautiful face. The bubbly joy she seemed to overflow with was eclipsed for a moment – by grief. "Daddy couldn't take it," she said softly. "He loved that ranch. Life without it weren't nothing for him. And there was too much damn booze in that trailer. He began drinkin', just like his brother, and that was the end of it. He careened off the highway one night drivin' home drunk. Right into the Cimarron."

"Leigh," I said, reaching out to touch her hand. "I'm so sorry."

She smiled softly, her familiar warmth returning. "It's okay, baby. I'm still around. We all get our share of scars down the line, don't we?"

I nodded. "Yeah, we sure do."

She smiled. "Anyway. Mom didn't cope so well. We fought a lot, and I struck out on my own at just sixteen. I traveled all around – which is why my accent is so screwed up. Tulsa, Dallas, Albuquerque… I even worked on a ranch in Mexico for a few years… That was a crazy time. After that, I waitressed a bit. When the Upheaval came around, the traveling days would have been over, had it not been that I got a Class."

I leaned forward. "You got one at the start?"

"Hm," she purred, her blue eyes blazing. "Beastmaster, baby. Cowgirl style." She bit her lip as she looked me over. "Something you know all about, I bet."

I laughed loudly at her lewd joke, and she joined in, all the pain of old memories forgotten in the moment.

"Anyway," she continued. "In the first days, there wasn't a Coalition or a Frontier Division. Everybody was just kinda gettin' their bearings, y'know?"

I nodded, remembering those days as chaotic even within the safety of Louisville. It must have been a million times worse out in untamed lands. At least we had the city and the military and the police. Negotiations with the elves began almost immediately, and New Springfield — where I moved to later — was an early town to be formed under the predecessor of the Coalition in those days just after the Upheaval. By comparison, I'd had it easy.

"But before we continue," Leigh said, "let's get another round, huh? Talking's thirsty work!"

I watched as she headed off toward the back to get another round and came back. Settling back in my chair, I smiled and waited. I was looking forward to hearing the rest of Leigh's tale.

"Those early days were not very comfortable," Leigh said as she placed the tankard in front of me. "Lots of fightin'. People banded up and split and banded again. Towns were there one day and little more than burned-down ruins down the next. I was lucky with my Class because I could tame some of those weird Tannoris creatures bleedin' into our world. I had this Firepanther, Mr. Toasty..."

I laughed. *"Mr. Toasty?"*

She grinned and gave me a playful swat. "Watch it! I'm gonna tame you and make you my next Mr. Toasty if you don't mind your tongue!"

I licked my lips, sat back, and took a swig as I eyed her. "Sounds fun."

"Hmm, you don't know the half of it. Anyway, Mr. Toasty got me out of a lotta trouble. We hung around for a while, and we finally met a trader willing to take us west if we worked along the way. I helped him barter at frontier towns we passed through. When we came to Gladdenfield, I got the chance to open the store. I just knew this was where I belonged. The folks here, Caldwell among 'em, were friendly and took me in, helped me get established. And here I am!"

"And Mr. Toasty?"

She smiled softly. "Firepanthers don't like to stay in

one place, so I let him go. I didn't want him to get restless."

I shook my head in amazement. "Wow, Leigh. That is quite the story."

Leigh waved it off modestly. "Aw, when you grow up scrappy, you gotta make do. Anyway, I like it here. All's missing is a man." At that, she eyed me again in that way of hers, making my blood pump.

"No eligible bachelors in Gladdenfield?"

She shrugged. "Not for me. Maybe I'm picky." As she spoke, she scooted even closer until our knees were touching. "I'm sure some men around here are fine in theory – reliable, strong homesteaders and such. But you know how it is, baby. Sparks gotta fly. It ain't all about where someone lives and what they do. There's a kind of magic about it, don't ya think? Somethin' we can't measure or explain."

I nodded, relishing the warmth of having her so close to me. "I agree," I said. "Chemistry."

"Often," she hummed, big blue eyes on me, "you know it when you see it. And I mean *right away*."

The moment between us hung in the air. Our souls connected in that instant, and her lips parted slightly. I would have leaned in, and I think I would have kissed her at that moment if someone hadn't begun playing the piano, some half-drunk townsfolk breaking into song.

It broke the moment, but we both laughed at the jaunty little dance some of the townsfolk engaged in. When my eyes found hers again, I knew there would be another chance.

For a while longer, our conversation meandered happily, and I found myself captivated by her musical laugh and lively spirit. Out here, social norms were far looser, I was coming to realize, and it was so much easier to connect because we all had frontier life in common. We relied on each other as a community, and that made a lot of difference in how we acted.

And there was something infectious about Leigh's easygoing, mischievous attitude. She had a knack for pulling people out of their shell. I wanted to be around her more often, and I knew I would be. Time passed swiftly in Leigh's company, and I realized it would soon be getting late, and I wanted to get back to Diane.

"I really should get moving," I said. "I'm kinda eager to tell Diane all about these seeds for the alchemy garden."

"I understand," Leigh replied, standing as well and stretching lithely, her voluptuous body on full display as the buttons of her blouse nearly popped. "Come on, baby, I'll escort you outside." She smiled and looped her arm through mine. "I appreciate you keepin' me company today. All the pretty girls in town will be jealous."

I laughed, enjoying how close she was and how she bumped into me on each step as we headed outside. "I spent time with the prettiest and had a great time," I said sincerely.

At my Jeep, Leigh pulled me into a friendly hug. As we embraced, she whispered playfully in my ear, "You come visit again real soon now, y'hear?" Before releasing me, she discreetly nuzzled her soft cheek against mine, then gave me a kiss.

I smiled at her forwardness as we parted. "Count on it," I promised with a wave as I climbed into the driver's seat.

Leigh stood there, hips cocked, hands in the back pockets of her skin-tight jeans, brim of her hat shielding her pretty eyes from the sun. She watched me go as I revved the engine and pulled out.

The charming little settlement soon shrank in the rearview mirror as I navigated toward home through deepening dusk. But thoughts of the bubbly shopkeeper lingered, making the ride pass swiftly.

Chapter 29

The sun was on its way to dip below the treetops as I navigated the rugged trail back to the secluded cabin. Long shadows stretched across the landscape, signaling the day's end and marking the transition to another magical frontier night.

I smiled to myself as I drove, replaying the lively conversations with Leigh in my mind. Her playful humor and shameless flirting never failed to lift my spirits, and it had been interesting to get to know her a little better. But all the while, I had found myself missing Diane too. And now, as our cozy riverside dwelling came into view, I was happy to be home again.

I parked the Jeep and grabbed my pack filled with the new alchemy seeds before heading inside. The interior was illuminated only by flickering firelight, but it immediately felt welcoming.

Diane looked up from the bubbling stew pot hanging over the hearth and smiled radiantly when she saw me. "David! I'm so glad you're back." She came over to embrace me warmly. I held her close for a long moment, breathing in her sweet scent.

"It's good to be home," I murmured against her hair. Diane's presence was calming after the long day. When we parted, I gave her a lingering kiss.

"How was town? Did you see Leigh?" Diane asked curiously as we moved to the table.

I nodded, getting comfortable in the wooden chair. "I did. We had a nice chat, and she bought all the smoked fish. Oh, and I got these..." I showed Diane the wrapped alchemy seeds, explaining my plan to start an alchemy garden.

Diane's eyes lit up. "How wonderful! We can plant these right away. I know just the fertile spot."

But first things first, I was starving.

Over steaming bowls of Diane's hearty stew, I recounted my visit with Leigh in more detail, including her bawdy jokes and shameless flirting. Diane just laughed knowingly.

"That sounds like our Leigh! She has such a big heart underneath it all," Diane remarked fondly.

I nodded in agreement. Leigh's caring nature was obvious once you got to know her. "But she can be a talker, all right…"

Diane gave a chuckle. "I know! I love her for it!"

When we had finished eating, Diane shyly brought out her violin. "I wrote a new song today, while you were gone. Would you like to hear it?"

"I'd love to," I replied. Music was yet another way Diane bared her soul.

Tucking the instrument under her chin, Diane began playing a gentle, swaying melody. Then she sang in her sweet, lilting voice:

"My love, my heart, you are my home,
No matter where our lives may roam,
Whether parted or together,
My heart is yours, now and forever."

Her words struck a chord, and the sweet melancholy of her songs always brought about a measure of calm within me. I listened to the rest of the song with a gently easing mind, until her words were all that existed for me. It was a sweet song about waiting for one's love to come home, moving and tender.

When the final notes faded, I applauded enthusiastically. "That was beautiful," I said sincerely.

Diane blushed. "I'm so glad you like it. You are my inspiration." Her words made my heart surge with emotion. I drew her onto my lap by the fireside, needing to be close.

Diane settled against me contentedly, head tucked beneath my chin. I gently stroked her velvety fox ears and kissed her tenderly as we enjoyed the fire together.

She nuzzled against me with a pleased purr. "So," she hummed after a while. "What's the plan for tomorrow?"

"Well," I began, "I want to plant these alchemy seeds. I hope I can use my Identify Plants skill to learn a little more about them once they start growing. I also want to try if I can summon a minor spirit with the Woodland or Earth affinity and see if they can help me with the crops."

She lit up. "Oh, that's a perfect idea!"

I smiled into her silken hair. "Maybe they can make our job a little easier, huh?"

We spoke for a while longer, enjoying the fire as it slowly died down. Outside, the stars were on full display, and the nighttime sounds of the surrounding forests drifted to us through shuttered windows.

Eventually we turned in, climbing the ladder to the cozy loft hand in hand. As we lay nestled close beneath the blankets, Diane rolled over to face me, eyes luminous in the moonlight. I pulled her close, feeling my need rise as much as hers.

We kissed and touched, drowning in each other. Sure, we had not gone the full mile yet, but there were plenty of things we *could* do…

Chapter 30

The next morning, I awoke to find Diane curled against me, still asleep, her breathing slow and even. I smiled, watching her for a moment. She looked so peaceful with her hair mussed and her lips slightly parted. Our... nightly activities had been a lot of fun, and I could tell she — like me — was getting eager to move things to the next stage.

Still, I did not want to rush her. In her culture, this was a big step, and even though I was confident that it would be the *right* step, I needed her to reach that conclusion on her own terms and in her own time.

Careful not to disturb her, I slipped out of bed and went downstairs to wash up at the basin in the kitchen. After a quick wash, I dressed and started some coffee. Soon the smell of a fresh morning brew livened up the cozy space. I prepared a simple breakfast from our stores, laying out some eggs, dried meat, and bread on the table.

Just as I was finishing up, I heard Diane descending the ladder, tail swishing behind her. "Something smells delicious," she said brightly, giving me a quick kiss on the cheek.

"Morning, beautiful. I made us some breakfast," I said. We settled in at the table together, and I recounted an amusing tale Leigh had told me yesterday about a traveler trying to haggle prices with her and ending up with nothing — Leigh was too shrewd a saleswoman. Diane laughed, eyes crinkling happily, recognizing her friend well enough.

Over food, we discussed plans for the alchemy garden. Diane recommended a fertile spot by the riverbank that would get plenty of sunlight and moisture. Once we finished eating, we gathered tools and the precious seed packets and headed out into the mild morning air.

At the garden plot, we worked side by side tilling the rich soil in preparation for planting. The physical labor felt good, using muscles that had gotten soft during my city days. Diane hummed an upbeat tune as she hoed, fluffy tail swishing in time with the music.

When the earth was ready, we carefully planted the unusual alchemy seeds, following the diagrams on the packets showing proper depth and spacing. I activated my Identify Plants skill on each type as we planted it, curious to learn any details my magic could discern.

The information appeared in my interface, describing properties and uses. The gnarled Thauma Root would be key for potion bases, while the Wispsilk leaves improved mana restoration effects. The Magebread flowers were essential for crafting mana draughts. All in all, we had enough stuff here to make mana potions.

The only question was how…

"Fascinating," I mused aloud. "If these grow well, we'll have some reagents to start with. If we can get a good batch going, we'll probably earn enough to buy more seeds and improve our skills."

Diane nodded enthusiastically. "Oh yes,

homebrewed potions will be wonderful! No more relying solely on purchased potions and elixirs." Her eyes lit up. "Ooh, we could designate some of the harvest for sale! That way, we have some ingredients to experiment with, and we can sell the rest to Leigh."

I chuckled at her eager spirit. "Now you're thinking like an entrepreneur. But first, let's focus on just getting these seeds to mature properly with their magical properties intact."

We watered the freshly planted rows and stood back to admire our handiwork. The ordinary-looking seeds belied the mystical forces slumbering within. I was eager to see the plants flourish and experiment with crafting my own potions and concoctions.

When the sun had climbed high overhead, we stopped for a break, washing up in the river's glittering water. We sat together enjoying some bread and dried fruit beneath the dappled shade of a flowering tree.

As we ate, I turned to Diane. "You know, if these alchemy crops thrive, we could think about building a dedicated laboratory. A place to craft potions and work spells together."

Diane's eyes lit up at the suggestion. "That's a wonderful idea! Having an indoor space just for alchemy projects would be perfect." She tipped her head thoughtfully, taking a bite of bread. "If you want to learn more about outfitting an alchemy lab, you should talk to Waelin next time he's in Gladdenfield. He's an old elf alchemist who comes through every so often."

"Oh?" I asked curiously. "I don't think I've met Waelin yet."

Diane nodded. "He keeps mostly to himself whenever he's in town, but he's been practicing alchemy for centuries. Very knowledgeable about potion crafting." She smiled. "I've bought a few minor healing draughts from him before. If anyone can advise you on the ideal alchemy workshop setup, it would be Waelin."

"Interesting," I mused. Having guidance from a seasoned alchemist would be invaluable. "What's Waelin like? Is he friendly?"

"Hmm, friendly may be overstating it," Diane replied thoughtfully. "He's rather serious and keeps to himself. But I think he'd respect a fellow magic user wanting to learn. Just tell him I sent you."

I chuckled. "All right, I'll be sure to mention your name when I seek him out next time I'm in town." Picturing the seasoned elf alchemist, I imagined he had seen a great deal over his long life. I hoped he might be willing to share some wisdom.

Diane and I spent a pleasant hour sitting in the shade finishing our lunch.

After our leisurely lunch, I was eager to experiment with summoning some minor spirits to aid in the gardening work, just as I'd discussed with Diane the previous day. I still had a decent reserve of mana, so conditions were ideal for testing my emerging skills.

I smiled at Diane. "I'm going to try summoning a minor woodland spirit now to help us out. Let's head over to the plot."

Diane nodded eagerly. "Wonderful, I can't wait to see them in action again!" She gave my hand an encouraging squeeze as we made our way to the empty pasture area.

At the plot, I focused my will and extended my palm, channeling the necessary mana. The now-familiar swirling orb of elemental energy formed before me. It swiftly expanded, colors shifting. As I channeled the mana, my interface appeared, prompting me to select the spirit's elemental affinity. I chose Woodland.

The now-familiar swirling orb of energy formed before me and expanded into a spindly, leaf-headed spirit. It regarded me attentively, awaiting instruction.

Mentally, I directed it: "Nurture the plants in this garden. Increase their vitality and growth."

The spirit bowed and scurried over to the rows of freshly planted alchemy seeds. It began meticulously tending each one, its slender wooden fingers working the soil around the roots.

As it nurtured them, the seeds seemed to positively respond to its presence. Before our eyes, the first tiny shoots and leaves began to unfurl and grow at an accelerated pace. It was as if we were watching a timelapse video on fast forward.

"Incredible!" Diane gasped. "Look how quickly they're sprouting and maturing."

Indeed, what should have taken hours or even days was happening in mere minutes thanks to the spirit's influence. I noticed a faint glow building within its body as it worked. I was unsure of the mechanics behind it all, but the little guy had energy to do the entire plot, potatoes included.

When its power was spent, the summoned spirit dissolved away in a swirl of light. I saw that this special growth stimulation had depleted much of its mana reserves.

I also knew — on an instinctive level that seemed to come with the territory — that such a power could only affect a plant once a day. Unfortunately, I would not be able to summon multiple woodland spirits in rapid succession on a single day to let them grow my entire harvest in hours.

Still, this was awesome.

"Amazing!" I said. "If I understand correctly, those little spirits can do this once per day."

Diane nodded, clearly impressed. "If we summon these spirits regularly, we could accelerate the alchemy garden substantially! And the potatoes as well!"

I agreed. With cautious use of the woodland spirits' nurturing abilities, we could soon have a thriving crop of spell reagents. I made a mental note to continue experimenting with practical applications of my magic. I also wanted to try out the Earth spirit, but I had already used my Identify Plant skill three times and my Summon Minor Spirit skill once, so I had only 3 mana left — not enough for another Summon Minor Spirit.

Apparently, mana recovered while sleeping but not while just resting. I could really use those mana potions…

We turned our attention back to tending the garden,

carefully watering and inspecting the new sprouts. Thanks to the spirit's boost, they already looked days old rather than minutes. The mystical forces slumbering within the alchemy seeds were clearly responding powerfully.

When midafternoon warmth permeated the valley, we paused to drink some water and eat a light snack. As we sat sharing some bread and dried fruit, Diane turned to me.

"What do you think about going to explore the surroundings a bit more?" she suggested. "Since we have some daylight left, it could be nice to wander the riverbank or some nearby trails."

I smiled and nodded. "That sounds great," I agreed. There was still much of the frontier lands around our homestead left to discover. An afternoon ramble with Diane sounded perfect after the morning's hard work.

Chapter 31

After our snack, Diane and I decided to spend the rest of the sunny afternoon exploring the wilderness surrounding our homestead. We were eager to familiarize ourselves with the landscape and trails nearest to where we lived and worked.

I grabbed my backpack and did a quick check to make sure it was properly supplied for our hike. The small leather pack contained a metal flask filled with cool, clear water from the river.

I also had some packets of dried fruit and jerky, as well as a small folding knife. One could never be too prepared when venturing into the untamed frontier lands. You never knew when you might need some basic provisions.

Diane selected a sturdy wooden walking stick and slung her crossbow over her back. I noticed she opted for that over a firearm. When I asked her about it, she explained she preferred the crossbow because it was silent.

"And I only need one shot when I'm hunting," she said. "So why go for anything else?"

I chuckled and nodded, giving her that point. Of course, when the situation was different from just hunting deer — such as combat — a semi-automatic would prove a lot more useful.

Either way, I grabbed my rifle to bring along just in case. Despite the great beauty of the frontier, there were things out there that could be dangerous.

We set off on foot down a dusty path leading west from the cabin along the riverbank. The trail was narrow and winding, partially obscured in places by encroaching grasses and bushes. We had to tread carefully around knobby tree roots and loose rocks that protruded from the earth.

As we walked, I inhaled deep breaths of the fresh air, savoring the feel of sunlight coming through the swaying branches overhead. The play of light and shadow on my face and shoulders felt rejuvenating after being hunched over tending the garden plot all morning.

Diane kept a brisk pace but moved with fluidity, using her walking stick for balance on rougher patches of ground. She paused often to point out small wonders along the path — a flowering bush buzzing with fat bees gathering pollen, vines with succulent leaves creeping up the side of a weathered boulder, and other small marvels that her appreciation elevated from the mundane.

We spoke little, simply enjoying the serene sounds and sights of the frontier that surrounded us. The gentle gurgle of water tumbling over stones harmonized with the trills and warbles of birds calling out to each other among the branches. It was a marked contrast from the usual city ambience of traffic and machinery that I was accustomed to.

The faint aroma of wildflowers drifted on the breeze, mixing with earthy scents of decaying leaves and woodland mosses. Everything seemed more vibrant, the colors richer and textures more intricately detailed than back in civilization. It was an overload of the senses in the best possible way.

After roughly a mile, the forest path opened up into a sprawling sunny meadow dotted with swaying grasses and vivid purple and yellow flowers. We paused our leisurely stroll just at the edge of the tree line, standing side by side gazing out appreciatively at the scenic vista.

Wispy clouds drifted across the azure sky overhead as finches and sparrows flitted among the colorful blooms, singing merrily. The meadow seemed utterly peaceful and untouched.

"It's so beautiful here," she breathed.

I could only agree as I stood awed by the untamed landscape that now stretched out before us. Beautiful birds with long elegant tail feathers swooped through the air above the grassy clearing, their jewel-toned plumage catching the sunlight as they wheeled and dove hypnotically.

"It's magical," I said, finding no other word to describe the overwhelming beauty of it all.

Diane smiled and nodded in agreement, closing her eyes briefly as she inhaled a deep breath of the sweet floral air. "Isn't it? I never get tired of roaming these parts." Her fox tail swished contentedly behind her, brushing against the thigh of my jeans.

I grinned, always endeared by that cute mannerism of hers. We lingered a while longer on the outskirts of the flower-strewn meadow, neither of us eager yet to leave behind this idyllic spot we had chanced upon. But the day waited, and there were still more sights to explore down the winding trail.

At last we continued onward, skirting the sunny clearing and re-entering the shaded confines of the forest. The path grew rockier for a stretch as it began to cut through a series of forested hills. Knobby protruding roots and loose rocks required sure footing once more.

Diane nimbly scaled the stony incline ahead of me, seeming to intuitively find just the right placement for each step that would provide secure traction. Her lithe agility and balance were impressive. I scrambled up the slope a bit less gracefully in her wake, twice nearly turning my ankle before managing to crest the ridge.

At the top, we were met with an even more stunning panoramic view overlooking the valley below. From this new vantage point, I could see our tiny log cabin nestled against the shining blue ribbon of the

Silverthread River off in the distance. Wisps of white smoke emanated from the stone chimney, promising a warm hearth and comforting meal awaited us upon our eventual return.

The breathtaking vista stretched out for miles in every direction, an ocean of treetops interspersed with wildflower-speckled meadows that rippled in the breeze like waves below. Diane slid her hand into mine as we stood shoulder to shoulder admiring the awe-inspiring display of raw natural beauty laid out before us.

"It's really beginning to feel like home to you, isn't it?" Diane said softly, giving my hand a light squeeze. I tore my eyes from the sweeping landscape to turn and look at her. The lowering sunlight brought out glints of gold in her dark hair.

I nodded, returning the gentle pressure on her slender hand in kind. "It is."

This rugged but beautiful land was starting to feel like the place I truly belonged. No crowded city could ever compare to the profound sense of fulfillment offered by living closely attuned to the rhythms of nature.

We lingered for a while longer atop the ridge, admiring the stunning view. I could make out the palisade walls surrounding Gladdenfield Outpost in the distance, looking tiny and toy-like from this vantage.

All too soon, the steadily lowering sunlight signaled that it was time for us to turn around and begin carefully picking our way back down the rocky path. We needed to complete the loop trail and make it home before dusk fully settled over the valley.

Along the way, we paused occasionally so Diane could point out useful native plants growing alongside the path that I otherwise might have overlooked – some with sweet edible berries, others with leaves or roots that held medicinal properties when brewed as teas or pressed into salves.

I made mental notes of each plant's location and appearance; such valuable flora would prove handy to harvest sustainably in seasons to come. The wilderness provided everything one needed if you only knew where and how to look as Diane so adeptly did.

By the time we descended from the hills and the rushing Silverthread River came back into view between the trees, the sun was just a glowing orange orb hovering above the western horizon. We quickened our pace, eager to make it back within the comforting walls of the cabin before full darkness enveloped the land.

My legs and feet were pleasantly sore by the time we trudged up the front steps as dusk settled in. Despite being a relatively short hike, my body was still adjusting to the rigors and physicality of life out here, so far removed from the conveniences of the city. But it was a satisfying sort of tiredness, the reward of a day spent immersed in the wilderness.

Diane turned to me with a smile as we went inside. "Did you enjoy the walk? We'll have to explore more trails together when we can."

"I'd love that," I replied sincerely. "It was so nice getting familiar with the area around where we live."

We worked together preparing a simple but hearty supper. As we ate by the firelight, we reminisced fondly about the day's wanderings through the vibrant wilderness, making plans for future outings and adventures.

Eventually, we turned in for an early night, and after a little fooling around, I fell asleep with Diane in my arms — all to the tune of the nightly sounds of the forest.

Chapter 32

I awoke early, just as the first rays of dawn were creeping over the eastern hills. Diane was still sound asleep, so I dressed quietly and slipped outside, taking care not to wake her. Morning dew coated the meadow grasses, and my breath steamed in the chill morning air.

It was looking to become a fine day.

I stretched my stiff muscles and set to work gathering

fallen branches for firewood. Our supply was running low, and I wanted to get a good stockpile going. The forest floor was littered with deadwood from the large trees surrounding our cabin. I moved methodically from tree to tree, collecting any pieces of suitable size for our stove and fireplace.

The physical exertion soon had me sweating despite the cold. I worked up quite an armload of branches and kindling, cradling them awkwardly as I made my way back to the woodpile beside the cabin. Once unburdened, I made a few more trips until I was satisfied we had ample firewood.

After stowing the wood, I stood with my hands on my hips, observing the small clearing around the cabin. Several large trees at the edge had dead branches that looked hazardous. I decided this would be a good opportunity to fell them.

I retrieved my axe from the cabinet in the mudroom and got to work hacking at the base of a smaller tree. The blade bit deep into the gnarled trunk with each swing. Before long, the tree groaned and teetered before crashing to the ground in a tangle of branches.

The commotion brought Diane outside, shielding her eyes against the rising sun. "You're hard at work already, I see," she called.

I smiled and waved my axe in greeting. "Just getting some firewood and clearing out these damaged trees," I explained between swings at a larger trunk. "I also want to clear out some of these smaller trees encroaching on our terrain. We might even need to clear more plots in the future."

"Good thinking," Diane agreed.

My muscles strained as the steel axe head slammed into the sturdy wood again. With a thunderous crack, the tree splintered and toppled over. I let out a satisfied huff, pausing to wipe sweat from my brow. We would have ample firewood for quite some time thanks to my efforts.

"Here, let me give you a hand," Diane offered, grabbing a spare axe. Together, we made quick work of the remaining small trees encroaching on the cabin's perimeter. Soon, a sizeable pile of logs awaited splitting.

Around mid-morning, we decided to take a break. I was drenched in sweat, arms burning pleasantly from the demanding labor, but there were blisters forming, and I would have to stop soon. We sat together by the chopping block, gratefully passing a waterskin back and forth.

"You really got a lot done already," Diane said appreciatively, ears twitching as she took in the collection of felled trees.

I laughed breathlessly, still catching my wind. "Well, all this physical work is still new to me. But it feels good to really use my muscles."

Diane smiled. "You're a natural woodcutter. But don't overdo it, okay?"

Her concern was touching. I promised I would be careful not to strain myself.

After a quick snack of bread and jerky, we set back to work splitting logs for the fireplace. I wedged each segment of wood upright on the block before bringing the axe down in a smooth, controlled arc. The pieces split satisfyingly under each blow.

Nearby, Diane dragged sections over to be split or gathered the split firewood to be stacked. We soon established an efficient rhythm in tandem. The valley echoed with the steady chopping and occasional crack of wood splitting.

By late morning, we had finished processing all the logs I had felled earlier. My arms burned pleasantly as I added the last armload of split logs to the newly stocked woodpile. I dusted off my hands, gazing at the impressive mound of firewood with satisfaction.

Diane came up beside me, slipping an arm around my waist affectionately. "I think that'll hold us for a good long while," she said.

I nodded in agreement, pleased with our shared accomplishment.

The sun nearing its zenith, we decided to clean up for lunch. I stored my axe while Diane fetched some water from the river to wash with. The cool water felt amazing on my hot, grimy skin after the arduous chopping.

Refreshed, we moved into the shady interior of the cabin. Diane hummed merrily as she prepared a hearty lunch from our stores — crusty bread, cheese, fruits, and cold meats. The aroma alone made my mouth water after the tiring morning's work.

We ate eagerly, ravenous from the rigorous physical tasks. The simple food tasted incredible after working up such hearty appetites. Diane smiled across the table, her fluffy tail flicking contentedly as she watched me enjoy the well-earned meal.

Halfway through our leisurely lunch, I paused to massage my shoulders, rolling them slowly to ease the dull ache of repeated axe swings. Diane looked up from her plate sympathetically.

"Here, let me rub them for you," she offered. I turned my back to her, groaning in relief as her nimble fingers kneaded the sore muscles. Diane's strong yet gentle hands worked out each knot and kink perfectly. I was putty in her expert hands.

"Feels heavenly," I mumbled, my eyes fluttering shut. "You're amazing at this, thanks so much."

Diane chuckled. "My pleasure, you definitely earned a massage. Just be sure to take it easy this afternoon, okay?"

I nodded, knowing she was right. There would be plenty more days for felling trees and gathering firewood. After we finished eating, I planned to simply relax and let my body recover.

But for now, I focused on each soothing pass of Diane's skilled hands across my weary shoulders.

We spent the rest of the day relaxing, and it was good to take the pressure off for a little while. And of course, there was the added benefit of getting to spend the time in Diane's company. Having her soft and delicious body so close, massaging me as she let out a low, delighted purr, quick led to one thing.

And one thing led to another…

The next morning, I awoke a little before dawn. I was

eager to continue experimenting with my emerging magical powers. Thanks to the woodland spirit I had summoned yesterday, our newly planted alchemy garden was already sprouting and growing at an accelerated rate.

I dressed quickly and went outside into the gray light, careful not to wake Diane who was still sleeping soundly. The morning air was cool, but the blue sky promised another sunny frontier day ahead. At the garden plot, I focused my will and summoned another woodland spirit.

As before, the swirling orb of energy materialized before swiftly expanding into the spindly, leaf-headed form. I directed it mentally to nurture and stimulate growth in the alchemy crops. It immediately set to work scurrying along the planted rows.

Before my eyes, the sprouts grew visibly larger, leaves unfurling as the spiritual energy infused their growth. Within minutes, the plants had matured the equivalent of several days thanks to the spirit's influence. I smiled, pleased to confirm this effect could be reproduced daily.

Soon, the summoned spirit dissolved away in a swirl of light, its energy expended. Our alchemy garden already looked weeks rather than days old. At this accelerated rate, reagents for crafting potions wouldn't be far off.

Since I still had some mana left, I wanted to test summoning an earth spirit next to see if it could lend aid in other ways. I focused again, drawing on the necessary mystical energies.

This time when I cast the spell, I selected the earth affinity. The orb swirled before manifesting into a stout, rock-skinned humanoid form. It regarded me steadily, awaiting instruction.

Directing it with my thoughts, I commanded, "Enrich and aerate this soil to strengthen the crops. Make it as fertile and hospitable for the plants as you can."

Bowing, the spirit began passing its stony hands over the ground around each plant. Wherever it touched, the soil became darker, richer. I could see nutrients being converted and activated to feed the thirsty roots. The earth spirit was a veritable farming supercharger!

After completing its work, the summoned earth creature rumbled back over to me before dissipating. The garden plot now boasted incredibly fertile, loamy soil thanks to its efforts.

I marveled at the spirits' handiwork as I headed back inside the cabin. Already, my emerging powers were proving invaluable on the homestead. Between the woodland and earth spirits' specialized skills, our farm productivity increased substantially.

The use of magic for tangible tasks still amazed me. But I was also careful not to let reliance on it replace diligent physical labor. The spirits provided a boost, but tending the earth ourselves remained deeply rewarding.

I found Diane awake and tidying up inside the cozy cabin. She smiled brightly at my return. "You're up early! I hope you haven't overexerted yourself already," she teased.

"Don't worry, I just couldn't resist summoning some more spirits to help out around the farm," I explained. "You should see how much they accelerated the garden's growth overnight!"

Diane's eyes lit up. "How wonderful! I can't wait to see it." She brushed a hand affectionately across my back. "But first, how about some breakfast?"

I realized I was famished after the magical exertions. "That sounds perfect."

As we ate the simple hearty meal together, I told Diane about summoning both the woodland and earth spirits. She listened raptly, clearly amazed and impressed.

"Incredible!" she said when I had finished. "Those

minor spirits provide such specialized skills. It's amazing how useful those powers of yours are! But are you sure you can handle using your magic so much? You've only just begun!"

I grinned and nodded. "I'll be careful." Her concern warmed my heart — she already fretted over me like a wife. The thought made me smile.

After breakfast, Diane and I inspected the robust garden together. The enriched soil and accelerated growth were astonishing. If all went well, our first alchemical harvest wasn't far off. We were both eager to start brewing potions together using the homegrown reagents.

We spent the sunny morning tending to other tasks around the homestead side by side, pausing occasionally to exchange a quick kiss or caress. I treasured these moments alone together. Out here living close to the land, each day brought us closer.

When midday warmth spread across the valley, we decided to take a break for lunch and enjoy the fair weather. We packed some bread, dried fruit, and cold meat before spreading out a quilt beneath the shade of a flowering tree.

As we ate, Diane hummed a cheerful tune, her fox ears twitching happily in the dappled sunlight. A pair of butterflies danced around us, seemingly drawn to her sweet voice. It was peaceful and picturesque.

"So," she said after she finished, giving me a loving, sapphire-eyed look. "I think we should go into town tomorrow. Waelin might be there. And if not, Leigh could tell us when he comes around."

I nodded. "Yeah, that sounds like a good idea."

"Besides," she hummed, stretching lazily on the quilt. "I could use a day in town. I feel like talking to Leigh!"

I grinned. "Well, she *is* a lot of fun."

"You bet," she hummed. "And I always miss her after a couple of days."

"Well, that settles it then," I said. "We're going to Gladdenfield tomorrow!"

She gave a happy yip, her fox ears twitching, and I chuckled to myself as I finished my food.

Stretching out on the quilt beside Diane after we finished eating, I felt utterly content. We talked unhurriedly about pleasant topics — favorite memories, hopes for the future, and the progress we had made so far.

All too soon, the afternoon sun dipping lower told us it was time to pack up our picnic and head back. Arm in arm, we strolled contentedly to the cabin to start preparing an evening meal.

As Diane chopped vegetables and tended the stew pot, I built up the fire, eager for another cozy dinner together and the night that would follow.

Chapter 33

The next morning, Diane and I woke up early and hurried through breakfast, eager to get on the road to Gladdenfield. We were both looking forward to the little outing, eager to see the town and catch up on any news.

I gave the alchemy garden one final inspection, pleased to see the plants thriving and maturing rapidly thanks to the spirits' aid. With another round of nurturing today, they would progress even further.

I quickly summoned the woodland spirit and had it work its magic on the crops. The soil was more than rich enough; it would not need another treatment from the earth spirit. When I was finished, I headed over to the Jeep and began loading the few things we'd need for the road, including my rifle.

Diane finished tidying up inside the cabin, then joined me by the waiting Jeep, her fox tail swishing eagerly behind her. "All set?" she asked, her blue eyes bright.

"Ready when you are," I confirmed, opening the passenger door for her with a flourish. Diane giggled and hopped in. I slid behind the wheel and soon had the rugged vehicle rumbling down the winding path away from our secluded homestead.

The morning air still held a bit of nighttime chill, but the cloudless azure sky promised a hot afternoon ahead. Birds wheeled and glided between the towering trees lining the road, while forest critters scuttled out of the way of the vehicle. Everything here teemed with life.

As the Jeep roared along, Diane rolled down her window, smiling joyously as the wind whipped through her long hair. She was a vision of beauty as she sat beside me, and it gave me great joy that she and I always had a great time.

Before long, the fortified palisade walls of Gladdenfield came into view ahead. Diane waved cheerfully to the elf guards at the gates, who recognized us from prior trips. They returned her smile and waved us through.

Navigating the rutted dirt streets, I headed toward the town square where the markets and shops were located. By now, I knew the layout of the rustic settlement by heart.

After parking, we stepped out into the bustling streets of the town. Diane took my arm, her tail curling happily as she guided me from stall to colorful stall. Merchants called out greetings, offering samples of freshly baked pastries, spiced teas, and other wares.

As before, most of the people here were humans, but the occasional elf or foxkin walked around as well. The foxkin especially threw us curious looks — it was obvious that we were more than friends, and relations between foxkin and humans were rare.

As we walked, my mouth watered at the enticing aromas and exotic offerings. But we had to pace ourselves — it was still just morning. "Where to first?" I asked Diane.

She pursed her lips thoughtfully, her fox ears twitching. "Let's stop by Leigh's shop and say hello. She'll know if Waelin is around."

We found Leigh's general store open. Once we entered, the bubbly blonde perked up, immediately recognizing us.

She hopped out from behind the counter, every curve jiggling in her tight outfit of jeans and buttoned blouse, and she engulfed Diane in an exuberant hug. "Diane! So good to see ya!" She then winked at me. "And you, of course, handsome!"

Leigh's bubbly energy was always a pleasure to experience. When she was done with Diane, she gave me an equally fierce embrace that afforded me a generous glimpse of her freckled cleavage.

"Look at you two lovebirds!" Leigh exclaimed, ushering us farther into the store as she flipped around the sign to announce she was closed. "C'mon back, we got lots to catch up on!"

We spent some time seated together by the store counter as Leigh plied us with sweet tea and treats while chatting animatedly about gossip around town. I didn't follow every reference, but her lively storytelling style was inherently entertaining.

Eventually, I was able to ask if Waelin had been

through town lately. Leigh's eyes lit up knowingly. "Oh yes, you just missed him! But don't worry — Waelin will be back this way in a week, or so he said. And he'll be stickin' around for a couple of days since he has to restock on a couple of things."

I nodded, excited by the news that the alchemist would return so soon. I was really looking forward to getting into this alchemy adventure.

Diane gave me an encouraging pat on the knee. "Perfect, we can come back in a week or so, and you'll get to meet him for sure."

Leigh leaned forward eagerly, propping her chin in her hands. "Now what's this about Waelin? What're you two up to?" She threw me a suspicious look. "And with you buyin' all those seeds, hmm?"

I laughed and explained my emerging alchemy interests and desire to pick the ancient elf's brain about potion crafting. Leigh nodded along thoughtfully as I spoke.

"Well, ain't that fascinatin'!" she remarked. "I bet with your powers, you'd cook up some amazing concoctions. Be sure to let me sample any love potions you brew up, hmm?" She shot me a playful wink.

I chuckled while Diane gave her friend a gentle shove at the risqué joke. "Oh, stop it! Don't give him any strange ideas." But Diane's eyes were twinkling with amusement.

Leigh grinned mischievously. "Aw, I'm just teasin'." She gave Diane a little nudge. "But seems to me you two probably already got your own magic potion goin' on, if you catch my drift."

At that, Diane's cheeks flushed bright pink. But she was still smiling. "Oh hush, you!"

Leigh and I both laughed while Diane tried unsuccessfully to hide her blushing face.

The three of us bantered merrily together for a while longer before Diane mentioned wanting to browse the markets next.

"Well, don't let me keep y'all!" said Leigh, making a shooing gesture with her hands. "Go have fun together. But come back before you leave town for a proper goodbye!"

Diane gave her a quick hug. "We'll be back a bit later!"

Leigh nodded appreciatively before we took our leave.

Outside, the plaza was even more crowded, with shoppers mingling with merchants at the colorful stalls. Diane turned to me, her eyes sparkling. "Where to next?"

Taking her hand, I led her toward a tantalizing display of exotic baked goods. "I want to try some of this food," I said. "It smells great!"

After indulging in the baked goods, Diane and I browsed the lively market stalls, hand in hand. The diversity of wares was astounding – from mundane tools and produce to fantastical objects imbued with frontier magic. My curiosity was piqued examining a glowing blue crystal the elf merchant claimed could summon rainstorms when shattered.

Diane had to gently steer me away from the more extravagant magical items, reminding me we were on a budget. "Remember, we're just here to pick up a few necessities," she said with an amused smile. "We don't have much."

And that was true, of course: apart from the little coin we had procured selling the smoked trout to Leigh, we had nothing. Still, it was fun to just look around.

At a weapons stall stocked with all manner of swords, axes and bows, I noticed a band of adventurers gearing up for an expedition. They were a motley crew

— two humans, a dwarf, and a foxkin. Their leader, an old but brawny warrior woman, was briefing them on fighting giant spiders.

It was a glimpse into a very different frontier life from that of a homesteader. Diane followed my gaze, ears perking curiously. "Ah, looks like Clara's crew is preparing for another delve into the Wyvern Wood," she remarked.

I shook my head in amazement. "Takes guts to willingly head into spider-infested woods. That kind of adventuring actually looks exciting, though," I mused. "Maybe we could mount some expeditions of our own once we're a higher level, help clear sections of the Wilds near our valley."

Diane gave me an evaluating look, then smiled. "You may be right; some low-level adventures together could be rewarding. And there's always work making the land around Gladdenfield safer."

We lingered a while observing the preparations. I was fascinated by frontier adventuring life, though I knew it wasn't the right path for me currently. Helping Diane run our homestead was fulfilling enough for now. But in time, a little excitement would be interesting, especially if my summoning magic improved.

I also remembered the Dungeons that Caldwell and I had spotted on our drive down from New Springfield. It was good that such adventure was available, should I be interested in it.

Moving on, we knew we only had a little coin left from selling the smoked fish to Leigh. So we purchased just some basic food supplies that would last us a while — among them hardy vegetables, eggs, dried meat, and some cream. Those would replenish our stocks and keep things a little interesting in the kitchen.

Rather than ogling things we could not afford right now, we decided to chat with some of the traders to get news and rumors. An elf merchant told us he had heard rumors of valuable minerals discovered near the Shimmering Peaks. And a dwarven prospector mentioned sightings of strange new creatures emerging from the Dungeons to the east. Some forayed out at night, and although there had not been any attacks, the dwarf mumbled in his beard that it sure as hell was taking the Frontier Division long enough to deal with the threat.

It was all interesting information. Diane and I agreed we would have to focus on selling crops, doing some odd jobs around Gladdenfield, and maybe trying our hand at alchemy to earn more coin soon. But for today, we were content with the fresh food supplies to restock our larder.

By midday, when the market thronged busiest, we decided to take a break for lunch. We sat beneath a spreading tree just outside of town, sharing the baked goods purchased earlier along with some dried fruit and fresh water from my flask.

Diane nibbled contentedly on a honey-glazed pastry, her ears twitching happily. "Mmm, this is delicious," she mumbled. A few crumbs clung endearingly to her cheek. Chuckling, I gently brushed them away.

We talked unhurriedly as we ate. I told Diane more about my fascination glimpsing frontier adventuring life. She shared amusing tales of Clara leading her ragtag team on epic monster-slaying quests. Apparently, they had been level 3 for a long while now, as Clara was hesitant to take on higher challenges for more experience.

"And why should they?" I laughed. "If they're happy, then it's good enough."

Diane grinned and nodded. "I've been level 2 for a long time myself. There's no rush, but it's nice to know that advancement is an option for those interested."

As we talked, the sun dipped lower, and the afternoon market began to wind down with merchants packing up their stalls. Some would be here again tomorrow, and others would leave early in the morning to visit the next frontier town. We packed up the remains of our lunch and headed back into the bustling town square.

We did stop by Leigh's shop again to chat, though we didn't purchase anything else today. Leigh happily caught us up on the day's gossip and news.

Before leaving town, Diane and I made one final pass through the market stalls before they closed, simply enjoying the sights and sounds. We paused to watch a talented elven musician sing a melancholy song in the graceful elven tongue for coins from passersby. I tossed a few coppers into the elf's upturned hat, earning an appreciative nod.

When the mellow notes faded, Diane turned to me, eyes twinkling. "Shall we go have a drink together at the tavern? We still have some time before we need to return home."

I smiled. "I'd love to. Lead the way!"

Chapter 34

Laughing and talking, Diane and I headed to the lively tavern near the town square. We were just in time, as it was beginning to rain.

It was late afternoon, and patrons were starting to file in. We found a small table in the back corner, and I offered to grab us some drinks from the busy bar.

I stood waiting at the crowded bar, observing the

rustic tavern interior to pass the time. Lanterns lined the timber walls, casting a warm flickering glow. The savory aromas of roasting meat and fresh bread mingled with the earthy scent of tobacco from dozens of pipes. Up near the front, an elven minstrel plucked out a lively melody on his lute.

Patrons crowded the tables and lined the long bar, a mix of humans, elves, and the occasional dwarf or foxkin. Their lively conversations and raucous laughter filled the cozy space with convivial energy. Serving girls deftly wove between tables, sloshing brimming tankards as they took orders.

I smiled, soaking in the atmosphere. Places like this tavern were hubs of the frontier community. Here, deals were made, news spread, and weary travelers found roaring fires, stiff drinks, and hot meals.

As I waited my turn at the crowded bar, I felt a rough jostling elbow dig into my ribs. Wincing, I turned to see who had shoved me.

Beside me stood a wiry and unpleasant-looking foxkin male, glowering up at me. His coarse hair was unkempt, his ears folded back, and he wore threadbare clothes. I recognized him after a moment — the spiteful fellow from the road when Diane and I had first come to Gladdenfield.

"You're that human shacking up with Diane, ain't ya?" he growled accusingly, upper lip curled in a sneer. His breath stank of cheap ale.

I suppressed a sigh, realizing this little guy clearly had some issue with Diane and me being together. But I refused to let this belligerent stranger sour my cheerful mood.

"Something you want?" I asked. I wasn't going to take the bait and talk to this runt about my relationship with Diane. It was none of his business.

The foxkin scowled as he glared up at me. "Yeah," he spat. "We don't need your kind lurking around here. Why don't you head on back to the city where you belong?"

His words were deliberately meant to provoke, but I still refused to take his bait. Still, it was irritating to have our relationship questioned by this complete stranger. But if this was going to be a fight, I wasn't going to become known as a troublemaker in town and in the tavern by throwing the first punch.

"Look, man," I said evenly, keeping my tone free of confrontation. "I have nothing to say to you. Why don't you just mosey on and get another drink, huh?"

The foxkin's ears flattened back angrily against his skull at my measured response. Clearly, he had hoped to get a rise out of me.

"It's my concern when some outsider starts sniffing around our women," he snarled, then prodded my chest roughly with a bony finger. "Diane deserves a proper mate."

I just laughed at that and shook my head. "You're not talking about yourself, are you? Man, there are dwarves in here that are taller than you… and elven women that are more muscular."

The patrons in our immediate vicinity — they had all stopped their conversations to watch the situation unfold — began laughing at my comment. The foxkin — I now recalled his name as Anwick — bristled with impotent rage and sputtered something, but he was unable to come up with a comeback.

I shook my head. "We're done talking," I said coldly. Turning my back on him, I stepped up to the bar to place my drink order.

Suddenly, I felt a sharp yank on my shoulder as the disgruntled foxkin grabbed me.

I had expected it, of course, so my guard was still up. I spun around to face him again.

"Don't you turn away from me!" he snarled, spittle flying from his bared teeth.

My fraying patience finally reached its end. As the

foxkin reared back a clawed fist preparing to swing at me, I reacted on instinct. My hand shot out and grabbed his thin wrist in an iron vise-like grip before he could strike.

"Bad move," I hissed through gritted teeth, clenching his wrist tighter.

Before he could react, I swiftly brought my knee up hard into his gut, doubling him over with a pained wheeze. Keeping my hold on the foxkin's bony wrist, I half-marched, half-dragged his gasping form across the tavern floor toward the entrance.

Patrons hastily moved aside to clear a path, staring and murmuring. But no one made any move to intervene or protest my rough handling of the antagonistic foxkin. A few even glared at him with satisfaction, apparently familiar with his unpleasant demeanor.

Reaching the door, I shoved it open with my free arm and flung the foxkin out into the muddy street. He landed with a wet splat, still clutching his stomach. I slammed the door on him. Good riddance.

As I rolled my shoulders and prepared to head back, I heard a gasp behind me. Turning, I saw Diane rushing over, eyes wide with concern.

"David! Are you alright?" she asked anxiously,

looking me over for any signs of injury.

"I'm fine, really," I assured her. But Diane was not easily placated.

"That awful Anwick," she fumed. "I saw him grab you from across the room. What did he want?"

"Nothing important," I said dismissively, not wanting to upset her further. But Diane persisted, her protective instincts stirred. Sighing, I explained the foxkin's ugly remarks about me not belonging with her.

Diane's expression softened with sympathy. "I'm so sorry you had to deal with that," she said, gently caressing my cheek.

Then, to my surprise, she pulled me into a sudden deep kiss right there in front of the staring tavern patrons.

Everyone was still looking. After all, I had only just turned Anwick out. So everyone saw it. It was not like we had been hiding our relationship before, but now… well, now everyone knew.

I blinked in astonishment when she finally drew back, cheeks endearingly flushed. Diane lifted her chin defiantly. "There, now everybody knows we're together," she declared. "And I'm not ashamed of it. I'm proud of it. I want to be with you, David."

My heart swelled at her bold display of affection.

"Same here, Diane," I agreed, smiling down at her.

"Forget the drinks," she said, holding my cheeks with both hands as her eyes burned into me. "Forget everything. Take me home and make love to me, David. I want it. I need it. I've been wanting it so bad. And I don't want to wait a second longer…"

I'm not sure how exactly, but we were in the Jeep within seconds.

Chapter 35

I drove fast out of the town, barely pausing at the gate before heading down the trail that led to our homestead, watching the headlights of the Jeep bring more life to the greenery around us. But my mind was on Diane as she sat next to me. Her bosom heaved, and her eyes were full of lust as she watched me.

"David, slow down. We have some time before it's

fully dark. Let's take the trip home, slow and fun…" she purred, her voice husky.

She leaned over and began to nuzzle my ear with her lips, her breath hot and sweet against my skin. My foot slipped off the gas, and I could feel my cock harden as her fingers gently traced the muscles of my chest, causing a shiver to run down my spine.

"Keep your eyes on the road," she whispered, her tongue flicking against the lobe of my ear. Her fingers fumbled with my fly, pulling it open to reveal my eager arousal.

"I am," I managed to reply, my voice tight. We were crawling along the road now.

The thought of her touch, her mouth on me, was driving me to distraction. I gripped the steering wheel tightly with one hand, the other resting on her thigh, feeling the warmth of her through the thin fabric of her dress.

She pulled my cock out, her fingers cool against the heat of my skin. I groaned as she began to stroke me, her touch light and teasing, driving me crazy with desire.

"I love your cock, David," she murmured, her voice filled with admiration. She stroked my length, her fingers tracing the veins that pulsed with my arousal.

"I've been thinking about your cock. I want it so bad. I need to feel you inside me, David."

I watched her from the corner of my eye, her black hair shining, her sapphire eyes sparkling with mischief. Her fox ears twitched as she concentrated, her tail swishing behind her, matching the rhythm of her hand on me.

She leaned forward, her breasts pressing against my arm. I could feel her nipples hard against my skin, her arousal as evident as mine. Then, she looked around as if to see if anyone was spying on us. When she was satisfied, she bit her lip in the cutest way before she pulled her top up, her beautiful breasts bouncing free to my hungry gaze.

"Diane," I groaned, lust driving me. "You're gonna make me crash this damn car!"

"Just drive slow and touch me, David," she breathed, her eyes locked onto mine. I obliged eagerly, my hand leaving the wheel to cup her breast, my thumb rubbing over her hardened nipple, causing her to moan softly. Luckily, there was no one out here.

"Let me suck your cock again, David," she purred, giving me that teasing look.

With those words, she leaned forward, her lips brushing against the head of my cock. I gasped as her tongue flicked out, tasting me. She moaned again, the vibration from her voice sending shivers of pleasure through me.

"Diane," I groaned, my fingers tightening on her nipple, pulling at it. I wanted her so badly, my body aching with desire for her. She teased me, her tongue swirling around the head of my cock, her hand stroking me in time with her mouth.

"You taste so good," she murmured, her words sending a jolt of arousal through me. I watched as she took me deeper into her mouth, her lips wrapped tightly around me. I could feel her throat constricting around me as she swallowed, the sensation driving me wild.

My climax was building, my muscles tensing as the pleasure mounted. Diane seemed to sense this, her movements becoming more insistent, her mouth working me to the edge.

"I'm going to cum," I warned her, my voice strained with effort. She looked up at me, her eyes dark with desire, her hand working me faster. I could see her go faster, cheeks hollowed out as she prepared for my release.

With a final stroke of her hand, I erupted into her warm mouth. My orgasm washed over me, leaving me breathless. I could feel my cock pulse, shooting my seed into her waiting mouth.

She swallowed me down, her throat working to take everything I had to give. I watched her, my breath coming in short gasps as the pleasure continued to ripple through me.

She sat back, a satisfied smile on her lips as she wiped her mouth with the back of her hand, her eyes sparkling with satisfaction. "You taste so good," she murmured, her voice filled with contentment.

I managed a smile, my body still recovering from the intensity of my orgasm. "I'm glad I didn't crash the car," I told her, my voice hoarse.

She laughed softly, her fox tail twitching in amusement. "You're a good driver, baby," she retorted, her fingers tracing lazy circles on my thigh as she pulled her top back down. I could feel my cock twitch at her touch, the aftershocks of my orgasm still making me sensitive.

She giggled, her laughter like music to my ears, before she leaned over, pressing a soft kiss to my cheek. "This was just a taste," she whispered, her breath tickling my ear. "Tonight, I want to feel you inside me. I want to feel what it's like to have you cum in me, to have you fill me with your seed."

I grunted with lust, my heart racing. The anticipation of what was to come making me dizzy with excitement.

She settled back in her seat, her eyes on the road ahead. I could see the outline of her nipples through her tank top, her arousal clear. I reached over, my hand brushing against her thigh, the heat of her skin burning me.

"Tonight," she promised, her voice low and sultry.

I could hardly wait, the thought of having her beneath me making me hard again. I groaned, my hands tightening on the wheel.

I could see the cabin in the distance, resting in its place by the banks of the Silverthread River. I could imagine us there, tangled, our bodies slick with sweat. The thought made me groan, my cock throbbing in anticipation.

I could feel her eyes on me, her gaze heavy with desire. I turned to look at her, my eyes raking over her body. I could see her blush, her cheeks turning a beautiful shade of pink.

"You're mine tonight," I told her, my voice husky.

She met my gaze, her eyes sparkling with desire. "Yours," she agreed, her voice barely a whisper.

I turned my attention back to the road, my hands gripping the wheel tightly. I could feel her gaze on me, her eyes heavy with desire. I could hardly wait to get her home.

In the distance, the cabin dawned on the bank of the Silverthread River. The sight of our home elicited a possessive growl from me as I shot a look at Diane, biting her bottom lip naughtily.

We pushed through the door, almost falling into the mudroom as we kissed and lost each other in our embrace. Without breaking our kiss, I kicked the door shut behind me, then ushered Diane into the cabin's cozy living room. Her fox tail brushed against my legs, sending shivers of anticipation up my spine.

"David," she breathed into my ear, her voice husky with desire. "Take me, please." Her hands began to roam over my chest, tracing the lines of my muscles through the thin fabric of my shirt.

I made quick work of my shirt, discarding it onto the floor. Diane's gaze roamed my bare chest, her eyes sparkling with desire in the dim light of the cabin. Her fingers traced the lines of my body, her touch igniting a fire within me.

I watched as Diane peeled off her tight tank top, revealing her firm, round breasts. Her nipples were already erect, showing her arousal.

I took her in my arms, our naked chests pressed together. The sensation of her bare skin against mine was electrifying. We kissed hungrily, our tongues tangling in a dance as old as time.

"On the rug," I whispered, guiding her towards the braided rug in front of the fireplace. She complied without hesitation, her eyes never leaving mine as she lay down, her fox tail curling around her body.

I knelt down between her spread legs, my gaze traveling down to her lower body. She was wearing a pair of tiny shorts, which left little to the imagination. I hooked my fingers into the waistband, pulling them down to reveal her pussy.

Diane was wet, her arousal glistening in the dim light. I glanced up at her, finding her watching me with lust-filled eyes. "Please, David," she said, her voice thick with desire. "Please eat my pussy…"

I leaned in, my tongue darting out to flick at her clit. She gasped, her hands coming to rest on my head. I closed my eyes, focusing on the taste and feel of her, my tongue exploring her folds with practiced ease.

Soon enough, Diane was squirming beneath me, her

hips thrusting up to meet my mouth. Her moans filled the quiet cabin, the sound spurring me on. She tasted divine, her arousal coating my tongue as I worked her towards her climax.

I slipped a finger inside her, feeling her muscles clench around me. She was tight, so incredibly tight. I added a second finger, pumping them in and out of her as I continued to lick and suck at her clit.

Diane's fingers were tangled in my hair, her nails digging into my scalp as she urged me on. "Don't stop, David," she pleaded, her voice strained with pleasure.

I was relentless, my tongue and fingers working in tandem to drive her to the edge. I could feel her body tensing beneath me, her breath coming in short gasps. I knew she was close.

And so, I pulled back, watching as she caught her breath, frustration mastering her as I teased her. She gave a purr as she arched her back, needing more. Her chest was heaving, her breasts rising and falling with each breath she took. Her skin was flushed, a thin sheen of sweat coating her body.

Diane's hands roamed my body, her fingers tracing the lines of my muscles. She shifted beneath me, her legs wrapping around me as she pulled me closer. I could feel her arousal, a reminder of what we had just shared. "David," she moaned. "Oh… I… I want to cum… Please!"

I grinned and took her hand, guiding it towards my throbbing cock. She wrapped her fingers around me, her touch sending a jolt of pleasure through my body. I groaned; the sound muffled by her lips as our lips met in a fiery kiss.

Diane began to stroke me, her hand moving up and down my length. I could feel the pressure building as she moaned for the orgasm she needed from me.

I pulled back, breaking our kiss. Diane looked up at me, her sapphire eyes clouded with desire. "Give it to me," she said, her voice thick with need. "And after… Ahnn… Please fuck me after, David. Fuck me and cum in me!"

Those words were driving me crazy! I kissed her again, this time with more passion. I could feel her body responding to mine, her hips grinding against me. I let out a groan, the sound muffled by her lips.

Diane's hand was still on my cock, her fingers stroking me to the brink of orgasm. But I held back, wanting to savor this moment for as long as possible. I pulled away from her, my cock slipping from her grasp.

I moved down her body, my lips trailing kisses along her perfect curves. I tasted the salty sweat on her skin, the sweet tang of her arousal. I reached her pussy, my tongue darting out to taste her once again.

"Yes!" she called out, surrendering to my touch. "Oh, yes! Please!" She was wetter than before, her arousal coating my tongue. I licked and sucked at her, driving her towards the orgasm she needed. I wanted to see her cum, wanted to see her lose control.

And then she was there, her body arching off the rug as her orgasm ripped through her. I continued to lick her through her climax, her taste filling my mouth. She bucked and gasped under the throes of her delicious orgasm, calling out my name again and again.

When the lashing of her orgasm stopped and her arched back relaxed, her blazing sapphire eyes fixed on me. Her skin was deliciously sweaty, and her eyes were wide and smoky, the very definition of bedroom eyes.

"I want it, David," she purred, not breaking eye contact. "Please, take me. Claim me now."

With a groan of need, I moved in.

Diane's naked body sprawled under mine, sweat glistening on her ivory skin as she lay on our braided rug in front of the cold fireplace. My cock was so hard at the sight of her; it almost hurt.

"Fuck me, David," she said, her sapphire eyes ablaze with desire, her voice a husky purr that sent shivers down my spine and made my manhood twitch with anticipation.

I obliged her request with a grunt, positioning myself between her spread legs, my tip nudging against her womanhood that was still tight and sensitive from the orgasm she had just moments ago.

"Finally," she hummed as she felt my hard tip against her slick heat. "Oh, finally, David!"

I pushed into her slowly, the feeling of her tightness enveloping me was indescribable. Diane let out a low moan, her body arching upwards, pressing against mine.

The sensation was overwhelming, a heady mix of pleasure and lust. I pushed deeper into her; my cock fully sheathed within her. I had wanted this for so long, and now that I was here, it felt even better to be enveloped by her wet warmth than I had dared hope.

I began to move then, a slow rhythm that had her gasping beneath me. Each thrust was a delicious friction, a decadent dance of bodies and souls.

Diane wrapped her legs around my waist, pulling me

closer, deeper. Her nails dug into my back, leaving marks that I wore with pride.

She was so wet, so warm, so welcoming. I increased my pace, pounding into her with a fervor that matched the burning lust in her eyes.

"Oh, yes, David," Diane moaned, her hips meeting mine with each thrust. The sight of our bodies moving in unison was almost too much to bear. "Ahnn… Your cock… Uhnnn… It feels so good! Fuck me, David!"

I groaned with lust, feeling my impending release, the telltale tightening at the base of my cock. I wanted to prolong this moment, to savor her, to enjoy her.

So, I pulled out, much to her surprise. I flipped her over, positioning her on her hands and knees on the rug.

Diane's tail twitched in anticipation, adding an exotic allure to this intimate moment. "Oh, David," she purred. "Yes, like that!"

I entered her from behind now, her back arched just right, offering me a view of her perfect ass that was now mine to claim.

"Fuck, David, harder," Diane moaned. Her dirty words spurred me on, my thrusts becoming more animalistic, more primal. I fucked her, each thrust harder than the last.

Diane was so responsive, her body moving with me, her moans becoming louder, more desperate with each passing second. Her orgasm was building, I could feel it.

And then it happened. Diane's body tensed, her muscles clenching around my cock as waves of pleasure washed over her while I fucked her from behind. Her moans turned into cries of ecstasy, her body trembling as her orgasm took over.

I slowed down, allowing her to ride out her orgasm. The sight of her climaxing under my touch, the sounds of her pleasure echoing in the room was intoxicating.

But Diane wasn't done. "Flip me over, David," she pleaded, her voice raspy from her moans of pleasure. "I want to see you when you cum in me."

I obliged her wish, flipping her over once again. The sight of her, sated yet hungry for more was a sight to behold.

I entered her again, her womanhood still throbbing from her recent climax. Diane gasped, her nails digging into my shoulders as I set a brutal pace.

I pounded into her, my cock hitting all the right spots. Diane's body responded in kind, her hips meeting mine with every thrust. Her luscious breasts bounced with every thrust, and I grabbed her slim waist for leverage as I rammed into her again and again.

She wrapped her legs around me, her heels digging into my lower back, urging me to go deeper, to give her more. "Do it, David," she panted, "Cum in me. Please!"

Her pleas, the sight of her beneath me, her body welcoming me, was all too much. I could feel my orgasm building, a tsunami of pleasure that was ready to crash.

I gritted my teeth, trying to hold back, wanting this moment to last. But Diane was relentless, her body moving in a rhythm that was designed to push me over the edge.

"Diane," I groaned, my voice a low growl. Her name was a prayer on my lips.

And then it happened. I came with a roar, my body tensing as my release flooded her. Diane's name was the only word that left my lips as I experienced the most intense orgasm of my life.

Diane came with me, her body convulsing around mine as her third orgasm of the night hit her. Her screams of pleasure mixed with mine, filling the room with sounds of our shared ecstasy. And as she came, I gave her rope upon rope of fertile seed, filling her delicious pussy to the brim with what she so desired.

We rode out our orgasms together, our bodies

entwined in a dance of pleasure. I felt her heartbeat against mine, a rhythm that matched the throbbing of my cock inside her.

I collapsed on top of her, my body heavy with satisfaction. Diane's arms wrapped around me, holding me close as we both struggled to catch our breaths.

I stayed inside her as I lay on top of her, a sigh of long-postponed needs fulfilled escaping me. I had filled her up, just like she wanted to, and she breathed heavily in my ear.

Our naked bodies were sweating, chests heaving from the pleasure we had shared as we lay on the braided rug. Diane's body was warm and soft against mine, her fox tail curling around my waist. The ripples of our climax still echoed within me, matching the rhythmic pulsating of my cock, slowly subsiding.

"That was…incredible, David," Diane whispered, her breath tickling my chest, her voice sultry and sated.

I met her sapphire gaze with a smile, and I could see the satisfaction, the contentment there. Her fingers traced idle patterns on my chest, their touch light and teasing.

I chuckled, a deep rumble in my chest. "You're not so bad yourself, foxy lady." I flashed her a quick grin, running my fingers through her black hair and past the fox ears with white highlights shimmering in the dim light. Her breasts pressed into my chest, and my hands explored the familiar terrain of her athletic body as we basked in the afterglow.

With a sigh, I moved off her to lay down beside her, and Diane immediately snuggled closer, her fox tail unwinding from my waist to wrap around us both, providing a layer of warmth against the cool night air.

Her head rested on my chest, her ear twitching slightly as it brushed against me. "I love you, David," she murmured, her words sincere and filled with emotions.

I tightened my hold on her, my fingers tracing her back, feeling the smooth skin under my touch. "I love you too, Diane," I said.

We lay in silent comfort like that for a while, realizing the truth of this moment. The cabin was filled with a sense of peace and contentment, our bodies entwined.

I shifted slightly, turning to my side and pulling Diane closer. I tucked her head under my chin, feeling the softness of her hair and fox ears against my skin. Her fingers traced lazy patterns on my chest, each touch sending a ripple of pleasure through me.

"You're getting pretty cold," I said at last when I felt a shiver pass through Diane. "What do you say we light the fireplace, get a blanket, and relax for a bit."

She gave a happy sigh and nodded. "And maybe afterwards," she purred, trailing my chest with a slender finger, "we can do it all over again…"

Chapter 36

I awoke to soft sunlight giving its glow to the cabin. Beside me, Diane was still asleep, her head nestled on my shoulder and one arm draped lightly over my chest. Memories of our passionate night together came flooding back, bringing a contented smile to my face.

After all the flirting and longing, finally consummating our love had exceeded every expectation. Diane had been almost ravenous in her need, and the tenderness that followed was profoundly moving. I knew now without a doubt that I wanted to spend my life with this amazing woman.

Careful not to wake her, I softly stroked Diane's silken hair as she slumbered. The sight of her naked form curled against me, lips still kiss-swollen, made my heart surge with emotion. Last night had deepened our bond immeasurably.

After a few blissful minutes, Diane began to stir, stretching languorously. Her brilliant blue eyes fluttered open, and she smiled up at me. "Good morning," she murmured huskily.

"Good morning, my love," I replied, kissing her tenderly. We lay entwined a while longer, neither wanting to leave our cozy nest just yet. But eventually the new day beckoned.

I slipped from the bed and washed up using the basin in the kitchen while Diane dressed upstairs. Soon I heard her descending to start some coffee. The rich aroma was a welcome way to start the day.

Diane hummed cheerfully as she cooked up eggs and potatoes for breakfast. I came up behind her at the stove for a lingering kiss and embrace, thrilled at this new domestic intimacy between us.

"I think some celebrations are in order today," I remarked, giving her waist a squeeze before releasing her to finish cooking. Diane's answering smile was radiant.

We soon sat across from each other, steaming mugs of fragrant coffee on the table next to us. Diane reached over to place her hand over mine, her thumb idly stroking my skin. Our eyes locked, the unspoken connection humming between us.

We ate leisurely, focused only on each other's presence. Diane's fox ears twitched happily when I complimented the hearty frontier-style meal she had prepared.

Halfway through breakfast, Diane set down her fork, looking at me earnestly. "David, last night was the most incredible experience of my life. I've never felt closer to someone." Her voice was soft but full of conviction. "I know you are my mate now, in all ways."

I smiled and squeezed her hand. "And you are mine," I said. "It was special... Everything I hoped it would be."

She smiled and nodded. "I feel the same way," she purred.

"In fact," I said, giving her a naughty grin. "I'm hoping we can share it again before we start the day in earnest."

Diane burst out laughing, giving my hand a playful swat. "Oh, stop!" But her eyes danced with amusement.

I chuckled. "That's not what you said last night."

That sent Diane into renewed giggles. The sound filled my heart with joy.

When her laughter finally subsided, Diane shot me a grin. "You're too much sometimes." She leaned across the table to give me a sweet kiss.

We lingered at the table a while longer, hands joined, talking lightly about the day ahead. Diane mentioned wanting to do some more fishing, and I thought it was a good idea. For now, the smoked fish were turning out to be our best source of income. And even with the help of my spirits, the crops were not going to grow so fast that we'd harvest before we needed to purchase new supplies.

"And maybe I can do some trapping after I do my little trick with the woodland spirit," I said, keen to try out the effects of my Trapping skill.

"Great idea!" Diane hummed, looking at me with her big, blue eyes. "We'll get some good income going."

After breakfast, we worked side by side tidying up — Diane washing dishes as I put away leftovers. The domestic harmony was nice to experience, and we laughed and joked, with me swatting Diane on her shapely rump whenever I passed her by. When the kitchen was spotless, we had another cup of coffee and laughed and joked a little more.

But daylight waited outside, and tasks remained. After a soft lingering kiss, we collected our gear and began our work.

Outside, the valley air was still crisp but warming steadily as the sun climbed. Birdsong echoed from the encircling trees, signaling a fair day for work. I took a deep breath, savoring life's simple joys.

Diane slipped her slender hand into mine, giving it a light squeeze before she kissed me and headed in the direction of the Silverthread for a day of fishing. As she did so, I headed out to the plots and summoned my little woodland sprite. The happy, flickering creature did my bidding, imbuing the crops with its energy.

After that, I headed back inside and retrieved the gear I would need for a day trapping in the forest. I took my rifle and handgun to be sure, as well as something to eat and drink for when noon came around. Then, I headed out.

I hiked until I reached a promising spot about a mile from the cabin, where I noticed traces of a lot of squirrel and rabbit activity – droppings, nibblings, and the like.

Now, I was by no means an expert trapper, but I had some foundational knowledge to build upon. I knew what would be a good spot, and I knew what would be a bad spot. And even though I had only set up one trap so far, the knowledge of how to do it was strong in my mind. The big advantage of skills…

I activated my Trapping skill, and I was at once infused with knowledge on how to craft traps. It came naturally to me, and I only slowed down when I started to think too much about it all.

And so, I just followed my instincts.

Selecting a small clearing surrounded by bushes and boulders, I got to work setting some simple snares. Using some twine and supple branches, I fashioned small noose traps and placed them delicately in areas I thought would be animal runs.

Next, I prepared a deadfall trap, propping a heavy rock up with a stick that acted as a trigger. I placed some nuts and seeds as bait beneath it. If all went well, the rock would come crashing down on any critters lured in by the food.

After checking that the traps were well-camouflaged and concealed, I moved farther into the woods seeking spots to set up a couple more snares. I wove between the trees, eyes scanning the undergrowth for signs of game trails.

Eventually, I found a likely area dense with low bushes. Carefully parting the foliage, I spotted several small paths winding through that animals clearly used regularly to get to their drinking spot. Perfect for snare placement.

Once again, I activated my Trapping ability at the cost of 1 mana. The knowledge flowed into me, and I quickly fashioned small noose snares from cord and supple twigs and set them over the narrow trails. I took care to make sure the loops were suspended properly above the paths, positioning the sticks I used to tie the twine so they would cleanly release if triggered.

When I had finished with the woven-branch snares, I surveyed my handiwork with satisfaction. The assembled collection of traps blended surprisingly well with their surroundings. Perhaps my Trapping skill lent some additional bonus in their camouflage?

In any case, they were well-situated to potentially catch some tasty additions to the larder, assuming I checked them frequently enough so that any trapped animals did not spoil. I would have to collect any catches early next morning. Adding that to summoning a woodland sprite to enhance crop growth, I was looking at a busy morning routine for the coming days.

But we needed the food, and we could smoke the meat if the catches were bountiful.

Continuing my trapping expedition, I hiked farther west, trying to listen closely for any sounds of animal activity. The rustling of bushes or chatter of squirrels could help reveal good areas to focus on.

After about a half mile, I came upon a small stream winding through the trees. I walked slowly along the bank, scanning carefully. Surely this water source would attract thirsty animals.

Kneeling by the stream's mossy edge, I searched for any telltale animal tracks in the mud that might suggest a crossing point to target. Before long, I noticed a clearly marked deer trail leading down to the water.

Deer would be too large and powerful for my current traps, but I thought their path might be shared by smaller creatures worth snaring, and so I activated my Trapping ability once more. I carefully constructed another twitch-up snare over the trail, using a strong green sapling branch as my trigger.

Satisfied it was properly situated, I continued upstream until I found a slight dip in the bank where it seemed animals came down to drink. Another prime location for a trap, and so I activated the ability again and got to work.

Selecting a flexible branch, I fashioned a spring-loaded snare designed to nab any animal pausing on the bank by swiftly pinning them against the ground once triggered. After double-checking the positioning, I moved on.

By now, the sun had passed its zenith and the afternoon was waning. As I quickly ate the food I had brought with me, I estimated I had hiked a good two miles west from the cabin. My legs were pleasantly tired, but I was thrilled by the number and variety of traps I'd managed to set on this first foray.

As I turned back eastward, I kept my eyes peeled for any final promising trapping sites along the way where I might deploy another deadfall or snare trap before the day ended.

I passed through a grove of nut trees and thought they might attract squirrels and chipmunks. Kneeling by one of the thick trunks, I dug a pit and placed some nuts from my own lunch inside as bait, disguising the hole with a lattice of twigs and leaves. With luck, curious animals would fall in seeking the nuts. I also took plenty of nuts with me for our larder.

Judging by the sun sinking toward the treetops, I estimated a couple hours of daylight remained. But I was quite far from the cabin now, so I decided not to venture any farther today. Best to start heading back.

As I hiked the winding path back toward home, I felt deeply satisfied by my productive first trapping foray. If some of my snares managed to catch game by morning, it would be nice as it wasn't the best season for either. I looked forward to checking them at dawn.

The final leg of my return trip passed swiftly, lost in thought planning how to improve my trapline network. There were so many opportunities out here if one kept their eyes open.

Time was the bottleneck here. I would have to go around checking my traps. Balancing that with my other homestead duties might not always be easy. Luckily, Diane could help out with that as well. And who knows what kind of summoning solution I could come up with in the future.

By the time the shadowy forest outskirts around our cabin emerged up ahead, the afternoon was drawing to an end. The walk home had been a nice, invigorating affair.

Relaxing with Diane and sharing a delicious meal after my long but satisfying day sounded perfect. But first, I carefully cleaned and stowed my gear back in the mudroom.

Diane would probably still be down fishing in the river, so I had time to quickly wash up at the basin before starting dinner preparations. I was getting handy around the kitchen and looked forward to surprising her with a nice hot meal waiting when she returned.

I got to work cooking, my mind still brimming with thoughts of the untapped hunting grounds I had explored today. There were so many opportunities out here if one kept their eyes open.

Chapter 37

I stood in the kitchen for a few moments, considering my option. I wanted to prepare a special dinner to surprise Diane when she returned from fishing, and I needed it to be something really delicious to celebrate what had happened between us.

I headed to the simple but well-stocked pantry to take stock of our food stores and get inspired about what to cook. Thanks to our growing foraging skills with the aid of my and Diane's powers, as well as obtaining more supplies on recent trips to the lively markets in Gladdenfield, we had accumulated a decent variety of ingredients. I examined the neatly organized shelves in the cellar approvingly.

There were plump wild onions and mushrooms we had foraged earlier, and they seemed to be in very fine shape. I selected some of each, imagining how their savory flavors would combine deliciously once sautéed. In the pantry, there were jars of pungent herbs and spices — a treasure Diane had obtained from traveling elf merchants and had always kept in her pack. Such would add depth and complexity to any dish.

After gathering the ingredients, I carried them over to the rough-hewn wooden counter near the stove. I took my time chopping the vegetables by hand, enjoying the simple, satisfying motions. Doing such small prep tasks always settled my mind before cooking and allowed me some space to go over the day.

The mushrooms were an otherworldly azure shade, while the onions were similar to Earth varieties, with papery reddish outer layers and juicy white interiors once peeled. To be sure, I checked the mushrooms with my Identify Plant skill once more, finding they were edible and known to greatly soothe the stomach when dried and powdered and made into pills.

I diced them fine since they would be going into a hearty mushroom soup to start our meal. Once the colorful array of mushrooms and onions were neatly piled, I turned my attention to preparing the soup base. I poured some of the fresh cream we had traded for at the market into a heavy-bottomed iron pot along with some butter.

I set it over the warm stove flames from our cabin's cast iron stove and allowed the butter to melt slowly, letting it foam and swirl together with the rich cream. Once it was near simmering, I added the finely diced onions and mushrooms to the creamy base. I gently stirred them to coat evenly and allow their moisture to leach into the liquid.

As the vegetable pieces softened, I seasoned them with dried parsley, rosemary, salt, and pepper. I had also traded for a special ground spice blend an elf merchant claimed added an irresistible umami richness to any dish. This frontier soup would be deeply savory, so I added an extra pinch for good measure.

After cooking the mushrooms and onions in the creamy base for several minutes until softened, I gradually added in scoops of our precious hoarded reserve of bone broth from previous stews. The pot bubbled gently as the fragrant liquid incorporated fully. The hearty simmering soup already smelled incredible, the savory aroma filling the cabin and making my mouth water.

For the main course, I wanted something equally special to accompany the soup. I decided to pan-fry some fresh rainbow trout that Diane had caught earlier and dropped off at the cabin, using a light dusting of cornmeal for a crispy crust. Though a simple preparation, it would let the flavor of the freshly caught fish shine.

I carefully seasoned the firm white fillets with salt, black pepper, parsley, and a dash of cayenne for a bit of lively spice. After coating both sides of the fillets evenly in the fine pale cornmeal, I prepared the frying pan by heating some olive oil from my small reserve as well as a knob of creamy butter.

Once hot, I gently laid the crusted trout fillets in the pan. They sizzled pleasantly as they crisped on the underside. The satisfying aroma of the frying fish joined that of the simmering mushroom soup on the stove, filling the cozy cabin with mouthwatering smells that signaled comfort and home.

As the fillets browned, I chopped up some small

colorful bell peppers from our supply of fresh vegetables. Though ordinary Earth vegetables, their bright jewel tones made for an attractive and tasty accompaniment. I added them to the pan to cook briefly until just tender but still crisp.

I scrutinized the fried trout fillets nestled alongside the colorful sautéed peppers. They were as near perfection as I could get them, and they made for an appetizing presentation. I was pretty sure that this – my own version of a frontier dish – was something new to Diane.

To complete the hearty meal, I took out a mix of leafy greens from our foraging trips. I rinsed them at the sink before tearing the leaves into bite-sized pieces and putting them in a simple carved wooden salad bowl. I tossed them with a tangy vinaigrette dressing made by emulsifying water, olive oil, and apple cider vinegar from our pantry together with mustard and honey.

As I put the finishing touches on setting our hand-carved wooden table, I smiled appreciatively over the frontier-inspired spread I had managed to put together. Everything represented our self-sufficient new lives – fish caught from the river by Diane, vegetables foraged or traded for, and wild mushrooms picked from the Wilds.

The trout fillets sizzled invitingly atop the colorful peppers, while tendrils of steam rose in beckoning swirls from the bubbling pot of rich mushroom soup. I knew Diane would likely be returning home hungry after a long day wading in the cold rushing river currents to land prize catches of trout. My goal was to have our cozy dinner ready to serve the very moment she walked through the creaky cabin door.

As a final touch, I straightened up the kitchen until it was orderly and welcoming. Then I placed some vivid wildflowers I had picked on my trek home earlier into a simple carved wooden vase on the table to add a celebratory ambiance.

Soon after, I heard the anticipated footsteps outside, along with the lovely sound of Diane's voice humming a cheerful tune to herself. It was time to sit down and eat together.

Diane stepped inside the cabin, humming a merry tune to herself. She paused as the delicious smells of the meal I had prepared wafted over to greet her.

"Mmm, something sure smells good!" she exclaimed.

She took a deep inhale, her brilliant blue eyes widening as she scanned the interior of our rustic dwelling, her gaze finally settling on the lovingly prepared spread of food arranged on the rough-hewn wooden table.

Two places were set with cutlery and simple carved wooden plates. Those were nothing special but completed the rustic picture. In the center, a wooden vase held a colorful bouquet of vivid yellow and violet wildflowers. Their sweet fragrance added a hint of the great outdoors to our cozy indoor space.

"Only the best for my beautiful girl," I remarked with a grin, laying it on a little too thickly just for fun as I stepped forward and pulled out one of the chairs for Diane with a courtly flourish. "I hope you worked up a hearty appetite today."

"David, you charmer!" Diane laughed musically as she settled gracefully into the proffered seat. Her fluffy tail gave an eager swish behind her that signaled her delight as her ears perked upright. "This looks absolutely incredible."

She leaned forward and inhaled again, her keen fox nose twitching. I could tell she was trying to parse apart the layered aromas emanating from the covered dishes. There was the woodsy, earthy scent of the mushroom soup bubbling away, as well as the tempting smell of the herb-crusted trout fillets sizzling in the pan.

"All this, just for me?" Diane asked, clearly touched by the effort as her ears perked up happily. "You really outdid yourself. What's the special occasion?"

"The occasion is us," I said matter-of-factly as I took my own seat across from hers. "I'm happy here, Diane. With you. So I wanted to do something special." I made sure to hold her gaze intently with mine, so she knew my words held nothing but sincerity.

Diane's cheeks took on an endearing rosy tinge, and she dipped her head, abashed but clearly pleased. "Oh, David," she murmured but shot me a coy smile from under her long lashes. "That's so sweet."

I simply smiled back warmly and gave her hand an affectionate squeeze. "Now come on, let's eat before everything gets cold!"

Diane laughed brightly, the musical sound warming me to my core. "You won't get any arguments from me!" she declared.

With that, we both lifted our spoons in readiness. I had positioned the tureen of steaming mushroom soup closest to us, so we would start with that course first.

As Diane ladled some of the fragrant soup brimming with finely diced mushrooms and onions into her bowl, I caught her discreetly sniffing its woodsy aroma again appreciatively.

I grinned, knowing her foxlike sense of smell meant food aromas were incredibly enticing to her. Finally, we both dipped our spoons into the broth and sampled the soup.

Immediately, Diane's eyes lit up with delight. "Mmm! Oh wow," she exclaimed after swallowing her first spoonful. "David, this is absolutely incredible!"

I smiled, pleased to see her enjoyment as I tasted the soup myself. The flavors were deep and rich, the spices enhancing but not overpowering the fresh tastes of the foraged wild onions and mushrooms. It was perfect. Admittedly, I had *some* skill in cooking – it was just one of the things that was adjacent to survival skills because a good meal helps motivate more than dry hardtack does – but I had indeed outdone myself this time.

We continued to steadily ladle the soup, occasionally breaking off small hunks from the crusty loaf of bread in the basket on the table to dip in the fragrant broth.

The trout fillets arrived piping hot in a the pan straight from the stove, having crisped to perfection. Diane inhaled again appreciatively as I slid the fillets artfully onto our plates alongside the brightly sautéed peppers.

The fish was flaky and moist, my spice rub enhancing its natural delicate flavor. Diane's eyes drifted blissfully shut as she bit into the trout, making happy little sounds of satisfaction as she savored the tender morsels.

"Gotta say, I do love a man who can cook," Diane remarked airily between bites, cracking one sapphire eye open just a sliver to glance at me.

I let out a hearty laugh. "You can show me just how much you love a man who can cook later," I replied smoothly, one eyebrow raised.

Diane just shook her head, chuckling. We continued eating with relish, occasionally engaging in a bit of playful footsie under the table when not preoccupied with our meal. There was a new current of energy humming between us, born of heightened intimacy. Our eyes frequently locked, speaking wordlessly.

The fresh garden salad provided a welcome bright, crisp contrast to the richer dishes. As we gradually neared the end of the meal, I refilled our mugs from a sweating pitcher of sparkling water from the tap. It wasn't luxurious, but regular water could be rich and powerful when paired with a good meal and the right amount of thirst.

Diane drank deeply and then released a contented

sigh. "Simply wonderful, my love. That was incredible. Thank you again for making this special dinner just for us."

I waved away her thanks. "Of course, for you, I'd cook incredible meals every night," I said, then jokingly reconsidered. "Well, maybe not *every* night..."

Diane quirked an amused eyebrow at me. "I was just about to say: be careful making offers like that. I just might take you up on it!" Then she shot me a coy, heated look that made my pulse jump. "I'm more than willing to be on my best behavior if that helps motivate you..."

I leaned back in my chair, folding my arms casually behind my head as I returned her simmering gaze. "Is that a promise?" I asked lightly. "Because I know a few things about how a girl should be on her best behavior."

Diane grinned and swatted my arm playfully. "Oh, you!" But her eyes sparkled with mirth and concealed desire.

We finished up and cleaned up together, laughing and exchanging playful touches. Once everything was cleaned up — no small task, considering how expansive the meal had been — we retired to sit on the rug by the fire, Diane leaning back against me, her fox ears on occasion tickling me, as we watched the playful game of sparks and embers in the fireplace.

The fire crackled merrily, its warmth warding off the evening's chill. Diane rested comfortably against me; her head tucked under my chin. My hand idly stroked her arm as we relaxed together in contented silence.

After a time, curiosity stirred within me. "Diane," I began, "can you tell me more about Tannoris? What was it like there before your world merged with ours?"

Diane tipped her head back to look up at me, her eyes glinting with interest in the firelight. "You want to know about my homeland?"

I nodded. "If it's not too painful. I'd love to learn more about where the foxkin came from."

Diane settled back against me again with a thoughtful hum. "Well, it was very different from Earth in many ways. More… wild, untamed. Dense forests covered much of the land. They had trees like your redwoods, but some grew even larger."

She paused, gazing into the flickering flames as she gathered her thoughts.

"The forests seemed to go on forever," Diane

continued wistfully. "Rolling hills covered in vibrant green, leading up to majestic snow-capped mountains that pierced the sky."

She grinned up at me. "Officially, there were four seasons, but where I lived it was basically either warm or warmer. We didn't get much snow."

I chuckled at that detail. Diane's voice took on a lyrical quality as she described the primeval forests, painted with nostalgic brushstrokes. I could almost see the pristine realm in my mind's eye.

"Food was plentiful for those who knew how to live off the land," Diane explained. "Fish teemed in the rivers, and the woods abounded with game. Berries, tubers, and nuts were there for the taking."

Her lyrical description reminded me of the primeval forests that must have covered great swathes of Earth before humanity's spread. A pristine, Edenic realm.

"It sounds incredible," I remarked when she finished. "A hunter's paradise."

Diane nodded wistfully. "It was. My people were born to roam those forests. We moved with the seasons and with the prey, never staying in one place for long."

I gave her shoulder a comforting squeeze, sensing traces of nostalgia and loss behind her words. "Do you miss it?"

"Sometimes," Diane admitted softly. "The world here now has its own beauty, of course. But Tannoris will always be the homeland of the foxkin."

We lapsed into thoughtful silence, watching the flickering flames. Then Diane shifted to look up at me again, her eyes curious.

"What about you, David? Tell me about Earth as you remember it, before the Upheaval changed everything."

I considered where to begin describing Earth. "Well, for starters, magic didn't exist on our world before the Upheaval," I said with a wry chuckle. "No Classes, no spells or potions. Just ordinary people living ordinary lives in a world ruled by science and technology."

Diane's eyes widened with fascination. The notion of a world without magic was clearly a foreign concept to her.

"We only had things like electricity that powered devices and appliances," I explained. "Cars and trains to get around. Phones to communicate over long distances. Computers to store information."

Diane listened with rapt attention; her ears perked upright. She asked an occasional question to clarify, like how phones could let someone far away hear your voice. Being of the frontier, she had never learned much about technology.

I did my best to describe the concepts in terms she could understand. As we talked, it really hit me how much technology had once dominated day-to-day life. Now, such things no longer functioned out here in the Wilds where the magic disrupted them.

Diane nodded thoughtfully. "I've heard a lot about the technological marvels of humanity," she said.

"In the cities, like New Springfield where I lived before this, they still work. Most of them, at least. Those cities are wondrous in their own way," I explained. "Gleaming towers of steel and glass, packed with thousands of people and businesses."

Yet even as I described the technological marvels, I knew many things had been lost too in pursuit of them. The slower pace, the connection to nature, the tight-knit communities.

"Still, life back then wasn't perfect," I conceded. "It was easier in some ways, with all the machines and tools. But people weren't as hardy. And it was easy to feel alone in a massive city surrounded by strangers."

Diane nodded thoughtfully. "It's hard for me to imagine living packed together with so many others like that." She nuzzled against me. "I prefer a little more space."

I smiled down at her. "So do I."

We sat talking late into the night about our respective worlds, learning about each other. The differences were there, yet bonds of understanding gradually formed as we understood more about each other's culture and origins.

When at last we climbed the creaky ladder to our bed, I marveled at how far our disparate realms had already been merged into one new world. Out here, there was a wilderness the city people knew nothing about. And vice versa. In a way, I was lucky to know both.

But for now, nestled under the blankets with Diane, trading lingering kisses, our own little world was everything I needed.

Chapter 38

Over the next week, Diane and I settled into a comfortable routine tending to the homestead. Each morning, I was up early, summoning a woodland spirit to nurture the crops before heading out to check the traps I had set in the woods.

Sometimes Diane accompanied me on these predawn jaunts, her keen senses helping track any caught animals that had managed to limp away from my snares and traps. Other times, she slept in, then started breakfast while I reset traps and foraged.

The snares were proving quite effective at supplying small game to supplement our larder. Squirrels, rabbits, and quail regularly stumbled into the woven nooses or deadfalls. I had a feeling that – like with foraging – the use of my Class skill somehow increased the yield because the animals were all fat and healthy.

Diane taught me how to field dress and clean my catches properly. We smoked much of the meat, and the furs and feathers could be sold after scraping and stretching them.

While I focused on trapping and crops, Diane's days revolved around fishing. The Silverthread teemed with trout, and her skillful angling meant our storage barrels were steadily filling with the silvery fish.

Some we ate fresh, but much was preserved via smoking over a smoldering alderwood fire in the smokehouse we had jointly constructed. Some we designated for later sale; others went into our larder, which was expanding every day.

Come midday, we always reunited, hungry for the fresh meals Diane prepared from our self-caught ingredients. We traded stories from our mornings apart as we ate, laughing over mishaps or discussing plans. Then we tackled maintenance tasks or small home improvements before finally relaxing together as the long frontier dusk settled in.

Of course, every now and then, we had a little noon rumble. Since this was our land and we were free, we made love wherever we wanted — on the riverbank, on the grassy turf, under the shade of the trees, or anywhere in the cabin. It was honest and delightful, and we came to know each other's bodies as well as our own — better maybe.

One night over dinner, Diane suggested I give my trick to summon a minor water spirit another shot to increase the catch. "One with an aquatic affinity, like you did before, to help herd fish toward my line," she pointed out.

I smiled and nodded. "Sure, we could cheat a little," I agreed.

The next day during fishing, I successfully summoned a minor water spirit who dutifully herded the fish toward Diane's waiting hook. Our catch hauls increased noticeably.

Working together, we also cleared brush from around the cabin to expand the yard space. The physical exertion felt good. I was steadily growing accustomed to the rigors of frontier life and could accomplish far more demanding tasks without tiring now. Diane often joined me shoveling and chopping, her endurance equally impressive.

Our alchemy garden was flourishing under the continual care of woodland spirits. The Magebread flowers, in particular, produced abundantly, their blooms a deep azure. Thinking some of the flowers looked ready, I harvested and dried them. Perhaps I could show them to Waelin.

Nights were spent cooking meals together or relaxing by the crackling fire, often with Diane playing lively folk tunes on her violin. We traded stories from our respective worlds, constantly learning more about each other. The new intimacy between us gave these quiet times a special meaning. I treasured falling asleep holding her.

One afternoon when the summer sun beat down fiercely, I decided it was time to gather firewood. The stack was getting low again, and winter would be here before we knew it. Diane joined me in the woods with an axe of her own.

We took turns felling dead trees and dragging logs back on a makeshift sled. It was tiring but satisfying work. By sunset, we had amassed a sizable pile of firewood that would keep our hearth fed for weeks.

The smokehouse was another thing — it practically ate alderwood. So we harvested that wherever we could. With an eye on retaining sustainability, I summoned earth and woodland sprites to give the saplings a little bit of a boost. We'd be needing wood for the time to come, and I didn't want to clear out the entire forest around the cabin.

Another day, I checked the perimeter fence around our pasture plot, finding a section that had been damaged by a fallen tree branch. Together, Diane and I repaired the broken wooden posts and reinforced that area using spare lumber. Though the work was physically taxing under the hot sun, seeing the solid fence restored gave us pride.

Inside the cabin, Diane pointed out some missing chinking in the log walls that allowed drafts inside. I went to work re-stuffing the gaps with a mix of mud clay to seal out the elements. Meanwhile, Diane fixed squeaky floorboards upstairs using spare nails and her dexterous hands. Our efforts soon had the cozy dwelling snug and weathertight once more.

When not doing repairs or maintenance, Diane and I continued improving our skill with magic and weapons. I practiced manifesting spirits using my summon spells, discovering that they obeyed commands of combat as well, with the fire and storm spirits being particularly useful due to the flames and lightning they could call forth. They could only manifest attacks that worked on touch, but the effect was devastating.

In the meantime, Diane honed her archery using makeshift targets. Becoming self-sufficient out here required vigilance and many diverse skills, both mundane and mystical.

Our evenings were often spent planning projects for the homestead, like ideas for expanding the cabin or constructing an outdoor workshop and alchemy laboratory. Though we currently lacked the money or materials for major additions, we still enjoyed dreaming together. This place was truly home now, and improving it brought great satisfaction. Over time, we would amass the needed materials and shape it more to our desire.

As the full week passed in a blur of hard work and small enjoyments, I reflected on how much my frontier capabilities had grown. Tasks that once exhausted me could now be sustained much longer thanks to the rigorous activity. My trapline network supported a steady stream of smoked meat and hides to eventually sell, while Diane's surplus catches also piled up. And once the alchemy garden reached full harvest, we would have reagents to craft potions for sale or use.

Together with Caldwell, the Frontier Division had given me this chance to transform my aimless city life into one of purpose and meaning. Out here, Diane and I could forge our own future guided by our shared pioneer spirit. Each day brought its challenges yet falling asleep with her in my arms made even the harshest labor worthwhile. I had found my place in this strange, merged world.

The morning of the eighth day since we had established our comfortable work routines, Diane and I decided to take a rare break from chores and walk together to the ridge that afforded an incredible view over the valley. The sunlight filtering through the vivid leaves overhead was radiant, bringing out glints in Diane's dark hair as we strolled hand in hand up the winding path.

At the top, we settled comfortably together in the fragrant grass, simply admiring the breathtaking sweep of untamed frontier lands displayed below us. The Silverthread River wound like a glittering blue ribbon dividing the vista. Our tiny cabin was just visible nestled against its banks. Wisps of comforting chimney smoke promised warmth and rest awaited us there after our leisurely outing.

Diane snuggled closer against me as we sat, her head coming to rest contentedly on my shoulder. I tilted my head to gently kiss her forehead as I idly stroked her arm. Everything about this moment was perfect — the stunning scenery all around, the tender intimacy we shared.

"I'm so happy here with you like this," Diane murmured, nuzzling briefly against me. "I've never felt more at home anywhere."

"Me too," I agreed quietly, tightening my arm around her slender shoulders. "This is where I belong."

We lingered atop the hill for a long time, neither eager for the moment of closeness to end.

"So," Diane began, trailing a finger over my arm — more bronzed and muscular now than it had been at the beginning. "What's the plan for tomorrow?"

"I think we should go to Gladdenfield and sell the pelts, the feathers, and the surplus smoked meat and fish. Also, if Leigh was correct, the elf alchemist, Waelin, should be around."

She perked up and nodded. "That's a great idea. Do you want me to come with you?"

I nodded. "Yeah, a change of scenery will be good for

both of us."

She smiled and sidled closer against me. We could have stayed like that for a long time, but the sun shifting lower across the vivid sky eventually told us it was time to begin the descent back to the cabin. I knew a delicious dinner, warm fire, and cozy bed awaited us there.

Diane took my hand, helping me to my feet before kissing me sweetly. Then together we began the walk home, our hearts light with shared contentment.

Chapter 39

The next morning, Diane and I loaded up the Jeep with the various goods we had produced over the past week to sell in Gladdenfield. There were bundles of smoked trout and game carefully wrapped in cloth, as well as a sack of furs and pelts from the creatures caught in my traps.

All in all, we had two crates of goods. I also brought a

parcel of colorful feathers plucked from the forest birds I had snared. And, of course, to be sure, we also brought our weapons.

In addition, we took two jars of the dried Magebread flowers from our first alchemical garden harvest. Though not a huge haul, it represented our initial foray into potion-crafting ingredients from the homegrown crops. I was eager to see what the elf alchemist Waelin might pay for such reagents, however humble.

With our hard-earned wares loaded up, Diane and I climbed into the Jeep and set off down the winding trail away from the secluded homestead. The morning air was crisp but promised another fair day ahead.

As we bounced over the rugged terrain, Diane hummed cheerfully, her fox tail swishing behind the seat as she took in the passing scenery. I smiled over at her, always buoyed by her sunny spirit.

The ride was lovely. We drove up to the old storm-harried cottonwood and turned onto the road to Gladdenfield Outpost. As always, traffic increased when we drew nearer: there were other homesteaders, traders, and even an adventurer or two returning from some quest.

Soon enough, the fortified walls of Gladdenfield came into view up ahead. The guards nodded in recognition as we rumbled through the open gates into the settlement's main thoroughfare.

The market stalls were already bustling with activity this morning. We would sell most of our stock to Leigh, as she gave us fair prices and served as our main distributor to passing merchants and travelers.

I parked the loaded Jeep in front of Leigh's sprawling shop. As we entered the cluttered space, Leigh looked up from behind the counter and broke into a broad grin.

"Well howdy, you two!" she called brightly. "Y'all got a delivery for me today, huh?" Her eyes roamed appreciatively over the parcels and crates as we laid them out before her.

Equally, *my* eyes roamed appreciatively over the way her tight jeans hugged her blessed hips and the expanse of freckled cleavage left by her shirt, buttons straining to contain her.

Diane caught me looking and giggled. "I'll do the talking since David is preoccupied," she joked. "We have smoked quail, rabbit, and trout. We also have fox and rabbit furs and some colorful feathers from David's traps," she summarized.

Leigh let out an impressed whistle as she looked over all we had brought. "My my, y'all have been busy! This is quite the haul." She picked up a smoked trout fillet and took an exaggerated sniff. "Mmm, smells delicious! This is all a week's work?"

I nodded. "Yep. But we have the Classes for it: Scout and Frontier Summoner. I think we're pretty much geared to doing well in the Wilds."

"You sure are," she hummed. "Well come on, y'all, let's have a looksy!"

We spent the next while going over the pricing together as Leigh thoroughly inspected everything. She seemed particularly excited about the feathers, revealing those were good quality and would fetch a nice price from the town's fletcher.

"And those furs will fetch a fine price from some of those fancy city traders," Leigh declared. "They go crazy for exotic frontier accessories like these!"

I smiled proudly. "Just the beginning, but we were really pleased with the results so far," I replied.

Negotiations came next. I knew Leigh was shrewd, but she wasn't pulling any of her tricks on us. After all, she and Diane were practically family, and by the half-lidded looks she threw me and all the flirting that passed between us, I knew she had the hots for me too. However, she kept herself a little more under control in Diane's presence. I understood that; she wasn't sure what the situation was. But I could tell she was still interested.

As was I.

In the end, Leigh offered us a solid stack of coins for the wares we'd brought in. Currency out here on the frontier had defaulted back to coins of copper, silver, and gold since electronic transactions weren't possible. Paper was used less, but some of the city banks issued them and they were generally warily accepted.

When everything was finalized, I helped Leigh store our merchandise in the back while Diane tidied up at the counter and in the Jeep before giving the inventory list – which was to double as a receipt – a final look.

It felt good transforming our hard work into fair compensation. The frontier life was not easy, but deeply rewarding. And this was our first serious haul – proof that we had what it took to make it out here.

Back up front, Leigh passed Diane an impressive stack of mixed coins along with the payment paperwork. "There ya go, my friends. I'd call that a right profitable haul!"

Diane quickly verified the payment amount against the receipts, then made sure it was securely stowed in her belt pouch. I caught Leigh winking at me, clearly pleased with having brokered another good deal for us.

"Thank you kindly, Leigh," I said sincerely. "We

really appreciate you buying from us."

"Of course! Always happy to help out fellow frontier folk," Leigh replied warmly. "Y'all just bring me whatever you produce from here on out. I'll make sure it sells."

We spent a little while longer chatting with the bubbly blonde shopkeeper about news around town and the progress on our homestead. But eventually Diane reminded me about finding Waelin, so we bid Leigh farewell for now after she told us that the elf alchemist was renting a room upstairs at the Wild Outrider tavern.

Diane and I headed over to the Wild Outrider. We entered the tavern, still quiet for now, and saluted the innkeeper, who grinned at me, recognizing me from my scuffle with Anwick.

"Welcome back," he said, throwing out his arms in a welcoming gesture. "Not here to kick out any of my guests," he joked.

I laughed and shook my head. "Not unless they have it coming."

He nodded, turning a little more serious. "Anwick had it coming. It was about time someone put that man in his place." He leaned forward a little. "My name's Darnassus," he said, "but everyone calls me Darny –

Diane will tell ya."

She grinned and nodded.

"Anyway, you come by this evening and dinner's on the house, huh?" Darny said. "As a thanks for kicking out Anwick. I doubt he'll have as big a mouth as he had before when we see him again at the Wild Outrider."

"Thanks, Darny," I said, inclining my head. "We'll likely take you up on that offer; a little steak or a burger would do me good after eating trout all week."

Diane nodded enthusiastically. "Oh, sounds heavenly."

"By the way," I said, "we're looking for Waelin. Leigh told us he rented a room from you?"

Darny fluttered his lips. "Ugh, that old coot is liable to blow up one of my rooms these days with all his concoctions. But yeah, he's upstairs. Second door on the right. Be sure to knock!"

Chapter 40

Diane and I headed up the creaky wooden steps, and I knocked firmly on the door where Darny had indicated Waelin was staying. After a moment, the door cracked open, revealing a weathered elf with long white hair tied back neatly.

He peered at us over a pair of small spectacles perched on his nose. "Yes? May I help you?" His tone was more resigned than welcoming.

I quickly introduced Diane and myself, explaining my emerging interest in alchemy and learning potion crafting. The elf studied me for a moment, then sighed. "Well, come in then."

The simple room was crammed with books, vials, and other alchemical tools. Waelin gestured for us to sit at a small table with one hand while he cleared a stack of books away with the other. "Now then, what can I do for you two?"

I showed Waelin the two jars of dried Magebread flowers, hopeful for his appreciation of our first alchemical crop. But the elf just shook his head critically.

"No, no, I won't buy those. They are far too brittle. You've dried them out too much. If you use these, you'll get a weak concoction. But you shouldn't dry them anyway. That technique wastes much of the potency! It's dated! Instead, extract the nectar. That is where the potency lies" He went over some pointers on the ideal process for extracting the nectar of the delicate blooms. I made careful mental notes, disappointed but appreciative of the constructive feedback.

When I had absorbed his instructions, I could only conclude that Waelin was indeed knowledgeable when it came to alchemy. I made a friendly attempt to keep the conversation going, but he had completed his instruction, and his answers were reduced to grunts or single words. After a few attempts, he rose.

"I have much to do," he said. "Unless there is anything else, it is time for me to get back to work. You may use the instructions I provided and come see me again when I am in…" he thought for a moment as if he needed to remind himself where he was. "In Gladdenfield… When I am in Gladdenfield again, and we will see how you have fared, hm?"

Small talk was getting me nowhere, so I decided to just state what I wanted.

"Of course," I said. "I was looking for more instructions, to be honest. In addition to Magebread, I also grow Thauma Roots and Wispsilk."

His eyes twinkled for a moment. "Making mana potions, eh?"

I nodded. "But I don't really know where to begin."

"What Class are you two?" he grunted, shooting Diane a look as well.

"She is a Scout, and I am a Frontier Summoner."

"Hmph, well, those are not native alchemy Classes. You'll want to get the Alchemy skill with a skillbook."

I perked an eyebrow. "A skillbook?"

He nodded. "I have one," he said. "You may have it."

I blinked. That was generosity I had not expected. And as it turned out, I expected correctly. There was a catch.

He grinned. "That is if you are willing to perform a task on my behalf first."

I nodded slowly, intrigued by the elf's words. "What sort of task did you have in mind?"

Waelin's eyes glinted as he leaned forward in his creaky wooden chair. "There is a rare flower that only blooms by the light of the moon in a valley to the south. I need several samples for an important potion I am crafting. Retrieve this flower for me, and the skillbook is yours."

I glanced at Diane, seated beside me on a rough-hewn bench. A two-day trip south didn't sound too daunting, especially with her company. And securing an alchemy skillbook would be invaluable in advancing my budding potion-crafting skills. She nodded as if she had guessed my thoughts and hers were no different.

"We'd be happy to retrieve these flowers for you," I

agreed after a moment's consideration.

"Excellent," said Waelin, rising slowly from his seat. He shuffled over to a cluttered bookshelf crammed haphazardly with leatherbound tomes, vials of odd liquids, bundles of dried plants, and other alchemical paraphernalia. After scanning the shelf, he retrieved a particularly old and brittle-looking leather journal.

Waelin returned to the table and gingerly opened the tome, mindful of its fragility. He flipped through the delicate pages covered in elegant but faded handwritten script until he found the entry he sought. Turning the book toward Diane and me, he tapped a detailed ink sketch of a delicate blue flower with elegant curled petals and thin twisting vines.

"This is a Moon Blossom," Waelin explained, one long fingernail tracing the drawing delicately. "They grow only in the southern valley called Azure Dale. A fairly remote but tranquil area, or so I'm told. The flowers bloom exclusively at midnight by the glow of the moon. During that brief fertile window, they possess unique properties I need for brewing. It happens whenever the moon is out, but it lasts only a short while. Half an hour at most."

I studied the static sketch closely, committing the details of the Moon Blossom to memory. Even captured only in ink, the feather-like petals seemed to shimmer as if illuminated from within. The flower appeared similar to certain orchids from Earth, yet I could tell it held otherworldly magic.

"How many samples do you need?" Diane inquired, leaning closer to inspect the journal page curiously, her pert fox ears perked.

"Just a few petals," Waelin replied, passing us a small, waterproofed case. "Ten at least. Preferably more. That amount should be ample for my purposes."

Diane took the case, then glanced at me. "I know the way," she said. "It is indeed a tranquil region. With your Class revealed, we should be able to handle any threats. With fair weather, we should reach Azure Dale within two days' time."

"Good," I said before turning to Waelin again. "We'll leave at first light tomorrow and travel swiftly."

Waelin nodded approvingly, snapping the aged journal shut with care. "Excellent. Then return to me before the week is over. Then, I must depart Gladdenfield to continue my journey. Your payment awaits completion of the task."

His brusque tone made it clear our business was concluded. Diane and I stood from the rickety bench, both energized by the prospect of this excursion. To explore new regions together beyond our homestead's valley was an interesting venture. And the homestead could do without us for a few days, especially if I enriched the soil before we left.

Before leaving, I extended my hand to the stern elf alchemist. "We appreciate the opportunity," I said sincerely, meeting his piercing gaze. "You can count on us to bring those rare Moon Blossoms."

Waelin shook briskly, his palm cool and papery. "See that you do," he replied tersely. With that, he ushered us to the door of the cramped rented room. Diane and I exited out into the creaky upper hallway and descended the tavern stairs, our minds already buzzing with plans and preparations for the journey.

Once outside in Gladdenfield's bustling streets, Diane turned to me, eyes alight. "A wilderness adventure!" she exclaimed eagerly, giving my arm an enthusiastic squeeze.

I smiled, equally thrilled by the prospect of journeying through new and unexplored frontier lands with my favorite partner by my side. "It'll be nice to take a short break from our usual homestead routines for a couple of days. And having you along brings twice the joy and excitement."

Diane smirked, playfully bumping her hip against

mine. "Careful there, charmer. Don't let Leigh hear you say things like that. She's liable to insist on tagging along too if she knew we were venturing afar without her!"

I laughed heartily at the truth of that statement. "Too right, we'd never hear the end of it! Though I'm sure Leigh would find a way to make any expedition more… lively. I actually wouldn't mind her tagging along."

Diane nodded. "Hm-hm," she agreed. "She runs the store alone, though. I doubt she could spare the time."

Our excited talking continued as we made our way through Gladdenfield's bustling streets toward the lively market square. There were many essential supplies and provisions to acquire before embarking on our journey come morning.

At the rows of colorful stalls, Diane and I perused the wares for sale, selecting the most practical and portable items for travel. I purchased a variety of dried fruits and salted meats to supplement our rations, as well as a sturdy waterskin. I also acquired a substantial coil of braided rope, thinking such a useful item could prove invaluable on our trek. Diane picked out a simple dome tent and a bedroll big enough for both of us.

We did not feel the need to acquire additional weapons since we already had my rifle, my handgun,

Diane's hunting bow, and our personal daggers. Once confident we had obtained the necessary basic provisions, Diane and I made our way to Leigh's store. I knew our ever-gregarious friend would want to hear all about this new expedition we were undertaking.

As expected, the moment we entered the door, Leigh perked up from behind the counter, flashing her trademark broad grin. "Well, howdy again!" she called out brightly, her blazing blue eyes drifting over us before she tipped her hat. We greeted her and waited patiently while she finished up with a customer before bustling over.

"What can I do for ya?" Leigh asked, deftly straightening the items on a jumbled shelf while keeping her bright blue gaze fixed on us expectantly.

"Diane and I will be venturing out on an expedition for the next couple of days," I said. "Waelin has requested we retrieve a special flower that only blooms in a remote valley."

Leigh's eyebrows shot up at this, nearly disappearing under the brim of her ever-present cowboy hat. "Ain't that something!" she exclaimed before clutching her chest in dramatic dismay. "And here I'll be, stuck mindin' the shop while y'all are out explorin' and havin' fun without me!"

Diane smiled and moved to give her friend a fierce hug. "I know, I'll miss you too," she reassured the bubbly shopkeeper. "But this is important. David needs to learn more alchemy, and these rare Moon Blossoms could help. Waelin promised an alchemy skillbook as a reward."

Leigh whistled appreciatively. "Fancy reward! Those skillbooks go for a buck or two," she hummed before sighing in resignation. "Well, y'all just be extra careful out there," she admonished, fixing me with a stern maternal look. "And no gallivantin' into hazardous ruins or monster dens, ya hear! You wanna do that, you'd better bring me along." With those last words, she gave her own chest a pat that made her ample bosom bounce in a way that aroused my appetite for the curvaceous, sexy blonde even more.

"We'll be careful!" Diane assured her.

I raised my hands in acquiescence as I nodded at Diane. "Don't worry, I'll make sure we steer clear of unnecessary risks."

Leigh scrutinized me a moment longer before breaking into a grin, apparently satisfied with my sincerity.

"Alright, alright," Leigh acquiesced. "Y'all just hurry on back once you've got them flowers! I expect to hear every detail of what you find out there."

"Deal," I promised. Diane gave her friend one more quick fierce hug before we took our leave, both eager to conclude the remaining preparations for tomorrow's expedition.

There were still supplies to organize and pack, as well as weapons to check over and clean. We'd have to hike to Azure Dale as no roads led there; the Jeep would just get stuck.

Chapter 41

After getting our pack ready for our expedition, Diane and I were determined to first enjoy one last leisurely dinner and round of drinks together at Darny's tavern, the Wild Outrider.

Spying us entering, Darny waved a hearty greeting from behind the crowded bar. "Welcome, welcome!" he called out jovially. "Come on over, first round's on me tonight!"

Diane and I gratefully edged our way through the throng toward the bar where Darny was already lining up two overflowing tankards of frothy ale for us. I fished some coins from my pouch to pay, but the congenial innkeeper waved it off.

"For you, it's on the house," Darny insisted with a wink. "Now what brings you two back here today?"

As we sipped our drinks, I briefly explained about the alchemist's request for rare Moon Blossoms and our impending journey to retrieve them.

Darny's eyes widened with interest as he listened. "Well, isn't that exciting! Y'know, I might just have a map somewhere showing the route to that valley you mentioned. I got it from some adventurers passing through long ago. Let me go check in the back..."

Diane and I exchanged a look, and she gave a playful shrug as her tail swished. She had said she knew the way, but more information was always good.

We leaned eagerly across the bar while waiting for Darny to search through his accumulation of random artifacts, curiosities, and loot gathered over the years running the tavern. After some banging and curses from the back room, he emerged triumphantly waving a dust-coated scroll.

"Here we are!" Darny exclaimed. He unrolled the yellowed parchment atop the bar, anchoring the corners with empty tankards.

Diane and I peered closely at the faded but meticulously inked map detailing the surrounding region, forests, rivers, hills, and valleys for many miles in all directions.

I quickly spotted the Silverthread River winding south from Gladdenfield up to where it passed our own secluded homestead. And sure enough, southwest of town was a valley labeled 'Azure Dale' in ornate flowing script.

Diane traced the route with a delicate finger, ears perked intently. "Nothing new on here. It looks to be about two days," she assessed. "We'll have to move swift and sure to make it there and back before Waelin departs."

I nodded studiously, committing the landscape details to memory as best I could. Any information helping us navigate would prove useful. This map appeared quite old but accurate.

Darny smiled benevolently. "Take that map with you," he instructed. "Wouldn't want you two getting lost out in parts unknown. And do take care — the frontier holds many mysteries and dangers untold."

"We will, and thank you kindly for the map," I replied sincerely, carefully rolling the parchment and stowing it in my pack. Diane also expressed her gratitude for our friend looking out for us.

"Of course, of course!" Darny waved off our thanks. "You two just focus on fetching those flowers and getting back safe. There will be plenty more tales to be told around the fire when you return."

We promised we would be cautious and come back with riveting stories to share. For the next hour, Diane and I lingered at the bar chatting with Darny as he deftly managed pouring drinks and mingling with his patrons.

As we sat, he served us up some good tavern food — he had no steak, but his wife made a damn good burger that I almost attacked. As we ate and drank, the tavern was lively with raucous laughter, rousing conversations, and the occasional bawdy song breaking out.

Being surrounded by the eclectic mix of frontier folks — traders, adventurers, laborers, and homesteaders alike — always made me feel a sense of community. They were good people, hardened by wilderness life but generous towards their own. An isolationist city dweller no more, I now began to consider these people as my own.

But eventually, Diane and I decided it was time to gather our belongings and retire upstairs to the rented room Darny generously provided us. There we could finish any remaining preparations before getting some much-needed rest for tomorrow's early departure.

We expressed our sincere appreciation of Darny's hospitality before we bade him goodnight. "You just be sure to come back and regale me with your adventures!" he called after us with a jovial wave.

Our room was small but cozy, furnished simply with a sturdy bed, nightstand, and stool. Diane and I took turns at the washbasin cleaning the day's dust from the road off our skin while the other neatly laid out clothing and equipment for easy donning come morning.

Soon we were nestled under the thick quilted blankets together. Soon enough, the magnetism between us aroused us both, and we made love under the blankets as the laughter and song still drifted up from the tavern below.

When we were panting and sweaty, Diane curled against me contentedly, already looking forward to the trek ahead. "Just think of the wondrous sights we might see," she mused dreamily.

I smiled and kissed her forehead, sharing her

anticipation for the journey. With Diane snuggled safe in my arms, it was easy to drift off into an untroubled sleep, serenaded by the tavern's muffled convivial din from below.

Tomorrow would bring the open Wilds.

Chapter 42

The next morning, Diane and I awoke before dawn. After a quick breakfast in the tavern's common room and receiving well wishes from Darny, we gathered up our packs, weapons, and supplies. I did one final check to make sure we had everything crucial for the two-day trek to Azure Dale. Rope, camping gear, food rations, first aid kit. All set.

With preparations complete, Diane and I hoisted our laden packs and set off on foot through Gladdenfield's bustling streets. The gates stood open, and the elf guards nodded in greeting as we passed into the wilderness beyond. Leigh had promised to keep an eye out on the Jeep, and we had parked it around the back of her store for safety.

And just like that, we were on the trail!

I took a deep breath, savoring the fresh air as we left behind the hubbub of the settlement. Birds swooped between the towering trees lining the path south, ducking out of sight as we approached. Strange scents mingled on the breeze — earthy mosses, crushed leaves, sweet flowers I had never smelled before. This was true frontier land.

Diane set a brisk pace as if eager to immerse herself in the Wilds. I quickly fell into step beside her, adjusting my pack straps. The open sky promised pleasant weather for our trek to Azure Dale in search of the rare Moon Blossoms.

"Feels good to be off on an adventure together," Diane remarked, her keen eyes continuously scanning our surroundings. I could tell she was in her element out here.

"It really does," I agreed, breathing deep of the fresh

air. "And the company ain't half bad, either."

Diane smiled, giving my arm an affectionate bump with hers. We continued onward, the only sounds being our boots scuffing the dusty path and the melodious chorus of birds heralding daylight. Our breaths emerged as faint wisps in the cool morning air.

The terrain grew increasingly hilly and forested as we hiked southwest. The rising sun cast slanting rays between the towering trunks, illuminating floating motes of pollen. Strange scents mingled on the breeze — earthy mosses, pungent crushed leaves, sweet flowers. Everything here felt more raw, primal, and unspoiled than lands nearer settlements.

We paused periodically to drink from our waterskins and consult the map. By mid-morning, the path forked at a towering oak. One branch led further south while the other continued west.

"This way," Diane said confidently, already setting off along the southern fork without hesitation. I quickly rolled up the map and walked along with her. Though I hadn't thought to question it before, her innate sense of direction out here was enviable. Foxkin were clearly at home navigating these untamed lands.

Around midday, we stopped by a burbling stream to rest and eat a light meal. Using my Foraging skill, I located some wild onions, mushrooms, and edible tubers growing along the bank to supplement our travel rations. Diane added crumbled dried jerky and produced some flavorful herbs from her pack to enhance the simple foods.

Bellies full, we continued our steady southward trek as the sun arced across the sky. The land began gradually sloping upward as we entered increasingly hilly terrain. The mix of pines and deciduous trees thinned, giving way to more open meadows blanketed in swaying grasses and wildflowers.

I paused to pick a vibrant azure blossom, tucking it behind Diane's ear. "Brings out your eyes," I explained with a grin.

Diane laughed musically, touching the flower with a smile. Playful moments like this made the long miles pass swiftly.

As the afternoon waned, we crested a rise affording an incredible view across rolling hills and patchwork meadows leading to the misty foothills beyond. Somewhere within that beckoning vista lay secluded Azure Dale, but it remained hidden for now. We would seek it come dawn.

For the final hours until sunset, Diane and I pushed on at a steady pace across increasingly hilly and rocky terrain. When the vivid oranges and pinks of dusk began painting the sky, we paused to make camp for the night. I was bone weary but deeply content – there was something profoundly satisfying about a long day's hike through the wilderness lands.

We chose a flat area beneath some spreading trees near a babbling stream. Diane gathered tinder and firewood while I erected our small dome tent with the outdoorsman's ease. Soon we had a cozy campsite ready as the valley darkened.

Building a crackling fire lifted our spirits after the arduous day. We cooked up a simple but hearty stew using our rations and the edible plants I had foraged earlier.

As we ate, Diane assured me we need not worry about setting a watch overnight. She was accustomed to camping alone in these parts and knew the land well. Still, I volunteered to tend the fire for a bit longer and join her in the tent a little later so she could get extra rest. Diane smiled gratefully and soon turned in.

The glowing embers swirled upward into the night sky as I sat gazing into the mesmerizing flames. The occasional hoot or rustling from surrounding wildlife reminded me this untamed land belonged as much to Tannoris as Earth. When weariness crept upon me some time later, I joined Diane in the snug confines of the tent. I was asleep almost instantly, lulled by the muffled sounds of the frontier night surrounding our shelter.

The next day we awoke to the cheerful birdsong at dawn. After a quick cold breakfast, we broke camp efficiently and got underway just as pink and orange suffused the eastern sky.

Consulting the map, we had perhaps ten miles yet to cover. The increasingly rocky and uneven terrain slowed our pace somewhat. But the stunning vistas kept our spirits high — sweeping windswept ridges towering above pristine valleys blanketed in wildflowers.

Around midday, we came over a rise and finally beheld Azure Dale stretched out below us. It was aptly named — the narrow valley basin shimmered with myriad vibrant azure pools and ribbon-like streams that reflected the vivid sky overhead. Lusher and more verdant than surrounding regions, it looked almost oasis-like in its tranquil beauty.

We hurried our pace, eager to reach the picturesque valley floor before dusk fell. The sun was already tilting westward as we began our descent from the rocky ridge on a winding trail. I was grateful for Diane's surefooted guidance — more than once her quick reflexes saved me from a nasty fall on the hazardous slopes.

Just as the sun dipped behind the western peaks in a dazzling display of fiery orange and pink, we reached the valley floor. Lush grasses and mossy beds beckoned invitingly. But we still needed to find the ideal spot to safely witness the blooming of the rare Moon Blossoms when midnight came. Our adventure was nearly complete.

I smiled at Diane, cheeks flushed from exertion but eyes bright with exhilaration. She returned my grin, giving my hand a quick squeeze as we headed deeper into Azure Dale. And soon enough, the magical heart of Azure Dale opened up to us.

The silvery light of the moon filtered down through the towering trees as Diane and I hiked along the winding forest path. An air of hushed serenity hung over the darkened woods of Azure Dale. Our boots crunched softly on the leaf-strewn trail as we walked, eyes peeled for any signs of the elusive Moon Blossoms.

According to Waelin's instructions, the rare blue flowers only bloomed at midnight under direct moonlight. We were cutting it close, but I was confident we would make it. The aged map Darny had gifted us proved accurate, matching the terrain perfectly thus far. Diane's keen senses had also kept us on course through the trackless Wilds. There was nothing left to do but actually look for the blossoms now.

Rounding a bend, the shadowy forest opened up suddenly onto a sweeping incandescent meadow. Both Diane and I halted, inhaling sharply at the sight revealed.

Azure Dale lay nestled between soaring cliffs, illuminated by pure silver moonlight. Lush grasses rippled like waves across gently rolling hills. The valley floor was dotted with shimmering ponds that reflected the starry night sky perfectly. We needed no light, for this valley was touched by Tannoris — phosphorescent flowers grew all around, casting gentle light on the forest floor, purplish blue in the hue of night.

It was breathtakingly beautiful.

"I see where it gets the name from," I muttered, unable to pick out any single thing to look at — it was all so beautiful.

Diane, still holding my hand, hummed agreement. She was even prettier in the almost hauntingly beautiful light of the valley. "This is a very… Tannorian place."

I drank in the sight of the colorful flowers in the moonlight, the vast boles of trees reaching skyward behind them. Holding Diane's hand as we marveled at nature's colorful display, we felt like mankind's first awakened children in the forest, speechless and at the same time beyond speech at the beauty of it all.

Wisps of bluish mist clung close to the ground, swirling ethereally around Diane's ankles as we resumed hiking. The rocky cliffs surrounding the secluded vale were tinged aquamarine by the otherworldly moonlight. Strange night birds called mournfully to each other, their cries echoing across the dale.

"It's so beautiful here," Diane breathed as we crested a hill, gazing out across the valley's sweeping splendor. I could only nod silently in agreement, awestruck by Azure Dale's haunting nocturnal allure. This was a place out of time, untouched by civilization.

As we proceeded, I glanced frequently at the position of the moon. Its languid climb told me midnight was fast approaching. Somewhere amidst this rolling landscape, the elusive Moon Blossoms awaited blooming under their ephemeral lunar light.

We began a methodical search for the mystical plants. I used my Foraging skill as we explored, letting its innate attunement to nature guide my steps.

So far, the mystical intuition remained silent. But I trusted persistence would unveil the flowers. Diane kept close at hand, alert for any signs of the rare blooms. I was thankful that Waelin had showed us an image – it would have been impossible to find the slightest trace of the blossoms if he had not.

Strangely, the valley seemed devoid of wildlife. We encountered no grazing animals, heard no nighttime birds. An inexplicable hush lay heavy over the land, broken only occasionally by the rush of wind through the swaying grasses. The rhythmic sound reminded me of restless waves breaking on some far-off shore.

As we trekked deeper, the wispy mists thickened around us. Soon they coalesced into a light magical fog that reduced visibility to just a few yards. I could barely make out Diane's form at my side, though her presence was reassuring. We continued on slowly through the cloaking haze, treading with care on the spongy loam underfoot.

Gradually, the mist began thinning enough that the valley's features re-emerged around us. We had reached a formation of boulders dotted with vibrantly hued night-blooming flowers. Their petals produced an otherworldly azure glow, lighting up the flowers like a sea of scattered stars.

"Could these be the blossoms?" I asked eagerly, breaking the silence. I reached out a hand to gently brush one luminous indigo petal. It felt impossibly smooth, almost frictionless. But on closer inspection, they did not fully resemble the image Waelin had shown us.

I activated my Identify Plants ability, and a pulse of intuition told me these were not the flowers we sought. Instead, they were just flowers — with no other qualities than their beauty. We pressed on, undaunted.

Passing the ridge, we entered a wide hollow carpeted with swaying purple-hued grass. The strange mist had retreated to the valley's outer edges, leaving the air clear. As midnight approached, the moon hovered directly overhead, suffusing the area with amethyst light that seemed amplified, almost liquid in quality.

I felt strangely energized beneath the crisp lunar glow. It invigorated me despite the late hour. Diane walked with renewed vigor as well, her bright eyes scanning intently for any sign of Waelin's elusive Moon Blossoms. The focused energy between us was palpable.

"Over there!" Diane exclaimed abruptly, breaking the charged silence. She pointed toward the far end of the hollow where a dense copse of trees rose, leafy branches stark black against the moon's radiance. Her keen sight had detected something promising.

Together we hurried across the open space separating us from the shadowy grove. Our footsteps were hushed by the thick grass, adding to the vale's aura of intense, watchful tranquility. Approaching the tree line, I spotted the welcome sight of ethereal azure flowers nestled amidst the undergrowth. They appeared similar in shape to Waelin's drawing.

Kneeling to examine the nodding blossoms, I let intuition guide me and activated my Identify Plants skill. As I reached out a hand, one of the closed buds quivered and began slowly unfurling its delicate petals. Within seconds, the flower had opened fully, releasing its otherworldly sapphire glow.

My skill informed me that these blossoms had great restorative properties and could be used to cure several mana-related illnesses, but only when clipped at midnight. It also informed me that our search had come to an end.

"The Moon Blossoms," I whispered reverently.

All around us, more of the mysterious flowers were unfurling in response to the moon's light as it reached its zenith directly overhead. The copse was soon aglow with dozens of radiant blue blossoms. Their ghostly luminescence reflected in Diane's wide, wondering eyes.

Activating my Foraging skill, I selected the healthiest, most vibrant flowers. With utmost care, I snipped just below the head of each plant, collecting intact petals as Waelin had requested. They gave off a sweet, honey-like aroma.

Since there were more, I took several more of the petals, hoping to get as many as we could before the window of opportunity closed again. After all, these were likely valuable.

As we moved amongst the trees, fireflies emerged from the high branches in glittering swarms. Their flickering orange glow accentuated the Moon Blossoms' ethereal azure shine. Awestruck, we watched for a moment as around us the enchanted grove pulsed with hypnotic living light. This moment felt spellbinding, profound.

But then, the vivid radiance began to dim as the blossoms closed up with the moon's descent. Their petals sealed once more into tight buds as the copse's supernatural incandescence rapidly faded away. By the time I had stowed the delicate samples safely in their case, the flowers stood mundane again in darkness, as if they were nothing special.

Diane and I locked eyes, sharing smiles tinged with both elation and sorrow. We had witnessed rare magic this night. But the Moon Blossoms were ephemeral – already their unique floral glow existed just in memory. Yet the wonder of experiencing their blooming would remain with us.

I slipped the case holding our hard-won harvest into my pack as we turned to retrace our steps out of the hollow. As we hiked, I noticed the floating mist dissipated slowly, revealing a stunningly clear night sky strewn with constellations of blazing stars. The heavens glimmered brighter than I had ever witnessed, even far from civilization. It was as if some veil had lifted.

Drawing even with each other, Diane and I walked hand in hand back through the now-quiescent vale. A profound sense of fulfillment left me untroubled by the late hour. Our purpose here was accomplished. The rare blossoms were secured safely for Waelin's alchemy. And we had a few extra if needed.

Tomorrow we would begin the two-day return trek to Gladdenfield. But tonight, we would make camp beside one of Azure Dale's tranquil ponds that shone so perfectly beneath the receding moon. After witnessing such profound beauty, rest would come easily.

I gave Diane's hand a gentle squeeze, wordlessly conveying my joy at experiencing this journey together. Her answering smile held all the radiance of the departed blossoms.

Chapter 43

After a short hike to one of those enchanting ponds of Azure Dale, Diane and I found a nice spot with firm ground and a tranquility that appealed to us both. I glanced around the small forest clearing we had found and nodded.

"This looks like a good spot to settle in for the night," I said. "Beautiful and peaceful."

Diane agreed, setting down her pack with a sigh of relief as she stared at the wisps of mist resting on the pond, colored blue and purple by the phosphorescent flowers behind. "What a night! I've never experienced anything like this."

I smiled, sharing her enthusiasm for discovering new places together. We worked efficiently to set up camp, gathering firewood and rolling out our sleeping rolls. We wouldn't need the tent tonight, judging by the clear sky. And despite the pond, there were no mosquitoes. Within twenty minutes, a cheery fire crackled merrily, warding off the evening's chill.

We ate a simple meal of bread and dried meat, relaxing near the flames. The surrounding forest was quiet save for the occasional hoot of an owl or rustle of leaves. I was tired but content. Diane was yawning.

As I finished eating, I noticed a familiar hovering box at the edge of my vision — my character interface. It must have been there for a while, but I hadn't noticed in Azure Dale's vibrant display. I opened it at once.

I had leveled up!

"Diane!" I said excitedly. "We must have gotten enough experience points from this journey. I just reached level 2!"

Diane's eyes widened. "Oh, how wonderful!" she

exclaimed. "Gaining your first level is always such a special milestone."

I nodded, still astonished. It was thrilling to tangibly see the results of our hard work reflected in my stats.

Some of my skills had leveled up — apparently they didn't do so in between gaining levels but only on advancement. In addition, my interface displayed an alert that I had unlocked three new spells to choose from as a reward for leveling up.

"Let's see here..." I mused, reviewing the options. I could learn Tranquility Aura, which would provide a calming presence to those around me. Or Summon Dancing Lights to call forth a display of wispy lights to confuse, distract, or to simply provide light. But the third spell immediately caught my eye — Summon Domesticant.

Focusing on the option, I learned it would allow me to summon a little house spirit, called a domesticant, that looked like a cute ghost. I could summon only one at a time at this level, but it stuck around for a long time.

I quickly conveyed my choices to Diane, but I already knew in which direction my mind was going. "I think I'll choose Summon Domesticant," I declared. "A little spirit like that could really help around the homestead."

Diane nodded approvingly. "Ooh yes, the domesticant can be very helpful with chores and keeping things tidy. And they're so cute! Plus, they're known to be the best housekeepers!"

That settled it.

I selected the new spell, watching as the notification confirmed my choice. Next, I took stock of my improved stats and abilities:

Name: David Wilson

Class: Frontier Summoner

Level: 2

Health: 30/30

Mana: 15/15

Skills:

Summon Minor Spirit – Level 4 (4 mana)

Summon Domesticant – Level 1 (6 mana)

Identify Plants – Level 3 (1 mana)

Foraging – Level 4 (1 mana)

Trapping – Level 4 (1 mana)

In addition to gaining a new spell, my health and mana had increased. Focusing on the other skills clarified that the abilities were now more potent and lasted longer. That was good; with a little luck, the minor spirits could make our crops grow even faster. And foraging and trapping would yield an even greater bounty!

"Done," I said to Diane, then quickly explained the changes I had noticed.

Diane squeezed my hand. "I'm so proud of how quickly you're progressing. It took me years to get to level 2! You're on your way to becoming a master summoner!"

We talked a while longer as the fire slowly burned down to glowing embers. I described ideas for new ways to use my summoning spells in synergistic ways. Diane listened eagerly, interjecting with her own creative suggestions. It was fun dreaming up new strategies together.

Eventually we climbed into our cozy bedroll, nestling close beneath the blankets for warmth. Tomorrow we would set out early to head back to Gladdenfield. But tonight, I was content falling asleep with my arm around Diane, knowing I was one step closer to unlocking my full potential.

Chapter 44

The next morning, I awoke eager to test out my new Summon Domesticant spell before breaking camp. Diane was still asleep, so I quietly slipped out of our bedroll and walked a short distance away into the woods.

I walked until the glow of our campfire was obscured by thick trees. Finding a small clearing surrounded by leafy underbrush for cover, I planted my feet and concentrated on summoning forth the necessary mana for the spell. I visualized drawing mystical energy up from the earth, feeling it flow into my core like currents of liquid light.

As the power built within me, I extended my open palm and spoke an incantation: "I call upon the realms beyond the veil. Send forth your loyal servant to answer my summons!"

The air before me began to shimmer, before a swirling orb of energy materialized and rapidly expanded. It solidified into the form of a cute ghost-like creature around two feet tall.

The summoned creature looked like a little bedsheet-ghost out of a child's cartoon, with cute, twinkling eyes, and an expressive mouth that appeared as little more than a black opening in its face. Its wispy lower body faded away into mist. The domesticant chirped and blinked at me expectantly, awaiting instructions.

I focused my thoughts, establishing a wordless mental link, and directed the domesticant to gather firewood. It nodded eagerly, then drifted off into the underbrush with surprising speed.

Before long, it emerged carrying an impressive bundle of sticks, the pile comically large compared to its tiny frame. But the stout creature hummed cheerily as it floated over unburdened by the weight.

When the domesticant reached me, I gestured to indicate where I wanted the wood piled. It set to work diligently, stacking the branches neat and orderly. Once finished, it hobbled back and chirped proudly admiring the results of its efforts. The domesticant seemed to take inherent satisfaction from even these simple tasks.

For the next test, I pointed toward the nearby pond just visible through the trees. Via our mental link, I instructed the domesticant to fill my canteen. It grabbed the canteen, bobbed its head in acknowledgment, and whisked off.

Moments later, it returned at surprising speed considering its wispy form, the canteen sloshing. The domesticant proudly presented its accomplished chore to me. The creature was proving extremely obedient and capable.

As I pondered what other tasks to assign my diminutive helper, the scent of frying fish wafted over from camp along with a telltale pop and sizzle. Diane must be awake cooking up some freshly caught trout over the fire for breakfast.

Gesturing for the domesticant to follow, I made my way back through the trees toward the clearing where wisps of smoke marked our campsite. The summon kept pace at my heels, hobbling along contentedly.

When we reached the camp, Diane looked up from tending the skillet and broke into an astonished grin.

"Well, who do we have here!" she exclaimed, setting the cooking aside to come inspect my companion. "Looks like a real domesticant spirit, David! That's amazing!"

The domesticant preened under Diane's admiration, its eyes curving happily as it studied her in turn.

"What an adorable little cutie!" said Diane, bending down to get a closer look.

The domesticant seemed to smile bashfully at that, looking at the ground shyly.

"These helpful house spirits are so wonderful for getting chores done around the homestead," Diane remarked to me.

I agreed, already picturing all the ways a tireless helper like this could aid our self-sufficient frontier life. Expanding the cabin, tending crops, foraging, crafting, repairs — the possibilities were endless. The domesticant could even function as a scout or lookout.

While Diane finished up the hearty breakfast of trout and tubers, I decided to test one more task for my summon. I gestured toward the tent and supplies, sending a mental command for the domesticant to start breaking down camp.

The diligent creature immediately got to work, humming a cheerful tune as it bustled about. Its dexterous hands made short work of tasks that would have taken Diane and me much longer.

The domesticant beamed proudly at having been helpful, rocking back and forth on its heels when finished. I made sure to send feelings of gratitude and praise through our mental link, sensing those emotions pleased the hardworking summon.

They weren't mindless slaves; so much had been affirmed by the deerkin woman in my dreams. Perhaps they could even refuse summons if they really disliked the one doing the summoning.

When it came time to depart, I tasked the domesticant with one final chore – erasing all traces of our campfire. It grabbed a sturdy branch and set to vigorously sweeping away all the ashes and embers, scattering them into the woods. Within minutes, no signs of our overnight camp remained.

Kneeling so I was at eye level with the waiting domesticant, I spoke aloud. "Thank you for all your valuable assistance, friend."

The domesticant smiled happily at the heartfelt

thanks, bobbing its head in acknowledgment as it chirped. Then its form dissolved into swirling mist, returning to its own realm now that its summoning was complete.

I straightened up and turned to Diane with a grin. "Well, I'd say that test run was a great success! This spell is sure to come in handy at the homestead."

Diane nodded enthusiastically. "Absolutely! That helpful little domesticant was so quick and capable. You'll have to summon it often once we're back – so many possibilities!"

The promise of extra help with frontier life, thanks to my emerging powers, lifted my spirits. I gazed around the tranquil grove that had been our campsite, sad to leave beautiful Azure Dale but eager to apply my new skills.

Diane came over and gave my hand an affectionate squeeze. "Come on, let's get moving," she said gently. "We've got a two-day hike ahead back to civilization."

After one final survey to ensure we left no trace, Diane and I hoisted our packs and set off to retrace our steps out of secluded Azure Dale. Consulting the map, I was confident we could reach Gladdenfield by tomorrow night if we maintained a steady pace.

The return trip was noticeably easier due to knowing

what lay ahead. Diane led the way with her innate sense of direction guiding us confidently out of the valley and onto the forested ridge overlooking it. We fell into comfortable conversation, reminiscing fondly about Azure Dale's wonders.

Around midday, we stopped to eat and rest beside a lively stream. I delighted Diane by using a bit of summoning magic to manifest a playful water spirit. It pranced gaily atop the rippling stream, performing a dance like a living liquid sculpture before dissolving away once more. Diane cooed her appreciation at the little trick.

The dense forest soon gave way to more open meadows blanketed in swaying grasses and vibrant wildflowers. Birds with colorful plumage swooped overhead, their calls echoing across the rolling landscape. We occasionally had to consult the map when we came upon obstacles, but Diane's instincts kept us on course.

As the sun sank toward the distant western peaks, we became more attentive of our surroundings, trying to find a safe place to camp for the night. My feet were sore, but it was a dull ache of accomplishment. Each step brought us closer to journey's end and a well-earned rest.

When the stars emerged in full glittering force, we found a suitable site for our camp for the night despite knowing we could have pressed on through the entire night to reach Gladdenfield is we had to. The site was sheltered by an overhanging rock, with plenty of trees growing around to make sure the flickers of any fire wouldn't stand out too much.

While Diane built up the fire, I summoned another helpful domesticant to get our modest camp in order. It scurried about, chirping cheerily as it prepared our simple bedrolls and gathered more firewood. Within minutes, all was in readiness for a peaceful night under the stars.

In the morning, we wasted no time breaking camp and getting underway at first light. As the sun climbed, civilization gradually encroached in the form of wider wagon ruts crisscrossing the once pristine landscape. Birdsong was replaced by the creak of laden carts drawn by beasts of burden.

By midday, Gladdenfield's timber palisade and guard towers came into view, backdropped by verdant forested hills. Diane and I picked up our pace, feet quickening at the prospect of soft beds, hot meals, and friends' smiles awaiting us.

Chapter 45

Diane and I made our way directly to the Wild Outrider tavern upon arriving back in Gladdenfield. We were eager to complete our errand for Waelin and receive the promised alchemy skillbook.

The innkeeper Darny greeted us heartily as we entered. "Welcome back! I can see by those dusty packs you two have ventured far. Come, sit and tell me of your travels."

We thanked him but explained we needed to see Waelin first. Darny nodded in understanding and pointed us toward the elf's rented room upstairs.

I knocked firmly on the aged wooden door, which soon creaked open revealing Waelin's weathered face peering out. He squinted at us over his spectacles. "You've returned. One hopes successfully."

By way of answer, I retrieved the waterproofed case from my pack and presented the delicate Moon Blossom petals within. Of course, it only contained the number we agreed on. The rest was for us. Waelin inspected them closely, then finally grunted in satisfaction.

"Acceptable. You've upheld your end of our bargain." He shuffled over to a trunk and withdrew a leatherbound tome which he handed to me. I eagerly accepted the alchemy skillbook, thrilled to finally acquire this valuable skill.

Waelin waved his hand in dismissal. "I must resume my work. But know you've done me a service, and in turn I've imparted valuable knowledge." With that, he shut the door, signaling our business was concluded.

Not the nicest guy, but at least he wasted nobody's time.

Clutching the priceless tome, I turned excitedly to Diane. "Where to next? I want to start reading this right away, but I think we should go see Leigh first."

Diane smiled, linking her arm through mine. "Let's go share the good news with Leigh before you disappear for days on end studying that book!"

I laughed, allowing her to guide me downstairs and back outside onto Gladdenfield's bustling streets. It was a busy and dusty day, with traders and townsfolk clogging up the streets. Apparently, a big group of elven traders had made their way to Gladdenfield.

The sight of Leigh's cluttered storefront was welcoming after days of wilderness travel. Diane pushed open the door, setting off the merry jangle of bells. Leigh looked up from an inventory ledger and instantly broke into a huge grin, and I had to admit that seeing her cute, freckled face and her big blue eyes made me feel like I was coming home.

"Well, look who it is!" she exclaimed. In a flash, she had bustled out from behind the counter to envelop first Diane then me in fierce hugs.

"We leave y'all alone for a few days and you're already wanderin' halfway across the frontier!" Leigh said, pretending to scold us even as her eyes shone with affection. "You're a bunch of adventurers if ever I saw one."

Diane quickly summarized our journey to Azure Dale and successful retrieval of the rare Moon Blossoms for Waelin. Leigh listened raptly, oohing and ahhing over the tale of ethereal magic we had witnessed blooming under the midnight moon.

I chipped in every now and then with my two cents but was content to let Diane convey the story to her friend and to catch the occasional admiring look from Leigh.

When Diane finished the account, I added, "And along the way, all that experience was enough for me to reach level two!"

Leigh's eyes went round as gold coins. "Level two already? Land sakes, now that's what I call progress! And Diane here was already level two when I met her." She nudged her friend playfully. "This guy's gonna leave us in the dust!"

Diane just smiled, clearly proud of my advancement. I went on to describe unlocking the Summon Domesticant spell and how much the helpful creature had aided us breaking camp.

Leigh listened raptly; chin propped on one hand. "Ain't that something! Those little fellows sure can work. You'll have to bring it by the shop sometime so I can get a look at the cutie… and put it to work."

I laughed. "I will," I promised. "But they like being treated well, so best be nice!"

"Yeah," Diane agreed. "Or it'll spoil your milk!"

I grinned, then fished the alchemy skillbook from my pack and showed it to Leigh. "And this is my reward from Waelin for fetching those Moon Blossoms. It's going to teach me alchemy!"

Leigh let out an impressed whistle, running a hand over the engraved leather cover. "Now that there is a fine prize! Waelin must've been mighty eager to get those petals to give up such a valuable book." She winked conspiratorially. "But I'd say you earned it fair and square."

She then touched her plump lip with a slender finger. "Wonder what he needed them petals for, though… He never came to me for them." She looked at me again. "What're they good for again? Healin' or some such?"

"Yeah," I replied. "Mana-related ailments. I have a few extra of them, and I might try using them to make a concoction myself once I've leveled up my skill a bit."

"Interestin'…"

Diane gave her friend a poke that made the busty blonde yelp, giggle, and swat Diane's finger away. "Don't pry in other people's business!" Diane warned her. "Especially elven alchemists."

"You're right, of course," Leigh agreed. "Still, a girl's curious." She then smiled at me. "So, are ya gettin' started on that book, darlin'?"

I nodded. "I can't wait. It'll really help expand my abilities." Just holding the ancient tome filled me with anticipation.

"Well, you should know: it'll be expended after you read it. I know it don't look like it, but a skillbook is an expendable item. Only one person can learn the skill. That's why they're so valuable."

"That's good to know."

Diane placed her hand on my shoulder. "It should still be for you," she said. "With your Identify Plant and Foraging skills, you'll be a better alchemist than me."

I nodded my thanks at her, and Leigh clapped her hands decisively. "Well, this calls for celebration! You leveled up, got an incredible new spell, and now you'll be an alchemist to boot! We gotta commemorate somehow."

Diane's blue eyes sparkled with enthusiasm. "Oh, Leigh's right! Reaching level two is a big milestone. We should celebrate your accomplishments, David."

I rubbed my neck, but inwardly I was touched and excited by the prospect of celebrating with two of my favorite ladies. "You're both too kind, but if you insist..."

"We sure do!" Leigh confirmed, planting her hands on her denim-clad hips decisively. "Now let's all meet up at the tavern tonight, and we'll have ourselves a real nice time. Dinner's on me!"

Laughing happily together at the cheerful prospect of camaraderie, celebration, and hot food after our wilderness journey, Diane and I thanked Leigh again for the generous dinner invitation.

Diane and I would spend the rest of the day relaxing at the Wild Outrider, hopefully getting Darny to run us a bath. After that, we'd walk around town a little before picking Leigh up from her store.

Chapter 46

After a relaxing day at the Wild Outrider, Diane and I dropped by Leigh's store as she was closing up. Together, the three of us entered the warmly lit interior of the Wild Outrider tavern together, scanning the crowded room until Leigh spotted a nice open table in the back corner.

"There's a good spot," Leigh said, leading the way for

Diane and me to follow. I couldn't help smiling, proud to be out with Diane and Leigh, who were easily the two prettiest women in the whole rustic tavern this evening.

Leigh had changed into an off-the-shoulder blouse for the occasion that showcased her freckled cleavage in a way that was sure to turn heads. The top buttons were undone, hinting at the swells of her full breasts. Her usual cowboy hat was absent, allowing her golden locks to cascade freely over her shoulders. Her hips swayed enticingly as she walked ahead of us to the table, and my mind could not help but explore the avenues of what could happen when I got those hips naked and on me.

Meanwhile, Diane looked enchanting in a simple but figure-flattering summer dress in her favorite shade of sky blue — she had borrowed the garment from Leigh. The fabric clung subtly to her shapely form. She had left her hair down as well, so it framed her delicate features beautifully. The style showcased her pointed fox ears, but it didn't have a hole for her tail, and she did her best to keep it down so as not to offer a flash of her lingerie.

As for myself, I wore my rugged outfit from the trip down to Azure Dale — both girls had assured me that nobody at the Wild Outrider would mind and that I looked hot to boot. Of course, I had cleaned up a little, with Darny offering me a bath and a razor.

We slid into our chairs at the corner table Leigh had scouted out. She had clearly selected it with care. It was positioned perfectly to have a clear view of the tavern's interior while being partially secluded. Shadows danced mesmerizingly on the log walls from the fire crackling merrily in the room's giant stone hearth.

"Don't you two clean up nicely," Leigh remarked approvingly, looking first at Diane, then myself as we got settled. "Gotta say, Diane, that dress makes your figure look real nice. And David, well you just look like a hot cowboy in need of a ride."

I laughed at that and shook my head. "Leigh, you *really* don't mince words around, do you?"

"Leigh minces many things," Diane cooed. She then winked at her friend, smoothing her tail along the billowing fabric of her light dress, stopping it from shooting up. "Anyway, thank you, Leigh," she said. "And might I say you're looking as beautiful as ever this evening."

"Well, ain't you sweet," Leigh said, openly basking in the flattery. It was clear the blonde — who put a lot of work into her appearance — appreciated the compliment. Her full lips curved into an appreciative smile. "Hope you like what you see too, David," she added, giving me a playful side-eyed glance.

I chuckled, taking an inaugural sip of ale from the foaming tankard Darny slammed in front of me. "Ladies, you both look beautiful as always," I said sincerely. "I'm the luckiest guy here tonight."

It was the simple truth. Diane and Leigh made an utterly captivating pair – different as night and day yet both stunning in their own way. Every man in the rustic tavern was likely envious of me for arriving with them.

Leigh gave me a light swat on the arm, grinning. "You charmer." But she looked immensely pleased by the compliment, her cheeks flushing a pretty pink.

We passed a lively hour eating, drinking, and swapping stories. Leigh waved down a barmaid to bring us a platter of cheeses, crusty bread, and smoked meats to share. She also kept our mugs brimming with smoothly poured ale from the pitcher at our table. As we nibbled and drank, Leigh entertained us with humorous tales about troublesome customers she'd dealt with.

"So this fellow rolls up with a wagon absolutely overflowing with pelts to trade," she regaled animatedly. "Fox, beaver, rabbit – you name it. But they were in such a sorry state – mangy, moth-eaten, crawling with lice!" Leigh described trying politely to explain why she couldn't pay top coin for such low-quality wares. "But this guy kept insisting they were pristine luxury furs fit for nobility! He accused me of trying to swindle him! Eventually, I just had to give him five coppers just to get him out of my shop." She fluttered her lips. "And I paid him another five to take those mangy-ass furs with him…"

Diane and I laughed uproariously picturing the scenario. Leigh's imitation of the man's indignant voice was so spot-on I nearly choked on my ale. She was a natural entertainer and seemed utterly in her element, her eyes sparkling as she held court.

When Leigh finally paused in her amusing anecdotes, Diane seamlessly picked up the conversational thread. In her gentle voice that hinted alluringly of far-off lands, she captivated us with a vivid tale of one of her journeys when she was younger and traveled down the Silverthread River, which eventually took her to a blasted, craggy land with many elven ruins.

I listened, enraptured, as she described the secluded and haunting, primal beauty of that rough land, which was home to several clans of — rather unfriendly — goblins. The way Diane spoke painted the fantastical sights into my mind's eye with exquisite clarity.

This was where I recognized the artist in her — the poet and song wright. I could nearly smell the wildflowers growing from the cracks in the sun-blasted rocky soil and hear the mournful calls of mysterious animals echoing down the plains. Leigh seemed spellbound; chin propped on one hand as she hung on Diane's every word.

When Diane had finished recounting the wonders of her journey in meticulous detail, I snapped out of the trance her lyrical words had woven. It was then my turn to regale our table with rousing tales of city life — of the strange things people did when they were living so close to one another.

And I had plenty of stories of weird roommates, power-hungry managers, but also plenty of the friendly and good people just trying to scrape by in the city. Diane's blue eyes went wide at my tales, clearly intrigued by my stories. She peppered me with questions about city life. Leigh, in her turn, was fascinated by tales of how New Springfield and Louisville — both cities where I had resided — had fared since the Upheaval.

Throughout all the tales and conversational detours, the friendship and affection flowing between the three of us felt utterly natural. We played off each other's quips and stories with an easy rapport, keeping the laughs flowing merrily.

I marveled at how both women's engaging personalities perfectly complemented one another. They were so different, but they were good friends, and they had this rhythm — a kind of back-and-forth — that I integrated seamlessly with.

Leigh's bubbly exuberance and naughty humor could make even the sourest soul crack a smile. Meanwhile, Diane's thoughtful manner and lyrical voice perfectly balanced her friend's rambunctiousness.

Together, they made the lively discourse flow effortlessly in an ever-changing rhythm, and I was enjoying it a lot.

As the hour grew later, our plates gradually emptied of food, but none of us felt inclined to end the magical conversation just yet. There was such an easy rapport between us — it seemed a shame to cut short these precious moments of connection.

Leigh, ever the shrewd hostess, picked up on the mood at the table. She insisted we share "just one more" round of laughs together over a final drink. But wisely, she called for steins of dark ale instead of anything stronger to avoid dulling our wits.

The rich, yeasty ale provided the perfect finale to our satisfying meal. As we sipped slowly, I observed the interplay between Leigh and Diane with fascination. Their friendship was so clear in the fond smiles and warm laughter across the tabletop when emphasizing some joke or point. The two were really close.

Yet the energy shifted when either focused their attention back on me, eyes taking on new intensity. It made my pulse quicken inexplicably. I wondered if they perceived the subtle change as well.

At first, this talk about harems had been new to me — a bit hard to believe, maybe. But now, as I witnessed these two beauties together and saw how they interacted, I was beginning to believe that it would be possible for them to have a harmonious relationship with a man — provided that was the right man for them both.

Me.

Maybe it was the drink, but I was starting to understand — starting to believe. And I wanted it too. There was no denying that.

We lingered long over the drinks, speaking in hushed

voices about lighter topics or sitting in comfortable silence simply enjoying one another's presence. Beneath the table, legs occasionally grazed, and knees nudged in a delicate dance that sent my heart racing despite myself.

At the end of our second round of drinks, a mood of cozy intimacy permeated the table, yet edged with tentative anticipation — a subdued crackling just waiting to ignite if given the chance. I sensed that tonight had sparked something new between the three of us. It felt natural, yet fragile and unspoken.

But it was late, and dawn would come early as always. We had already kept poor Leigh from her bed long enough. As much as a part of me yearned to linger in this perfect moment forever, I knew it was time we said our farewells. We would spend another night at the tavern — I had had too much to drink to drive.

As Darny started closing up, we said goodbye to Leigh. She leaned in close to me, pressing her delicious body against mine as she hugged me. She kissed me on my cheek — but only just: the corners of our lips touched. She awakened a feral hunger in me as she pressed those curves against me, and my arousal rose.

She must've felt it because she pushed a shapely thigh against it. It was almost too much teasing, and she pulled back and shot me a smoky look.

"This was fun, David," she said. I could only grunt my agreement as Diane shot us a knowing look before hugging Leigh and wishing her a good night.

We went to our room, and it took a long, long time before Diane and I finally slept — as it turned out, the teasing and romantic tension had affected her just as much...

Chapter 47

The next morning, Diane and I packed up the Jeep and said our goodbyes to Darny and Leigh – she had a bit of a hangover, but that didn't seem to be a detriment to her usual bubbliness – before embarking on the twenty-minute drive back home to our secluded cabin along the Silverthread River.

I steered the rugged vehicle carefully along the

winding dirt road leading out of Gladdenfield, keeping a watchful eye out for jutting rocks or treacherous ruts that could damage the axles or undercarriage. Diane smiled over at me from the passenger seat, clearly happy to be heading home after our eventful journey.

Leaving the settlement behind, we were soon surrounded by wilderness once more. Vividly colored birds darted between the soaring trees lining the trail, while strange animal cries echoed from deep within the forest. I inhaled the earthy frontier air deeply, letting it settle my spirits after the bustle of civilization.

The silvery ribbon of the Silverthread River eventually came into view through the trees up ahead, growing steadily nearer. Before long, the log cabin Diane and I called home emerged, sheltered against the flowing water. We were home.

I pulled the Jeep to a stop beside the house and shifted into park. Diane hopped out, smiling as she turned in a slow circle, taking in the cozy homestead.

"It's good to be back," she said contentedly.

I came around and drew her into my arms in agreement, holding her close.

Together we unloaded our packs and equipment, returning items to their proper places inside the cabin. It already smelled of home — wood smoke, wild herbs, with hints of our frontier life like leather and earth.

Once everything was put away, I headed out to inspect our garden and crops. I was eager to see the progress since we had been away with no woodland spirits to accelerate growth. Diane opted to remain inside and tidy up from our journey.

As I walked, I reveled in the crunch of twigs beneath my boots and the murmur of the nearby river. The valley seemed especially tranquil and beautiful after our days away.

At the garden plot, I saw that the moonlight tater plants looked about the same as when we had left. Clearly, they had continued to grow with the moonlight, but without the woodland spirits, they were not overly large. Still, they seemed to be coming along well at a normal pace.

I made my way over to inspect the rows of magical alchemy plants next. The gnarled Thauma roots were extending creeping tendrils deeper into the fertile soil. The Wispsilk's serrated leaves rustled softly, while more ripe indigo Magebread beckoned.

Using my Identify Plants skill, I verified all the alchemical specimens had nearly reached ideal potency for harvesting. Soon, I could begin extracting reagents and crafting my first restorative potions and elixirs using the new alchemy knowledge from Waelin's gifted tome. The prospects filled me with eager anticipation. Also, studying the tome by the fire, Diane lazing against me, was an image of rustic homeliness that I greatly looked forward to.

My mana reserves were restored after resting in town, so I decided to go ahead and summon some spirits to help out around the homestead. Their specialized skills could aid in harvest and growth.

I focused my will as I had done several times before, drawing on the necessary mana to manifest a woodland spirit. Extending my open palm, I spoke the incantation that now came naturally: "I call upon the realms beyond the veil, send forth your servant of nature to answer my summons." Once the interface popped up, I chose the woodland spirit.

The familiar swirling orb materialized in front of me and swiftly expanded into the spindly, leaf-headed form of the woodland spirit. It hovered patiently, awaiting my instructions. Through our wordless mental link, I directed it to nurture and stimulate the crops, accelerating their growth and preparing them for harvest.

The spirit bowed and floated over the garden, moving its slender wooden fingers over the plants.

Before my eyes, the crops visibly matured and swelled, boosted by its mystical influence.

When the spirit had expended its energies, it vanished in a swirl of light. The garden looked weeks more mature thanks to its efforts. Next, I summoned an earth spirit using the same process but selecting the earth affinity instead. The stout, rock-skinned creature materialized, and I directed it to enrich the earth, invigorating the soil with its mana to better nurture our crops. It did so before returning to its own realm.

Satisfied with the spirits' aid, I headed toward the pasture plot we had cleared and fenced. The area awaited occupants, and I imagined it filled with goats, chickens, maybe even a milk cow or two someday. For now, it was ready and waiting whenever we could afford to acquire livestock.

Near the pasture stood the simple log smokehouse Diane and I had jointly constructed. I pulled open the creaking door, smiling to see the rafters prepared for fresh catches from our traps. Our hard work trapping, fishing, and preserving food was paying off.

After checking on the various homestead infrastructure, I returned to the front step of the cabin and sat down, gazing with satisfaction across our humble but thriving frontier home. In just a short while, so much diligent work had transformed this rustic dwelling into a productive, comfortable home.

We spent the remainder of the day foraging, checking the traps, and tending to the homestead. Finally, the setting sun signaled the day's end as I lingered on the porch, watching vivid colors paint the sky. Crickets and frogs struck up their evening chorus.

All was peaceful. I was filled with profound gratitude for the opportunity to live this fulfilling life.

The cabin door creaked open behind me followed by soft footsteps. Diane joined me on the step, slipping her arm through mine and resting her head on my shoulder contentedly.

"It's so nice to be back home," Diane hummed softly.

I turned my head to smile down at her upturned face, feeling immense fondness. "You took the words right out of my mouth," I replied, stroking her long dark hair.

We sat together without speaking for a time, watching the glittering display of the setting sun as daylight gradually faded. I treasured these quiet shared moments of connection with Diane.

When twilight deepened, I gave Diane's shoulders a squeeze. "Ready to head inside, have a bite to eat, and relax by the fire?"

Diane lifted her head from my shoulder, eyes shining.

"Absolutely," she replied with a smile.

Standing, I drew Diane close, tipped her chin up, and gave her a lingering kiss beneath the darkening sky. Then together, we turned and headed indoors to enjoy a simple but hearty frontier meal side by side in the glowing firelight.

Once inside, Diane and I started to prepare dinner together, enjoying being together as the day drew to its close.

I gathered some of the wild onions and herbs I had foraged today while checking on the traps. As I did so, Diane retrieved spices from the pantry. I smiled, seeing the haul of wild edibles we had gathered ourselves. Foraging was hard but rewarding work.

At the sink, we washed the wild onions, playfully bumping hips as we worked side by side. I stole glances at Diane's profile, admiring her delicate features in the dimming evening light filtering through the cabin windows.

Once the onions were clean, we carried them over to the rough-hewn wooden table. I sliced the onions while

Diane readied the herbs and spices. Her brilliant blue eyes were warm when they met mine.

"This is nice, making a meal together," Diane remarked as she worked.

"It really is," I agreed. "But I would say that even cleaning out latrines would be nice if I did it with you." I leaned in to give her a quick kiss on the cheek as she chuckled at my joke. Diane's resulting smile made my heart swell.

When the onions were prepped, we moved to the stove where I started sautéing them in a skillet with butter and olive oil. Diane added pinches of the dried herbs and spices, filling the kitchen with mouthwatering scents.

Next, I began preparing the grouse I had retrieved from a snare earlier. By now, I knew how to expertly butcher and dress the wild game. It was a fat one, something I believe I owed to my high Trapping skill, and we would both have more than enough tonight. Once prepped, I seared the bird in the skillet as Diane stirred the simmering onions.

Working side by side with Diane like this came naturally, our actions fluidly in sync. Out here, far from distraction, shared purpose guided our days. Each task, no matter how humble, held meaning when done together. It was also a lot more fun than cooking alone had ever been.

Once the hearty frontier-style roast grouse was in the oven, I gave the sizzling onion mixture a final stir while Diane sliced rustic bread. The simple act of preparing food fostered an intimacy unique to our life out here.

Soon we were seated across from each other at the worn table. I smiled appreciatively at the spread of freshly roasted grouse paired with the savory sautéed onions. Though simple, the steaming meal looked utterly appetizing.

Diane met my gaze as we tapped our mugs together in a silent toast before digging in. We ate leisurely, focused only on each other's company. The fire crackled merrily, warding off the evening chill seeping through the log walls.

"Delicious grouse, David, thank you," Diane said sincerely when the meal was finished. She reached across to squeeze my hand. "You're getting to be quite the frontier chef."

I chuckled. "Well, I learned from the best." It was true – Diane had skillfully schooled me in preparing hearty, rustic cuisine with whatever ingredients we had on hand.

Together we cleared away the dishes, moving in easy

unison around the cozy kitchen space. Diane hummed softly as she washed up. I smiled, the homely display of her humming a song as she cleaned up warming my heart.

When the last plate was dried and put away, I stoked the glowing embers in the stone hearth. The fire sprang back to life, bathing the cabin interior in flickering amber light. Diane fetched more split logs to stack near the stove in anticipation of cooler nights ahead.

Soon we were nestled comfortably on the braided rug before the fireplace, side by side. I had one arm draped around Diane; her head snuggled against my shoulder. My other hand held the leatherbound alchemy skillbook given to me by Waelin. It was time to dig into the lore a little more.

Diane peered curiously at the arcane symbols etched on the tome's cover. "What wonders will it teach you?" she mused.

I smiled, equally eager to unlock the book's secrets, and content to do so while my hand ran through her hair or scratched behind her fox ears as she lazed beside me.

We sat in cozy silence, watching the mesmerizing dance of sparks swirling up the chimney. Outside, but muted by the sturdy log walls, the usual night sounds of the wilderness gradually took over from the fading birdsong — the rustling of nocturnal creatures in the underbrush, the distant cries of prowling beasts echoing through the valley.

But within our snug shelter, all was tranquil. Curled against me, Diane soon dozed off, her breathing slow and steady. I smiled down at her sleeping face, so at peace. Careful not to jostle her awake, I cracked open the alchemy book balanced on my knees.

As expected, the pages were densely packed with meticulous text and detailed ink diagrams of exotic plants, mysterious equipment, and step-by-step instructional illustrations. I would need to study it intently to fully unlock its secrets, and that was a job best begun — and finished — before we would have another alchemical harvest. I didn't want to ruin the Magebread again. I let my eyes trace over the elegant script, getting a feel for what knowledge lay in its pages.

Once I had a general sense of the layout of the book and the lessons it would convey to me, I wanted to begin reading in earnest. Of course, I was also a little tired from the long day, but the excitement of discovery kept my eyes open a little longer.

I wanted to delve a little deeper before Diane and I

would retire for the night…

Chapter 48

Settling in comfortably on the braided rug with Diane dozing beside me, I continued my study of the ancient leather-bound alchemy tome. My pulse quickened as I turned past the introductory pages to the first chapter, detailing fundamental alchemical principles.

The elegant but faded script described how skilled alchemy drew upon mystical forces from both Earth and Tannoris. Diagrams showed spheres depicting the two realms, with a nexus between them illustrating their merging during the event we called the Upheaval. This mystical convergence allowed alchemical reactions utilizing ingredients from both worlds.

I read how reagents could be extracted from plants via various methods — pressing, distilling, grinding using a mortar and pestle. Simple potions combined two or three reagents, while complex concoctions required precise steps and exotic components. Effects ranged from restorative draughts to elixirs granting enhanced abilities.

One section covered harvesting reagents during specific seasonal or celestial phases to preserve their innate magic. The book advised paying close heed to lunar cycles when gathering nocturnal blossoms or fungi. Proper timing was crucial.

My eyes widened reading about potent witch hazel and wisp stalk extracts used by master alchemists, seeking to brew transformative philters and libations. But such advanced creations were still far beyond my novice level. I focused on memorizing the fundamental techniques.

After covering extraction processes, the tome delved into assembling an alchemy workshop. Diagrams showed an ideal layout for distilling equipment, supplies storage, and a brewing station. I studied them closely, picturing constructing such a space in our cabin.

A full chapter was devoted to step-by-step potion brewing instructions. I read avidly about preparing bases using purified water or oil. Reagents were then combined in precise amounts, following strict recipes as the concoction was then heated over a flame. Every measurement had to be utterly exact to achieve the desired effect. Too much or too little of any ingredient would spoil the brew.

As I read on about proper brewing procedures, the concepts grew more complex, incorporating astrological timing and invocations in Tannorian to maximize potency. My eyelids were growing heavy, but I pressed on. There was so much to absorb.

A section on crafting potion vials showed sturdy but intricately etched glassware adorned with mystical sigils. These were enchanted to contain and stabilize the magical liquid inside without contamination or degradation. Unfortunately, acquiring such rare vials would not be feasible anytime soon.

For now, simple mason jars or emptied potion bottles would substitute to hold my amateur efforts. Still, gazing over the elegant illustrations, I yearned to one day brew draughts fine enough to store in such ornate alchemical vials. It would signify true mastery of the esoteric art.

One chapter profiled a variety of common potion types like healing tonics, vigor elixirs, mana draughts, and more. My pulse quickened reading the recipe for a minor mana potion. It seemed within reach using reagents from our garden.

I studied the required ingredients – purified water, Wispsilk leaf extract, Magebread nectar, and Thauma Root. Precise measures were provided for each. My mind raced, imagining the immense benefit such restorative draughts would provide by restoring my mystical energies. I would not need to purchase expensive potions.

The mana potion recipe alone was worth the price of Waelin's tome. I could already envision my alchemy worktable adorned with bubbling vials and bottles filled with iridescent tonics and dramatics. A glance at the dark night sky outside the frosted window reminded me it was getting late. But I was lost in the book's pages.

Reluctantly, I decided to stop for the night on the detailed chapter regarding brewing curing salves. My eyes ached from squinting at the cramped scrawling script by firelight. But my mind swirled with newfound alchemical knowledge that would prove invaluable on the frontier.

Carefully closing the aged tome, I set it on a side table within easy reach. I would study it again at the earliest opportunity. For now, warm drowsiness was settling over me as I leaned back comfortably and gazed into the fading fire.

Soft breaths still came from Diane curled beside me in tranquil slumber. Gently, I caressed her shoulder, whispering her name to rouse her just enough so we could head to bed together. She stirred and blinked up at me groggily, then smiled.

"Finished reading?" she asked through a yawn as she slowly sat up, silken hair adorably mussed.

I nodded, unable to stifle a yawn of my own. Diane's nearness made the notion of retiring to our cozy shared bed highly appealing.

"For tonight," I said. "But there's so much more to study. We'll have to start planning that alchemy workshop soon."

Diane hummed her agreement, fox ears twitching slightly as she woke up fully. I decided I would sketch some initial workshop designs on the morrow.

Banking the glowing embers safely, I rose and helped Diane gently to her feet. After I splashed my face with cool water from the basin in the kitchen, we climbed the creaky loft ladder together, readying ourselves for sleep.

Diane changed into an oversized linen shirt that made her look cute as she stood there rubbing her eyes and yawning. Soon we slipped beneath the quilted blankets.

I lay on my back, gazing up at the shadowy rafters overhead as Diane nestled close. Her arm draped lightly over my chest in a loose embrace. I already missed the flickering firelight but knew I would be asleep soon.

"You'll be crafting incredible potions in no time," Diane murmured encouragingly, her eyes shining even in the darkness.

I smiled at her confidence in me. With diligent study and practice, I hoped to justify it.

"I can't wait to get started," I replied through another yawn, the lateness of the hour finally catching up with me. "But for now, sleep calls."

Diane uttered a sleepy "Mm-hmm" of agreement, nuzzling even closer. Soon I sensed her breathing grow slow and even once more.

As weariness seeped into my limbs, I let my heavy

eyelids drift shut. Visions of bubbling brews and mystical sigils danced in my slumbering mind. Tomorrow I would study the ancient text again and make more plans. But for now, I was content to hold Diane close and let restful sleep take me under.

Morning would come soon enough, bringing another productive day of hard-earned achievement. But on this night, limbs pleasantly weary from a long day's work, it was enough simply to sleep peacefully with my beloved by my side.

Chapter 49

Over the next week, Diane and I came back to our comfortable routine caring for the homestead. I was up early most mornings, using my abilities to summon spirits that could aid with the crops and garden.

Meanwhile, Diane focused on fishing and foraging, making sure we kept our larder full and would have plenty of goods for trade. Whenever we had work around the house – like hauling stockpiled supplies, cleaning, and making the beds – I summoned the domesticant, who chirped happily as it did its work.

My snares were supplying rabbits, grouse, and quail to vary our diet. Diane and I properly cleaned them together. What we didn't eat fresh, we smoked to preserve over the alderwood fire in the smokehouse. Thanks to Diane's keen eyes and reflexes and my ingenious traps, we were building up quite the stockpile for our second trade run into town.

Around midday, we'd reunite for the meals Diane prepared from our self-caught ingredients. We talked and laughed as we ate, discussing plans or sharing what we had done so far. I reveled in these homely moments together; she and I were forming a family together, becoming closer and closer in both the ways of the body and those of the mind.

In the evenings, I studied the alchemy book by firelight, absorbing its intricate details on potion brewing while Diane relaxed nearby playing tunes on her violin, singing, and writing new songs about the things we had experienced. She was fascinated watching me study the ancient tome. Gradually, I gained understanding of using alchemical tools and preparing reagents.

One night, I showed Diane a diagram of an ideal alchemist's laboratory. "We could build something like this near the cabin," I suggested. "It would give me a dedicated brewing space."

Diane's eyes lit up. "Let's start gathering supplies," she urged enthusiastically.

And so, we began collecting materials on the side, using whatever spare time we had to get lumber, stone, clay, and other building supplies we would need for the future laboratory. I was already imagining the possibilities. It would start out humble — as all things on the frontier — but I would be able to build it up and expand it over time, using the proceeds from our homestead to acquire more complicated equipment.

Within a week, I neared the end of the dense book. Its teachings were finally unlocking this intricate skill. As I turned the pages, Diane nestled contentedly beside me. The final section covered using runes and sigils to focus energies. Turning the last page, I felt a pulse of energy.

A notification appeared: 'Alchemy Skill Unlocked!'

I'd done it — the knowledge was now mine!

Seconds later, the book vanished as Leigh had warned. But its teachings would stay with me, many of them now innately available through my new Alchemy skill, which a quick check-up on my character sheet revealed was at level 1.

I explained to an elated Diane what had happened. "You'll be an amazing alchemist in no time," she exclaimed, embracing me. I would justify her confidence through practice. We talked late into the night about my plans for the workshop and first brewing attempts.

The next morning, I checked the garden eagerly. The moonlight taters were nearly ready for harvest. But I was most excited about the alchemy crops. Thanks to the spirits' aid, they had reached maturity.

Activating my Identify Plant skill, I inspected each plant, assessing their potency. The gnarled Thauma Roots pulsed with concentrated mana. The Wispsilk leaves shimmered with dew. And the Magebread flowers beckoned, fragrant and heavy with petals. Now I could begin extracting the reagents.

Using a small knife, I carefully harvested leaves, petals, and root sections, collecting the valuable ingredients into glass jars. My skill guided me in selecting the choicest portions from each plant without destroying them — that way, they could regrow. Soon I had a promising stockpile of components.

Inside, I proudly showed Diane the reagent jars. She sniffed each curiously. "I can't wait to see your potions!" she said. Her confidence inspired me to start brewing with the harvested ingredients.

But first, we wanted to celebrate. At breakfast, Diane surprised me by breaking out precious hoarded honeycomb. Drizzled on our food, it was an indulgent treat.

"Where did you get this?" I asked through delicious mouthfuls.

Diane just smiled. "I found it out during one of my solitary jaunts." She laughed at the memory. "Let me tell you, the bees were not eager to part with it. I never ran so fast in my entire life! I was saving it for your breakthrough."

"That's so sweet of you, Diane," I said, moved by the gesture of her going through all this trouble just to add a little special something to the celebration.

We tapped mugs, giddy over the special breakfast and what it signified. My career as an alchemist — albeit a novice one — had officially begun.

Over the next days, between chores, I began gathering more materials and planning the layout for my alchemy workshop, using the book's diagrams as a guide. I wanted to have everything ready to begin constructing soon. Diane was eager to help however she could.

Of course, producing viable potions would take much study and practice. But holding the leatherbound book's teachings in my mind, I felt confident mastery would come in time. Perhaps I'd botch a few batches, but no one ever learned anything by shying away from making a mistake or two. Diane was endlessly supportive, reassuring me experience would bring results.

In the evenings, we would relax together comfortably by the fire as before. Though the tome itself was gone, our time together remained a ritual. Diane would work on mending clothing or carving useful household items from wood during these quiet moments. Sometimes, I'd summon the domesticant to have it help her out around the house, or we'd just laugh together at the cute little ghost-like creature's antics.

Other nights, if the weather was fair, we would enjoy a moonlit stroll around the homestead grounds or sit gazing up at the dazzling night sky snuggled close beneath a blanket.

Our days fell into a steady comforting rhythm — hard work, simple meals, good conversation. And in between, stolen moments alone together as our passion kindled. We were truly partners now in all aspects of life.

Chapter 50

During those days of rewarding labor spend with Diane, I devoted all the spare time I could get between working on the homestead to planning and designing the layout for my alchemy laboratory. This dedicated space would allow me to properly practice the potion crafting techniques from Waelin's tome.

I carefully reviewed the diagrams and instructions in

the book, making sure I understood the ideal placement and purpose of the various apparatus – the brewing station, ingredient shelves, distilling equipment, etc. Proper workspace configuration was crucial for efficiency and safety when working with volatile reagents.

Using scraps of parchment and a bit of charcoal, I sketched some basic drafts showing potential arrangements within our cabin space. Diane would occasionally peek over my shoulder, offering suggestions about light sources or equipment access.

Her input was quite helpful, but we soon decided the laboratory would have to be outside the walls of the cabin. It would be safer if something went wrong.

"Plus, it might smell," Diane remarked, wrinkling her cute nose.

I had laughed and agreed. Better to build a little shack for the workshop, close to the bank of the river.

Once I had a rough layout in mind, I was ready to start gathering materials and tools. First I took stock of usable items already on hand, like tables, shelves and jars that I could use. The domesticant happily helped me inventory supplies, working hard and fast while chirping happily.

Next I ventured outside to locate suitable stones and

lumber to construct new furniture and surfaces. The domesticant dutifully stacked larger rocks into tidy piles as I chopped firewood and sawed planks using my woodcutting skills.

Over the following days, the domesticant and I slowly transported the accumulated building supplies to an empty area near the cabin where the lab would take shape as a separate outbuilding. Diane helped tidy up and make space as I hauled in materials. Picturing the finished laboratory kept me motivated.

Late one evening by firelight, I finalized my detailed sketch of the ideal laboratory layout. The design featured angled workbenches, ingredient shelves arranged by type, and space for a dwarven-made copper distiller I hoped to someday acquire.

Diane listened attentively as I described my vision for the workshop. "It sounds perfect!" she said. "I know you'll brew wondrous potions there. And I can assist you."

I gave a satisfied nod. "Yeah. And the domesticant will be useful as well as a kind of lab assistant."

The next morning, I was eager to commence construction on the new outbuilding. While Diane worked outside, I began measuring and marking off the space near the river for the lab's footprint. The domesticant stood by, observing the process with curiosity.

When the boundaries were delineated, I retrieved my saw and got to work cutting boards and wooden beams to size. The repetitive motions were soothing, putting me in a productive mindset.

Sawdust soon coated my clothes and the ground. As I worked, the Domesticant — with the aid of an earth spirit I summoned — got to work clearing and leveling the ground for my construction project.

I couldn't help but feel a little wondrous as I worked hard, with my magical minions scuttling about me to put in their own hard work. Having them around would save me days of labor, and I was excited to see how skilled they actually were: the earth spirit did most of the leveling through its control of the soil, while the domesticant cleared the ground, chirping as if it couldn't be happier.

By the day's end, I had finished sawing lumber for the walls and the furniture. My shoulders ached, but I was satisfied with the tangible progress. The domesticant dutifully swept up the mess when I finished cutting boards — it was tireless. The ground was also sufficiently leveled and cleared.

Over the following days, I focused on starting

construction of the outbuilding that would become my alchemy workshop. I began by preparing the foundation, digging trenches and filling them with stones. The domesticant assisted by fetching rocks and dumping them into the trenches as I leveled them.

After that, I slowly assembled the framework for the alchemy lab's structure, starting with rough beams of sturdy wood driven into the ground to form the frames of the timber walls. Focusing intently on the build was meditative. Each night I reviewed my plans, modifying details as needed. Diane helped position pieces as I affixed joints.

Once the frames for the walls were laid down, I began assembling the log walls using my woodcutting skills. Felling and hauling additional logs was hard work, but the structure soon began taking shape. Diane and the domesticant helped lift beams as I hoisted them into position and locked them into place.

After the walls were up, I installed the roof beams and shingled the pitched roof to create an enclosed shelter. The shingles were made of wood, but the earth spirit had assisted in making a coating of clay that would protect them and waterproof them. The domesticant swept up debris and fetched tools as I focused on carpentry. Seeing the building take shape with each passing day was deeply fulfilling.

When the basic structure was complete, I installed a rough wooden door I had built and cut out windows to let in light and fresh air.

Inside, I got to work laying the stone floor using shale hauled from the nearby river. The domesticant did the lifting while I positioned and leveled each piece. Mortar made by the earth spirit helped each flag fit snugly. Soon we had transformed the interior from bare earth into a solid surface.

Using clay, straw, and wooden planks, I then constructed the walls for a dedicated reagents pantry accessible from the laboratory. The little add-on storage room – almost like a walk-in closet – would help organize ingredients and projects.

Next, I began assembling the framework for the alchemy lab components – a sturdy workbench, storage shelves, and apparatus stands. I focused methodically on measuring, sawing lumber, and assembling components. The space gradually assumed its intended purpose.

In the evenings by the fire, I mixed clay, sand, and straw to create insulation and chinking material for the walls, occasionally summoning my earth spirit for help to get the measurements right. Though rudimentary, it would help control temperature and seal out drafts.

Diane contributed by kneading clay and forming it into chinking bricks. These were fun nights, even though we got ourselves — and the cabin — very dirty. Luckily, the domesticant was always there and always cheerful, happy to help us clean the place up after another clay-filled night.

It was amazing to me how much could be achieved with just the materials available in nature. I had made shelters in the wild before, and I had been an avid treehouse-builder when I was still a kid, but some of that knowledge had drifted to the background until housing became something that had to be done with machinery. And yes, machinery speeds the job up — it's a great tool.

But it's not impossible to manage without it, contrary to what many believe.

Over several exhausting but gratifying days, I filled gaps between the timber walls using the clay mixture. The domesticant brought buckets of materials as needed, its wispy form unaffected by the weight. Soon the shelter was insulated and weathertight.

I installed a stone hearth against one wall and extended the chimney up through the roof. It would vent fumes from brewing operations and provide warmth during winter months. Diane helped me mortar the chimney stones into place.

When the hearth was complete, I began adding finishing touches to increase functionality. Sturdy wooden shutters carved for the windows helped control light and airflow into the workspace. I used some spare hinges we found in the cabin. The domesticant swept up sawdust and tidied as I sawed and sanded.

Next, I built the dedicated reagents pantry accessible through a doorway off the main workshop. Shelves lined the walls to neatly organize ingredients and materials.

At last, the humble but serviceable outbuilding was ready for its intended purpose. Though initially sparse, my new alchemy workshop would shelter me from the elements and allow room to grow my budding skills.

After all our shared labor, the finished structure stood as a demonstration of the progress Diane and I achieved together on the frontier.

Chapter 51

After completing my new alchemy workshop, I was eager to begin using the space to process ingredients from my earlier harvests and attempt brewing my first potion.

I carried the jars containing my earlier harvested ingredients into the new workshop — gnarled Thauma roots with their faintly glowing flesh, Magebread petals so vibrantly azure they almost seemed to glow, and Wispsilk leaves that pulsated with power.

Along with my – admittedly – limited tools, I set everything out neatly atop the wooden worktable I had built along one wall beneath a shuttered window that let in ample daylight.

I began by selecting several Thauma root tubers from the jar and trimming away the knobby ends using a small sharp knife. As I did so, I took care to activate my Alchemy power and follow the instructions I had memorized from the skillbook as well as the ones that – through the absorption of the skillbook's content – had become part of my intuitive knowledge.

The knife was simple but perfect for delicate alchemical tasks. I sliced each trimmed root horizontally into thin discs, sectioning them to expose the supple inner flesh. This central part of the Thauma root contained the concentrated magical essence which appeared as a faint luminescence when revealed.

I decided first to try bruising some of the sliced roots using a mortar and pestle. The mortar was crafted from a heavy, dense black stone with a rough-hewn texture to aid in grinding. I placed a few thin slices of the Thauma root into its bowl-like cavity, then began rhythmically grinding them into a pulp using the blunt stone pestle. I started slowly, coaxing out their innate magic.

Soon a thick, viscous glowing paste had formed in the mortar. By pulverizing the cellulose fibers of the root vegetable, I had released its inner radiance while keeping the mystical energy potently concentrated within the extracted paste. Using a small funnel, I carefully decanted the crushed root pulp into one of several mason jars I had set out, stoppering it securely.

After cleaning the stone tools for reuse, I turned my focus next to the Magebread. Their delicate azure petals glimmered iridescently in the mottled sunlight streaming through my workshop's windows. Using wooden tweezers so as not to damage the fragile blooms, I selected one flower and gingerly plucked free the minute black seed flecks concentrated at its center where petals joined the stem.

These seeds I could use to plant some more Magebread if so required. I sprinkled a pinch of the tiny seeds into a ceramic bowl for later processing.

Next, I employed a thin stirring rod to gently coax nectar from the Magebread tender inner petals where they naturally secreted a sweet, shimmering syrup. I took utmost care extracting the precious viscous fluid, transferring each accumulated droplet into a separate jar using the rod.

This process required immense focus and a delicate touch to harvest the minute amounts of glistening nectar contained within each flower. But gradually I collected enough to produce my first potion – or so I had measured. Its inherent mystical properties would lend potency when added as a reagent.

Next, I turned to the Wispsilk leaves. Holding one of the serrated leaves up to the window, its translucent surface shimmered beautifully in the sunlight. Placing several on my worktable, I used the stone mortar and pestle again, this time gently grinding the Wispsilk into a fine jade-hued powder.

The powder retained the faint translucency of the leaves, and I funneled this as well into a capped jar for safe storage. The crushed Wispsilk would help bind the disparate elements of a brew together.

Surveying the three jars of processed ingredients I had extracted and prepared – luminescent Thauma paste, gleaming Magebread nectar, and crushed magical Wispsilk powder – I felt deeply satisfied.

From an untrained amateur, I was taking my first toddler steps to become an adept alchemist through study and practice. These harvested elements from our garden were the first fruits of my labor. Soon I would combine them into viable potions.

But before attempting an initial brewing, I first devoted great care to purifying my instruments and workspace. Using boiled water, I thoroughly cleaned the small iron cauldron — a spare from the kitchen that we didn't use — and all the assorted jars, funnels, tongs, stirring rods, and other tools to be employed.

Handling reagents called for immaculate equipment to avoid contamination. I also wiped down the wooden tabletop and stone hearth until they were spotless.

With preparations complete, I was ready to begin my inaugural attempt at brewing a minor mana potion. Transferring the cleaned cauldron to the hot coals lining my workshop's stone hearth, I filled it with fresh cool stream water that I first ran through a fine linen cloth. Purity of the base liquid was vital.

As the cauldron gradually heated, I prepared the precious harvested ingredients according to the memorized recipe. Carefully tilting the vial, I allowed the exact amount the glowing Thauma root paste to fall into the now-steaming water. The viscous stuff swirled hypnotically before dispersing through the clear liquid.

Next, I added the concentrated Magebread nectar. I employed the stirring rod to control the minute measure precisely, drop by drop. The nectar suffused the brew with flecks of molten gold as it blended with the steaming water.

Finally, I added the powdered Wispsilk leaves from their jar, watching the fine jade-hued flakes settle onto the base liquid's surface before absorbing into the concoction. This binding element would harmonize and stabilize the combined reagents' disparate mystical energies.

As I attended the cauldron, lightly stirring its contents using a rod, I watched my first concoction with fascination. Gradually, the clear liquid within the gently bubbling cauldron shifted to a pearlescent lavender as the elements came into mystical harmony. Delicate azure wisps arose, twirling serenely before dissolving in the air. Though still in its preliminary state, the liquid undeniably thrummed with gathering magical force.

My pulse quickened — the concoction was coming together!

As a side effect of the alchemical process, most of the water steamed away at great speed until a veritable mist hung over the cauldron. I needed to step away for a moment, and when the mist had settled, the cauldron contained only a little bit of liquid. Before my eyes, the liquid settled into a pale, opalescent silver-blue, signifying the proper mystical fusion and stability.

It was now time for the next step.

I lifted the cauldron using sturdy iron tongs and transferred it to a rack to cool off. It took only a little while before it was ready to be taken from the cauldron, and I poured the concoction into a mason jar.

For all these processes, glass would have been superior as it stood less chance of contaminating the concoction, but we simply didn't have such supplies yet, and according to my newfound knowledge, using the mason jar was still better than letting the brew stabilize in the iron pot.

Finally, the culminating step — decanting the stabilized potion into a delicate vial. So far, we had only one vial — a delicate glass thing that had contained spices. I had cleaned it thoroughly. It needed to be glass, or else the potion would diminish in hours.

As I tilted and poured the viscous liquid, it glowed serenely with azure radiance, reacting to the glass. Securely stoppering the vial sealed its magic in stable suspension.

I had successfully produced my very first potion!

Holding the fragile vial up, I gazed in awe at the mesmerizing bluish liquid, scarcely believing I had crafted it with my own hands. Though merely a minor restorative mana draught, it marked a momentous step forward in my mastery of alchemy. Much remained to be learned, but I had proven to myself that success was possible. I resolved to continue improving through steadfast dedication to my craft.

Making careful notes on the entire brewing process in my journal, I documented each step and observation for later study, knowing consistent replication would be key. But then, it was time to share my success!

Eager to test my very first brew, I stowed the glass vial in my coat pocket and carried my journal outside to share this triumph with Diane.

Chapter 52

I hurried outside into the valley's golden late afternoon light, searching for Diane. I soon spied her down by the garden plot, pulling up plump moonlight potatoes into her basket.

"Diane!" I called excitedly as I approached, causing her fox ears to perk up. "You'll never believe what I've managed to brew up!"

Diane set down her basket, brushing the soil off her hands as she turned to me with an intrigued smile. "By the look on your face, I'm guessing it must be something momentous!" she replied.

I nodded eagerly, pulling the delicate glass vial from my pocket with utmost care. "Look – my very first attempt at crafting a mana potion!" I declared proudly. The opalescent silver-blue liquid swirled gently inside the fragile vial.

Diane's brilliant blue eyes went wide. "Your first potion!" she exclaimed. "Why, that's incredible!" She leaned in for a closer inspection of the glowing elixir. "I can feel the magical energy radiating from it already. You've done it!"

I grinned broadly. "It wasn't easy, but all that studying finally paid off. I wanted you to be the first to witness the fruits of my labor." Diane's unwavering faith had helped motivate me through the many long hours of effort.

"Please, you simply must try it right away," Diane urged, fairly quivering with excitement. "We have to see if it works to restore your mystical energies as intended!"

I nodded in agreement, thrilled by her enthusiasm. "Alright, let's give it a test run." I glanced at my character interface, noting my current mana reserves were at 2 after casting several spells and using several skills today. Then, with utmost care, I removed the stopper from the vial. A wisp of sweetly scented vapor emerged as I raised the open vial to my lips.

Tilting my head back, I drank the potion in one go, swallowing every precious droplet. The delicate floral flavor tingled pleasantly on my tongue. A few seconds later, I felt renewed currents of arcane energy flowing into my mystical core as the potion took effect.

Opening my eyes, I checked my interface — my mana reserves had increased by the expected amount! I was now back at 12, which meant the potion had restored 10 mana! It was a success!

I whooped and pumped my fist exuberantly. "It works! I can't believe I actually did it!" I swept a thrilled Diane up in my arms and spun her around joyously. She giggled musically, sharing my elation.

"I knew you could do it!" Diane exclaimed. "And on your very first try, no less! Why, you're a natural alchemist, my love." Her pride and excitement for me shone in her sparkling sapphire eyes. I set her down reluctantly, still smiling from ear to ear.

"That was just a start — I still have much to learn," I replied modestly, though inwardly I was immensely pleased by her glowing praise. "But at least now I know it's possible to progress in the art." With study and care, I might one day craft truly miraculous elixirs.

Diane gave my hands an encouraging squeeze. "Even starting small is an impressive accomplishment. Just think of the wonders you'll brew once you gain more experience!" I loved how she envisioned only success in my future endeavors. Her optimism lifted my confidence.

We walked together back toward the cabin as the valley slowly sank into dusk. Our fingers remained loosely entwined, the comfortable silence broken only by a few chirping crickets. Above, the first faint stars winked into view through purple gossamer clouds.

Back inside, I carefully stowed the now empty glass vial on a high shelf. Though I itched to begin my next brew, I knew patience and diligence were key. Each step built gradually towards mastery.

While I tidied my workspace, Diane prepared a simple but hearty stew from our recent bounty. Soon, we were seated across from one another at the worn wooden table as we had so many times before. But tonight, an air of celebration hung over the cozy scene. We tapped our mugs together in a wordless toast before digging in.

"To many more triumphs to come," Diane said earnestly, catching my eye over the table. I smiled in thanks, my mind spinning with the possible avenues to explore.

We talked animatedly over dinner about ideas for future brews and potion types I hoped to attempt in time. Diane listened raptly, interjecting with her own creative suggestions. Her enthusiasm fueled my ambition to push my fledgling skills ever farther.

When the food was finished, we cleaned up together as had become our comfortable ritual. Diane hummed softly as she washed dishes while I tidied and swept with the help of the domesticant spirit. The little creature's assistance with tasks kept the cabin well in order.

As the last plate was dried and put away, I impulsively swept Diane into my arms from behind in a playful hug. She laughed that magical laugh I adored, a sound sweeter than a bell, and swatted my arm lightly in mock admonishment. I nuzzled her slender neck, breathing deep her rose-vanilla scent. We stood like that for a while, in silent enjoyment of one another.

When darkness fully claimed the valley outside, we retired to the fireplace as we did most nights. But this evening's mood held a new charge — a sense of shared accomplishment and anticipation for the promise of future triumphs together.

Nestled comfortably beside me on the braided hearth rug, Diane idly toyed with my hair as we lightly talked about our day and speculated on what the future might yet bring us. My fingers traced slow circles on her shoulder, gradually straying lower along her back and waist. Soon, tender caresses eclipsed conversation, our lips meeting in sweet passion beneath the dancing firelight.

As the flickering flames gradually burned low, we finally ascended together to our waiting bed in the loft above. And within that sanctuary that was wholly ours, we celebrated again — not with words, but with action.

Later, as I drifted off in contented weariness, Diane lay safe in my arms. And my final thoughts before sleep's veil descended were of the bright future ahead.

The next morning, I awoke eager to further hone my nascent alchemy skills by attempting to brew several more mana potions. My first effort had only yielded a single vial, but with practice, I hoped to refine the process and increase my yield.

Diane smiled supportively over a simple breakfast as I outlined my plan to spend the day focused solely on potion-crafting. "That's a wonderful idea, my love. With more mana draughts on hand, you'll be able to summon twice as many helpful spirits!" she said.

I grinned and nodded. "Well, we'll be selling a couple of them, too. I expect we'll get a good price!"

After we ate, Diane headed outside to tend the garden and smokehouse while I prepared my workspace. I carefully sorted my remaining harvested reagents and purified a large vessel of fresh water. Once my tools were meticulously cleaned, I was ready to begin.

Consulting my handwritten brewing notes, I combined and processed the ingredients in sequence as before, striving for precision in each step. Thauma paste, Magebread nectar, Wispsilk powder — all were measured out exactly according to the formula I had memorized.

As I gently stirred the steaming concoction, it once again gradually assumed its distinctive pearlescent lavender hue, wisps of azure vapor twirling hypnotically above the gently bubbling liquid. When the color stabilized, signaling mystical fusion, I removed the cauldron from heat.

After decanting the finished potion into the sterile jar and letting it stabilize there, I was left with another concoction. I poured it into another vial – Diane had been so sweet to transfer out spices and salt into clay jars so I could use the thoroughly cleaned glass containers for my alchemy.

Energized by this success, I immediately prepared another batch using the same meticulous steps, striving for consistency between brews. Soon a second vial held another portion of glowing mana draught.

I continued steadily brewing all morning, pouring all my focus into the intricate work. Around midday, drawn by the alluring scents, Diane peeked into the workshop. I proudly showed her the yield so far – the fruits of hours of steadfast labor.

"Amazing work!" Diane marveled. "At this rate, you'll have stockpiled more mana potions than you can use!" She gave me a quick kiss on the cheek in congratulations before returning outside so I could resume uninterrupted.

I turned my attention back to the bubbling cauldron, beginning another meticulous brewing. When this one finished, I would have yielded a total of four full vials of shimmering mana draught.

By late afternoon, that number had upped to five, and my mystical focus was waning after the lengthy demanding effort. I was also running out of ingredients from our first harvest. But I was too exhilarated by my successes to stop now. Ignoring my weariness, I started one final brew for the day, determined to hone my consistency.

This last batch progressed beautifully, the coagulating color perfectly matching the others. As afternoon cooled into evening, I finally decanted the fruits of this day's dedicated alchemy practice into the sixth waiting glass vial.

Weary but profoundly satisfied, I carefully labeled each container 'Mana Potion – Minor' before storing them. I was tired and had used up all my ingredients, but the work had been immensely satisfying. I could only imagine my Alchemy skill would increase on my next level.

I summoned my chirpy domesticant, and we tidied up my workspace together. The domesticant was a lot faster at cleaning than I was, and it didn't mind me slacking a little as I was tired from standing over the cauldron all day.

Soon after cleaning up, Diane entered the cabin looking nearly as tired as I felt after a long day working outdoors. But her brilliant smile returned when I proudly presented the day's bountiful alchemical yield.

"David, these are amazing!" she gasped, gingerly handling the six filled vials. Her eyes widened seeing the substantial volume I had managed to brew solo in a single day. "You've grown so skilled already."

I smiled at her effusive praise. "Well, I wanted to really hone the process since our first success. But repeated practice is still key." I slid my arm around her waist, drawing her close. "Although having your support definitely helps keep me motivated."

Diane nestled happily against me. "Of course, I'll always be your most eager cheerleader," she promised. We stood a moment admiring the gleaming potion vials side-by-side before I broached an idea I'd formulated while brewing.

"You know, with a decent stock of mana potions now stored up and all the other smoked meat, fish, furs, and moonlight potatoes, I'm thinking we have enough goods produced to do another trading run into Gladdenfield soon."

Diane's eyes lit up at the suggestion. "That's a great idea! All of our goods should fetch a nice profit from Leigh."

I nodded enthusiastically. "It's high time we turned

all our hard work into some more coin. We can purchase some better tools. And we're in need of nails and screws as well… I'd really love to make some furniture." I pinched her pretty butt, making her yelp. "A bigger bed, for starters…"

She laughed and nodded. "Hmm, that would be nice. Also, I think we might want to get some fuel for the Jeep. Out here, that's likely to cost a pretty penny."

I nodded. Getting fuel out into the Wilds was tough. The roads here weren't good enough for large tankers, and the way magic fiddled with technology made it difficult to use other methods of transportation. Most of it came by jerry can or barrel as far as I was aware – at great expense and risk. Still, we needed the Jeep, and the Jeep needed fuel.

"We'll see if Leigh can cut us a nice deal."

"I'm sure she will," Diane hummed. "*If* she actually has fuel. It might be something we'll need to get from other traders."

We passed a peaceful evening meal together discussing plans for expanding the homestead with our hoped-for proceeds from selling our stockpiled goods in Gladdenfield.

Before retiring for the night, we agreed the surplus trout, some of the smoked meat, the furs, two sacks of moonlight potatoes, and my manufactured potions would comprise a worthwhile trading haul. Tomorrow we would spend the early morning preparing, then set off early on the familiar journey into town to visit Leigh's lively shop once more. We'd be there by noon.

I drifted off to sleep with Diane nestled snugly beside me beneath the quilts, my mind abuzz with new ideas for improving my potion-crafting abilities and imagining what wonders I could manifest next using these fledgling skills I was cultivating.

Chapter 53

The next morning, Diane and I awoke early to begin preparations for our trading run into Gladdenfield. After a quick breakfast, we started gathering the goods we had produced to sell — two sacks of moonlight potatoes, bundles of smoked trout and game, a parcel of furs and feathers, and my stock of six mana potions.

I did one final check to ensure we had the essentials

for the drive into town while Diane finished bundling the merchandise. Soon everything was securely loaded into the back of the Jeep. I grabbed my rifle to be safe and helped Diane into the passenger seat before climbing behind the wheel.

The morning air was fresh on our faces as I cranked the engine to life. Diane smiled over at me, clearly excited for our little shopping excursion. We were both eager to transform our hard work into coin to continue improving the homestead.

I steered the rugged vehicle carefully along the winding dirt road away from our homestead. Diane hummed cheerfully as I drove, her gaze taking in the sights of the vibrant scenery. Soon enough, we turned onto the main road to Gladdenfield Outpost.

The drive was always pleasant, but today it seemed busier than usual. After several miles, we began passing laden wagons and travelers on foot far more frequently. They slowed us down considerably as it took some time for them to make room and let us pass. Still, we were in no hurry.

"The road sure is crowded," I remarked to Diane. "Any idea what's going on?"

Diane's blue eyes lit up. "Oh, the Aquana Festival must be starting soon! Travelers come from all around for the celebrations. I'd forgotten it was that time of the year already."

I glanced over at her curiously. "Aquana Festival? I don't think I'm familiar with that one."

Diane nodded. "It's an ancient elven holiday celebrating water spirits. The elves have passed down traditions around it for centuries."

She went on to explain, "During the Aquana Festival, elves make pilgrimages to sanctified groves and springs deep in the wilderness to make offerings and give praise to various water deities. They believe doing so ensures bountiful rains and healthy rivers for the year ahead."

I listened with fascination as Diane described some of the elaborate rituals and ceremonies involved. "In Gladdenfield, they recreate one of the ceremonial processions. Many elves will also trek deep into the Springfield Forest where there is a sacred place said to be blessed by the water spirits."

Diane continued, "The whole festival lasts a week. Most businesses in town will close down as the inhabitants leave to make their pilgrimage. Before it starts, travelers flood in and keep the taverns and inns busy." She grinned broadly. "During that time, food and drink are more expensive. It should help us get a good price for our wares!"

I nodded along as she spoke. "A good price sounds interesting, but so does the festival itself."

She shot me a smile. "Oh, you want to partake?"

I laughed. "Well, I don't know! Can we? Do you need to be an elf or… of a certain religion or something?"

"Oh no!" she said. "No, everyone can come, although plenty of elves partake. As long as you're respectful of the customs, it won't be a problem at all."

"Well, I'm getting more excited for this by the moment."

She laughed, sitting up in her seat as she placed a slender hand on my arm. "You're getting me excited too!"

"So what do you say?" I asked, shooting her a grin.

She shrugged playfully. "Yeah!"

I grinned and nodded. "Provided we can get the homestead in order so it'll do without us for a week, I think it would be fun!"

She nodded vigorously. "It'll take some preparation, but we can do that!"

We continued onward, moving cautiously around the increased traffic cluttering the road. Many were pilgrims headed for Gladdenfield, and there was a fair number of elves among them. Their joyful songs drifted through the open windows as we drove past.

After a little under an hour of careful navigation down the crowded road, we reached the widened main thoroughfare that led directly to Gladdenfield's gates. The crowds grew denser as we approached, forcing me to inch along behind laden carts. It was going to take a little longer than expected. Everyone seemed in high spirits, though, colorful banners and garlands fluttering from wagons and cars.

At last we reached the settlement walls where elf sentries smiled and waved us through after a quick inspection, accustomed to seeing our rugged vehicle by now. Inside, the lively streets absolutely thronged with revelers. Gladdenfield was the busiest I'd ever seen it.

Finding a place to park along the main square was impossible. After slowly circling, I was finally forced to leave the Jeep in a cramped side alley and continue on foot, hoping it would be unbothered in the press. Still, folks around here weren't interested in vandalizing property, so I felt confident it'd be fine.

Diane stayed close to me as we nudged our way through the colorful chaos toward Leigh's shop. Snatches of music competed from every corner as minstrels played for tips from the crowds. The air hung heavy with enticing aromas of freshly baked goods and sizzling meats.

Everyone seemed to be drinking, singing, or dancing even though the festival had yet to officially commence. Little foxkin kits scampered about underfoot, chasing each other and giggling. Their laughter lifted my spirits along with the general mood of revelry.

At last Leigh's storefront emerged up ahead, its familiar cluttered facade never a more welcome sight.

"All right," I said, laughing as I dodged a foxkin scamp running past. "Let's get the business part of our little visit over with."

As we entered the shop, the bells jangled merrily to announce our arrival. Leigh looked up from behind the counter and broke into a huge grin.

"Well, look who it is!" she exclaimed. In a flash, she had bustled out to engulf first Diane, then me, in fierce hugs. As always, it was a delight to have Leigh push her voluptuous self up against me, and her nearness sent a jolt of excitement down my spine.

By now, I knew the bubbly blonde shopkeeper well enough to understand that she wasn't like this with everyone. With other customers, she was reserved, businesslike, and not flirty at all, and I was pretty happy with this special treatment.

"Y'all are lookin' mighty fine today," Leigh said, giving me an appreciative up-and-down look as she stepped back. "Especially you, David. Ya just get more handsome every time I see ya."

I chuckled while Diane gave her friend a playful nudge. "Oh, hush, you two. We're here on business, remember?" Though Diane's eyes were twinkling with amusement.

Leigh grinned unrepentantly. "Well, alright, if y'all insist. Let's take a look at what you brought me."

Diane and I laid out our goods on the counter – smoked meats and fish, bundles of furs, colorful feathers, the sacks of potatoes, and finally my six potion vials.

Leigh let out an impressed whistle. "My, my, quite the haul! The smoked meats and fish will sell like hotcakes once the festival crowd starts pourin' in – perfect stuff for the trek to the hot springs in Springfield Forest."

"Hot springs?" I said, perking an eyebrow.

Diane nodded happily. "Yes, the destination from Gladdenfield are the hot springs. There's a lot of them in Springfield Forest, and the elves consider them sacred."

Leigh nodded her agreement. "Oh, and these fine furs are sure to fetch top dollar from them fanciful city elves."

She turned her focus to the potions, gently lifting one of the glass vials. "And these here are the fruits of your alchemy labor, I see!" Leigh exclaimed. "They positively shine with magic." She fixed her radiant blue eyes on me. "This is very impressive, David!"

I grinned proudly. "Just a few mana potions, but hopefully the first of many successful brews."

Leigh nodded approvingly. "I know just the merchant to sell these to. Folks 'round here will pay plenty for potions, especially the adventurers and craftsmen." She winked at me. "And I'll make sure you get every coin you deserve, darlin'."

Diane and I then settled in to negotiate fair prices for all our goods. True to her word, Leigh offered us excellent terms, especially on the potions, which she insisted on paying a premium rate. I had to laugh when she tried to dramatically haggle over the potatoes just for sport.

When we had finally concluded our trading, Leigh passed Diane an impressive stack of mixed coins along with the payment paperwork. "There ya go! Y'all been working mighty hard, and it shows."

Diane quickly verified the payment amount against the receipts, then made sure it was securely stowed. I made a mental note to stock up on some iron strongboxes to keep our savings more secure.

As I helped Leigh store our merchandise in the back, she asked about the festival.

I explained Diane and I were thinking about coming for the festivities once our business was concluded. Leigh's eyes lit up excitedly at that.

"Well, that's just perfect! I was hoping you two would come by when it begins. I'm closin' up shop and will be at the springs all week! Why don't you come along? We're gonna have us some real fun!" She leaned in close with an impish smile, pushing her ample breasts against my arm. "And I can think of no one finer to enjoy it with than you two."

I chuckled while doing my best to ignore her intentionally distracting proximity. "We're looking forward to it. Diane tells me it's quite a spectacle."

"Oh, it surely is!" Leigh agreed enthusiastically. "Though the real highlight is the feastin' and drinkin' and dancin' all night with good company, if you ask me." She shot me a wink that brought heat to my cheeks.

By the time we finished stowing everything in the back, other customers were filtering into the front of the shop. Leigh flashed me an apologetic smile. "Duty calls, darlin'. But y'all come on back this evenin' once I close up, okay? We'll kick off the festivities right!"

I laughed. "We need to go by the homestead before we can actually join up! There's stuff we need to put in order."

She waved it off with a playful scoff. "There's plenty of time for that! You stick around tonight; I'll let you sleep in my guest room. You'll have plenty of time tomorrow and the day after to get your affairs in order. But you have to join the party here in town for at least one night! Things get pretty wild even before we kick off the Aquana Festival!"

I exchanged a look with Diane, and she was making big eyes, almost hopping with excitement. There was no saying no to that. "All right," I conceded, laughing.

Leigh clapped her hands and hopped up and down, making her full bosom jiggle. "Perfect!" she purred. "Y'all come back when it's closin' time. We'll eat, drink, and have ourselves a time!"

I promised we would, and Diane and I then stepped back out into the colorful chaos and bustling crowds packing Gladdenfield's streets.

"Where to first?" I asked Diane, slipping my hand into hers so we didn't get separated.

"How about we browse the markets?" Diane suggested. "With what Leigh paid for our goods, we can afford some indulgences."

I readily agreed. "We can also see if we can find some useful tools and other equipment we might need. We'll just store it at Leigh's and take it with us in the morning."

Diane nodded and guided us toward the rows of stalls laden with wares while I took in the sights and sounds of the pre-festival excitement. We passed jugglers, musicians, food vendors hawking skewers of exotic meats, and colorful garlands fluttering everywhere. The mood was joyful but slightly manic.

At one stall selling baked goods, Diane convinced me to try a hot, sticky honey-glazed pastry twisted into a figure-eight shape. It was delicious, the dough just the right balance of crispy and chewy. Diane's smile was smug, knowing she had picked just the thing to satisfy my sweet tooth.

"All right," she said when I finished the treat. "Now let's see about those tools!"

Chapter 54

Diane and I browsed the lively market stalls of Gladdenfield Outpost, on the lookout for useful tools and supplies to purchase with our newly earned coin. My eyes widened, taking in the incredible assortment of wares for sale. From mundane implements to artifacts imbued with magic, the diversity was astounding.

At one booth, an elven merchant displayed an array

of etched alchemical glassware and paraphernalia. I inspected the elegantly crafted alembics, beakers, vials, and other vessels appreciatively. High-quality equipment like this would aid my brewing considerably.

After comparing several sizes, I purchased a set of three glass beakers and a sturdy clamp stand to hold them over a flame. I also purchased several purpose-built vials to store my concoctions. The merchant wrapped them carefully in cloth for me before taking my payment. Though not cheap, I knew these tools would prove a wise investment.

Next, we perused a stall stocked with farming tools and equipment. I selected a new shovel, rake, and hoe to expand our stock of implements in case something broke or Diane and I wanted to use the same tool at the same time. The stout dwarven-crafted steel heads looked built to last. Diane found a nice hand trowel for delicate gardening tasks.

At another booth, I acquired a bundle of screws, nails, wood glue, and other useful hardware for doing repairs and future projects, as well as varnish to treat and season wood for construction. The metalwork had clearly been salvaged from old human settlements but was still serviceable. Diane picked out a roll of oilcloth for preserving dried foods.

After finding a stall with seed packets, we eagerly browsed the exotic selection. Many seeds promised magical properties or rapid growth spells. I chose quick-growing onion and tomato varieties to add to our garden.

Our last major purchase was several jerry cans of fuel for the Jeep from a trader who had come from New Springfield. It was expensive, but fuel came at a premium out here. Since we relied heavily on the vehicle, we needed it. I bartered the price down a little before taking our heavy but precious can.

Once we felt suitably equipped with new tools and supplies, Diane and I headed for a quieter corner of the market to share some freshly baked meat pies and enjoy a brief respite from the crowds. It was nice to sit and relax together after walking around all morning. The market's lively sounds and scents surrounded us as we ate.

When the meat pies were finished, we spent the rest of the afternoon walking around and checking out the sights. When we got tired of the crowds, we headed over to the Wild Outrider and got old Darny to let us relax in one of his rooms with a balcony. We looked over the crowds and drank some coffee, letting the brew invigorate us.

When it was getting late, we gathered up our purchases and slowly navigated our way through the colorful chaos back towards Leigh's shop. The main streets absolutely overflowed with newly arrived pilgrims chanting songs in melodic elven tongues, laughing, and joking.

The journey back was slow going due to the sheer volume of bodies cramming Gladdenfield's thoroughfares. Several times we had to change course to avoid logjams of wagons unloading wares. But the mood remained festive despite the close quarters. Local children dashed about giggling and playing games amidst the throngs of adults.

After considerable nudging and excuse me's, we finally reached Leigh's store. I was able to wave and get her attention through the window glass. Leigh nodded to show she had seen us and continued assisting the patron she was with. We loitered patiently nearby for her to finish up.

Fifteen minutes later, the customer emerged carrying a bulky parcel. Leigh followed them out long enough to wish them a happy Aquana Festival. Then she turned to us beaming. "There y'all are! I was starting to wonder if you two started the party without me."

I assured her we just took our time browsing the markets. Diane and I carried our purchases inside.

"Seems like you found some good stuff!" remarked Leigh approvingly as she looked over our acquisitions. "Them fancy beakers oughta help with your potion crafting. And that there's a fine shovel for a bare-chested man with sweat beading on his chiseled body to do some diggin' with, hm?"

I laughed while Diane grinned and shook her head at her friend's overt flirting. "We tried to pick out useful items built to last." The hardware and tools had indeed looked sturdily constructed.

"And these new seeds will add some variety to our garden," I added, showing Leigh the vegetable packets.

She nodded knowingly. "Oh yes, those quick-grow seeds are real handy! With your skills, you'll have more onions and tomatoes than you can eat."

Diane and I exchanged amused smiles at the thought of overrun garden plots. Producing steady surpluses was important, but Leigh's enthusiasm was endearing. We passed a pleasant interval chatting with the energetic shopkeeper about our purchases and plans as she tidied up.

When Leigh paused to assist another browsing customer, I turned to Diane. "Maybe we should store these supplies upstairs in Leigh's guest room for now? I don't want to leave them out in the Jeep overnight."

Diane nodded. "Yes, that's a good idea. Let's ask if we can keep everything here until morning."

After conveying the plan to Leigh, she readily agreed to store our purchases upstairs. "Of course, y'all can keep your things in the spare room! C'mon up and I'll show ya."

Leigh led us up a narrow staircase behind the counter to a cozy apartment built above the shop. She showed us to a tidy guest room containing a bed, wardrobe, and dresser. "Here's where you two lovebirds can bunk down later," Leigh said with a playful wink.

Together, Diane and I arranged all our tools, supplies, and parcels in the room for safekeeping. I did a quick check to ensure nothing was crushed or damaged. Everything looked good.

"This is perfect, Leigh. Thank you for letting us store this here until morning," I said.

"Of course! Couldn't have y'all leavin' all your new goods out on the street," Leigh replied.

With our purchases secured upstairs, we headed back down just as Leigh was locking up for the evening. "All set!" she announced cheerily, pocketing her keyring. "Now let's have a glass of wine and dress up a little!"

She shot Diane a wink. "We'll make you the belle of the ball… Right after me, that is."

I chuckled. "Alright, I get the feeling this is gonna take a while."

Diane laughed, shooting me a playful wink. "It just might!"

"Well, you relax here for a bit, David, baby," Leigh said. "And we'll come and show our outfits. I got some ale in the larder."

I winked and nodded. "All right, you girls take your time!"

Chapter 55

After Leigh and Diane disappeared upstairs, I made myself comfortable on a worn leather armchair near the store's front counter. I propped my feet up leisurely as I let my gaze wander over the diverse array of curiosities crowding the rustic space.

The sheer variety of items lining the shelves was astounding. There were bolts of embroidered cloth, bundles of dried herbs, jars of preserved fruits, and stacks of thick, dusty tomes. One shelf held an assortment of carved wooden toys and figures. Another was bursting with clay pots and urns of every shape and size imaginable.

Along the far wall stood floor-to-ceiling racks cluttered with tools and equipment — fishing poles, shovels, axes, lanterns, and countless other iron, wood, and leather implements. Sturdy backpacks stuffed full of travel gear were lined up on the worn floorboards beneath. It was a frontier paradise.

After a time, I rose and went behind the counter, cracking open the small barrel of ale Leigh kept stashed away. The cool, bitter liquid helped slake my thirst after the warm, dusty chaos of the festival crowds outside.

As I sipped, my eyes continued roaming the fascinating wares surrounding me. Assorted animal traps dangled from the rafters overhead, along with bunches of dried herbs and braids of garlic and onions. My fingers trailed over an intricately tooled leather saddle perched atop the counter.

Everything here brimmed with the promise of adventure. My excitement about joining the Aquana Festival grew as I lingered in Leigh's lively shop. Out here beyond the city walls, traditions still held strong. I was honored to take part.

After helping myself to another mug of ale from the tapped keg, I reclaimed my seat and propped my feet up once more. The hour grew late as I awaited Leigh and Diane's return. Lively music and raucous laughter drifted in through the open windows as revelers packed the crowded streets outside.

At last, I heard footsteps on the stairs and straightened up eagerly. A moment later, Leigh emerged looking radiant in a figure-hugging blue gingham blouse tied below her ample bosom and a knee-length ruffled skirt. Her golden curls cascaded freely over her shoulders, but other than a bit of mascara to bring out her eyes, the natural beauty wore no makeup.

"Well, what do you think?" Leigh asked, slowly turning in place so I could admire her outfit from all angles. The way the fabric clung accentuated every delicious curve. She looked utterly captivating.

I let out an impressed whistle. "Leigh, you look absolutely beautiful!" I said sincerely.

Leigh beamed, clearly delighted by my reaction. "Why, thank ya kindly." She shot me a playful wink. "But just you wait 'til you get a load of Diane, sugar."

Right on cue, Diane descended the stairs behind

Leigh. My jaw nearly hit the floor.

She wore an off-the-shoulder emerald gown made from some shimmery, almost sheer material that hugged her slender curves enchantingly all the way down to mid-calf. The neckline showcased her delicate collarbones while the flowing skirt gave enticing glimpses of her toned legs as she moved. Her inky hair was swept up, accentuating the graceful arch of her neck.

Diane paused, suddenly looking self-conscious under my openly awestruck gaze. She smoothed her hands over the dress nervously. "Well? What do you think?"

I swallowed, finding my voice. "Diane… you are absolutely breathtaking," I managed. I slowly approached her, unable to take my eyes off her incredible beauty. Taking her hands in mine, I leaned in for a soft, lingering kiss. "You're gorgeous," I murmured against her lips.

Diane's cheeks flushed prettily. Behind us, Leigh let out a delighted laugh. "He ain't wrong, girl!" she cooed. "Ain't ever seen you look so fine."

Blushing harder, Diane shot her friend a grateful smile before turning back to me. "Shall we head out?" she asked almost shyly.

I offered her my arm gallantly. "Lead the way, my

dear." As we made for the door, I added sincerely, "Really, you look absolutely stunning."

Diane's answering smile was radiant as she gave my arm an affectionate squeeze. Together, we stepped out into the colorful chaos and revelry packing Gladdenfield's streets, ready to join the festivities.

Our first stop was the row of food vendors lining the lively streets near the town square. My mouth watered at the sight of sizzling meat skewers, fragrant mushroom and vegetable pastries, and decadent cream-filled confections dripping with honey being sold under the starry night sky. We sampled a bit of everything as we strolled leisurely past the sumptuous outdoor offerings.

When our appetites were sated, we headed to where Darny had set up an outdoor bar along the edge of the square, already overflowing with revelers. I gently guided Diane through the packed crowd using my height advantage until we secured a small standing table. Leigh forced her way up to the makeshift bar and returned with three brimming tankards of frothy ale for us, winking as she set them down.

Sipping the smooth brew beneath the glittering blanket of stars, we relaxed and took in the energetic outdoor atmosphere. The space was filled to capacity with drinking, laughing revelers. In the corner, elven minstrels played a lively tune on shawms and lutes accompanied by a steady drumbeat. More than a few festival-goers were up and dancing merrily, their forms blurred by clouds of pipe smoke.

Leigh regaled us with humorous tales about past Aquana Festivals she had partaken in over the years. Many involved copious drinking, impromptu bonfires, and at least one instance of being trotted around town in a wheelbarrow by two shirtless dwarves. Diane and I laughed uproariously picturing the outrageous scenarios.

As Leigh launched into yet another amusing anecdote, a staggering patron bumped our table, rattling the mugs perilously. He slurred out an apology before lurching off again into the crowd. Drunk, but friendly.

Diane shook her head in amusement, absently straightening her mussed hair. I took the opportunity to gently tuck an errant strand back into her unruly bundle of locks, my fingertips grazing her silken skin. Her eyes softened, and she gave my thigh an affectionate squeeze beneath the table.

When our drinks were drained, Leigh insisted on buying another round. As she headed up to wrestle her way through the densely packed mob at the makeshift bar, Diane leaned close so I could hear her over the din.

"This is so much fun," she said. "I haven't seen this many people hanging out and having a good time in ages!"

I grinned and nodded, taking in the good-natured revelry going on around us. People were dancing to jaunty tunes and capering, and the ale flowed freely. Everyone seemed to be having a good time; I saw no sour faces or people arguing. They were partying with the zest of people who don't get a chance to let loose like this too often.

Minutes later, Leigh returned bearing three more foamy tankards. Our night wasn't over yet!

As the night wore on, Gladdenfield became even livelier and more raucous as revelers continued flooding into town. Diane, Leigh, and I slowly made our way through the chaotic streets, stopping frequently to chat or joke with passersby.

At one point, we came across a pair of shirtless dwarves arm wrestling on an overturned barrel. A crowd had gathered to cheer them on. Leigh whooped and hollered right along, clapping enthusiastically when one dwarf finally slammed his opponent's hand down in victory.

"Reminds me of the Dwarf Brawlin' Tournament they used to hold here ages ago," Leigh remarked with a grin. "Folks used to come from all over to see those rowdy competitions!"

"What happened to them?" I asked, grinning as another dwarf forfeited the match because he wanted to take a swig of ale.

She thought for a moment. "Fewer dwarves of late, I suppose. I know there's more of 'em these days in Ironfast, another frontier town huggin' the Shimmerin' Peaks."

We lingered a while longer watching the impromptu rematch before moving on. I smiled down at Diane, enjoying seeing her so carefree and spirited in the festive atmosphere. A rosy glow lit her cheeks from laughter and ale. Several times I caught Leigh openly admiring us together, an almost wistful look in her bright eyes.

At a crowded stand, we managed to procure spiced wine served piping hot in carved wooden mugs. I sipped the potent mulled concoction carefully, the rich flavors warming me through. Beside me, Leigh dramatically fanned herself between gulps.

"Hm, this stuff'll put some fire in your belly!" she exclaimed. I had to chuckle at her boundless enthusiasm for all of life's pleasures, big and small.

We encountered many friendly faces along our meandering path — fellow traders, adventurers, and townsfolk who recognized Leigh. She made a point of introducing Diane and me to anyone we hadn't met, proudly presenting us as her dear friends. I was touched by the warmth in her voice when she said it. And she wasn't wrong — I felt close to her, and I liked her.

In more ways than one.

Farther out on the streets, we paused to listen to a talented Bard plucking out lively folk tunes on his lute. His melodies set toes tapping and hands clapping.

When he finished one song, Leigh shouted, "Play 'Fire Eyes' next!" The Bard grinned and obliged, strumming the familiar upbeat melody he had clearly performed many times before.

As the rollicking tune filled the street, Leigh grabbed my hands, pulling me into an impromptu do-si-do.

Laughing, I spun her around before we switched partners so I could swing Diane next. Our boots scuffed up little puffs of dust as we danced together under the torchlight. Passersby hooted and clapped along until the song ended with a flourish.

"Now that's how you kick off a festival!" Leigh declared breathlessly.

I wholeheartedly agreed. Dancing together had lifted our mood even higher. Diane's eyes shone as she caught my gaze. Impulsively, I pulled her close and kissed her right there in the bustling street. She returned it eagerly heedless of any onlookers.

When we finally parted, Leigh let out an approving whistle. Diane's cheeks were endearingly flushed. Together, we continued navigating the crowded thoroughfares.

I was glad the girls had linked arms with me to avoid getting separated in the crush. Everywhere, laughter and snatches of music filled the smoky air.

The mouthwatering aroma of frying pastries stopped us in our tracks outside a food stall. My stomach rumbled hungrily, reminding me it had been some time since our last nibbles. Leigh insisted on treating us, waving away my offered coins and passing steaming pastries filled with spiced meat and vegetables into our hands.

We stood elbow to elbow leaning against a wall,

munching contentedly. These late-night festival snacks were just what we needed to maintain our energy and high spirits. As we ate, a band of foxkin kits raced by, weaving between legs in pursuit of a leather ball. Their playful laughter perfectly matched the mood of revelry everywhere.

When only crumbs remained of our snacks, Leigh neatly licked her fingers clean before suggesting we pop into a nearby curiosities shop she wanted to show me. Apparently, some of the stores were still open.

Inside, we browsed shelves cluttered with strange artifacts, relics, and trinkets from Tannoris. My eyes lingered on an intricate compass whose needle constantly spun without settling on any cardinal direction.

When I asked the shopkeeper, he claimed it had been salvaged from the ruins of a great elven mage's tower following the Upheaval. It used to point at the nearest source of mana. The shopkeeper demonstrated, but the needle continued its aimless, chaotic spinning. Though broken, it was a fascinating relic hinting at ancient magics. A little reminder of how fantastic the world had become.

Back outside, the crowds seemed to have doubled in just the brief time we were indoors. Everywhere, revelers linked arms, singing and swaying tipsily. The overall mood was one of cheerful camaraderie – strangers embraced like old friends. Several times we were pulled into the impromptu dances and tunes. Diane, Leigh, and I always made sure to stay linked so as not to lose one another in the crush.

Leigh seemed utterly in her element, chattering merrily, joking, and twirling playfully. She really came alive – even more so than normal – and when I caught her looking at me, cute blush on that pretty freckled face, I knew I was falling. And I *wanted* to fall.

We paused along the fringes of a crowded town square where a group was passing around bottles of potent moonshine brewed from forest tubers. Leigh eagerly accepted a swig before passing it to me. I winced at the throat-searing strength of the hooch but still took an obliging gulp. Warmth immediately spread through my chest.

Diane tried just a small sip, nose wrinkling at the harsh burn. Her sensitivity to taste and smell meant such spirits were too overwhelming. But she smiled indulgently as Leigh passed the bottle along to others.

We joked around and talked with the group of hooch-swigging locals for a while, learning they were homesteaders like us. Most of them grew non-magical crops, and none of them had a Class that actually seemed to support homesteading. It turned out many people got strict combat Classes, which really wasn't all that useful unless you planned on dungeon delving until you ran into something stronger than you. Skillbooks to learn actually useful trades and skills were rare to come by. More than one of them whistled in admiration when I told them I was a Frontier Summoner — it was one of those rare Classes that could do fine in and out of combat.

By now, the moon had climbed nearly overhead, silvering the scene with its spectral glow. Everything shone softly around the edges, as if viewed through a veil. Time ceased to hold meaning in any normal sense. Some primordial spirit possessed us all, kindred in our joy.

The three of us stayed arm in arm, swaying dreamily to bursts of distant music, laughing, talking, or just enjoying the night. All was right in our tiny corner of the joined worlds.

We scored a few candied apples and got some fresh energy from them. Leigh, with her usual blithe charm, offered me a sticky bite of hers. I grinned and accepted, letting the sweetness fill my mouth as I kept my eyes playfully locked with hers. Leigh's own eyes sparkled brighter than the sugar.

"The night is young, my friends!" Leigh declared merrily after that. She scanned the crowds expectantly. "And it's about to get wild!"

Right on cue, a rollicking fiddle tune I vaguely recognized began drifting over from a nearby tavern window flung wide to the balmy air — it was the Wild Outrider of all places, and it sounded like the party was starting at Darny's. Leigh's face lit up when she heard it.

"Ooh, listen! Now that right there is my absolute favorite festival reel," she purred, grabbing my hands excitedly. "What say we mosey on inside and have us a proper dance, hmm?"

Before I could reply, she was already eagerly towing Diane and me along by our wrists toward the source of the upbeat fiddle music. Laughing, I exchanged an amused glance with Diane as we allowed ourselves to be pulled along in the bubbly blonde's wake toward the lively tavern.

At the entrance, Leigh finally relinquished her grip on our wrists, pausing just long enough to smooth back wild blonde locks that had escaped during our night of revelry so far. Her eyes shone with anticipation.

"Ready for some real fun?" she asked brightly,

waggling her eyebrows at Diane and me. With that, she shoved open the wooden door, releasing a wave of laughter, singing, and fiddle music into the street.

Still grinning, Diane and I followed our vivacious friend into the crowded tavern, eager to join in the spirited festivities that seemed to culminate here.

Chapter 56

Stepping into the boisterous interior of the Wild Outrider tavern, our senses were immediately overwhelmed. Everywhere, patrons were up and dancing joyously to the rollicking fiddle and drum music, while raucous laughter and singing echoed around the timbered walls.

Leigh grinned and grabbed both Diane's and my

hands, towing us right into the heart of the chaotic fray. I exchanged an amused glance with Diane as we allowed the bubbly blonde to guide us onto the makeshift dancefloor.

There was barely room to move amidst the densely packed bodies twirling and stomping to the infectious beat. But Leigh was undeterred, nudging revelers aside to secure a tiny pocket of space for our impromptu trio.

Facing us with an impish smile, Leigh began leading us through the quick steps of a traditional frontier folk dance. We locked arms and spun in tight circles together as Leigh clapped and stomped her feet to the wild beat. Diane and I did our best to mirror Leigh's deft movements and follow her lead.

Despite a few inevitable collisions and trodden toes from other dancers crowded in tight, we managed to fall into a rhythm together. The upbeat fiddle strains and pounding drumbeats made it impossible not to feel energized. Soon, we were breathless and laughing at our frequent mistakes, but utterly caught up in the music's lively tempo.

As the first rollicking song ended, Leigh shot me a playful wink. "Not too bad for a city boy!"

Before I could respond, a new tune struck up and she immediately whirled back into motion, blonde tresses fanning out. Chuckling, I turned my focus to keeping up with her and Diane.

The next few melodies brought more traditional folk dancing with linked arms spinning in tight circles. But soon, the music shifted to a sultrier, slower beat accompanied by the gentle song of the Bard — a love song, no doubt to slow things down a little before tankards went flying. Without hesitation, Leigh slid her arms up around my neck, pulling my tall frame down closer.

"Hope you don't mind me cuttin' in, darlin'," Leigh murmured near my ear. Her warm breath and sudden nearness made my pulse skip. Diane laughed and gave an encouraging nod, touching both mine and Leigh's shoulder to show her approval.

With a teasing smile up at me, Leigh began guiding us into a graceful swaying two-step. As we slowly revolved amidst the other coupled-up dancers, I found myself acutely aware of every point our bodies met. Her full hips and soft bosom pressed to mine made focusing difficult. She got an immediate physical reaction from me as my shaft hardened.

She felt it; I was certain of that, but she just bit her bottom lip as she looked up at me with those big, half-lidded blue eyes and pushed closer, almost grinding on me. I shot Diane a quick look, but she just gazed lovingly at us — she really experienced no jealousy at all.

The hand Leigh had resting on my upper back stroked idly up and down, fingertips digging in just slightly in a way that sent pleasant tingles through me. We moved in easy unison, gazes locked.

The tempo was languid but Leigh still managed to occasionally brush her thigh firmly between mine. I had to wonder if it was intentional. From her coy smile, I had a feeling it was.

When the song ended, Leigh leaned up, bringing her face temptingly close to mine as though she meant to kiss me. My pulse roared in my ears. But at the last second she diverted, merely whispering, "Thanks for the dance, baby," and stepping casually out of my embrace.

I was left standing stunned, hot, and bothered, watching Leigh make her way over to where Diane waited off to the side, looking amused but unconcerned. They were speaking in low voices and Leigh shot me a look over her shoulder paired with a crooked smile. The girls giggled, and I had to wonder what they might be discussing regarding me.

I got the feeling that things were about to... *progress.*

But then the music picked up again, lively and fast, so I pushed the thought from my mind for now.

Rejoining the girls, I decided to direct my invitation to Diane this time. "Care to dance with me, my lady?" I asked, making an exaggerated bow and extending my hand toward her in an overly aristocratic manner.

Diane laughed at my antics, and her eyes lit up as she accepted at once. I led her onto the floor just as the fiddler tore into a breakneck reel.

Diane followed my movements gracefully as I guided us through spins and turns amidst the blurred forms of the other daring couples. Though pressed close by the crowd, only my lovely partner existed in those breathless moments.

Diane's slender body followed my lead flawlessly. When the frenzied song ended, she gave me a soft kiss that left me dazed but grinning.

Leigh cut in next with a playful shoulder nudge to Diane. "My turn again!" she insisted and swept me up once more. Another fast-paced song had just begun, and Leigh seemed determined to wear me out with her enthusiastic style of dancing. She whooped loudly as we twirled, encouraging me to do the same.

When she took a moment to shake her pretty behind for me in the most tantalizing manner, I gave her a hard smack that made her yelp and shoot me a coy look. A jiggle went down her butt, and I pictured myself doing all sorts of naughty things to that pretty ass. All thoughts of fatigue vanished, caught up in Leigh's infectious energy and beaming smile.

The music and dancing continued, song after song. I partnered up with both Leigh and Diane in turns, sharing lively reels and laughing through frequent missteps. Out here, propriety mattered little — we threw ourselves wholly into the communal merriment.

Bodies glistened with sweat, cheeks glowed from exertion, bosoms heaved to catch breath between melodies. The shared joy was a tonic sweeter than any served at tonight's revel.

When at last the band slowed the tempo, I drew Diane close, relishing the feel of her in my arms. We swayed together gently. Over her slender shoulder, I glimpsed Leigh watching us with a soft smile. When our eyes met, her gaze warmed, and she gave a tiny nod of approval.

As the mellow song ended, Leigh parted the crowd, moving toward us. "How 'bout we all sit and catch our breath a spell?" she suggested, looking us both over approvingly.

I realized then how parched dancing had left me.

Diane and I readily agreed.

After staking claim to a small corner table, Leigh headed to the bar and returned minutes later precariously bearing three overflowing tankards of mead. Its sweetness helped soothe my dry throat and roiling pulse.

We talked and laughed together, our bodies still thrumming from exertion and shared elation. A sheen of perspiration glistened on Leigh's freckled décolletage, and I tried not to stare. But the way her eyes twinkled knowingly told me she noticed anyway.

Much later, after further dancing, drinking, and story swapping, exhaustion finally began creeping upon our merry trio. The crowds had thinned somewhat as other revelers trickled away into the night or passed out at their tables. The music still played, lively but no longer at a frenzied volume.

Leigh stifled a delicate yawn behind one hand. "Suppose we oughta consider turnin' in for the night soon," she murmured. Her eyes were tired but content, cheeks still endearingly flushed. "Can't have y'all passin' out before the festival even starts tomorrow!"

Diane nodded her agreement, likewise looking pleasantly worn but radiant. I knew we would all sleep deeply after the night's rousing revelry. As the band struck up one final farewell tune, a spry jig, Leigh's expression brightened once more.

"One more dance before we go?" she entreated, looking between Diane and me hopefully. Unable to resist the prospect or her charm, we allowed ourselves to be led into the energetic throng one final time.

But soon enough, the music wound to a close, the fiddle's last notes drowned out by raucous cheers. As patrons began filtering toward the door, Darny's voice cut through the din: "Last call, folks! Everyone clear out after that, so your old innkeeper can grab some shuteye before the festival really begins!"

Laughing together at his gruff but good-natured tone, Diane, Leigh, and I moved to make our own departure into the night. We went into the streets, where revelers who couldn't let go of the evening just yet roamed about and sang bawdy songs. Laughing, joking, and with a girl on each arm, we made our way to Leigh's place.

Chapter 57

Arm in arm, the three of us made our unhurried way through Gladdenfield's chaotic streets toward Leigh's cozy apartment above her shop. Revelry still spilled from every doorway and open window despite the late hour, but we were pleasantly exhausted after a long night of festivities.

At Leigh's door, she fished out her key ring and

unlocked it with fumbling fingers, giggling at her slight tipsiness. "There we go!" she declared triumphantly as the lock clicked open.

Once upstairs, Diane immediately flopped onto a plush sofa with a contented sigh, her limbs boneless with fatigue. I couldn't help but smile at how adorable she looked sprawled there. Leigh shot me a knowing grin, clearly having noticed my admiring gaze.

"Whew, I'm beat!" Leigh exclaimed, kicking off her boots. "You two make yourselves at home while I slip into somethin' more comfortable." With a playful wink, she sashayed toward the bedroom, her hips swaying enticingly.

I quirked an eyebrow as I watched her disappear inside. With Leigh, "something more comfortable" could mean almost anything, from flannel pajamas to barely-there lingerie. Though after the teasing flirtation tonight, I suspected she might opt for the latter. The thought sent a pulse of heat through me that I tried to tamp down.

Sinking onto the couch beside Diane, I slipped an arm around her shoulders, and she snuggled against me contentedly. Her fox ears twitched when I pressed a soft kiss to the top of her head.

"Mmm… that feels nice," Diane murmured

appreciatively. Her fingers trailed lightly up and down my chest. I could tell the lively night had made her a little hot and bothered, and she certainly wasn't the only one...

We traded unhurried kisses, our bodies molding together. Soon we were both a bit flushed and breathing quicker when Leigh's approaching footsteps made us separate.

"Hope I'm not interruptin' nothin' too fun," Leigh said airily as she emerged from the bedroom.

I had to concentrate on keeping my jaw from dropping at the sight of her.

The curvy shopkeeper now wore a slinky satin nightgown in a delicate shade of peach that hugged every inch of her voluptuous figure. The thin straps showed off her lightly tanned, freckled shoulders, and the low neckline perfectly framed her ample cleavage. But most amazingly, the thing was practically transparent! Her tight, high-rise thong was visible underneath, and I could see how high her full bosom sat on her chest. She was voluptuous and curvy in a delicious and mature way, and the freckles just emphasized her beauty.

Beside me, Diane let out a delighted giggle. "Leigh, look at you!" she exclaimed. "Wherever did you get such a darling little nightie?"

Leigh preened, smoothing the satiny fabric down over her hips. "Oh, this old thing? Won it a couple years back in a game of Wicked Grace with a fancy city elf trader."

She did a slow pirouette to show off the back, which dipped enticingly low, but my eyes were mainly drawn to how her lingerie clung to her full backside. "Had to promise the scoundrel free drinks at the Wild Outrider if I lost the hand. Luckily, I won!" Leigh shot me a sly sideways look through her lashes. "Ain't no beatin' me at cards."

I chuckled. Even exhausted from a long night, Leigh's bubbly energy and shameless flirting remained in full force. The alluring nightgown certainly amplified her beauty. I tried valiantly to keep my eyes above neck level as she moved closer.

"Here, I brought y'all some extra nightshirts and things to sleep in," Leigh said cheerily, handing Diane and me small bundles of folded garments. "They're clean, just been in storage is all."

After thanking her sincerely, Diane and I took turns washing up and changing in the little water closet. My loaned nightshirt was softly worn and just slightly too small, but clean. It reached just above the waistline, and

I wore my boxers underneath. I folded my dusty frontier clothes neatly, leaving them atop the dresser.

When Diane emerged from changing, she wore an oversized linen shirt that hung nearly to her knees. Her shapely legs peeped out beneath the hem as she walked. The casual garment accentuated her slender beauty.

Leigh let out an approving whistle. "Ain't you just the cutest thing in that big ol' shirt!" she teased affectionately. Diane did a playful twirl, and the loose fabric rose up to flash a little thigh.

"I see London, I see France…" I joked.

Diane swatted my arm amidst their laughter. But her cheeks were rosy, clearly enjoying our light flirtation. It kept the warm mood from the streets going.

I chuckled and pulled her in for a hug, and she answered with fiery intensity that went straight down my spine.

Diane then shot a smile at her friend and blushed a little before gesturing at the plush couch. She bit her lip for a moment, then grinned at Diane. "Let's sit on the couch for a bit," she hummed, her voice a little husky. "All three of us! We can talk and relax a little."

Those words sent an excited prickle down my skin, and my heart was beating fast as Diane led me to the couch and beckoned Leigh over again.

The three of us sank onto the supple leather sofa together, hip to hip, relaxing in comfortably casual intimacy after the camaraderie of the night's revelry. Outside the open window, raucous laughter and snatches of song still echoed up from the festival crowds below.

Leigh shifted, crossing her smooth bare legs casually. The motion caused her nightgown to ride up, exposing an enticing expanse of toned thigh. She caught me peeking and gave a playful wink. Diane just rolled her eyes in amusement at our antics.

"Well, after all that dancing, I'm feeling mighty parched again," Leigh declared. "How 'bout a nice nightcap before bed?"

Diane and I readily agreed that a drink sounded perfect. Leigh bounced up and headed to her kitchenette, returning shortly with three glasses of amber liquid tasting of honey and spice, which spread cozy warmth through my limbs. We tapped our glasses together in a wordless toast, our eyes sparkling.

I had a feeling this was going somewhere pretty soon…

Chapter 58

Leigh shifted her weight on the couch, and now her hips touched mine. Even better, the motion had caused her flimsy satin nightgown to hike up even more, revealing the way her thong clung to her tight little pussy in a camel toe. My cock bucked, outlined in my boxers.

"So, how're things goin' between y'all?" Leigh

drawled, the lilt in her husky voice making my mind swim; she was just so sexy. Her eyes were bright and teasing in the dim candlelight of her apartment.

Diane bit her lower lip, a blush creeping up her cheeks. "It's… it's been good," she stammered, her sapphire eyes flickering to me nervously.

Leigh let out a hearty laugh, throwing her head back and causing her voluminous blonde hair to cascade down her back. Her breasts jiggled with the motion, the areola of one rosy nipple escaping from the flimsy fabric of her nightgown.

"Y'all fucked, huh?" she asked, the wicked grin on her face making my heart race.

I chuckled at the bold question, but Diane turned as red as ketchup. She just stammered something along the lines of yes.

"Guilty as charged," I openly admitted, my eyes flickering to Diane who was now even fidgeting with the hem of her oversized shirt.

"Well now," Leigh purred, scooting closer to me on the couch. Her thigh brushed against my own, a jolt of electricity shooting up my spine at the contact. "No need to be bashful, sugar. It's a normal thing to do for lovers."

She leaned in closer, her free hand crawling up my

thigh as her naughty gaze dipped to my cock, outlined firm in my boxers. "Did his cock taste as good as it looks, Diane?" she asked, her voice dropping to a sultry whisper.

Diane's eyes widened at the question, her cheeks flaring a deep red before she gave a playful chuckle. "Maybe you should find out," she hummed, teasing her friend right back.

That one made my heart skip a beat, though. This was getting hot and heavy pretty fast! I loved the way Leigh's dirty talk was making Diane squirm, but my fox girl was competitive and gave Leigh as good as she got. And both women were getting turned on by their banter. I could see the arousal in their eyes.

"Maybe I should..." Leigh purred as her hand continued its journey, her fingers brushing against the outline of my hardening cock in the most teasing way.

God, the things I wanted to do to this woman!

"And did he fill that tight little pussy of yours?" Leigh purred, taking it up a notch as her eyes locked on Diane's.

"Hmm," Diane hummed, tucking a strand of her black hair behind her ear as she watched Leigh's fingers tease. "He did. Maybe you can watch him do it again?"

My breath hitched as Leigh's fingers traced the length

of my cock through my boxers, her touch teasing and tantalizing. I looked at Diane, whose eyes were glued to Leigh's roaming hand. She rubbed her thighs together, giving a little mewl of arousal at the sight of Leigh so casually prickling my rod with her fingers.

Leigh smiled naughtily at Diane's reaction, her fingers continuing their dance. "Are you sure I can taste him too?" she asked, her voice dripping with a wicked sweetness.

Sweet mother of mercy. I sat back and grinned, letting these two work out who could get on my cock first. If this was the so-called 'elven marriage', I was sold…

Diane gave a naughty nod. She was blushing as this was all a little dirtier than what she was used to, but she wasn't giving up, and she was enjoying the play. This, I could tell by the naughty twinkle in her eyes.

"Do it," she said. "See if you can get him off like I do."

Leigh giggled, and her hand shifted, her fingers brushing over my balls. I couldn't suppress the groan that escaped my lips, the sensation sending waves of pleasure coursing through my veins.

"Does Diane suck a good cock, David?" Leigh drawled, her voice husky as she continued to tease me.

I bit my lip, my gaze flickering between the two women. "She does," I confirmed, my voice barely a whisper.

Leigh's grin widened at my answer, her blue eyes sparkling with mischief. "Well, ain't that somethin'," she said, her hand leaving my cock to play with a loose strand of her golden hair.

Diane shifted in her seat, her tail swishing behind her. I could see the way her nipples strained against the fabric of her oversized shirt, the sight making me even harder.

"Think you can do better?" Diane teased Leigh, her sapphire eyes ablaze as she licked her lips.

Leigh's giggle filled the room once more, the sound as intoxicating as her touch. "I ain't sure," she drawled, her hand returning to my cock, her wide blue eyes fixing on me. "I can try, though…"

I groaned, my hips bucking instinctively into her touch. The heat of her hand through the thin fabric of my boxers was driving me wild, my breath hitching with anticipation.

Leigh's fingers expertly traced the outline of my hard length, her touch feather-light yet torturously slow. Diane watched, her eyes glazed with desire as she bit her lip.

"I think you should," she purred, and I glanced at Diane, who was now squirming in her seat. The sight of her, so aroused and fascinated at the way her friend was touching and teasing me, was incredibly erotic.

My heart pounded in my chest as Leigh's grip tightened around my cock, her thumb brushing over the head through the fabric of my boxers. A shiver of pleasure ran down my spine, my weapon throbbing under her touch.

Diane leaned in closer, her breath hot against my ear as she addressed Leigh. "We should make this interesting," she said, her words sending a thrill of anticipation through me.

"*More* interesting?" I muttered.

"A competition!" Leigh agreed.

I swallowed hard, my gaze flickering between the two women. Diane seemed as intrigued by the idea as I was, her sapphire eyes filled with curiosity and desire.

"Hm-hm," she hummed, shooting the Leigh a smile. "A competition between friends… A little contest to see who sucks David's cock the best?"

My eyes widened for a second, but my cock gave a happy buck at the suggestion.

Diane gasped and blushed at Leigh's dirty suggestion, but Leigh just pushed up closer against me, the couch creaking as her transparent nightgown slipped away to reveal her other nipple as well.

"Come on, baby," she hummed at Diane. "A friendly competition! Winner gets a pussy full of cum..." She threw me a wink.

My kind of competition...

Diane's mouth fell open, surprised by her friend's dirty suggestion, but then her eyes narrowed, and she gave a naughty little giggle. "All right," she purred. "Let's see what you got..."

Leigh started by teasing me a little more through my boxers, her slender fingers tracing the outline of my erection. She then pulled back, arching a dark blonde eyebrow as she grabbed the hem of her disheveled nightgown and pulled it over her head, her big tits bouncing free of the flimsy garment. The sight of her in just a thong made my heart pound in my chest.

Then, she bent down to kiss me, her lips meeting mine in a passionate exchange. I had been wanting this for a while, and the softness of her lips only fueled my desire. Her tongue explored my mouth, and I could taste the sweet flavor of her.

My hands moved up to knead those big breasts of hers, and the purr of pleasure that escaped her as we kissed told me how sensitive and sensual she was.

Diane watched us from a corner, her hand slipping beneath her oversized shirt. Her cheeks were flushed, and her breath hitched as she watched Leigh and me. Her fingers moved rhythmically under her shirt, and I could tell that she was touching herself.

Leigh then removed my boxers, her eyes flickering with admiration as my erection sprung free. "Such a pretty cock, baby," she purred, shooting me a naughty look. "I've been wanting to taste it for a while now."

She gave it a few teasing strokes, her touch making me shiver with pleasure. Then, she spat on it, her warm saliva making my cock glisten in the dim candlelight.

She then moved to kneel in front of me, her large breasts swaying slightly as she positioned herself. Her mouth descended on my cock, and I couldn't help but groan at the feeling of her lips around me.

She leaned forward, and seeing her big ass in the skimpy thong was incredibly arousing. The material barely covered her, and the sight of her round buttocks made my cock twitch in her mouth. My mind swam with pictures of me doing the dirtiest things to that butt, Leigh screaming with pleasure as I fucked her senseless…

Her pace increased, her head bobbing faster on my cock. Her lips slid up and down my length, the wet, warm feeling of her mouth making my toes curl. I could feel my orgasm building, and I knew I wouldn't last much longer.

Diane had shimmied her panties to the side, her fingers working on her pussy as she watched Leigh and me. Her breathy moans filled the room, adding to the erotic atmosphere. She looked incredibly sexy, her fox tail twitching in time with her fingers.

Diane moved closer to us on the couch, her hand still buried in her panties. She leaned in to kiss me, her lips meeting mine in a hot, messy exchange. Her taste was different from Leigh's, more tangy and wild.

As we kissed, Diane's fingers moved faster on her pussy. I could hear the wet sounds of her fingers slipping in and out of her, the sight and sound making me even more aroused.

Leigh continued to work on my cock, her pace relentless. I could feel her tongue swirling around my tip, the sensation driving me crazy. Her hand cupped my balls, giving them a gentle squeeze.

Diane broke our kiss, her breath coming in short, ragged gasps. Her hand moved faster under her shirt, her fingers working furiously on her clit. Her moans grew louder, her eyes locked on Leigh and me.

"She's… Ahn… She's good," Diane muttered. "Look at her go… Working… Ahnn… working so hard for your cum, David."

The sight of Diane pleasuring herself made me only more aroused. I could feel my orgasm building, the pressure in my balls becoming unbearable. I tried to hold back, not wanting the pleasure to end. But Leigh's tongue and mouth were relentless, her rhythm unchanging.

Leigh sensed my impending orgasm and redoubled her efforts. She took me deeper into her mouth, her lips pressing against my base. Her tongue swirled around my tip, the sensation driving me closer to the edge.

Diane's moans filled the room, her fingers moving furiously on her pussy. She was close too, her body trembling with the effort as she fingered herself while I fucked her friend's mouth. "Fuck, Leigh," I groaned. "I'm… I'm gonna cum."

She popped my cock out her mouth for a moment, jacking me off as she did so. "Cum for me, baby," she hummed. “I want it.”

“Yeah, cum,” Diane agreed. “Cum… ahnn… cum in her mouth.”

Leigh took my cock back in her mouth and went faster, gagging and slobbering, until my orgasm came up from my very toes. With a grunt, I thrust between her lips and released, my cum shooting into Leigh’s mouth.

At the same time, Diane climaxed, her body shaking with pleasure as she watched me pump a hot load into Leigh’s mouth, her eyes hazy as she reveled in the forbidden delights.

My orgasm was intense, my body shaking with the effort. I could feel my cum spurting out, filling Leigh’s mouth. She swallowed what she could, but some of it dribbled down onto her breasts. The sight of her big tits covered in my cum was incredibly arousing.

Finally, Leigh pulled away from my cock, her lips still glistening with my cum. She licked her lips, tasting my essence. Her blue eyes met mine, and she gave me a satisfied smile.

“Damn, David,” Leigh hummed, licking her lips clean and giving a chuckle. “You cum so much, baby.”

Then, she shifted her naughty gaze to Diane. “See if you can top that, honey…”

I sat back as Diane, blushing and giggling, hopped down from the couch and got onto her knees next to Leigh. As she did so, she pulled off the oversized shirt, revealing her cute panties and firm breasts. The sight of her like that next to Leigh's voluptuous body made me half-hard again.

"Jack him off, baby," Leigh encouraged, her hand already wrapped around my engorged cock. "Make him nice and hard." Diane's sapphire eyes sparkled with mischief as her delicate fingers closed around me.

Diane began slowly, her hand stroking me with a tantalizing rhythm that made my breath hitch. Her fox ears twitched adorably, and her tail swished from side to side as she worked my cock.

"That's it," Leigh's voice was breathy, her accent a sweet melody to my ears as she encouraged Diane.

As Diane pumped me faster, Leigh's fingers fluttered to the edge of her thong. She shimmied it aside, revealing her glistening pussy, a sight that made my cock twitch in Diane's hand.

Leigh began fingering herself, her eyes never leaving

mine, her fingers delving deep into her wetness. "You cummin' in my mouth got me all hot and bothered," she breathed as her delicate fingers explored that pretty pussy. I couldn't wait to get my cock in there; the hot little vixen was probably a perfect fuck.

Every stroke of Diane's hand and every flick of Leigh's fingers sent jolts of pleasure coursing through me. I beckoned Leigh closer, urging her to join me on the couch.

"Let me taste those beautiful tits," I murmured, my voice husky with desire. Leigh clambered onto the couch, positioning herself next to me.

My mouth found her breast, my tongue tracing her nipple before I sucked it into my mouth. Leigh moaned, her hand guiding my other hand down to her already soaked pussy. "That's it, baby," she hummed. "Touch my pussy like that."

The taste of her skin was intoxicating, the feel of her soft breast in my hand and her slick folds under my fingers drove me wild. I probed her depths with my fingers, finding her sweet spot with ease.

Leigh gasped as she reached around, peeled her thong to the side, and slipped a slender finger into her tight asshole as she rode my fingers. "Oh, baby," she crooned. "I can't wait till I get to feel that cock of yours… Hm… I'll let ya fuck any hole you want, baby."

Damn, she was driving me crazy! Meanwhile, Diane's mouth was working wonders on my cock. Her lips glided over my length, taking me deep into her throat. Her technique was flawless, and the sight of her bobbing head between my thighs was driving me to the edge.

I could feel the tension building, my balls tightening as my climax approached. Leigh's sensual moans and Diane's expert blowjob were pushing me to my limit.

My fingers moved faster inside Leigh, matching the rapid pace of Diane's mouth. Leigh's moans were getting louder, her body trembling as she got closer to her climax.

"Oh David," she moaned. "I'm so close… I'm gonna cum for you, baby…" Her words spurred me on, my fingers moving even faster inside her.

Then, with a loud cry, Leigh's body arched, her orgasm crashing over her like a tidal wave. Her pussy clenched around my fingers, her juices coating my hand.

"Oh fuck, David!" Leigh cried out, her body trembling. "I'm cumming… I'm cumming so hard…" Her dirty talk was like music to my ears, her orgasm a symphony of pleasure that echoed through the room.

At the same time, I felt my own climax rushing towards me. My hips bucked, thrusting my cock deeper into Diane's throat.

"Diane," I gasped, pulling my cock out of her mouth. "I'm gonna cum…"

Diane pulled away but stayed on her knees in front of me, pushing up her breasts. "Cum for me, David," she begged, her eyes wide and eager. "Cum all over me…"

With a roar, I came, my hot cum spurting out and coating Diane's beautiful breasts. The sight of her sitting there, my cum dripping down her tits, was crazy sexy. I watched as she smeared my seed over her breasts, her fingers playing with her nipples as she did so. She moaned, her eyes closing in pleasure. This was a new side of her, and I loved it!

"Oh fuck…" I groaned, taking in and treasuring the sight of her like this. Diane looked up at me, her fox ears twitching adorably.

"Did you enjoy that?" she asked, her voice sultry. I could only nod, my breath coming in ragged pants.

Meanwhile, Leigh was still coming down from her orgasm, her body still trembling. She looked at me with lust-filled eyes, a satisfied smile playing on her lips.

"That was… amazin'," she purred. "I came so hard…"

I smiled at her, reaching out to stroke her cheek. "You were incredible, Leigh," I told her, my voice sincere. "Both of you were…"

Leigh blushed, but her smile didn't waver. She glanced at Diane, and I followed her gaze.

Diane sat on her knees, her pretty tits glazed with cum, like the image of some goddess of lust. At the sight of her like that, completely surrendered to her desire for me, I was almost ready to go again at once.

"Damn, girl," Leigh hummed, still panting from her own orgasm. "I concede… You won." She grinned naughtily. "That means you get a pussy full of cum…"

With my hand still on Leigh's tight and wet slit, my eyes fell on Diane. Lost in her lust, she rose from her knees. Her pretty chest was glazed with my hot cum. Some had even trickled down to her cute panties.

"David," she murmured, her voice heavy with desire. "I need you…" The sapphire fire in her eyes burned brighter. "I need you to fuck me."

Leigh's giggle echoed in the room, sultry and full of wicked delight. "That's right, Diane," she said, her hand still moving on her own body. "You did win fair and square. Now, let's see our man claim his prize."

I felt a surge of desire course through me, making my cock twitch. With a low growl, I pulled Diane up to me, her soft body molding to mine as our lips met in a searing kiss. My hand slipped into her cute panties, and I felt she was ready for me.

I broke the kiss, my gaze meeting hers. I saw her anticipation, her need, and I couldn't resist. I pulled her onto the couch and pushed her over to place her on all fours, her fox tail twitching with excitement as she gave a little yelp at my somewhat rough handling.

"Oh, yeah," Leigh moaned from her spot, her hand cupping her own large breast. "Fuck her like that, David. Give her what she's been begging for."

My hands found Diane's hips, pulling her closer. I felt the heat of her, the wetness, and I couldn't help but groan. The tip of my cock pressed against her, teasing her entrance.

"Please, David," Diane begged, her voice a husky whisper. "Fuck me. Hard."

With a deep, guttural groan, I pushed into her. She was tight, so damn tight, and I saw stars. I grabbed her fox tail, using it as leverage as I began to thrust.

Diane's moans filled the room, each one louder than

the last. Her fingers clutched the leather of the couch, her body trembling with each thrust. A ripple went down her perfect ass with every thrust, and even though I had come twice already, my pleasure already rose at the sight of that perfect body all for me.

I fucked her hard, my hips slamming against hers with each thrust. Her ass was up in the air, presented to me, and I couldn't resist giving it a hard smack.

Diane's response was immediate. A loud, wanton cry slipped from her lips, her body arching beautifully.

Leigh's voice cut through the room, her words dirty and encouraging. "That's it, David. Make her scream."

I could feel my climax building, the pressure mounting. But I didn't want this to be over just yet.

I slowed my thrusts, savoring the feel of Diane around me. My hands roamed her body, exploring every inch of her. I could hear Leigh's heavy breaths, her gasps and moans growing louder.

"Don't stop, David," Leigh moaned. "I wanna to see you fuck her hard. Make her yours, baby."

With a growl, I picked up my pace again. I was fucking her rougher now, faster, with her cheek pressed against the creaking leather of the sofa. I could tell by the way she was moaning, the way her body was shaking, that she was close.

"Oh, David," Diane cried out, her voice filled with pleasure. "I… I'm going to… Oh, God!"

I felt her tighten around me, her body convulsing as she came. It was one of the most beautiful sights I'd ever seen.

"That's it, Diane," Leigh cooed. "Let him feel how good he's making you feel."

Diane's orgasm was long and powerful, her body shaking with each wave of pleasure. It was all I could do to keep my own climax at bay.

"David," Diane gasped, her voice breathless. "I want… I want you to fill me."

"She's earned it, David," Leigh said, her voice filled with passion. "Give her all of that hot cum."

My own climax built up, the pressure mounting. All this dirty talk, their beautiful bodies, glistening with sweat. I couldn't hold back any longer.

With a grunt, I thrust one last time, my cum spurting out to fill her. Diane's body shook under the power of my orgasm, her cries filling the room. I growled with lust as I emptied my balls in her fertile womb, eager to give her and Leigh exactly what they wanted. Then, with a sigh, I was spent.

"Oh, David," Diane moaned. "That was… incredible."

I collapsed next to her on the couch, my arm wrapping around her. I could feel her body still trembling, the aftershocks of her orgasms still coursing through her.

Leigh's giggle filled the room, light and full of satisfaction. "Well, that was certainly a sight to see."

I raised my head, meeting Leigh's gaze. "I hope you enjoyed the show," I said, my voice filled with amusement.

"For sure," Leigh purred. "You filled her up nice and good, baby! Hmm, she'll be walkin' funny for a day or two."

I chuckled in between gasps for breath as I gave Diane's round butt a slap. She giggled and shook her ass for me as she lay down on the couch beside me.

I glanced over at Diane, her fox ears perked up in satisfaction as she snuggled up against me. Her tail twitched idly as she basked in the afterglow. Leigh's curvaceous body sprawled lazily in my lap.

I ran my fingers along Leigh's arm, tracing the freckles that dotted her skin like stars in the night sky. "You two are amazing," I said, the words rumbling from deep within my chest. Diane's sapphire eyes sparkled as she turned to look at me, her lips curling into a satisfied smile.

"Well," she drawled, her fingers lightly tracing a path down my legs. "You ain't too bad yourself." She yawned, covering her mouth.

"But I think it's time for bed now," Leigh said, breaking away from my gaze to stretch. I grunted in disagreement, my eyes wandering over her voluptuous body.

Man, I still wanted to fuck her. And hard, too.

Leigh chuckled teasingly at my reaction, her eyes sparkling with mischief. She stood; her body silhouetted by the soft candlelight. I watched as she ambled towards her bedroom, her round ass swaying enticingly. I licked my lips at the sight, my cock stirring at the thought of what was to come.

"If you want more, you'll have to come to the Aquana festival," Leigh called out as she disappeared into her room. "We can do a few more friendly competitions when we get there, baby," she hummed. "Maybe we can see which butt bounces the best!"

At that, she gave her round butt in its thong a slap, making it jiggle.

Diane and I laughed, and I licked my lips at the prospect. "Oh, we will be definitely going," I said.

"Or *coming*," Leigh joked with a wink before she sashayed into her bedroom, leaving Diane and me chuckling as we snuggled on the couch.

Frontier life… it's the best.

Finished and eager for early access to my next book? Check out my Patreon: patreon.com/jackbryce

THANK YOU FOR READING!

If you enjoyed this book, please check out my other work on Amazon.

Be sure to **leave me a review on Amazon** to let me know if you liked this book! Like most independent authors, I use the feedback from your review to improve my work and to decide what to focus on next, so your review can make a difference.

If you want early access to my work, consider joining my Patreon (https://patreon.com/jackbryce)!

If you want to stay up-to-date on my releases, you can join my newsletter by entering the following link into any web browser: https://fierce-thinker-305.ck.page/45f709af30. You can also join my Discord, where the madness never ends… Join by entering the following invite manually in your browser or Discord app: https://discord.gg/uqXaTMQQhr.

Jack Bryce's Books

Below you'll find a list of my work, all available through Amazon.

Frontier Summoner (ongoing series)

Frontier Summoner 1

Country Mage (completed series)

Country Mage 1

Country Mage 2

Country Mage 3

Country Mage 4

Country Mage 5

Country Mage 6

Country Mage 7

Country Mage 8

Country Mage 9

Country Mage 10

Warped Earth (completed series)

Apocalypse Cultivator 1

Apocalypse Cultivator 2

Apocalypse Cultivator 3

Apocalypse Cultivator 4

Apocalypse Cultivator 5

<u>Aerda Online (completed series)</u>

Phylomancer

Demon Tamer

Clanfather

<u>Highway Hero (ongoing series)</u>

Highway Hero 1

Highway Hero 2

A SPECIAL THANKS TO...

My patron in the Godlike tier: Lynderyn!
My patrons in the High Mage tier: Christian Smith

All of my other patrons at patreon.com/jackbryce!

Stoham Baginbott, Louis Wu, and Scott D. for beta reading. You guys are absolute kings.

If you're interested in beta reading for me, hit me up on discord (JauntyHavoc#8836) or send an e-mail to lordjackbryce@gmail.com. The list is currently full, but spots might open up in the future.

Made in the USA
Monee, IL
11 December 2023